Dragon's Island
and
Other Stories

Dragon's Island and Other Stories

Jack Williamson

Five Star • Waterville, Maine

This collection is a work of fiction. Names, characters, places and incidents are either the product of the author's imagination, or, if real, used fictitiously.

Five Star First Edition Science Fiction and Fantasy Series.

Published in 2002 in conjunction with
Tekno-Books and Ed Gorman.

Cover illustration by Ken Barr.

Set in 11 pt. Plantin by Rick Gundberg.

Printed in the United States on permanent paper.

Library of Congress Cataloging-in-Publication Data

Williamson, Jack, 1908–
Dragon's Island and other stories / Jack Williamson.
p. cm.—(Five Star first edition science fiction and fantasy series)
Contents: Stepson to creation—Guinevere for everybody—Dragon's Island.
ISBN 0-7862-4314-7 (hc : alk. paper)
1. Science fiction, American. I. Title. II. Series.
PS3545.I557 D73 2002
813′.52—dc21 2002067510

Dragon's Island and Other Stories

Table of Contents

Introduction

The invention of a new technology can change the way we live. One early example is the use of fire, the art of flaking stone another. Writing was later, printing far later. Most of them came thousands of years apart, but recently the pace has grown faster. The last century gave us electronics, nuclear energy, and genetic engineering.

The creation of new species had begun ten thousand years ago, when we turned wolves into dogs. It went on with the domestication of plants and other animals, which transformed us from hunter-gatherers to city builders, but only as an art. Genetic engineering as a science had to wait for James Watson and Frederic Crick to discover the double helix of DNA.

Until then, the idea had made great science fiction. I was fascinated long ago by H. G. Wells' *The First Men in the Moon.* His Selenites are shaped to play their roles in a hive-like society; they hardly exist as individuals. Aldous Huxley, in *Brave New World*, has people also grown to fit. He makes a telling point: his brave new world is planned and run by intelligent men of good will. His Savage, however, brought up in New Mexico as a free individual, finds its perfection intolerable. He hangs himself.

My own *Dragon's Island* was published in 1951, a few years ahead of Watson and Crick. I believed for years that I had coined the term "genetic engineering." I'm still proud of this passage in the epigraph:

Man may now become his own maker. He can remove the flaws in his own imperfect species, before the stream of life flows on to leave him stranded on the banks of time with the dinosaurs and trilobites—if he will only accept and use the new science of genetic engineering.

But the torch is passing on. The editors of the OED seem to have found the term in a science paper published in 1949. As Andy Warhol observed, everybody is famous, if only for fifteen minutes.

Stepson to Creation

The multiverse creates itself.

It had no beginning; neither will it end.

Each new universe is wombed as a fire-egg, born through a contracting black hole. Expanding in space-time, ripening new black holes, it sows the eternal manifold with new fire-eggs of its own. Cooling, each new cosmos gives birth to galaxies and suns, to worlds of life and change, sometimes to intellect.

Flowing out of chaos, the multiverse is blind. Its law is chance. It has neither plan nor will. Its creatures are chance atoms, tossed together in the flux of mindless force. Such were the premen, who called themselves men.

Evolved by chance mutation on the hallowed planet Earth, the premen came by chance upon the art of genetic engineering and so became their own Creators, the mortal precursors who fathered the Four Creations.

The first act of Creation formed the trumen, the perfected human race, purged of all ancestral evil and planned to supplant the premen.

The second act of Creation produced the mumen, the variform men, shaped to fit their several functions in many universes.

The third act of Creation gave being to the stargods themselves.

Still merely premen, blind to the splendor of true perfection, the Creators then neglected to rest from their triumphs, but went on instead to father yet another creation. The issue of their error was a race of demons, creatures of power without beauty, mind without truth, desire without justice. Evil revivals of the ancestral beast, they rebelled against their makers and the gods, seeking to usurp the whole multiverse.

The god Belthar perceived their emergent malevolence. Returning across space from his own domain, he reconquered the holy Earth, ended the folly of the Creators, and erased their monstrous last creation.

In benign solicitude, the supreme Belthar continues to rule the sacred planet, granting power to his variform defenders, wisdom to the trumen, sons to their most fortunate daughters, and mercy to the surviving premen. His sovereign will gives law to chaos, and his omniscience illuminates the multiverse.

His glory endures forever.

— *The Book of Belthar*

ONE

Two naked waifs, paternity unknown. A black halfgod, the proud son of Belthar himself. A lovely young goddess, touring the sacred sites of her ancestral Earth. A yelping dog and a frightened rat. A red-scaled mutant guardian, its third eye flashing thunderbolts.

Old chaos in collision with stellar divinity . . .

The god Belthar had leveled the crown of Pike's Peak for his North American temple. All black granite, it could hold half a million chanting worshippers. It was empty, however, on that chill spring morning when a small skimmer marked with the triple triangle of the Thearchy dropped to a parking terrace on the slope beneath it.

The halfgod Quelf left the skimmer with five attendant sacristans. His mother had been a dancer who satisfied Belthar. Inheriting her dark grace and his father's towering power, he was commonly arrogant, but his bold tread faltered as they reached the elevator.

"Leave your boots," he told the blue-robed trumen. "There's a live goddess here."

He had long ago learned the mixture of impudence and flattery that pleased his godly father, but Zhondra Zhey was a casual transient from remote stellar dominions, a dangerous unknown.

"She's a starship pilot." He bent to set his own boots in the rack. "Visiting Earth while her ship's in orbit. The Lord has ordered us to serve her."

The sacristans straightened and stared, but shuffled after him into the elevator without comment. He had taught them silence.

They emerged between great black columns under the rim of the vault, which was a blue-black star-map, all aglow with shifting lines that showed the space-routes of the explored multiverse. Heads bent, they marched out across the polished floor, which mirrored all those far dominions. The central altar was a vast black disk that held the sacred apartments. Kneeling beneath it, holding up his offering, the halfgod intoned a formal invocation to the goddess.

Before he was done, she appeared at a high window, gestured as if to check him, and stepped out into the air. Wearing only her aura and the diamond star of her space-pilot's rating, she dropped to the granite bench before him and floated just above it, anchored to the stone with only one rosy toe.

"You—Your Divinity!"

Conflicting impulses shook his voice. Pink and slim beneath her golden nimbus, the goddess was still no more than a lovely child, not out of her second century, yet already overwhelmingly alluring. Fond of young girls, he was used to taking what he wanted. But no mortal virgin had ever come clothed in her perilous power.

"Favor, Great One!" Torn between lust and terror, he dropped his eyes to the casket of rare Terran gems he had brought. "Humbly, we implore your gracious acceptance of our insignificant gift." Sweaty hands quivering, he raised the casket. "Eagerly, we await your all-wise instructions—"

"Stand up, Quelf." Her Terran diction was pure, her tone gently chiding. "I want no gifts."

"Forgive us, Your Divin—"

The casket had slipped from his fingers. Her slender hand moved slightly. Flowing from it, her shimmering nimbus reached out to catch the casket, lifted it over his head and into the hands of a startled sacristan behind him.

"Save your offering for the premen," she said. "I think they need it more than I do. I've come to see their reservation. Please arrange it."

Clumsily, he stood up.

"We obey." His avid eyes were fixed on that tempting toe. "However, if Your Divinity deigns to tour the holy planet, there are better sights. The Asian Temple, which is Belthar's dwelling. His statue on the Andes—"

"I'm going to Redrock."

"Indulgence!"

Her mild tone had given him courage to look up, and her bright-washed beauty stabbed him with a hotter regret that he had not inherited all his father's privileges and powers. She waited, aloof, aware, a little amused.

"If Your Divinity cares about the aboriginal life, there's

the European Zoo. The Terran creatures there include a fine preman habitat."

"I prefer to visit the people at Redrock."

"People?" His rising tones echoed unthinking scorn. "They're miserable animals. Wallowing in their own filth. So squalid that the Lord Belthar has ordered their removal—"

"That's why I'm here. The premen created us. I'm afraid that fact has been forgotten. I want to see them while there's time."

"Forgiveness!" he protested. "But those stinking beasts at Redrock are the last dregs of a dying race. The real Creators died for their final folly a thousand years ago. If Your Divinity is concerned with history, we humbly suggest the Museum of Terran Evolution in Antarctica. There's a Smithwick Memorial Hall, with authentic reconstructions of the genetic engineers in their laboratory—"

"Take me to the reservation."

"Your Divinity, we obey."

Redrock was a straggle of brown mud huts beside an irrigation ditch that was also a sewer. Four larger buildings enclosed the grassless plaza: the jail, the town hall, and the twin chapels of Thar and Bel, dedicated to the god of Earth in his major aspects of wisdom and love.

By Quelf's command, old wooden doors wore new blue paint. Litter had been raked from the mud-rutted road, and a strip of gold carpet rolled along it from the chapel of Bel on the plaza to the agency mansion on its green-terraced hill above the odors and vermin of the town.

The premen had been warned, and the landing skimmer was greeted with an apprehensive hush. The sacred procession emerged on the plaza and marched up the carpet toward the agency. Two mutant soldiers stalked ahead, the dry sun burning on black crests and ruby scales. The halfgod followed, dark nose held high, as if offended by every reek around him. Four blue sacristans carried the canopied chair of honor, the divine tourist smiling out as if delighted with everything she saw.

A dog barked.

A child screamed.

A brown rat slithered out of an alley, darted across the carpet. A dirty mongrel darted after it, yelping with excitement. A small naked boy splashed across the green-scum ditch, running after the dog. They veered toward the goddess.

Quelf hissed an order. One muman guardian spun to face the intrusion. Lightning stabbed from its black-lensed crest. The dog's body spun across the carpet and tumbled into a puddle.

"Make way!" the halfgod shouted. "Make way for Her Divinity!"

The boy looked five years old. Brown and thin, he wore only splashes and smears of drying mud. Planted at the center of the gold carpet, he stared up at the holy procession with dark wet eyes.

"You—" A sob racked and choked him. "You killed Spot!"

"Davey!" A tiny girl shrieked from the alley behind him. "Come away, Davey. Don't let the deadeyes hurt you."

The boy stood fast.

"Off!" the halfgod snapped. "Off the road!"

"Killer!" The boy shook his grimy fist. "I'll make you sorry!"

"What?" Anger stiffened Quelf. "You insolent pup!"

He gestured at the scar-marked mumen. Both bent their lenses toward the boy. Violent pathmaker beams hissed around him. Yowling, the naked girl came splashing to him through the gutter.

"Hold everything!"

The goddess froze them with that gold-toned command. Levitating from the chair, she came sailing over the halfgod and the mumen and sank toward the carpet in front of the boy. Smiling, she paused to watch the girl, who was darting to pick up the dog.

"Who are you children?"

The boy studied her solemnly.

"I'm Davey," he said at last. "Davey Dunahoo."

"But I have no name." The girl came panting back to his side, lugging the limp body of the dog, which seemed heavier than she. "They call me—" In the reek of the charred brown fur, she sneezed twice. "They call me Buglet."

"Don't you have parents?"

"I never had a father." Davey stopped to consider her again. "My mother was a girl at La China's. A drunk man stabbed her." Gravely, he nodded at the girl. "Spot found Buglet lying in the weeds beyond the dump. She was sick. She can't remember who she is."

"Where do you live?"

"Nowhere." He shrugged. "Anywhere."

"In the street," the girl piped. "When it rains El Yaqui lets us sleep in his barn. Sometimes he finds a bone for Spot."

"Mercy, Your Divinity." The halfgod came striding around the mumen. "The reception is waiting for us." He glowered at the muddy urchins. "I've warned you off the road."

"You can kill dogs." The boy stared back. "But you can't kill the Multiman—"

"Blasphemy!" the halfgod roared. "Belthar will put a stop to that—"

The goddess raised a shining hand.

"Multiman?" She turned to frown at Quelf. "Who is Multiman?"

"A wicked heresy. Forbidden by the Thearchy, but still current among these stupid premen." He grinned at the defiant children. "I believe their removal will put an end to it."

She floated back to the children.

"Please forgive us." She settled toward them, smiling. "I do want to help you. Won't you tell me what you need?"

The boy stared blankly, but the girl crept forward with the dog in her arms.

"If you're a goddess, please make Spot alive again."

"I can't do that." She gave Quelf a quick wry glance. "Not even Belthar could reanimate your pet."

"The Multiman could," the boy insisted. "If he had come."

He took the dog from Buglet's arms. Silently he turned, to wade back across the ditch to the mud-walled alley. Buglet splashed after him. The goddess glided back to her chair, and the procession marched on again through the sharp sewer reek.

A few sun-browned children in blue-and-white uniforms watched from the schoolyard. At one corner, a withered woman sat on a wasted donkey, waiting impassively. At El Yaqui's trading post, a dozen men looked up from the drinks and the games on their sidewalk tables, and a plump dark girl in a bright-red wrapper leaned from a second-floor window to stare at the passing goddess.

At the end of the carpet strip, on the clean green lawn beneath the white marble steps of the agency, the preman leaders and the truman agent waited, robed in official white. Bowing to the chair, the agent humbly begged the favor of the goddess. The premen were eager to entertain their sacred guest in the agency garden.

Zhondra left her chair and levitated after him, to inspect the display of preman arts and crafts. A dark silent youth stood sweating beside a plow, the garden wall behind him hung with sample plants of cotton, corn, beans, and hemp. A one-legged smith bent over his anvil and forge, shaping hot metal, preparing to shoe a mule. Two shy girls in clean white gowns showed a relief map of the whole reservation, its red buttes and canyons modeled in clay. A row of silent matrons offered tacos and hamburgers and rice balls, with mescal and beer and tea.

The goddess tasted politely. When she asked to make the premen a gift, the agent called for El Yaqui. A lean, grave man with brooding eyes and a far-off smile, he accepted the casket of gems with a silent bow that seemed indifferent.

"Your Divinity, these are the premen." Following the goddess back to her chair, Quelf spoke with a covert satisfaction. "You'll find no Creators among them."

"Yet they look more unfortunate than harmful. I see no cause for their destruction."

"But they aren't to be destroyed," the halfgod protested. "They are simply to be resettled. On a virgin world in the Ninth Universe."

"Why?" Her violet eyes probed him. "Is Belthar afraid of heretics?"

"If my Lord Belthar dreads anything, I'm not aware of it. The problem is simply living space. The premen never accepted civilization. Out of place in our sacred culture, they're dwindling away. Only a generation ago, the survivors from the other continents were gathered here. Now they're too few to make efficient use of the land they occupy."

"This wasteland? Who needs it?"

"The Lord Belthar has graciously approved an engineering project of my own." He beamed with self-approval. "A dam across the lower canyon. Desalting plants and tunnels to fill a wide new lake with Pacific water. The entire reservation will be flooded."

"Your own project?" She looked away at the tall red buttes and the vast bare flats, and keenly back at him.

"The actual plans were drawn by truman engineers, but I'll have a palace on the lake. And—"

"I see." Her cool voice cut him off. "What about this Multiman."

"Pure myth." He chuckled. "Preman logic is the joke of the planet. Though the Lord Belthar has been their ruler for a thousand years, they still cling to irrational beliefs in their old imaginary gods. Buddha, Brahma, Allah—the list is endless. The Multiman heresy may well be a distorted folk recollection of the Fourth Creation." He chuckled again. "The Lord Belthar took care of that."

"Not if you ask Davey Dunahoo." With a thoughtful glance at the straggle of huts, she levitated into her chair. "Perhaps Belthar is wise to get the premen out of his universe."

TWO

Zhondra Zhey went on to visit the Museum of Terran Evolution. She paid a formal visit at Belthar's Asian Temple, but felt no regret when the god of Earth was not in residence. Her starship loaded with a precious cargo of gum from the seed-pods of a mutant poppy that flourished on the Terran highlands, she took it on to dominions of the Thearchy in another universe, guiding it through contact planes that no mortal pilot could sense or penetrate.

She had left instructions, however, with the Redrock agent, San Six. He spoke to El Yaqui, who sent a preman magistrate to look for Davey Dunahoo and Buglet. They were found in the brush beyond the town dump, solemnly building a mud-mortared rock pyramid above the ashes of their dog. Silent and afraid, they were escorted to the agency.

"I don't bite." The genial agent came to meet them at the door of a huge room hung with bits of ancient preman art. "In fact, I've got good news for you." He made them sit in hard chairs too big for them. "First, however, I must ask you something." He leaned intently toward them across his bare enormous desk. "Who has spoken to you, about Multiman?"

Though he was smiling cheerily, his brown eyes seemed very keen.

"Everybody." Davey squirmed on the hard chair and looked at Buglet. "But most people don't believe."

"Who does believe?"

"My mother did." Davey stared up at a tall case full of rusty preman weapons. The agent sat and watched, till at last he went on: "She was born on the old Asian reservation. She was beautiful. A halfgod saw her and took her away to be a bride of Belthar. She was never chosen, but the halfgod took her for himself. When he didn't want her any more, he sent her here. She worked for La China, and she used to say I had many fathers. She hated all the gods and the whole Thearchy. I guess that's why she wanted to believe in the Multiman."

"What exactly did she say?"

Davey looked at Buglet till she nodded.

"She said he was made in the Fourth Creation—but he's no demon. He escaped Belthar's attack. He lives in hiding. He's immortal, waiting for his time and gaining power while he waits. When he comes out, he'll be greater than all the gods—Master of the whole multiverse. My mother said he would bring justice to the premen."

The agent reached to touch a button, and Davey guessed that some machine had been storing all he said.

"Thank you both." The agent smiled again, leaning back in his tall chair. "It's my duty to learn such things, but you needn't be afraid. The Lord Belthar is more tolerant of heresy than your old preman deities used to be. He knows that you premen are afflicted with imaginations too strong for your perceptions of reality. Anyhow, the church has been instructed to overlook the insane faith so many of you have in your old imaginary gods and demons. After all, I suppose you couldn't endure all the pains and dangers of your brief lives without your saviors and your saints, your werewolves and your warlocks." His gaze grew sharper. "Of course, if anybody did believe in this Multiman, we would have to act."

Davey moved uneasily in his chair, but Buglet shook her head. He shrugged and said nothing.

"Anyhow, there is good news for you." With a wider smile, the agent waved all talk of heresy away. "The goddess remembers you. She regrets what happened to your pet, and she likes what she calls your irreverent independence. She wants the two of you to become special wards of the agency. We're to see to your care and education."

"Thank—thank her!" Buglet gulped. "She's nice."

"She's kind." Davey sat very straight. "But we don't want anything."

"Why not?" The agent squinted at them unbelievingly. "You premen! I've been your keepers for a dozen years, and I still don't understand you."

Davey looked down and said nothing. The trumen were too much of everything—too quick and too keen and too strong, too modest and too happy and too generous. The agent seemed too content that his race had been designed to replace the old imperfect premen, yet too careful not to hurt them with any display of his own superiority.

"We—we thank you, sir!" Buglet stifled a sob. "The goddess is good, but she couldn't help Spot."

They squirmed off the chairs and started for the door.

"Don't go yet," the agent called. "My son wants to meet you."

San Seven was a stocky brown-eyed boy; their own age, but inches taller. Warm with instant friendship, he led them off to the long gameroom and showed them his toys, strange bright machines and moving models of men and gods and aliens. He showed them his books, which were filled with living pictures and mysterious symbolism. He took them into a great clean kitchen and filled them with foods and drinks they had never imagined. When he asked them to stay at the agency, so that they could really be his friends, Buglet accepted before Davey could say no.

Though they didn't like being apart, there was a whole huge room for each of them. One tall wall in Davey's room was a wonderful window that could open on starships in space or worlds in other universes. When San Seven was showing them the buttons that worked it, Davey asked to see the place where the premen were to go.

"Here's the planet where my uncle lives." Hastily, San Seven fingered the buttons to make a picture of jewel-colored towers clustered on smooth blue hills, with a double sun hung in the greenish sky. "My mother wants us to move there, when the agency is closed."

"It's lovely!" Buglet said. "You are very lucky."

"Please," Davey insisted. "Show us our new home."

"Another time." San Seven began explaining again how to shift the pictures.

"Now," Davey said.

With an unhappy shrug, San Seven punched the buttons to show them Andoranda V. It was all naked rock and mud flat and sand dune, with rivers of red mud staining the storm-beaten seas. The sky was yellow dust, spilling blood-colored rain.

Buglet turned white beneath her grime, and Davey clenched his fists.

"A very remarkable planet." San Seven spoke fast without looking at them. "It's off in Universe Nine. It does have creatures enough in the sea—I've seen great dark monsters fighting things as big as starships. But its native life never adapted to dry land. You premen will have the continents all to yourselves."

"No—no trees!" Buglet whispered. "No grass."

"Not yet. But we're working to establish Terran land-life."

"I don't like it," Davey muttered. "We won't go there."

"You'll own the whole planet." San Seven tried to smile. "And we're trying to improve it for you. We've had a pilot station there for several centuries." The picture flickered to show a row of rusting metal huts around a circle of rock blasted flat for landing shuttles. The huts were banked high with dirty snow and nothing moved anywhere. "We're trying to terraform the planet, but the engineers have run into problems. Terran plants die. Seeds don't sprout. Even our engineers are sterile there—they're reporting some unknown lethal factor that kills all desire."

"So we'll die there."

"There won't be children—but of course the starships will bring supplies. The Lord Belthar will preserve you."

"We won't go."

"The Lord says you will." As if to soften that hard finality, San Seven added, "Though you'll probably be allowed to stay here till the lake begins to fill."

He tapped the buttons again, to show them Quelf's new dam, a dark ridge reaching from one bleak red mesa to another, construction machines still swarming over it.

"But we premen made you," Buglet was whispering. "We made the mumen and the gods. Now you want to take the last poor scrap of our own world and send us off to die—"

"I'm sorry." San Seven reached to touch her shoulder, but she shrank from his hand. "Our Lord is merciful," he insisted. "You can't blame him and you can't blame us. My father says the whole trouble is that you premen just can't compete, because too many of your ancestors were spoilt creations."

Davey stiffened angrily.

"It's only what my father says." San Seven moved cautiously back. "After all, the Creators were still premen. Though I know they did make us and the gods, they often bungled. Their greatest failure was the Fourth Creation—the demons that the Lord Belthar had to destroy. But there were other misbegotten things, my father says, that escaped from the lab to corrupt the blood of the premen. By now, my father says, you're all stepchildren of the Creators."

Buglet caught Davey's lifted arm.

"But of course you aren't to blame, any more than we are." He smiled at them gently. "Though it's simply stupid to expect some new god to save you. I know the Creators were premen, but the Creation is over. The Lord Belthar won't let it happen again."

He hurried them back to the gameroom to let them play with his toys. Davey sat down instead to look at a book. The live pictures delighted him, changing scenes as he moved his finger along the edge of the page, but the text baffled him with many-colored patterns that flashed on and off too fast for him to see their shapes.

Hopefully he asked, "Can you teach me how to read?"

"Our symbology doesn't work like preman print." San Seven looked apologetic. "It isn't linear, with one simple symbol after another. It's multiplex, instead. Each display is a whole gestalt. I'm afraid it's too hard for you. Come on down to the basement. There's a free-fall gym you'll enjoy."

Trying to forget that they were premen, they followed him down to the gym. They did enjoy the null G-belts, flying as easily as levitating gods, till San Seven called them to meet his mother. A calm cheery woman, she made them wash themselves in a steamy, strange-smelling room and dressed them in her son's clothing. She said they must start going to the preman school.

San Seven went with them on the first day to show them what to do, but his own training came from special machines in a room at the agency. When Davey asked to use these, he flushed and mumbled that they were too difficult for premen.

At the school, their fellow students were all bored and sullen. Their lessons were about all the other worlds of the Thearchy except Andoranda V, the only one that they could ever expect to see. They laughed at Davey and Buglet when they spoke of the Multiman—and sometimes jeered them for being the agent's pets.

Davey asked the preman teachers about the Creators and the Multiman, but all they knew came from the words in the *Book of Belthar*, which the school chaplain droned every morning before their studies began.

With pocket money now for tacos and rice when they were tired of the strange foods at the agency, or a cactus ice at the sidewalk cafe, they made more preman friends in town. The wisest, people said, was La China.

She was El Yaqui's wife, strange odored, silent and black

and nearly too fat to move. Shapeless in a faded blanket, she sat behind her ancient cash machine in the wide door of the trading post, taking money for meals and beer and mescal, for stuff off the shelves, for the girls upstairs. Her dark Asian eyes saw everything, but when Davey asked what she knew about the Multiman, her only answer was a sleepy smile.

"Maybe he's only a story," Buglet decided at last. "Maybe we'll have to let them send us off to that awful world where no life grows."

"My mother believed," Davey always insisted. "I won't give up."

One morning on their way to school they found a strange skimmer on the plaza beside the chapel of Thar. Branded with a black star inside the triple triangle, it had brought six gray-robed monks of the Polaris order, who scattered over the reservation to ask for preman antiques and look for preman ruins. Their dean came to the school.

"The gates are closed at Prince Quelf's dam." He was a short fat man who kept licking his lips as if his words had a good taste. "The lake will be rising fast. We want to gather all the preman artifacts we can, before the water gets here. If you know of any old records or tools or weapons—or where any old buildings stood—please help us preserve them for history."

"I think they're looking for the Multiman," Buglet whispered to Davey. "Don't tell them anything."

Meeting that night in the adobe town hall, the senate voted to let the monks explore Creation Mesa, which legend said had been the actual birthplace of the trumen and the gods. Though El Yaqui had always been as silent as his wife about the Multiman, he called softly next morning as Davey was passing:

"Venga, muchacho!"

El Yaqui was brown as the earth, bald as a pebble and quick as a spider. Coming late to the reservation from far high mountains where the church had left them alone, his people had brought strange words and strange things. In the hungry times before the goddess came, he had been generous to Davey and Buglet with bowls of milk and bits of sun-dried goat meat, and he still liked to share his desert lore and his peyote buttons on fiesta days. Breathing fast, Davey followed him down the stairs behind the bar and back through the stale stinks of spilled beer and mescal to a serape hanging on the wall.

"I think you are now ready to become a man." Hard brown fingers squeezed his arm, as if that had been the test. "You have asked about the Multiman. Really, I know nothing—there was no Multiman in the dry *sierra* from which my people came. Yet there are certain ancient artifacts I must show you, before the monks take them."

Behind the faded serape was a tiny room carved out of raw earth. A preman book with torn and yellowed pages lay open on a cloth-covered box, and a tiny flame burned beneath the image of an agonized man nailed to a cross.

"The book tells of a preman god." El Yaqui knelt before it, his brown hand jumping like a spider. "The son of the god was killed. The book promises that he will return to aid his true believers. I once thought that perhaps it foretold the Multiman's awakening."

"Do you—" The musty little pit seemed suddenly very cold, and Davey found himself quivering and voiceless with awe. "Do you believe?"

El Yaqui stood up slowly.

"I believe in the stargods," he said. "I have seen them and felt their power."

"Then why—" Davey frowned at his hard dark face, mysterious in the flicker of the candle. "Why do you keep these things?"

"Because they were my father's," El Yaqui said. "A powerful sorcerer and a very wise man. He knew the language of this book, and he used to read the story of the tortured god to me. He could take an owl's shape to watch the churchmen, and a coyote's shape to escape them. He expected the old god's forsaken son to return and rescue the premen. But he is dead. The waters will be rising over Redrock. The monks of Polaris have come to take the cross and the book for their museum of preman heresies."

Bending, he blew out the candle.

Buglet was waiting at a sidewalk table under La China's sleepy smile when Davey came out of the bar. She looked at him, and her bright face clouded.

"Davey, I'm afraid." Her small voice shivered. "I'm afraid of Andoranda V."

"I think we must learn all we can," he told her as they walked on to school. "All about the trumen and all about those worlds that are not for us. If there is no Multiman, I think we must plan to leave the reservation and hide among the trumen."

She stopped to stare at him, eyes round and huge and dark.

"I know the penalty," he told her. "But no penalty could be quite so bad as Andoranda V."

They learned all they could at school, though term by term their teachers seemed more and more stupid and indifferent, their fellow students less and less concerned with anything except sex and drugs and vandalism. They heard that the tunnels were flowing, heard that water was already deep in the lower canyons, heard that their camp was ready on Andoranda V. They saw the new square mountain rising, far-off in the north, which San Seven said was to be the foundation for Prince Quelf's palace. They listened to the fat gray Polarian dean, who sometimes dined at the agency and talked about the excavations on Creation Mesa.

Davey kept hoping the monks would uncover some hint that the Multiman was real, but the digging went slowly. There was only legend to tell where the old labs had stood, and the preman workers came only when they needed mescal and La China's girls. Beneath the barren dunes and the desert brush, all they had found was the story of Belthar's attack from space, written in buried craters and glassy flows of lava. Davey's last spark of hope was nearly dead, when Buglet had her dream of the Creation.

THREE

Unfolding like some desert flower, Buglet had begun to call herself Joan Dark after the heroine of a tragic preman legend she had heard from La China's girls. Taller that year than Davey, with straight black hair and yellow-gray eyes, she was suddenly alluring. Half the boys in school were in hot pursuit, and he was haunted with a secret dread that some churchman might see her and take her away for Belthar or himself.

Moody that morning, she met him with only a smile. They walked in silence down the hill from the agency and along the muddy road toward school. She was deaf to the whistles of two preman boys setting the sidewalk tables for La China. Unaware of the black-starred skimmer that dived by them, gray monk staring. Blind to the new arroyo that rain had cut in the trail ahead.

"Don't brood, Bug." He caught her arm to steer her past the ditch and trembled from the contact. "The lake's still miles away. We may have months yet to find something, though I don't know what—"

"Maybe I do."

He heard the hope in her voice and saw then that she was not despondent, but full of some confused elation. They had come to the plaza, which was stacked with big yellow plastic shipping containers, waiting to be packed with the effects of the premen for the long star-flight to Andoranda V. She led him back among them, off the trail.

"Last night I had—I guess it was a dream."

Her eyes were lemon-colored in the reflected light from the containers. She stood peering into the empty sky above them, as if searching for something she couldn't quite make out.

"But it was real, Davey. Real as anything! It didn't fade when I woke up, the way dreams do." Her troubled eyes came back to him. "Yet it's hard to talk about. Because I was somebody else. The places and people and ideas—they're all so new."

Shivering, she caught his hands.

"I'm getting a headache, just trying to remember."

He didn't beg her to tell about it; they understood each other too well for that. Instead he beckoned her farther away from the trail, and they sat face to face on two empty containers. Eagerly, he waited.

"It's like a memory, though it never happened to me. In it, I'm Eva—Eva Smithwick." She was hesitant, groping. "The last of the Creators. But the Creation wasn't the instant miracle they talk about in church. It took hundreds of people, working for hundreds of years."

She stopped to think again, unconsciously combing a black-shining sheaf of her hair with slim white fingers.

"The real Creators—the leaders—all belonged to one

great family—Adam Smithwick and his descendants. I believe—Eva believed that the family itself had been the actual first creation."

Leaning closer, he caught the faint sweet exciting scent of her hair.

"You can't guess how hard it is." Her tawny eyes flashed him a wry little smile. "It's all terribly real. So plain I'll never forget. But when I try to talk about it the words aren't there. Even the language Eva spoke wasn't yet our Terran. After all, I'm still *me.*"

"I'm glad."

With only a grave, pleased nod, she went on searching out the words that rang so strangely when she spoke them. "The first actual creators must have been Adam's parents. They had been geneticists, working to control mutations in lab animals and then in human beings by micro-manipulation of chromosomes—"

She saw his puzzled expression and paused to think again.

"They had been working with the genetic code, trying to revise the blueprint for a new body and a new mind carried by the germ cell from parents to child."

"I can understand that," he said. "From exobiology class."

"Adam's parents had both been in trouble. His father had to leave a country called England when people learned about his experiments with humans—I guess they were already afraid of what he might create."

Gazing at the yellow containers, Davey nodded somewhat grimly.

"His mother was a refugee from what was called a labor camp in another country—she had been sent there because she wouldn't work in a secret genetic project to grow military clones. Adam was born in Japan. He grew up to be the best geneticist anywhere.

"The reason was, his own genes had been improved. Anyhow, that's what Eva thought. She must have been his great-granddaughter." Buglet stopped again, frowning with effort, twisting the strands of bright-black hair. "Sorry, Davey. It's all in broken bits. I need time to fit them together—and we're already late for school."

"Forget school."

She sat very still for awhile, her searching eyes fixed on things beyond the yellow boxes and the dusty sky. "Adam—" She brightened again, remembering. "Adam came to North America to be the first director of a new space clinic. Men were exploring the planets by then, and he was already the greatest specialist in space medicine.

"Secretly, he was already creating the trumen. I guess he had learned from the the misfortunes of his parents, because he kept the secret well. He arranged for the trumen to be accepted as the normal children of his wives—he was married three times in all—and children of his friends and associates.

"They looked like premen, of course. They were simply better. Stronger and smarter. Immune to all the old diseases. Free of all the old genetic defects. Rid of all the animal jealousies and aggressions that have always kept the premen in conflict with each other. Their social adaptiveness kept them out of trouble. For a whole generation, their existence wasn't suspected at all."

She paused again to think.

"People like San Seven wouldn't be suspected," Davey murmured. "He's as normal as anybody. Just brighter and nicer."

She hardly seemed to hear him.

"Darwin—Darwin Smithwick was the next Creator.

Adam's last child and probably himself another special creation. He made the mumen—mutant creations shaped to meet all the different challenges of space. With their new senses, the mumen began finding the first shortcuts to other star systems through the contact planes—up till then, the finite speed of light had limited exploration."

Her lemon eyes smiled at something he couldn't see.

"To the premen of those days, the Creators themselves must have seemed like gods. They were nearly immortal. Adam lived and worked a hundred years. Darwin even longer. Before he died, the trumen were changing history. Never fully revealing themselves—at first not even aware they were a new species—they had become the leaders in everything.

"War ceased, because the trumen saw that it was stupid. They dissolved the old contending nations into a new world republic. They revised social systems to end crime and disorder. They invented new sources of energy and food, found a new equilibrium with the environment. There was a long age of peace and abundance, till the premen revolted."

"They had never known—"

Half a mile across the town, the school bell had begun to ring. Buglet moved as if to slide off her yellow perch, but Davey checked her with a gesture. Frowning in a way that charmed him, she went on again, groping for the words she recited in a grave slow voice that hardly seemed her own.

"For a hundred years and more, the trumen had been the faithful public servants Adam Smithwick wanted. Under them, the premen were better off than they had ever been. As Darwin wrote in his journal, the world had become the paradise the old preman prophets and philosophers had always dreamed about. Most of the premen must have understood that their new leaders were too useful to be destroyed, because the rebellion was delayed a long time, even after the truth was pretty well known.

"When it came, the rebellion was savage. As illogical as always, the premen refused to see that they had nothing at all to gain. Their own irrational leaders magnified the number and the powers of the trumen. In a wave of insane panic, they overturned the world republic to revive the old conflicting nations and parties and unions and classes. Trumen were mobbed and slaughtered. War came back. Famine and disease and misrule.

"Yet, through most of that dark age, the premen seemed about to win. They had the numbers, billions against a few tens of thousands. They had their old aptitude for senseless violence. They seized or burned most of the cities. Trying to kill the Creators, they wrecked the space clinic. Darwin Smithwick had to hide in an old copper mine.

"In the end, of course, the premen lost. Numbers meant nothing. Though the trumen lost most of the Earth, they found refuge in space. No fighters themselves, they brought muman soldiers to defend their strongholds around the spaceports. And Huxley Smithwick made the stargods.

"Darwin's son, Huxley had grown up in hiding—most of the time in that abandoned mine. He learned his father's crafts of creation and improved on them. When he escaped to space, he carried three new synthetic life-cells in cryogenic flasks. Alpha and Beta and Gamma.

"Those names seem to have come from the phonetic symbols of some lost language. Huxley separated the new beings for their own safety, arranging for proxy-mothers to bear them on three different planets. Not really divine, not yet immortal, they were gifted enough. He called them his three Valkyries, from the warrior women in some forgotten preman legend. When they were old enough for battle, he sent them back to face the rebels.

"Though their powers were limited, they had been designed for battle. Withdrawing from simple space at will, they were untouchable. They could levitate where they pleased, unstoppable. With one flash of a nimbus, they could kill a preman leader or explode an arsenal. After two or three encounters, the premen panicked.

"Huxley recalled his Valkyries to space, and the trumen tried to restore the world republic. For reasons they couldn't understand, the effort failed. Defeat had changed the premen. They refused to trust anybody, or to accept any aid, or even to help themselves. As Eva saw it, they had suffered an emotional wound that never healed. And I guess that's the way Redrock began."

Buglet wrinkled her nose at the sewer stink drifting between the yellow containers.

"The two cultures grew apart as the centuries went on—and the premen lost most of their own. When the world-state came back, it was a union of the spreading truman enclaves, with the premen left out. I wonder—"

Her breath caught, and her voice was again her own.

"I wonder if San Six is right—if the premen really are the mongrel stepchildren of creation. Because they just gave up. They quit trying. In government. In science and art. In everything. When the troubles ended, they still owned most of the planet. But they died of their own strife, their own plagues, their own despair. Their numbers dwindled as the trumen grew. Again and again they gave up land, till Redrock is their last stronghold—"

"You and I are premen," Davey objected gravely. "Really, Bug, do you feel so inferior?"

Her yellow eyes blinked.

"I guess I was still thinking Eva Smithwick's thoughts."

With a quick little smile, she reached to touch his arm. "We're different, of course. We can't do what the stargods can. We aren't even as sharp as San Seven, in a good many ways. But we're—ourselves."

"We're just as good—as good as anybody!" A gust of anger shook his voice, and he sat bleakly, silently until it had passed. "Go on, Bug." He bent toward her hopefully. "Is there anything about the Multiman?"

"Maybe." She frowned at the yellow boxes. "It's like trying to fit the pieces of a broken pot together when half of them are gone. I don't know what I know. I have to put the scraps of Eva's memory into a language I can speak.

"But Huxley Smithwick had a daughter—"

Absently combing at her hair, she forgot to go on.

Davey watched the monk's skimmer sail above them toward the dig on Creation Mesa, and listened to the hooves of a mule clopping along the trail.

"When the war was over, Huxley came back from space." She nodded to herself, as if to confirm the recollection. "He built the laboratory—the exobiology lab—where the old space clinic had stood. There he created mates for his three Valkyries.

"The first of the stargods. True immortals, with keener senses to explore the multiverse and greater powers to control it. The mumen had begun encountering advanced and sometimes hostile alien cultures, and he thought they needed stronger champions than the Valkyries.

"In his old age, talking to his daughter, he confessed that the gods had been a blunder. Even at the time, he was aware of the danger, but he thought he was taking precautions enough. Like the Valkyries, those first gods were implanted in the wombs of proxy-mothers, to be born and raised on other worlds. Trying to guard himself, he gave them an avoidance compulsion, to keep them light-years away from Earth.

"Eva was his daughter and his student, herself perhaps his greatest creation—but not immortal, of course. The last Creator. She took over the lab when he died. By that time, the extent of his blunder was clear. The gods were far too powerful, too scornful of their makers, with too much self and passion from their Valkyrie mothers, more anxious to extend their own divine might than to aid and shield the older human races.

"The first three gods made no trouble. Bound by that compulsion, they stayed away from Earth. But—after they had found their Valkyrie mates—their children inherited their immortality and all their powers, without the compulsion. Alarmed, Eva went to work on a new creation—"

"The Multiman?"

"Not by such a name." Buglet shook her head. "She was trying to design a new sort of being, greater than the stargods, with a better control of the multiversal environment and a stronger love for all the older races. But she had to rush her work, because she was afraid the jealous young gods would try to wreck it, to defend their own supremacy.

"There simply wasn't time—"

She stopped again, frowning at nothing, absently kicking at the next hollow box.

"That's about as far as I can go. About all Eva knew, when her memory somehow got mixed up with mine. She was still busy in the lab on what we call Creation Mesa, working to perfect that new life-cell. Out in the multiverse, Belthar and his brothers and cousins were growing up, afraid of her work and free to attack her. The new creation wasn't ready to be implanted in a proxy-mother. She was making plans to hide it—"

"Where?" Davey whispered. "Where?"

Her lemon eyes looked through him, while she groped for Eva Smithwick's thoughts.

"The mine!" She smiled a little, as the details came. "In that old copper mine, where her father had hidden. It's under the end of the mesa. The centuries and the preman wars had already erased all the surface signs that it was ever there, and her father had dug an escape tunnel to it from the basements of the lab.

"She knew the gods would be looking for new creatures. To outwit them, she had set her engineers to work on a robot nurse that could keep the germ-cells frozen for years—maybe for centuries—till a safe time came for it to be incubated and developed."

"So he's out there?" He was breathless with excitement. "Asleep under the mesa!"

"I don't know, Davey." With a shrug of regret, she slid off the container. "That's where Eva Smithwick was in time. She didn't know what was going to happen. I've come to the end of the memory—if it was a memory."

"Do you think—" He caught her hands, and found them oddly cold. "Do you think we could find a way into the mine? Wake the Multiman?"

"That's all I know." Though the still air was hot around them, bitter with the smell of the yellow containers, something made her shiver. "If he's there at all, the monks will probably find him first."

FOUR

Their preman teacher scowled and their fellow students winked and tittered when they came late to school. Davey sat dumb all day, hearing nothing, vainly trying to imagine ways to reach and wake the sleeping Multiman before the gray monks found him. Working out on a null-G belt that afternoon, he was so preoccupied that he tumbled clumsily into the ceiling of the gym. When San Seven asked what the trouble was, a wave of terror swept him.

"Just worried, I guess," he muttered. "About Andoranda V."

"I'm sure you are." San looked at him almost too keenly. "If I can help, just ask."

He had to quench a spark of hope. San was his best male friend, but also a sharp-witted truman, faithful to Belthar. "Thanks," he said. "But I'm afraid there is no help."

On graduation night, he filed into the old adobe auditorium just behind Buglet, half-drunk with the scent and shine of her long black hair. Seated side by side, they listened to the commencement address. The speaker was San Six.

The occasion was significant, he said, because they would be the last graduates from Redrock. They would be carrying their memories and the traditions of the school to a far-off frontier world, where they would be facing novel and exciting challenges. To survive there, to succeed, to make their careers and nurture their ancient preman culture, they must call on the lessons they had learned from their faithful teachers and the aid they might earn through steadfast devotion to the gods—

Listening to the agent's mellow oratory and thinking of those empty containers waiting on the plaza, Davey tried not to shudder. He turned impulsively to Buglet, who looked very grave and pale in her dark robe, more alluring than a goddess.

"If we could run away together—" The whisper burst out before he thought. "If we could hide somewhere—live somewhere as trumen—"

He stopped, stifled by the fear of his own audacity. She

turned a little toward him, her lemon eyes wide. After one breathless instant, she nodded slightly.

"I'll come." Her lips moved soundlessly. "If we can find a way."

"But that's crazy." His wave of elation was already gone. "We've got to stay. Understand your vision—whatever it was. Look for the Multiman. If he does exist."

They went next morning to the Thar chapel, to ask for work at the excavation. The fat dean was sorry, but the monks had stopped hiring anybody. The dig had not been productive, and the new lake was rising fast. Within the next six-square of days, their expedition would be leaving Redrock.

"Anyhow," Buglet whispered to Davey. "I want to see where Eva lived. The place might wake another memory."

They rented two mules from La China and rode out for a picnic on Creation Mesa. A skimmer came sailing to meet them at the top of the trail, and a gray monk leaned out to warn them that the area was closed to visitors.

"Your permission, Master." Davey bowed respectfully. "We're only looking for wild flowers and a place to eat our lunch."

"Flowers?" the Polarian snorted. "All you'll find is cactus."

"There's a spring—" Buglet caught herself. "We heard there's a spring below the north rim."

"Dry rocks," the monk muttered.

But he let them ride on.

"There *was* a spring," Buglet whispered. "A thousand years ago. A tunnel, actually, dug to drain water out of the mine. It could be our way inside."

She rode ahead through the glaring noon, her brown mule clattering over naked rock and crashing through brittle brush. Davey followed eagerly, breathing the juniper scent, searching ahead for the green of a spring, but his bright hope died when they came to the rim. Buglet had stopped there, shading her eyes, peering blankly down at the desert.

"Things—things are wrong. Nothing looks quite like it should. Maybe Belthar's bombs caved the cliffs away. I guess the spring has dried up. Anyhow, I don't know where to look."

They hitched the mules to a piñon stump and scrambled down the slope looking for the scar of a drill, the red of iron rust, even one green weed. When they found nothing, Buglet chose another place to search, finally a third.

"No use." She was scratched and grimy, drooping in the heat. "I guess the monk was right."

They sat in the shade of a sandstone cliff to eat their bread and cheese. Late in the suffocating afternoon, they were riding back toward the trail when Davey slid off his mule.

"Bug, look!"

What he had found was half a red brick, one face burnt black. Kicking breathlessly into the gravel, he uncovered a gray mass of battered aluminum, an opal blob of fused glass, a blackened silver coin. Reining up her mule, Buglet peered off into the heat-hazed distance.

"Eva's view!" Her eyes grew wide. "From the parking lot behind the exobiology lab. Davey, this is where the monks think they're digging." With a quick little nod of recognition, she looked south across the mesa. "Actually, they're down at the site of the old mining town."

"Shall we tell them?" Davey frowned doubtfully up at her and down at the opal ball. "If we do, they may find the Multiman—and maybe kill him. If we don't, the lake will drown him."

She sat for a moment staring down at the gravel as if her yellow eyes could penetrate it. "The escape tunnel from the lab to the mine must be fifty feet down. Farther than we could hope to dig. I think we'll have to risk help from the monks."

When the pudgy Polarian dean came that night to dinner at the agency, Davey showed him the bits of brick and metal and glass. Squinting at them, he forgot his appetite. They went with him next morning in the skimmer to guide him to the site and watched while he explored it with strange machines.

"Probes," he told them. "Sonic and magnetic and gravitic. They're mapping the solid masses and the metallic bodies under the gravel and rubble. Broken walls. Pavements and foundations. Old excavations. An important site. I wish we had found it sooner."

"Since we found it," Davey begged, "may we work here?"

"Till you leave," the dean agreed. They drove stakes for him that afternoon and helped stretch the colored cords that outlined the foundations of the buried lab. Davey went to work next morning with a spade, tossing gravel against a sloping screen, while Buglet knelt in the dust to scrabble for artifacts.

"You're right above old Huxley's tunnel," she told him. "If we can ever dig that far down."

His hands were raw blisters before the long shift ended, but he had begun to uncover ancient masonry, walling his narrow pit.

"An old elevator shaft," Buglet told him, and dropped her voice. "Old Huxley's escape tunnel opens from the bottom of it." She frowned uneasily. "If we can somehow get into it first—"

Day after day, he shoveled rubble into a bucket, to be hoisted and sifted above. Foot by laborious foot, he cleared the ancient shaft. The pit was hot and his muscles ached. but he dug through a level of broken porcelain and glass that came, Buglet said, from the biochemical lab. He dug past a shattered archway into what she said had been a cold room for a colony of alien methane-breathers. He dug on down beside a vast concrete slab that had covered a bomb shelter. Dripping muddy sweat, reeling with fatigue, still he shoveled rubble.

But time ran fast. From the windows of the skimmer, as the monks took them home after work, they began to see dusty sunsets burning red in the rising lake. The preman magistrates had begun scattering the yellow shipping containers through the town, one to every dwelling. Most of the other premen stopped coming to work, but they kept on.

Breathing the dust of dead centuries, Davey piled the bucket with broken stone and muck, with charred wood and rusty iron, with stray bones and battered bullets. Spitting bitter mud, he worked on down beyond the floor of the buried shelter.

"Just a few feet more!" Buglet's tawny eyes shone. "The tunnel opens from the south side of the shaft. There was a false wall to hide it. I don't think the monks suspect it yet."

Energized with eager hope, yet half afraid that the wall had broken, that some flood had washed debris through to choke the tunnel, he toiled through most of another day. Abruptly, in mid-afternoon, the Polarian foreman called him out of the pit. Work had stopped. The expedition was departing.

"Sorry to go," the dean told the agent at dinner that night. "Because of your excellent hospitality. And because we've finally located the true site of creation. We could spend our lives here, uncovering relics of the holy progenitors. But the church has ordered us out."

He reached to spear a second steak.

"Enjoy yourself," the agent urged him genially. "Everybody's going. The transport's in orbit at last. Long overdue.

Delayed somewhere to wait for a pilot. Now we've only three days to clear the premen out."

Afraid to look at Buglet, Davey reached under the table for her hand. Cold and quivering, her fingers clung to his. San Seven sat across the table, watching them with a troubled intentness. He followed when they left the dining room.

"Davey—" His uneasy whisper stopped them. "Bug—please!"

He beckoned them into his own room and closed the door. Nearly always cheerily confident, he looked so pale and nervous now that Davey thought he must be ill.

"You heard—" Nervously, he went back to listen at the door. "Andoranda V—unless you get away—"

Unless we find the Multiman, Davey thought.

With a tiny gesture, Buglet warned him to say nothing.

"I'm not used to this." San Seven was breathless and sweating. "I've never broken the code before. But we—we've grown up together. I love you both. More than my truman friends—"

Buglet ran impulsively to kiss him.

Davey grinned gratefully, his own throat aching.

"I'm no—no criminal." He was almost sobbing. "Not till now." Brown fingers trembling, he thrust a tiny envelope at them. "I got into Father's office. Stole forms. Forged truman passports."

We'll never need them, Davey thought. *Unless—*

"Invented identities for you. Priests of Bel. You belong to the wandering order of Yed. Your society owns no property and observes no discipline. Your obligation is to preach the Lord Belthar's boundless love. Understand?"

"We've seen the priests of Yed."

Davey nodded. "They used to bring their message to us premen. Wearing rags. Sleeping on the chapel floor. Begging food at El Yaqui's. Preaching Bel to everybody." He grinned his gratitude. "A clever way to help us hide!"

"We can't repay you." Eyes dark and wet, Buglet accepted the envelope. "But we'll always remember—"

"Perhaps you shouldn't thank me." San Seven shrugged a troubled apology. "I'm not a skillful forger. You're likely to be picked up, and you know the penalty for trying to pass yourselves as trumen."

Death.

"We know," Bugiet whispered. "It's not as bad as Andoranda V."

"Anyhow," he mumbled, "I wanted you to have a chance."

With a guilty haste, he looked out to see that the hall was empty and rushed them from his room. They slipped away from the agency and hurried through back streets to the trading post.

"The starship's in orbit," Davey told La China. "They'll be shipping us out. We want to remember the mesa by moonlight. We'd like to rent two mules."

"Take them." She blinked sleepily across her cash machine. "Take these." Her fat black fingers dug into the drawer for a heavy roll of coins. "Take—take anything you need." Her husky voice caught. "If I were young enough, I'd be running with you."

"Maybe—" Davey whispered. "Maybe the Multiman can help."

"There's no help." She smiled dreamily. "I'm dying tonight."

They saddled the mules and followed dark alleys out of town. The moon was full, the desert all silver and shadow.

"It's all so beautiful," Buglet murmured. "Too lovely to leave."

The dig on the mesa was silent, black cranes jutting like skeletal arms into the sky. They hitched the mules and he showed Buglet how to run the bucket. Down in the narrow pit he dug desperately.

One jagged mass of fallen concrete was too heavy to move. With no tools or explosive to break it up, he burrowed around it. His headlamp found a dark hollow behind it, and he smelled musty dampness.

"Bug!" His voice boomed back from the walls of the pit, magnified into a monstrous bellow. "We've found the tunnel—open!"

She rode the bucket down. Thrusting and prying with the shovel, hauling bare-handed at muddy concrete masses, they widened the opening. Before it was big enough for him, she dived through. For a moment she was lost in the dark.

"We've found the Multiman!" Her face came back into the light, grime-streaked and eager. "If Eva really left him here."

They strained together to move another boulder, and he slid down beside her. Roughly cut through dark sandstone, the narrow passage was so low they had to stoop. Sloping steeply down, it brought them at last into a wider shaft, where drops of falling water crashed and echoed.

"Which way now, Bug?"

She shrugged uncertainly.

"The robot nursery—" Her voice brought chattering echoes out of the dark, and she dropped it to a whisper. "The nursery hadn't been installed. All I know is Eva's idea. She wanted a high spot, safe from flooding. She wanted easy access to it from the lab, through Huxley's tunnel."

The shaft curved and sloped, where the miners must have followed a wandering vein. Ancient timbers had gone to dust, letting it cave. They climbed it, till a larger rockfall stopped them. Crawling through the jagged crack above the boulder mound, they saw the loom of a huge, dark-cased machine.

"No!" Buglet gasped. "Oh, no!"

Davey's searching headlamp struck dull glints from the rock-piled floor around the silent machine. Once a thick glass shell had covered it, but that lay shattered into dusty fragments beneath a great stone mass from the ceiling. Clambering down the slope, he let his light play over broken glass and rusting metal. Nothing moved, and the air had a reek of old decay.

"Dead!" Buglet sobbed. "The Multiman is dead."

FIVE

Still damp with sweat, Davey shivered. That cold cavern had suddenly become a tomb—for Eva Smithwick's last creation, for the premen waiting exile to Andoranda V, for all their dreams. Though they stayed an hour, digging under the great glass shards in search of something more than rust and dust, they found no hope.

"Nothing!" Davey flashed his lamp on the boulder that had crushed the machine. "It happened too long ago. A quake, I guess."

Buglet stood trembling in the gloom, fingering a broken scrap of stainless metal. She shaded her eyes from his light. "Belthar's bombs, more likely."

"What now, Bug?" He peered at her hopefully. "Shouldn't there be a spare machine? A second Multiman?"

"I don't know." She dropped the useless metal fragment and started a little when it jangled on broken glass. "Eva was afraid the machine might fail. She did think of a spare. But—" With a tired shrug, she turned to stare at the dead pile of rock and wreckage. "I don't know anywhere to look."

Her small sad voice sent a surge of pity through him. He reached to touch her trembling shoulder, and suddenly they clung together. The warm strong yielding feel of her body spun him into a chasm of emotion. He crushed her hard against him.

"I—I love you, Bug!" he gasped. "We've got to live. That means we've got to run. With money from La China and passports from San, I think we have a chance." He looked into her lemon-gray eyes, contracting under his light. "Are you game?"

Eyes wet and bright, she kissed him again.

The full moon was already low when they came out of the excavation. They rode the mules east to the mesa rim and down a long rocky slope. Dawn met them far from Redrock, on a vast bare flat.

"They'll soon miss us." She kept watching the sky behind. "They'll come hunting."

The tired mules were stumbling, but they pushed on to the next sandstone ridge. From the shelter of a red-walled canyon there, they saw the glint of the early sun on a skimmer that flew low, searching across Creation Mesa.

Hiding out through that blazing day, they finished the tortillas and smoked meat they had brought from El Yaqui's. By turns, they watched and slept. Climbing the canyon, after the skimmer was gone, they found a rock pool where they drank and watered the mules. From the top of the ridge, just before sunset, they looked out of the reservation into truman country.

A straight and endless line cut off the desert. On the preman side, red buttes and dead brush shimmered in a haze of smothering heat. Beyond the line, young orchards and ripe grain patterned the fertile truman lands with tender green and mellow gold, laced with narrow blue canals.

"A wall!" Buglet whispered. "A wall around the reservation."

"Death if we cross." He spat muddy froth. "Andoranda V if we don't."

Dismounting to rest the mules, they sat resting on a rocky ledge, looking down into that richer world. Harvest machines like bright insects were crawling over the golden wheat. The reddening sun picked out the lean white towers and mirror domes of a truman town on one far hill.

"There are too many trumen," Buglet murmured solemnly. "Too few of us."

As they rose to go on, Davey looked back and caught his breath. The desert behind was a vast empty basin, the long blue shadow of Creation Mesa creeping across it. One tiny red speck had left the shadow, creeping after them beneath tiny puffs of sunlit dust.

"A muman soldier," he decided. "On our trail. Using a null-G belt."

"Then it will catch us." Alarm darkened her yellow eyes. "We can't outrun a flying belt."

"We can try." He gave her a small grim smile. "Our trail will be harder to follow in the dark. If we can get across the line, we'll be trumen—with passports to prove it."

In the hazy dusk, the sweat-lathered mules slid and scrambled down the ridge. In the early dark, they plodded on and on across the next bare gravel plain. When one mule went lame, Davey dismounted to lead it. Before moonrise, the other stumbled into a dry arroyo, pitching Buglet over its head.

Davey found her lying in the bottom of the rocky gully, unable to speak. Her breath was gone. When she got it back, she whispered faintly that she wasn't hurt at all. Except for a twisted ankle.

The mules, they saw, could carry them no farther. She sat on the arroyo rim, nursing her ankle, while he unsaddled and freed them. In the first pale light of the moon, he cut two leather thongs from the saddles, knotted a pocket between them, and searched the arroyo bed for pebbles to fit the pocket.

"A weapon?" she asked.

"A sling," he said. "One summer El Yaqui taught me how to use a sling for rabbits."

"For rabbits, maybe." Her eyes were huge and black in the moonlight. "Not for muman deadeyes."

He wrapped her ankle with another thong and found her a dry yucca stalk for a cane. More slowly now, they toiled on. At midnight, by the high moon, they were climbing a long rolling slope which brought the far-off town into view again, its domes now glowing rose and gold.

"The reservation line." He pointed at a straight dark streak across the next low hill. "We'll be there by daylight."

Buglet limped on beside him. At the crest of the ridge, she stopped with a gasp of dismay. He thought she had hurt her ankle again, until she pointed into the broad valley ahead and he saw the shimmer of the moon on water.

"The lake—" she whispered. "It has cut us off."

They hobbled on until the ridge they followed had become a narrow spit of sand jutting into a wide arm of Quelf's filling sea.

"Water all around us," he muttered huskily. "And the deadeye behind."

They waded out through the drowned brush and cupped water in their hands to drink. He stood a long time staring out across that unexpected barrier.

"Trapped." Wearily, he splashed back to the shore. "But we tried."

"We tried," she echoed bitterly. "Now I guess we wait."

Waiting, they lay in a dry sand hollow. Buglet loosened the thong around her swelling ankle and rested her head on his shoulder. She felt very light and fragile, tragically vulnerable. Breathing the sweetness of her hair, he thought of many things to say, but nothing really mattered now.

"Stepchildren," she whispered once. For a time she was breathing so evenly that he thought she was asleep. Her low voice startled him. "It's a strange thing, Davey. When you remember that we premen made the trumen and the mumen and the gods."

His throat ached, and he only stroked her glossy hair.

Brush crackled and pebbles rattled.

Standing stiffly, they watched the mutant guardian coming down the ridge. Naked except for harness and belt, it was taller than a god. Its red scales were black and silver in the moonlight, but the deadly lens in its crest glowed crimson. Though its gliding bounds seemed slow, each covered many yards.

Buglet kissed Davey and gripped her yucca stick. He fitted a pebble to his sling. Rising and pausing and falling through a last flowing leap, the guardian crashed into a grease-wood clump twenty yards from them. It stopped there, splendid in its towering power. The wind brought its scent, an odor like pine.

"Greetings, premen!" Its voice was a trumpet blaring. "From Allaya K, guardian of the gods. To Davey Dunahoo, male. To Joan Dark, female. By order of the church, you are under arrest. Drop your weapons and walk forward."

Davey glanced at Buglet. Somehow she was smiling, fine teeth glancing white in the moonlight. He whirled the sling to test the pebble's weight.

"Now hear your charges," that cold voice pealed. "Jointly

and individually, you stand accused of theft from the preman woman known as La China. You stand accused of complicity in her death—"

"She isn't dead!" Buglet gasped. "She gave us the money and the mules."

"She was found hanging in the mule barn behind the trading post," the hard official tones boomed on. "You also stand accused of flight to escape transfer from Redrock. Any display of resistance will forfeit the clemency requested by San Six, agent of Belthar. Drop your weapons and walk toward me."

Davey gulped. "We aren't coming."

"Do you refuse to obey a lawful command?" the muman bugled. "Are you not aware that the penalty is death?"

"They want to send us to Andoranda V," Buglet said. "That is death."

"Listen, children." Another gliding bound brought the guardian halfway to them, so close that he could see a half-familiar pattern of darker scales across its gleaming torso. Its voice was suddenly softer, chiding, almost feminine. "Don't you know me?"

"No—" Buglet started. "You killed Spot!"

"A savage animal was charging the goddess," its new voice chimed instantly. "I struck it down at Prince Quelf's command. I followed my duty to the Lord Belthar then, as I follow it now. But I beg you to surrender. Even premen should be too smart to defy the church and the gods. Please put down your silly weapons."

"We—we just can't!"

Buglet brandished her yucca wand.

"Fools!" The muman's voice rang cold again. "You give me no choice."

The guardian crouched. Its black crest swelled. Its third

eye volleyed pathseekers, arrows of violet brightness probing for a mark. When they found the brittle stick, thunder cracked. The stick exploded into blazing splinters.

"Dav—"

With that stifled cry, Buglet slid down to the sand.

"Take warning, preman!"

That lethal eye swung to Davey, alive with painful fire. Sharp as needles, the ionizing pathseekers stabbed his arm and shoulder. His nostrils stung with their lightning scent, and all he could hear was their hurried *hiss-click, hiss-click, hiss-click.*

He whirled the sling around his head.

"Give up!" the mutant boomed. "Or—"

His wrath and grief lent force to his stone. It went true, but the guardian had flung out its arm, as if brushing at a gnat. He heard the pebble thump against the yielding scales, heard it clatter on the gravel. Dancing nearer, the muman lit the brush around them with its killing eye.

"Idiot!" Its laughter rang like an iron bell. "You premen! You're still only animals, for all your human form. Blind to logic. Slaves to raw emotion. Cowards when you ought to fight and brave when only flight can save you. I guess it's no wonder you've lost your last reservation."

Its seeing eyes challenged him.

"Will you yield now?"

Gasping for his breath, Davey had no voice. His whole body quivered. Tears blurred his eyes, until the guardian was a shimmering pillar of silver and crimson. Fingers numb and clumsy, he fitted another pebble to the pocket. He spun the sling again. If he could smash—

"You've fury enough," the mutant mocked him. "But fury isn't force. If you elect to die here—"

Red fire exploded from that hateful eye.

Aiming at it, he tried to release his missile.

But time had paused. A red-purple fog had erased the towering guardian and flooded all the moon-gray sky. Blind, he still could somehow sense the deadly bolt hurled at him.

Desperately, with his last reserves of nerve and will, he tried to catch it, turn it back.

He knew the effort was folly, and he thought it had failed. That cold fire-fog became a roaring tornado around him, dragging him into a bright abyss he didn't understand. Bewildering images flickered and vanished in his mind, too quick for him to grasp them. Dazing thunder crashed—

"Davey!" Buglet was sobbing. "Can't you move?"

Numb and trembling, he sat up. The world seemed strangely still. The calm lake lapped around them. The mutant soldier lay sprawled a few yards away, its crested lens dark and dead, staring into the moonlit sky.

"You stopped it, Davey!" Breathless with elation, she was hovering over him, brushing at the sand on his face. "Just in time."

"I thought—thought it had stopped me." He stopped to get his own breath. "The finder beam was jabbing at me. I saw the lens blaze. I knew it was striking. I do remember trying to turn the bolt—"

"You did it!" Her voice was hushed with awe. "The bolt never reached you. I saw it curve back toward the guardian's heart. Somehow, you made it kill itself."

Unsteadily, he stood up. Sparks from Buglet's splintered stick still glowed around them on the sand, and the air was edged with its smoke. Bewildered, he stared down at the fallen soldier. The mighty limbs were twisted and rigid, and the extended talons had ripped long scars in the sand.

"If I stopped the bolt—" He shook his head. "I don't know how!"

"Maybe—maybe I do!" A sudden elation had quickened Buglet's voice. "When it hit my stick, something happened to me. The shock knocked me down. For just an instant, I must have blacked out. By the time it was striking at you, I was awake again. With another memory, Davey! A later link to Eva Smithwick's mind.

"Now I know—"

Her voice faded out.

He felt numb and light and strange, the way he had felt once on the desert, chewing bitter peyote buttons with El Yaqui. Staring down at the enormous armored body lying on the sand, he couldn't remember for a moment what it was. When he looked back at Buglet, she was wrapped in a dust-devil of whirling golden motes. Her excited voice came out of its thundering vortex, still so faint he could hardly hear.

"—more than stepchildren," she was saying. "More than just rejects from the genetics lab, bungled mutants or spoiled gods. Davey, we're the actual Fourth Creation!"

Trying to move closer, to hear better, he was swept with her into that whirl of fire. The bright motes became winking images, like the truman symbology he had never learned. He knew they had meaning, but it was always gone too fast for him to grasp.

"Demons?" Swaying giddily, he fought for breath and balance. "Are we—demons?"

Her reply seemed intolerably delayed. Her slim form was frozen, as if the air had congealed around her, her face a stiffened mask. He stood there, numb and shuddering, until the thunder waned and that bright vortex let them go.

"The demons were a lie." Time had begun to flow again, and her rigid face thawed into a slow and bitter smile. "A lie invented by the gods to excuse their murder of the Creators. The real Fourth Creation was something greater than any god. It was the being we've been calling the Multiman. He is hidden in us!"

"But—" His tongue felt too thick for speech. "That smashed machine—"

"Only a decoy." Receding, those flakes of whirling fire still seemed more real than the moon, and her voice too faint and slow. "It's all clear now, since I have this later recollection. Eva had known from the first that the robot nurse would be too easy to find and destroy. She was looking for a more subtle way to hide her last creation. She found it long enough before Belthar came back—in the cells themselves."

Still too numb and dull to think.

He waited.

"What she did was to rebuild that last synthetic germ cell, to conceal its true nature. She had always given a share of her time to clinics on the preman reservations, and she was planning to use her last tour there to plant copies of the cell in preman women. The children, for many generations, were to be apparently premen, maybe even a little subnormal—too harmless-looking to alarm Belthar."

Her white smile brightened.

"Of course all I know is what she planned but she meant to be back here at the mesa lab when Belthar struck, working desperately to get her decoy machines completed and installed in the mine. I believe that's what happened. She herself was the real decoy, waiting for Belthar to wreck the lab and kill her. Out on the reservations, those preman-like children were born. They grew up to hand their special genes down to another generation. And the gods never suspected the truth."

Her eyes were black and huge, and her low voice quivered

with something near terror.

"Davey, those genes have come down to us!"

Breathing unevenly, he waited for that far-off thunder to fade from his ringing ears, for the last flecks of fire to dissolve in the cold moonlight.

"So that's how—" His voice was hoarse and strange. "How you got Eva Smithwick's memory?"

"The things we must know were engineered into the germ cells. Designed to lie latent, generation after generation. Till something triggered them."

"Bug, I can't—can't realize!" Though time was flowing again he felt dull and cold and slow. He reached uncertainly to touch her arm, but his hand shuddered and drew back. "You're a goddess, Bug. Greater than a goddess!"

"We don't yet know what we are."

"We?" With a stiff little grin, he shook his head. "I don't remember anything. There's no Multiman waking up in me. Sorry, Bug, I'm just a preman."

"What do you think happened to the deadeye?" She nodded at its body. "I think—I know we both carry the created genes, though different powers have begun to awaken in us."

He stood trembling, as if the wind off the lake had chilled him.

"Why?" He gaped at her. "Why us? Why now?"

"Danger is the stimulus, I think."

"I never expected—" He had to get his breath. "Bug, what are we going to be?"

"I know what Eva planned." Her dark eyes shone. "The being we called the Multiman is sleeping in us, Davey. In both of us. Waiting to be waked. We're the Fourth Creation born to challenge the gods!"

He blinked at her, shocked by the audacity of that.

"I don't feel equal to the gods." He shrugged uneasily. "In fact, I'm tired and cold and hungry. And we're in a bad spot, Bug. We've just killed a muman guardian. The whole church will be hunting us now—"

"We ought to welcome danger, Davey." She was smiling in the moonlight. "It's the stimulus we need, to make us what we must be."

"I imagine we'll see danger enough."

She looked down at the body, her smile slowly fading.

"It does frighten me," she whispered at last. "To think what Eva planned for us to do. To repair the errors of the gods. To build a better multiverse for all the human races." Her cold hand caught his. "That was to be our destiny—but I don't know how to begin."

"First of all, let's get off the reservation."

Testing her hurt ankle, she winced and nearly fell.

"We'll fly," he told her. "With the deadeye's belt."

Bending to loose the mutant soldier's harness, he found the nipples the sleek scales had hidden. Beneath the bluster and the armor she had been female. He felt a pang of astonished sadness that excitement washed away.

Buglet snuggled against his belly, her fragrant hair against his cheek. He snapped the belt around them and turned up the nullifier. The sandspit and the mutant body dropped behind. The cool dawn wind caught them, swept them on across the moon-flecked lake toward trumen country.

Guinevere for Everybody

The girl stood chained in the vending machine.

"Hi, there!" Her plaintive hail whispered wistfully back from the empty corners of the gloomy waiting room. "Won't somebody buy me?"

Most of the sleepy passengers trailing through the warm desert night from the Kansas City jet gaped at her and hurried on uneasily, as if she had been a tigress inadequately caged, but Pip Chimberley stopped, jolted wide awake.

"Hullo, mister." The girl smiled at him, with disturbingly huge blue eyes. The chains tinkled as her hands came up hopefully, to fluff and smooth her copper-blond hair. Her long tan body flowed into a pose that filled her sheer chemistic halter to the bursting point. "You like me, huh?"

Chimberley gulped. He was an angular young man, with a meat-cleaver nose, an undernourished mouse-colored mustache, and three degrees in cybernetic engineering. His brown, murky eyes fled from the girl and fluttered back again, fascinated.

"Won't you buy me?" She caressed him with her coaxing drawl. "You'd never miss the change, and I know you'd like me. I like you."

He caught his breath, with a strangled sound.

"No!" He was hoarse with incipient panic. "I'm not a customer. My interest is—uh—professional."

He sidled hastily away from the shallow display space where she stood framed in light, and resolutely shifted his eyes from her to the vending machine. He knew machines, and it was lovely to him, with the seductive sweep of its streamlined contours and the exciting gleam of its blinding red enamel. He backed away, looking raptly up at the glazing allure of the 3-D sign:

GUINEVERE
THE VITAL APPLIANCE!
NOT A ROBOT—WHAT IS SHE?

The glowing letters exploded into galaxies of dancing light that condensed again into words of fire. Guinevere, the ultimate appliance, was patented and guaranteed by Solar Chemistics, Inc. Her exquisite body had been manufactured by automatic machinery, untouched by human beings. Educated by psionic processes, she was warranted sweet-tempered and quarrel-free. Her special introductory price, for a strictly limited time, was only four ninety-five.

"Whatever your profession is, I'm very sure you need me." She was leaning out of the narrow display space, and her low voice followed him melodiously. "I have everything, for everybody."

Chimberley turned uncertainly back.

"That might be," he muttered reluctantly. "But all I want is a little information. You see, I'm a cybernetics engineer." He told her his name.

"I'm Guinevere." She smiled, with a flash of precise white teeth. "Model 1, Serial Number 1997-A-456. I'd be delighted to help you, but I am afraid you'll have to pay for me first. You do want me, don't you?"

Chimberley's long equine countenance turned the color of

a wet brick. The sorry truth was, he had never wholeheartedly wanted any woman. His best friends were digital computers; human beings had always bored him. He couldn't understand the sudden pounding in his ears, or the way his knobby fists had clenched.

"I'm here on business," he said stiffly. "That's why I stopped. You see, I'm a troubleshooter for General Cybernetics."

"A shooter?" Psionic educational processes evidently had their limits, but the puzzled quirk of her eyebrows was somehow still entrancing. "What's a shooter?"

"My company builds the managerial computers that are replacing human management in most of the big corporations," he informed her patiently. "I'm supposed to keep them going. Actually, the machines are designed to adjust and repair themselves. They never really go wrong. The usual trouble is that people just don't try to understand them."

He snapped his bony fingers at human stupidity.

"Anyhow, when I got back to my hotel tonight, there was this wire from Schenectady. First I'd heard about any trouble out here in the sun country. I still don't get it." He blinked at her hopefully. "Maybe you can tell me what's going on."

"Perhaps I can," she agreed sweetly. "When I'm paid for."

"You're the trouble, yourself," he snapped back accusingly. "That's what I gather, though the wire was a little too concise—our own management is mechanized, of course, and sometimes it fails to make sufficient allowances for the limitations of the human employee."

"But I'm no trouble," she protested gaily. "Just try me."

A cold sweat burst into the palms of his hands. Spots danced in front of his eyes. He scowled bleakly past her at the enormous vending machine, trying angrily to insulate himself from all her disturbing effects.

"Just four hours since I got the wire. Drop everything. Fly out here to troubleshoot Athena Sue—she's the installation we made to run Solar Chemistics. I barely caught the jet, and I just got here. Now I've got to find out what the score is."

"Score?" She frowned charmingly. "Is there a game?"

He shrugged impatiently.

"Seems the directors of Solar Chemistics are unhappy because Athena Sue is manufacturing and merchandising human beings. They're threatening to throw out our managerial system, unless we discover and repair the damage at once."

He glowered at the shackled girl.

"But the wire failed to make it clear why the directors object. Athena Sue was set to seek the greatest possible financial return from the processing and sale of solar synthetics, so it couldn't very well be a matter of profits. There's apparently no question of any legal difficulty. I can't see anything for the big wheels to clash their gears about."

Guinevere was rearranging her flame-tinted hair, smiling with a radiance he couldn't entirely ignore.

"Matter of fact, the whole project looks pretty wonderful to me." He grinned at her and the beautiful vending machine with a momentary admiration. "Something human management would never have had the brains or the vision to accomplish. It took one of our Athena-type computers to see the possibility, and to tackle all the technical and merchandising problems that must have stood in the way of making it a commercial reality."

"Then you do like me?"

"The directors don't, evidently." He tried not to see her hurt expression. "I can't understand why, but the first part of my job here will be to find the reason. If you can help me—"

He paused expectantly.

"I'm only four ninety-five," Guinevere reminded him. "You put the money right here in this slot—"

"I don't want you," he interrupted harshly. "Just the background facts about you. To begin with—just what's the difference between a vital appliance and an ordinary human being?"

He tried not to hear her muffled sob.

"What's the plant investment?" He raised his voice, and ticked the questions off on his skinny fingers. "What's the production rate? The profit margin? Under what circumstances was the manufacture of—uh—vital appliances first considered by Athena Sue? When were you put on the market? What sort of consumer acceptance are you getting now? Or don't you know?"

Guinevere nodded brightly.

"But can't we go somewhere else to talk about it?" She blinked bravely through her tears. "Your room, maybe?"

Chimberley squirmed uncomfortably.

"If you don't take me," she added innocently, "I can't tell you anything."

He stalked away, angry at himself for the way his knees trembled. He could probably find out all he had to know from the memory tapes of the computer, after he got out to the plant. After all, she was only an interesting product of chemistic engineering.

A stout, pink-skinned businessman stepped up to the vending machine, unburdened himself of a thick briefcase and a furled umbrella, removed his glasses, and leaned deliberately to peer at Guinevere with bulging, putty-colored eyes.

"Slavery!" He straightened indignantly. "My dear young lady, you do need help." He replaced his glasses, fished in his pockets, and offered her a business card. "As you see, I'm an attorney. If you have been forced into any kind of involuntary servitude, my fee can certainly secure your release."

"But I'm not a slave," Guinevere said. "Our management has secured an informal opinion from the attorney general's office to the effect that we aren't human beings—not within the meaning of the law. We're only chattels."

"Eh?" He bent unbelievingly to pinch her golden arm. "Wha—"

"Alfred!"

He shuddered when he heard that penetrating cry, and snatched his fingers away from Guinevere as if she had become abruptly incandescent.

"Oh!" She shrank back into her narrow prison, rubbing at her bruised arm. "Please don't touch me until I'm paid for."

"Shhh!" Apprehensively, his bulging eyes were following a withered little squirrel-faced woman in a black-veiled hat, who came bustling indignantly from the direction of the ladies' room. "My—ah—encumbrance."

"Alfred, whatever are you up to now?"

"Nothing, my dear. Nothing at all." He stooped hastily to recover his briefcase and umbrella. "But it must be time to see about our flight—"

"So! Shopping for one of them synthetic housekeepers?" She snatched the umbrella and flourished it high. "Well, I won't have 'em in any place of mine!"

"Martha, darling—"

"I'll Martha-darling you!"

He ducked away.

"And you!" She jabbed savagely at Guinevere. "You synthetic whatever-you-are, I'll teach you to carry on with any man of mine!"

"Hey!"

Chimberley hadn't planned to interfere, but when he saw Guinevere gasp and flinch, an unconsidered impulse moved him to brush aside the stabbing umbrella. The seething woman turned on him.

"You sniveling shrimp!" she hissed at him. "Buy her yourself—and see what you get!"

She scuttled away in pursuit of Alfred.

"Oh, thank you, Pip!" Guinevere's voice was muted with pain, and he saw the long red scratch across her tawny shoulder. "I guess you do like me!"

To his own surprise, Chimberley was digging for his billfold. He looked around self-consciously. Martha was towing Alfred past the deserted ticket windows, and an age-numbed janitor was mopping the floor, but otherwise the waiting room was empty. He fed five dollars into the slot, and waited thriftily for his five cents change.

A gong chimed softly, somewhere inside the vending machine. Something whirred. The shackles fell from Guinevere's wrists and flicked out of sight.

SOLD OUT! a 3-D sign blazed behind her. BUY *YOURS* TOMORROW!

"Darling!" She had her arms around him before he recovered his nickel. "I thought you'd never take me!"

He tried to evade her kiss, but he was suddenly paralyzed. A hot tingling swept him, and the scent of her perfume made a veil of fire around him.

"Hold on!" He pushed at her weakly, trying to remind himself that she was only an appliance. "I've got work to do, remember. And there's some information you've agreed to supply."

"Certainly, darling." Obediently, she disengaged herself. "But before we leave, won't you buy my accessory kit?" A singsong cadence came into her voice. "With fresh undies and a makeup set and gay chemistic night-wear, packed in a sturdy chemyl case, it's all complete for only nineteen ninety-five."

"Not so fast! That wasn't in the deal—"

He checked himself, with a grin of admiration for what was evidently an astutely integrated commercial operation. No screws loose so far in Athena Sue!

"Okay," he told Guinevere. "If you'll answer all my questions."

"I'm all yours, darling!" She reached for his twenty. "With everything I know."

She fed the twenty into the accessory slots. The machine chimed and whirred and coughed out a not-so-very-sturdy chemistic case. Guinevere picked it up and hugged him gratefully, while he waited for the clink of his nickel.

"Never mind the mugging, please!" He felt her cringe away from him, and tried to soften his voice. "I mean, we've no time to waste. I want to start checking over Athena Sue as soon as I can get out to the plant. We'll take a taxi, and talk on the way."

"Very well, Pip, dear." She nodded meekly. "But before we start, couldn't I have something to eat? I've been standing here since four o'clock yesterday, and I'm simply famished."

With a grimace of annoyance at the delay, he took her into the terminal coffee shop. It was almost empty. Two elderly virgins glared at Guinevere, muttered together, and marched out piously. Two sailors tittered. The lone counterman looked frostily at Chimberley, attempting to ignore Guinevere.

Chimberley studied the menu unhappily and ordered two T-bones, resolving to put them on his expense account. The counterman was fresh out of steaks, and not visibly sorry. It was chemburgers or nothing.

"Chemburgers!" Guinevere clapped her hands. "They're made by Solar Chemistics, out of golden sunlight and pure sea water. They're absolutely tops, and everybody loves 'em!"

"Two chemburgers," Chimberley said, "and don't let 'em burn."

He took Guinevere back to a secluded booth.

"Now let's get started," he said. "I want the whole situation. Tell me everything about you."

"I'm a vital appliance. Just like all the others."

"So I want to know all about vital appliances."

"Some things I don't know." She frowned fetchingly. "Please, Pip, may I have a glass of water? I've been waiting there all night, and I'm simply parched."

The booth was outside the counterman's domain. He set out the water grudgingly, and Chimberley carried it back to Guinevere.

"Now what don't you know?"

"Our trade secrets." She smiled mysteriously. "Solar Chemistics is the daring pioneer in this exciting new field of redesigned vital organisms. Our mechanized management is much too clever to give away the unique know-how that makes us available to everybody. For that reason, deliberate gaps were left in our psionic education."

Chimberley blinked at her shining innocence, suspecting that he had been had.

"Anyhow," he told her uneasily, "tell me what you do know. What started the company to making—uh—redesigned vital organisms?"

"The Miss Chemistics tape."

"Now I think we're getting somewhere." He leaned quickly across the narrow table. "Who's Miss Chemistics?"

"The world's most wanted woman." Guinevere sipped her water gracefully. "She won a prize contest that was planned to pick out the woman that every man wanted. A stupid affair, organized by the old human management before the computer was put in. There was an entry blank in every package of our synthetic products. Forty million women entered. The winner was a farm girl named Gussie Schlepps before the talent agents picked her up—now she's Guinevere Golden."

"What had she to do with you?"

"We're copies." Guinevere smirked complacently. "Of the world's most wonderful woman."

"How do you copy a woman?"

"No human being could," she said. "It takes too much know-how. But our computer was able to work everything out." She smiled proudly. "Because the prize that Miss Chemistics won was immortality."

"Huh?" He gaped at her untroubled loveliness. "How's that?"

"They call it cloning. A few cells of scar tissue from her body were snipped off and frozen, in our laboratory. Each cell, you know, contains a full set of chromosomes—a complete genetic pattern for the reproduction of the whole body—and the legal department got her permission for the company to keep the cells alive forever and to produce new copies of her whenever suitable processes should be discovered."

"Maybe that's immortality." Chimberley frowned. "But it doesn't look like much of a prize."

"She was disappointed when they told her what it was." Guinevere nodded calmly. "In fact, she balked. She didn't want anybody cutting her precious body. She was afraid it would hurt, and afraid the scar would show—but she did want the publicity. All the laboratory needed was just a few cells. She finally let a company doctor take them, where the scar wouldn't show. And the publicity paid off. She's a realies actress now, with a million-dollar contract."

"One way to the top." Chimberley grinned. "But what does she think of vital appliances?"

"She thinks we're wonderful." Guinevere beamed. "You see, she gets a royalty on every copy sold. Besides, her agent says we're sensational publicity."

"I suppose you are." A reluctant admiration shone through his mud-colored eyes, before he could bring his mind back to business. "But let's get on with it. What about the Miss Chemistics tape?"

"The contest closed before our management was mechanized," she said, "while old Matt Skane was still general manager. But when the computer took over, all the company records were punched on chemistic tapes and filed in its memory banks."

He sat for a moment scowling. His eyes were on Guinevere, but he was reaching in his mind for the tidy rows of crackle-finished cabinets that housed Athena Sue, groping for the feel of her swift responses. The thinking of managerial computers was sometimes a little hard to follow, even for cybernetic engineers—and even when there was no question of any defective circuits.

Guinevere was squirming uncomfortably.

"Is something wrong with my face?"

"Not a thing." He scratched his own chin. "I heard you tell your legal friend, back there at the vending machine, that you aren't a human being within the meaning of the law. What's the difference?"

"The original cells are all human." She dabbed at her eyes with a paper napkin and looked up to face him bravely. "The differences came later, in the production lines. We're attached to mechanical placentas, and grown under hormone control in big vats of chemistic solutions. We're educated as we grow, by psionic impulses transmitted from high-speed training tapes. All of that makes differences, naturally. The biggest one is that we are better."

She frowned thoughtfully.

"Do you think the women are jealous?"

"Could be." Chimberley nodded uncertainly. "I never pretended to understand women. They all seem to have a lot if circuits out of kilter. Give me Athena Sue. Let's get out to the plant—"

Guinevere sniffed.

"Oh, Pip!" she gasped. "Our chemburgers!"

The counterman stood rubbing his hands on a greasy towel, staring at her with a fascinated disapproval. The forgotten chemburgers were smoking on the griddle behind him. Her wail aroused him. He scraped them up and slapped them defiantly on the counter.

Chimberley carried them silently back to Guinevere. He didn't care for chemburgers in any condition, but she consumed them both in ecstasy, and begged for a piece of chemberry pie.

"It's awfully good," she told him soulfully. "Made from the most ambrosial synthetics, by our exclusive chemistic processes. Won't you try a piece?"

When they approached a standing cab out in the street, the driver stiffened with hostility. But he took them.

"Keep her back," he growled. "Outa sight. Mobs smashed a couple hacks yesterday to get at 'em."

Guinevere sat well back out of sight, crouching close to Chimberley. She said nothing, but he felt her shiver. The cab went fast through empty streets, and once when the tires squealed as it lurched around a corner she caught his hand apprehensively.

"See that, mister?" The driver slowed as they passed a block of charred wreckage. "Used to be one of them mechanized markets. Mob burned it yesterday. Machines inside selling them. See what I mean?"

Chimberley shook his head. Guinevere's clutching hand felt cold on his. Suddenly he slipped his arm around her. She leaned against him, and whispered fearfully:

"What does he mean?"

"I don't quite know."

The Solar Chemistics plant was ominously black. A few tattered palms straggled along the company fence. A sharp, yeasty scent drifted from the dark sea of solar reaction vats beyond, and blue floodlights washed the scattered islands where enormous bright metal cylinders towered out of intertwining jungles of pipes and automatic valves.

Chimberley sniffed the sour odor, and pride filled his narrow chest. Here was the marvelous body to Athena Sue's intricate brain. It breathed air and drank sea water and fed on sunlight, and gave birth to things as wonderful as Guinevere.

The driver stopped at a tall steel gate, and Chimberley got out. The rioters had been there. The palms along the fence were burned down to black stumps. Rocks and smashed gaping black holes in the big 3-D sign on the side of the gray concrete building beyond the fence, and broken glass grated on the pavement as he walked to the gate.

He found the bell, but nothing happened. Nobody moved inside the fence. All those dark miles of solar reactors had been designed to run and maintain themselves, and Athena Sue controlled them. A thousand fluids flowed continuously through a thousand processes to form a thousand new synthetics. Human labor was only in the way.

"Your almighty machine!" the driver jeered behind him. "Looks like it don't know you."

He jabbed the bell again, and an unhurried giant with a

watchman's clock came out of the building toward the gate. Chimberley passed his company identification card through the barrier, and asked to see somebody in the office.

"Nobody there." The watchman chuckled cheerfully. "Unless you count that thinking machine."

"The computer's what I really want to see, if you'll let me in—"

"Afraid I couldn't, sir."

"Listen." Chimberley's voice lifted and quivered with frustration. "This is an emergency. I've got to check the computer right away."

"Can't be that emergent." The watchman gave him a sun-bronzed grin. "After all the hell yesterday, the directors shut off the power to stop your gadget."

"But they can't—" Alarm caught him, as if his own brain had been threatened with oxygen starvation. "Without power, her transistors will discharge. She'll—well, die!"

"So what?" The watchman shrugged. "The directors are meeting again in the morning, with our old legal staff, to get rid of her."

"But I'll have her checked and balanced again by then," he promised desperately. "Just let me in!"

"Sorry, sir. But after all that happened yesterday, they told me to keep everybody out."

"I see." Chimberley drew a deep breath and tried to hold his temper. "Would you tell me exactly what did happen?"

"If you don't know." The watchman winked impudently at the cab where Guinevere sat waiting. "Your big tin brain had developed those synthetic cuties secretly. It put them on the market yesterday morning. I guess they did look like something pretty hot, from a gadget's point of view. The item every man wanted most, at a giveaway price. Your poor old thinking machine will probably never understand why the mobs tried to smash it."

Chimberley bristled. "Call the responsible officials. Now. I insist."

"Insist away." The brown giant shrugged. "But there aren't any responsible officials since the computer took over. So what can I do?"

"You might try restraining your insolence," Chimbeley snapped. "And give me your name. I intend to report you in the morning."

"Matt Skane," he drawled easily. "Used to be general manager."

"I see," Chimberley muttered accusingly. "You hate computers!"

"Why not?" He grinned through the bars. "I fought 'em for years, before they got the company. It's tough to admit you're obsolete."

Chimberley stalked back to the cab and told the driver to take him to the Gran Desierto Hotel. The room clerk there gave Guinevere a chilling stare and failed to find any record of the reservation. Another taxi driver suggested his life would be simpler, and accommodations easier to arrange, if he would ask the police to take her off his hands, but by that time his first annoyed bewilderment was crystallizing into stubborn anger.

"I can't understand people," he told Guinevere. "They aren't like machines. I sometimes wonder how they ever managed to invent anything like Athena Sue. But whatever they do, I don't intend to give you up."

Day had come before he found an expensive room in a shabby little motel, where the sleepy manager demanded his money in advance and asked no questions at all. It was too late to sleep, but he took time for a shower and a shave.

His billfold was getting thin, and it struck him that the auditing machines might balk at some of his expenses on account of Guinevere. Prudently, he caught a bus at the corner. He got off in front of the plant, just before eight o'clock. The gate across the entrance drive was open now, but an armed guard stepped out to meet him.

"I'm here from General Cybernetics—"

He was digging nervously for his identification card, but the tall guard gestured easily to stop him.

"Mr. Chimberley?"

"I'm Chimberley. And I want to inspect our managerial installation here, before the directors meet this morning."

"Matt Skane told me you were coming, but I'm afraid you're late." The guard gestured lazily at a row of long cars parked across the drive. "The directors met an hour ago. But come along."

A wave of sickness broke over him as the guard escorted him past an empty reception desk and back into the idle silence of the mechanized administrative section. A sleek, feline brunette, who must have been a close runner-up in the Miss Chemistics contest, sat behind the chrome railing at the dead programming panel, intently brushing crimson lacquer on her talons. She glanced up at him with a spark of interest that instantly died.

"The hot shot from Schenectady," the guard said. "Here to overhaul the big tin brain."

"Shoulda made it quicker." She flexed her claws, frowning critically at the fresh enamel. "Word just came out of the board room. They're doing away with the brain. High time, too, if anybody wants to know."

"Why?"

"Didn't you see 'em?" She blew on her nails. "Those horrible synthetic monsters it was turning loose everywhere."

He remembered that she must have been a runner-up.

"Anyhow," he muttered stubbornly, "I want to check the computer."

With a bored nod, she reached to unlatch the little gate that let him through the railing into the metal-paneled, air-conditioned maze that had been the brain of Athena Sue. He stopped between the neat banks of pastel-painted units, saddened by their silence.

The exciting sounds of mechanized thought should have been whispering all around him. Punched cards should have been riffling through the whirring sorters, as Athena Sue remembered. Perforators should have been punching chemistic tape, as she recorded new data. Relays should have been clicking as she reached her quick decisions, and automatic typewriters murmuring with her many voices.

But Athena Sue was dead.

She could be revived, he told himself hopefully. Her permanent memories were all still intact, punched in tough chemistic film. He could set her swift electronic pulse to beating again, through her discharged transistors, if he could find the impossible flaw that had somehow led to her death.

He set to work.

Three hours later he was bent over a high-speed scanner, reading a spool of tape, when a hearty shout startled him.

"Well, Chimberley! Found anything?"

He snatched the spool off the scanner and shrank uneasily back from the muscular giant stalking past the programming desk. It took him a moment to recognize Matt Skane, without the watchman's clock. Clutching the tape, he nodded stiffly.

"Yes." He glanced around him. The billowy brunette and the guard had disappeared. He wet his lips and gulped. "I—I've found out what happened to the computer."

"So?"

Skane waited, towering over him, a big, red, weather-beaten man with horny hands shaped as if to fit a hammer or the handles of a plow, a clumsy misfit in this new world where machines had replaced both his muscles and his mind. He was obsolete—but dangerous.

"It was sabotaged." Chimberley's knobby fist tightened on the spool of tape, in sweaty defiance.

"How do you know?"

"Here's the whole story." He brandished the chemistic reel. "Somebody programmed Athena Sue to search for a project that would result in her destruction. Being an efficient computer, she did what she was programmed to do. She invented vital appliances, and supplied a correct prediction that the unfavorable consumer reaction to them would completely discredit mechanized equipment. So the saboteur reprogrammed her to ignore the consequences and manufacture Guinevere."

"I see." Skane's bright blue eyes narrowed ominously. "And who was this cunning saboteur?"

Chimberley caught a rasping, uneven breath. "I know that he was somebody who had access to the programming panel at certain times, which are recorded on the input log. So far as I've been able to determine, the only company employee who should have been here at those times was a watchman—named Matt Skane."

The big man snorted.

"Do you call that evidence?"

"It's good enough for me. With a little further investigation, I think I can uncover enough supporting facts to interest the directors."

Skane shifted abruptly on his feet, and his hard lips twitched. "The directors are gone," he drawled softly. "And there isn't going to be any further investigation. Because we've already gone back to human management. We're junking your big tin brain. I'm the general manager now. And I want that tape."

He reached for the chemistic spool.

"Take it." Chimberley crouched back from his long bronze arm, and ignominiously gave up the tape. "See what good it does you. Maybe I can't prove much of anything without it. But you're in for trouble, anyhow."

Skane grunted contemptuously.

"You can't turn the clock back," Chimberley told him bitterly. "Your competitors won't go back to human management. You'll still have all their computers to fight. They had you against the wall once, and they will again."

"Don't bet on it." Skane grinned. "Because we've learned a thing or two. We're going to use machines, instead of trying to fight them. We're putting in a new battery of the smaller sort of auxiliary computers—the kind that will let us keep a man at the top. I think we'll do all right, with no further help from you."

Chimberley hastily retreated from the smoldering blue eyes. He felt sick with humiliation. His own future was no serious problem; a good cybernetics engineer could always find an opening. What hurt was the way he had failed Athena Sue.

But there was Guinevere, waiting in his room.

His narrow shoulders lifted when he thought of her. Most women irked and bored him, with all their fantastic irrationalities and their insufferable stupidities, but Guinevere was different. She was more like Athena Sue, cool and comprehensible, free of all the human flaws that he detested.

He ran from the bus stop back to the seedy motel, and his heart was fluttering when he rapped at the door of their room.

"Guinevere!"

He listened breathlessly. The latch clicked. The door

creaked. He heard her husky-throated voice,

"Oh, Pip! I thought you'd never come."

"Guin—"

Shock stopped him when he saw the woman in the doorway. She was hideous with old age. She felt feebly for him with thin blue claws, peering toward him blindly.

"Pip?" Her voice was somehow Guinevere's. "Isn't it you?"

"Where—" Fright caught his throat. His glance fled into the empty room beyond, and came back to her stooped and tottering frame, her wasted, faded face. He saw a dreadful likeness there, but his mind rejected it.

"Where's Guinevere?"

"Darling, don't you even know me?"

"You couldn't be—" He shuddered. "But still—your voice—"

"Yes, dear, I'm yours." Her white head nodded calmly. "The same vital appliance you bought last night. Guinevere Model 1, Serial Number 1997-A-456."

He clutched weakly at the doorframe.

"The difference you have just discovered is our rapid obsolescence." A strange pride lifted her gaunt head. "That's something we're not supposed to talk about, but you're an engineer. You can see how essential it is, to insure a continuous replacement demand. A wonderful feature, don't you think, darling?"

He shook his head, with a grimace of pain.

"I suppose I don't look very lovely to you any longer, but that's all right." Her withered smile brightened again. "That's the way the computer planned it. Just take me back to the vending machine where you bought me. You'll get a generous trade-in allowance, on tomorrow's model."

"Not any more," he muttered hoarsely. "Because our

computer's out. Skane's back in, and I don't think he'll be making vital appliances."

"Oh, Pip!" She sank down on the sagging bed, staring up at him with a blind bewilderment. "I'm so sorry for you!"

He sat down beside her, with tears in his murky eyes. For one bitter instant, he hated all computers, and the mobs—and Matt Skane as well.

But then he began to get hold of himself.

After all, Athena Sue was not to blame for anything. She had merely been betrayed. Machines were never evil, except when men used them wrongly.

He turned slowly back to Guinevere, and gravely kissed her shriveled lips.

"I'll make out," he whispered. "And now I've got to call Schenectady."

Dragon's Island

ONE

The city snarled. Its sudden hostility was a bitter taste and a biting scent of menace, and a livid glow of danger over everything he saw, and cold peril crawling up the back of his neck. Though his ears heard no warning, alarm crashed inside his brain.

Dane Belfast met that shocking impact when he opened the door of his New York hotel room, at seven that March morning. The unexpected force of it took his breath and drove him backward. He retreated into the doorway, groping dazedly to discover what had hit him.

The maroon-carpeted corridor lay empty. He listened, thinking there must have been some shot or scream, but he could hear nothing more alarming than the muted mutter of traffic on Madison Avenue, twenty floors below. He sniffed to test the air for smoke, but he found no actual odor more disturbing than the faint, stale human scents of tobacco and perfume.

His straining senses found no threat of anything, and he tried at first to ignore what he had felt. He was a scientist, a research geneticist. He had found mysteries enough in the working of the genes and chromosomes, whereby like gives birth to like. He had no time for the inexplicable.

He caught his breath and carefully brushed a fleck of lint from the overcoat folded on his arm and started resolutely out again toward the elevator. You didn't need to be a professional biologist to know that danger by itself has no taste or feel or warning glow, and he tried for a moment to believe that he had been stricken with a sudden synesthesia—that abnormality of perception in which sounds are seen in color and colors tasted.

But he wasn't ill. He had never been, not even with a cold. Even after the crushing strain of these last months, he felt too hard and fit to be yielding to any fevered imaginings. He was only twenty-five, still clothed in the indestructible vigor of youth. Everything had been all right, until the moment when he opened the door.

He hastily explored the day before, but he could recall no disturbing incident—certainly no taste or scent or feel of peril. Bad weather had delayed his plane, so that he arrived too late to call on the man he had come to see. He had gone out alone to eat and see the lights of Times Square. He watched a fight on the television set in a bar, while he drank three beers, and then returned to his hotel. New York had not been snarling then.

He was trying now to swallow that acrid taste of evil, but it clung to his tongue. He blinked against that colorless glare, but still it washed the corridor with a dreary enmity. And danger halted him again, before he could close the door of his room. An invisible yet strangely actual barrier, it delayed him for a few uneasy seconds—long enough to hear the telephone ringing.

He hurried back inside to answer.

"Dane?" The voice was a young woman's, low-pitched and pleasant. "Dr. Dane Belfast?"

She sounded as if she thought she knew him, but he hadn't

been East since the time long ago when he and his mother came along with his father to a medical convention. He had no friends in New York; no girl friends, certainly.

"I'm Nan Sanderson," she was saying, but he couldn't remember ever meeting anybody named Sanderson. "Of the Sanderson Service. We're on Fortieth, just a few blocks from your hotel. Would you come over to our office this morning, say at eleven?"

"Huh?" He felt sure he had never heard of the Sanderson Service, and he wondered for a moment how the firm had got his name. He had not announced his coming even to Messenger, the financier he meant to see. "What are you selling?"

"Nothing," she answered quietly. "Unless you'd call it life insurance. Because you're in danger, Dr. Belfast. And we can probably save your life."

Her voice had a ring of conviction, and her words opened the room to the dark illumination he had met outside. Now that danger-sense was no longer a possible illusion. It was suddenly something real, that he had to accept and explain.

"Danger?" he whispered blankly. "What enemies have I?"

"Enough!" Her hushed voice had a hurried urgency. "Deadly enemies, working cleverly in secret, desperate enough to poison your food or shoot you in the back or stab you while you sleep."

Five minutes ago, he might have laughed at that. Now, however, he could feel the frosty breath of peril seeping around the closed door, and taste the venom of hate lingering on his tongue.

"That sounds pretty drastic." He couldn't help shivering. "Who would want to murder me?"

"One man who might is John Gellian."

He repeated that name. Its sound was strange, and he

tried again to deny the possibility of danger. He had injured nobody. His research goals had been unselfish. He had nothing anyone could want desperately enough to kill him for it.

He reached absently to touch his flat pocketbook. Most of his savings had gone to meet unpaid bills at the bankrupt laboratory, after his father died and Messenger's donations were cut off. The five twenties he had left were not a tempting bait for robbery.

"I can't talk long," the girl was saying. She gave him an address on Fortieth. "Will you be here at eleven?"

"But I can't be in any real trouble," he insisted. "Unless—" He caught uneasily. "Is it because of my research?"

Like his father, he had been looking for a way to reach and change the genes, to reshape the traits of inheritance they carried. That secret of creation might have been enough to surround him with greedy enemies—but he had failed to find it.

Tantalizing keys to all the mysterious wonder and power of life, the genes were too small to touch and turn with any process they had tried. Their repeated failures must have worn out Messenger's faith in the project, and Dane knew they had finally killed his father. He had been ready to give up, himself, before he found the old letters in his father's desk.

Letters from Charles Kendrew—written in the 1930s by that pioneer geneticist, about his daring plans for the great new science he called genetic engineering. Letters from Messenger, dated many years later, promising funds to carry on Kendrew's unfinished work.

Those letters were in Dane's scuffed briefcase now. They had brought him to New York. They contained exciting evidence that a workable process for creating useful genetic mutations had already been discovered, probably by Kendrew himself, and that Messenger had made a fortune from it.

That circumstantial evidence was what he meant to talk to the financier about. He expected an explosive interview. Any process for making directed mutations could be more important to mankind than the methods of setting off atomic fission. If Messenger had anything to hide, the letters might become a dangerous possession after he had been confronted with them.

But Messenger hadn't seen them yet. Neither had anybody else. Whatever his motives, he had given nearly two million dollars in all to the laboratory. That entitled him, Dane felt, to the benefit of a considerable doubt. The evidence was too uncertain to establish any crime, and he still hoped that the financier could explain it innocently.

All Dane wanted was another chance to realize Kendrew's magnificent dream. If Messenger was already exploiting some crude mutation process, as the letters suggested, he wanted to learn it, perfect it, and see it applied as Kendrew had intended—to benefit mankind and not a corporation.

Dane was not, however, an enemy of property. He regretted his own shortage of funds as merely a temporary handicap. He was quite willing to let Messenger's company make an incidental profit on all the creations of genetic engineering, and he had been reasonably confident of fair treatment—until he opened his door and met that dark blaze of danger.

Now he wasn't sure of anything.

"I've been doing some genetics research," he explained to the girl on the telephone. "It might have been important, but it didn't pan out. If anybody thinks I discovered anything worth stealing—"

"No, Dane, it isn't that," she broke in quickly. "But your predicament is truly desperate. Look out for Gellian. And we'll be expecting you at eleven."

"Wait!" he whispered. "Can't you tell me—"

She had hung up. He replaced his own receiver and reached absently for his handkerchief to wipe the sweat from his clammy palms. He had failed to learn anything about the Sanderson Service, but he knew he would be there at eleven, hoping to escape the cold pall of danger around him.

Her warning had convinced him that his disquieting sensations were due to some real cause outside himself, but it seemed to him now, as he turned from the telephone, that they were already fading. He realized uncomfortably that the net result of that glare and reek and taste of harm had been to keep him here long enough to receive her call.

Until he had more data, however, the nature of that danger-sense seemed likely to remain mysterious. He gulped a glass of water to ease the dryness in his throat, and then unlocked his briefcase, suddenly afraid the contents would be gone, with all his clues to that secret science.

He found them safe—the time-yellowed letters in the neat hand printing of Charles Kendrew, and the notes from Messenger typed on the expensive letterheads of Cadmus Corporation, and the penciled drafts or the carbon copies of a few of his father's replies.

He locked the case gratefully, and took it with him when he started out again. He met no shock of new alarm, and that pitiless bloom of danger had dimmed to a haunting memory by the time he reached the lobby.

Almost himself again, he ate ham and eggs in the hotel coffee shop, although that danger-sense had left a bitter after-taste that dulled his appetite. He went back to the lobby, and called the office number on Messenger's letterhead from a public telephone booth.

Mr. Messenger wasn't in, a sleek voice purred. Mr. Messenger seldom came in before three in the afternoon, and he was usually in conference after three. Mr. Messenger's schedule didn't permit appointments, but Dane could leave his name. He left his name, and said he would be waiting to see Mr. Messenger at three.

It was still nearly two hours before he would be expected at the Sanderson Service. Hoping to find some illuminating fact about that firm or Messenger's company or even about somebody named John Gellian, he bought an armful of newspapers at the stand in the lobby and started back to read them in the dubious sanctuary of his room.

"Excuse me—aren't you Dr. Belfast?"

The inquiry was softly spoken behind him, as he left the newsstand. Somehow, it awoke a momentary echo of that disconcerting danger-sense. He spun apprehensively, and saw a sullen flicker of dark hostility that picked out and identified the tall man hurrying after him.

"I'm Belfast," he admitted huskily. "I suppose you are John Gellian?"

"Of the Gellian Agency." The stranger gave him a stern little smile. "May I have a moment of your time?"

TWO

Dane had stepped back defensively, but that flash of danger made visible had already faded. John Gellian was left with a look of harassed good will. With an uneasy nod, Dane followed him away from the newsstand, toward an unoccupied corner of the lobby.

Dane studied the stranger sharply, and failed to find the implacable enemy that Nan Sanderson's call and his own shock of danger had led him to expect. John Gellian was a rawboned, dark-skinned man of about thirty-five, vigorous and muscular but slightly stooped, as if from overwork. Something about him was puzzling.

There was a veiled desperation beneath the gravely courteous restraint of his manner. His nervous movements and his worried frown seemed to reveal some cruel inner conflict, of ruthless purpose fighting crushing handicaps. He looked grimly determined, yet thoroughly afraid.

Perhaps he was ill. Waiting anxiously to find out what he wanted, Dane had time to see the haggard brightness of his eyes and the bad color of his skin and the lines of pain cut deep around his mouth. He was fighting some grave sickness, Dane decided, and haunted with a consuming fear of death.

They reached a group of chairs in an empty corner, away from the newsstand and the desk and the busy elevators, but Gellian made no move to sit. He swung abruptly to face Dane, his hollowed eyes unexpectedly sharp.

"I wasn't expecting you to know me." His voice was still oddly soft. "Do you mind saying how you knew my name?"

Dane smiled warily. "I might ask the same question."

"We're a private detective agency." Gellian smiled disarmingly. "We have been investigating you, with a view to offering you a place on our staff. When our operatives reported that you were in town, I decided to talk it over with you."

Somewhat astonished, Dane shook his head. He had riddles enough of his own to solve: the strange disappearance of Charles Kendrew; the peculiar prosperity of Messenger's company; the nature of the Sanderson Service and the source of that baffling danger-sense.

"I'm afraid you have the wrong man," he said. "I'm not a criminologist."

"What we need is an expert geneticist," Gellian answered quietly. "Our reports seem to show that you have just the sort of background we require. I understand that you are free, since the Kendrew Memorial Laboratory went out of existence, and we're able to pay whatever you want."

"Thanks," Dane said. "Thanks, but really I'm not interested."

"You will be," Gellian promised softly. "When you know what we're doing. Because we aren't the usual sort of agency. We don't run down missing husbands or people who fail to pay their bills. We're fighting a war—"

A sudden vehemence had lifted Gellian's voice, but he checked himself sharply to glance around the lobby as if afraid of being overheard.

"The job will interest you." His voice sank cautiously. "But, before I tell you any more about it, I'd like to know something about your work at the Kendrew laboratory."

"I'm not looking for a job," Dane insisted. "But there's no secret about our research there. In fact, our results have all been published. We were studying mutations—the sudden changes in the genes that give the offspring new traits, not inherited from either parent."

Gellian nodded impatiently. "But what was the purpose of your work?"

"When my father set up the laboratory, he was hoping to find a method of directing mutation—a process for creating new varieties and species at will, without waiting on the random process of natural variation the way plant and animal breeders have always done. We spent twelve years and two million dollars on the project, and finally gave it up."

"I know, I know." Gellian shrugged nervously. "Our people on the West Coast reported your failure." His hollowed eyes narrowed keenly. "What they didn't report is where you got the two million."

"My father's secret." Dane felt his fingers tighten on the

handle of the briefcase, as he thought of the letters from Messenger inside. "The gifts were anonymous," he went on quickly, hoping Gellian hadn't noticed his reaction. "We promised not to reveal their source."

"Perhaps that doesn't matter." Restlessly, the gaunt man looked around the lobby again. "Or perhaps you'll decide to tell me later. Anyhow, here's a more important question." His anxious eyes came back to Dane. "Why was your laboratory named for Charles Kendrew?"

Dane thought he felt the chill of danger creeping back into the lobby, and thought he saw the dark flicker of it on Gellian's haggard face again. It made him shiver a little, but he could see no harm in the question. He answered soberly:

"Kendrew was an old friend of my father's. A gifted geneticist, born before his time. Forty years ago, he began trying what we just failed to do. But a family tragedy broke up his life. He abandoned his work and dropped out of sight, back in 1939, years before I was born. My father was hoping to carry on from where he quit—"

"But he didn't quit!" A hushed violence quivered in Gellian's voice. "He never abandoned his work. He disappeared deliberately, to carry on his unholy experiments in secret."

"You're mistaken," Dane said sharply. "I've seen letters Kendrew wrote about his work, and it wasn't unholy. I know he meant nothing but good—"

"I don't know his intentions," Gellian cut in, grimly. "But I've seen the results."

The frosty breath of peril hung bitter in the air. Staring in wonder, Dane shivered again. His clutch on the briefcase stiffened. Those letters held tantalizing hints of Kendrew's success, but he had found no actual proof.

"What results?" he whispered eagerly.

"Mutants!" Gellian's deep-sunk eyes had a haggard glitter, but his quiet voice seemed sane enough. "I thought that ought to interest you, Belfast. The fact is that we have both been working on the same problem, from our different angles. Don't you think we should join forces?"

"I don't know." The icy pressure of danger made it hard for Dane to breathe. "I've wondered, of course, what happened to Kendrew." He stared at Gellian's face, which seemed cruel and cold beneath that dark light. "Where are these mutants you've seen?"

"All around us." The lines of pain looked deeper in Gellian's hollowed cheeks, and he peered behind him again like a man afraid. "Superhuman monsters!" His hushed voice shook. "Hiding among mankind, and waiting to overwhelm us."

"Huh!" Dane stepped uneasily back from his trembling vehemence and that pall of sensed peril around him. "You don't mean—mutant men?"

"They aren't men!" Gellian stalked after him, gaunt hands knotted and quivering. "They're a new species. Not-men, we call them. They were bred from human beings, by Kendrew's wicked science. They look like men. They try to pass for men. But if you had ever met one, you could feel the difference."

Dane stood hunched apprehensively. His nostrils had caught a sharper scent of danger, and its bitter taste was on his tongue again.

"I told you we're at war," Gellian went on bleakly. "Our agency is a little group of loyal, determined men, organized to fight Kendrew's creatures for survival—the same way I suppose the last desperate Neanderthalers fought our own mutant Cro-Magnon forebears, a hundred thousand years ago. Only, we know the danger. We're getting a faster start than the Neanderthalers did. In spite of all the gifts and powers Kendrew gave his monsters, we intend to win."

"They can't exist," Dane muttered huskily.

But couldn't they? He had the letters in his briefcase, and he knew that human mutants were no more impossible than the mutant plants that Messenger's company was growing in New Guinea. He wet his lips, and tried to swallow that clinging bitterness.

"Wait till you meet them," Gellian challenged him. "They're so clever that it's hard to see the difference, but you'll feel it then—like ice in the marrow of your bones."

"I've been feeling—something." Dane couldn't help glancing behind him, as uneasily as Gellian had done, and he had to catch his breath. Was that what he had sensed—the veiled enmity of monstrous mutant minds, striving with unknown powers to overwhelm humanity?

"Yes?" Gellian whispered quickly. "Feeling what?"

"Danger." He shook his head uncomfortably. "Ever since I opened the door of my room this morning. I can't understand it, because I've no reason to be afraid of anybody."

"But you do. You were in danger from the moment we decided to take you into the agency—those *things* seem to have an uncanny knowledge of our plans against them."

"I don't know what to think," Dane murmured uneasily. "I'm sure old Kendrew meant no harm, and this seems too dreadful to believe—"

Gellian's fingers checked him, digging savagely into his arm. The rawboned detective stood silent for a moment, swaying on his feet as if weak from fatigue or perhaps from the illness visible in him. Then he straightened, with a stubborn effort.

"Let's step over to the office, if you can spare a moment." His voice was mild again; self-control had returned. "If you still have any doubts about our proposition I can show you all the proof you want."

THREE

The Gellian Agency occupied the seventh floor of a shabbily respectable old building near Madison Square. The harried-looking detective had said nothing more in the taxi about that secret war, and Dane looked around him with a puzzled alertness as they left the elevator.

The receptionist was a slim, shy-faced Negro girl, whose limpid eyes seemed to light with devotion when she spoke to Gellian. The operator at the switchboard behind her was a dazzling Nordic blonde, and the trim brunette busy at the teletype machines beyond was Chinese.

"Yes, we come from every race," Gellian commented softly. "From every human race. Our old racial quarrels have come to seem pretty stupid, now that we're fighting side by side against these things of Kendrew's."

He took Dane back into a comfortable private office. The Chinese girl followed to bring him a yellow sheaf of messages torn from the machine. He read them, while the creases of pain cut slowly deeper into his thin, sick face.

"Ask Miss Hunter to get our Canberra branch on the phone," he told the girl abruptly, and then turned apologetically to Dane. "Sorry, Belfast, but this is urgent. I'll be back in a few minutes to talk about your place with us."

He gestured at a chair as he hurried out, but Dane felt too deeply excited to sit down. The ambiguous hints in those old letters had been enough to bring him to New York. Proof of Kendrew's genetic discovery would be—tremendous!

Dane was still reluctant to believe that the lost geneticist had created any sort of superhuman beings to crowd out mankind, but he was breathless with a driving anxiety to see the evidence Gellian had promised. He looked around him wonderingly.

He was still somewhat staggered by the idea of a secret conflict for survival between mutants and men, but the agency had a convincing air of matter-of-fact efficiency. The busy people here seemed calm and sane as clerks in a bank. And the organization must be surprisingly extensive, if there were branches as far away as Australia.

His searching glance paused on the books shelved behind Gellian's scuffed and cluttered desk. Instead of volumes on criminology and law, he saw recent works on the biological sciences. There was even a copy of his own research report, *The Biochemistry of Mutation.*

He turned from the books with an uneasy shrug, and the map caught his restless eyes. A huge map of the world, it covered most of one wall. Dozens of black pins had been stuck into it, and a scarlet cord was wound among them, ending upon a black-inked question mark.

Peering at the question mark, he shook his head blankly. The pins were scattered, as if at random, across the inhabited areas of five continents. He failed to see what they stood for, and the windings of the red cord seemed too intricate to mean anything.

Baffled, he walked on around the room and came to the tree. A decoration left from last Christmas, he thought at first, and he wondered why it hadn't been thrown out months ago. But it seemed to shine, in the dim corner where it stood, as if with a gray reflection of that danger-glow.

It was a small, dark-leaved evergreen set in a common red flowerpot. The pot had been weighted with pieces of dark rock and rusty scrap metal. A few bits of dusty tinsel still hung from the branches, and among them was a toy.

A rocket ship. He wondered for a moment why it hung neglected here, so long after Christmas. He had seen the pictures of two dark-eyed children on Gellian's desk, a girl and a boy. And the tiny ship was a thing to delight any child, with its bright sheen and the fine workmanship of airlock and landing gear and bell-flared exhausts. He was reaching to touch it, when Gellian came back.

"If you want proof of the mutants!" The gaunt man shrugged unhappily. "That was the sort that keeps us on edge. A child eight years old—clever enough to get away from our best operatives in Australia! We need men with your training, to tackle such cases."

Turning from the puzzle of that dusty Christmas tree, Dane shook his head.

"I'm not a detective," he protested. "I can't believe Charles Kendrew made any superhuman monsters—he certainly didn't intend to, when my father used to know him." He stepped quickly forward. "But I'm anxious to see whatever proof you have."

"I'll show it to you." Gellian sat down heavily at the desk, his back to the windows and the rain-dimmed uptown skyline. His troubled glance went to the pattern of pins and string on the wall map, and touched that exquisite toy shining on the little tree, and then paused sadly upon those children in the picture on his desk. For a moment he seemed tired and frightened and haggard with his illness, but then his gaunt body straightened defiantly.

"Wasn't Kendrew trying to create controlled mutations, as long as forty years ago?" Stern again, his hollowed eyes flashed back to Dane. "What makes you so sure he failed?"

"I'm not sure he failed," Dane said. "I suppose it's possible that he did invent some sort of mutation process, after he disappeared in 1939. But he wasn't irresponsible or stupid or wicked enough to create anything dangerous to mankind."

"The evidence says he did."

"But my father knew him," Dane insisted. "In fact, they used to work together. When my father got out of medical school, back in 1925, Kendrew hired him as a research assistant."

"For mutation research?" Gellian leaned anxiously across the desk. "What did they accomplish?"

"Nothing." Dane shook his head. "Kendrew did have sound ideas about such things as the similarity of viruses and genes, my father used to say. But the world wasn't ready. There were no electron microscopes or radioisotopes to explore the living molecules he theorized about. My father got discouraged, after several years of failure, and opened his practice as a surgeon."

"But Kendrew kept on?"

"In spite of everything," Dane nodded. "His financial support had collapsed, in those depression years. He left San Francisco, to take whatever positions he could find as an instructor. He used to write my father about his work in meager little college labs or at home, with only his wife for an assistant."

"Working to create our destroyers!"

"He meant no harm," Dane protested. "I'm quite sure of that, from things he used to write my father about his plans and dreams. If he sometimes hoped to change the world, it wasn't for the worse."

He could hear the echo of Kendrew's great hopes ringing in his own eager voice. In spite of Gellian's forbidding frown, he let his old enthusiasm carry him on.

"What are the genes? Only protein molecules, perhaps, strung like beads to make the chromosomes. But they are the pattern of life. They duplicate themselves, when a cell divides. They are the living templates that shape each new life in the likeness of the old—except when mutation changes the pattern. Suppose we could reach and rebuild them at will!"

Gellian nodded grimly. "So that's what he did?"

"What he tried to do," Dane said. "Can you blame him? Just think what success would mean! Plants and animals—and even viruses—could be transformed. Useful species could be improved, and harmful species made useful. Applied to man himself, genetic engineering could eliminate all the hereditary flaws and deformities with which each human generation now saddles the next. From what he used to write my father, Kendrew must have speculated about that. But he wanted only to improve Homo sapiens, not to replace us."

"I wouldn't be so sure of that." Gellian's haggard eyes narrowed probingly. "But what do you know about the circumstances of his disappearance?"

"His last letter was written from Albuquerque, in 1939." Dane leaned to set his brief case on the floor; those letters ought to interest Gellian, but he wasn't ready to show them. "Things must have been pretty desperate. Kendrew was jobless. His wife was expecting another child, and he was having a hard time finding milk for the first. Yet he was still the optimist, busy writing some sort of paper on genetic engineering."

"Huh?" Gellian stiffened eagerly. "What became of that?"

"It was burned, I imagine," Dane said. "Because the thing happened a day or two after he wrote the letter. His wife went berserk. She set fire to the house. She shot their baby daughter, and put three bullets into Kendrew, and then she killed herself."

"Why?" Gellian whispered. "Don't you know?"

"My father never knew." Dane shook his head. "He saved

the newspaper clippings about it, but they don't explain anything. Margaret Kendrew had been a scientist herself—a parapsychologist—but she had been enough in love to give up her own career when she married. My father used to say she had a splendid mind, and he couldn't understand what broke her sanity."

"She was sane enough!" Gellian said bitterly. "I can tell you what happened. She was a human being. She found out that her own children weren't! That little girl was the first of the things that had to be killed." His thin jaws hardened. "The great tragedy is that Kendrew survived, to make other mutants."

"Did he?" Dane's breath caught. "Do you know?"

"Fireman dragged him out of the burning house," Gellian said. "He recovered from the burns and bullet wounds, and got away to Mexico." The gaunt man rose abruptly, swinging toward the wall map. "There's the trail he left us."

"How's that?"

"The trail of the maker!" Gellian strode to the map, gesturing at the red cord wound across the continents. "Each pin marks the birthplace of a proven mutant. The string joins them, in order of occurrence. The first was Kendrew's own child, born in Albuquerque thirty-four years ago. The latest we've found is this infant prodigy born eight years ago in Australia."

"Is Kendrew really alive?" Dane had turned hopefully from the riddle of that twisted string, and he couldn't help flinching from Gellian's cadaverous face. "I mean, how do you link him with those later births?"

"We still don't know how the mutants are made." The gaunt man spoke deliberately, scowling as if with disapproval of his breathless interest in Charles Kendrew. "But it seems logical to assume that the man who made them was nearby when they were conceived." He gestured sternly at the map. "The maker must have been in Acapulco in 1940, and in Rio de Janeiro two years later, and in Manila in 1945. Kendrew followed that same trail, making each move at precisely the right date—so far as we can trace him."

"Pretty flimsy evidence," Dane objected. "There must have been thousands of travelers who went the same way."

"But very few geneticists," Gellian said. "None known to have been tinkering with the genes. We had eliminated many thousand suspects before we came across Kendrew—he doesn't seem to have published any work, and he was never well known. But I'm certain he's the maker."

Dane glanced at the map, with a doubtful frown.

"If that's your best evidence, how do you know there *is* a maker?" he demanded. "Mightn't it be that you're investigating cases of natural mutation?"

"You're too good a geneticist to be suggesting that." Gellian shook his head, with a bleak impatience. "I know there has been a lot of sensational speculation, ever since Hiroshima, about the effects of atomic radiations on the germ plasm. But these not-men aren't fission products!"

"Natural mutations are caused by several other factors, besides radiation," Dane pointed out.

"But mutations in nature are usually slight," Gellian answered quickly. "And usually bad. Nature can't create a successful new species with one tremendous step, the way these not-men were made. Natural evolution requires thousands of generations, to accumulate the tiny accidental chances that happen to be useful, and to eliminate those that don't."

Dane nodded reluctantly, and tried not to shudder at the sullen glow of danger coming back to Gellian's stern and hollowed face.

"That's true," he admitted. "If these mutants are different

enough from men to be classified as a new species, that would show manipulation of the genes by some intelligence."

"By Charles Kendrew's!" Gellian's emaciated features hardened, and his sick eyes glittered strangely beneath that dark illumination. "And the not-men are different enough," he muttered. "When you see how different, you'll regret your efforts to defend the evil genius who made them."

"Maybe." Dane stepped back watchfully; he had begun to see that this meeting might have awkward consequences. "But you haven't showed me anything to prove that Kendrew made these mutants—or even anything to show that they exist. If you've any real evidence, let's see it."

"Now we're getting places." Gellian nodded, with a quick, thin smile. "We've proof enough, and I want you to ask questions. Many hard-headed men pass through this office, on their way into our organization—financiers and statesmen and military leaders. Most of them seem doubtful as you are, at first. They usually ask the same questions—and join us gladly when they learn the answers."

His cold smile became disquieting.

"Men must join us," he added softly. "Just because they're men."

Dane shook his head uncomfortably. "I don't see why."

"There's no room on Earth for two master races," the gaunt man said. "The past proves that—the old Neanderthalers, and all the other past competitors of men."

"I'm not so sure," Dane murmured. "But let's see your evidence."

"There's what I used to show." Gellian gestured restlessly at a locked steel cabinet. "Such objects as a book of intellectual poems, written in Braille by a blind child. A symphony—a weird, metallic, dissonant sort of thing, hard to perform and painful to hear—composed by a boy of six. The notebooks of another infant prodigy, kept in cipher—the only section we managed to read is a criticism of the quantum theory."

"Are such things alarming?"

"They do seem harmless," Gellian agreed quietly. "Harmless as the first human footprints must have seemed to creatures still walking on all fours."

Dane stared at him, shaken with a sick amazement.

"Have you declared war on a few gifted children, just because they seem a little too precocious?"

"It's true that most of the things we fight are young." Gellian nodded impatiently. "Their youth is all that gives us any chance of winning." His stern face tightened. "We can't afford mercy, when even a mutant baby carries the seed of our destruction." His haggard eyes looked hard at Dane. "Can't you see that?"

Dane shrank from the cruel glare of danger shining on Gellian, and he shivered from the chill of it gathering in the room. The taste of peril was sharp in his mouth, and the odor of it choked him. But he straightened defiantly. Whatever the trouble ahead, he meant to take no part in any war on children, whether mutant or human.

"No," he said. "Nothing you show me could make me see that."

FOUR

Gellian's stare seemed hawklike for an instant, but then his frosty smile came back.

"You're human, and you want to be humane." He nodded disarmingly, his voice soft again. "Most of us did, in the beginning. But war is not humane. Don't make up your mind before you've seen the evidence."

"Let's see it," Dane said. "But it will have to be good."

"It is." Gellian nodded nervously again at that locked cabinet, but still he didn't open it. "We've other exhibits there, that I used to show before we had anything better. Generally they were good enough."

Dane stepped back watchfully. The gathering glare of visible danger was painful to his eyes, a sinister riddle that had to be explained. He didn't intend to be convinced that Kendrew had created any superhuman enemies of men, but he wanted desperately to find out what the missing geneticist had really done. He could already foresee trouble to come, if he refused to join Gellian. But he was looking for the secret of creation, and any fact he learned might be a useful clue. He waited silently.

"There's one item that always convinced the politicians," Gellian continued. "A detailed and cunning scheme for setting up a military dictatorship in America. It was found among the papers of a brilliant West Point cadet, who died of a brain hemorrhage before he graduated."

He gestured restlessly at the wall map.

"That ambitious not-man was Case 44. There's the pin that marks his birth—in Miami, twenty-four years ago. Though we've found no other evidence of Kendrew's movements during that year or since, the map shows that he went from Japan to South Africa about that time, and he must have stopped in Florida long enough to shift the genes that made that monster—I wish I knew how!"

With a baffled shrug, the haggard man swung back to the cabinet.

"Anyhow," he went on, "here's another item that always enlists the technically minded. It's a report written by a stool pigeon for the warden at Alcatraz. It describes the plans of another convict to blow up the prison with a lithium hydride bomb. The convincing technical point is that the atomic explosion was to be triggered with radium from the dial of a wrist watch."

"Not very convincing," Dane objected. "It takes a fission bomb, plus a lot of secret equipment, to set off any sort of fission reaction."

"Radium atoms fission," Gellian said gently. "In this case, the evidence shows that they set off a fusion bomb."

Dane stared skeptically. "When I left San Francisco yesterday, Alcatraz was still sitting in the bay."

"But you probably heard about the explosion and fire there last year."

"We felt the shock, out at the lab." He shook his head. "It must have been quite a blast—but a real H-bomb would have burned out the whole bay area."

"We had the facts hushed up, hoping to keep other notmen from repeating that experiment," Gellian said quietly. "But that fire was actually caused by a limited fusion reaction, set off in a few grams of lithium hydride by some process that the AEC hasn't yet discovered. The prisoner died in the blast, but the evidence is adequate. Besides the stool pigeon's testimony, there's the fact that the whole cell block was contaminated with radioisotopes—so strongly that the debris had to be dumped at sea."

"A homemade H-bomb!" Dane peered at the gaunt man, appalled. "If such a secret got out—"

"Compared to the secrets of genetic engineering, it would be pretty harmless," Gellian cut in grimly. "But it didn't get out. The explosion obliterated every trace of the gadget itself, and the stool pigeon's description is pretty sketchy. That shows you, though, what Kendrew's creatures can do—even the imperfect mutations."

He moved as if to leave the cabinet, but swung back with a troubled frown.

"There's another item I used to show, that's even more disturbing," he went on. "A letter, written before the last war by a patient in a state mental hospital. Addressed to the president. It's a protest against his diplomatic blunders—and it describes the results to come, with the dates and the places of all our first terrible defeats and disasters.

"At the time, of course, it looked like just one more crank letter. The investigators found that the writer was a girl in her early teens, confined as a hopeless manic-depressive case, and the letter was simply filed away. By the time it came into our hands—after all those dreadful events had confirmed her predictions—she had already hanged herself."

His sick eyes lifted.

"Almost frightening, don't you think?"

"Not to me," Dane protested. "Ordinary human beings seem to have such glimpses of the future now and then. My own mother did."

"I'm afraid," Gellian said softly. "Though not so much because of the ambitious cadet and the ingenious convict and the psychopathic seer—I think they were flawed creations. Slips of the maker's hand. He's still human, remember. Subject to error, even since he set up shop as a creating god."

The colorless cast of danger lay cold on Gellian's fleshless face, and Dane thought he shuddered.

"The things that frighten me are those precocious poems, and that uncanny music, and that notebook in cipher," he went on huskily. "Because they show the terrible abilities of the true not-men. The cadet and the prisoner and the seer were all unfit—they didn't even live to meet our agents. The fitter mutants have a greater capacity for survival." His sunken face grew hard again. "Greater than our own, if we let them grow up!"

Dane straightened impatiently.

"Let's see your evidence," he challenged the gaunt man. "Those documents—or something more convincing. You still haven't showed me any sufficient reason for hunting down bright children."

"But here it is." Gellian swung abruptly from the locked cabinet, toward the potted evergreen Dane had seen. "Our newest exhibit. As innocent, at first glance, as that blind child's poetry. Just a child's toy, hanging on a Christmas tree. But it has never failed to convince anybody."

Dane followed him to the dusty little tree.

"What's so odd about it?"

"Plenty." Gellian's voice sank dramatically. "The oddities are cunningly disguised, as you might expect—it was last Christmas day that we found the thing, in a raid on a Park Avenue apartment where we had hoped to trap a mutant girl. She escaped, as the more competent and dangerous ones generally do. But we did get this plant."

"I don't see anything—"

"Feel the leaves."

Dane reached to touch the needles, and pricked his finger on a point sharp as glass. The entire plant seemed curiously heavy and hard.

"Metal," Gellian said softly. "The roots are using up that scrap and ore in the pot. When we sawed off a branch for analysis—and ruined a good hacksaw blade—the report showed forty percent iron. And a dozen other metals, with even a trace of uranium."

His feverish eyes peered at Dane.

"Would you believe that?"

Dane had to catch his breath, but he nodded slowly.

"I do," he whispered. "Metals are essential, after all, to any sort of life. The iron in this plant is no more remarkable, I suppose, than the iron carrying oxygen in our own red blood cells."

Gellian was smiling bleakly.

"Then you find it convincing?"

"Exciting!" Dane bent over it eagerly. "A remarkable mutation. Real proof, I suppose, that somebody can manipulate the genes. I'd like to look at it, inside a good laboratory." He turned from it, back to Gellian. "But I don't see anything to make it so alarming."

"Then look at this." Gellian reached to touch the bright hull of that toy rocket, his thin smile fading. "It *grew* there—inside a sort of shell we were able to chisel off." His fearful eyes came back to Dane. "What do you think of that?"

Dane stooped to feel the toy. The metal was heavy and cold in his trembling fingers. Fragments of a dark, thick husk still clung to it, around the hard metal stem which attached it to the tree.

"Well?" Gellian said. "Isn't that enough?"

"A wonderful thing!" He straightened from it reluctantly. "Though, granting that somebody can rebuild genes, I suppose such a toy as this would be a good deal simpler to make than a human being—or a superhuman mutant."

He leaned eagerly to touch the shining hull again.

"It's beautiful!" he whispered. "But not very dangerous, so far as I can see."

"I think it was planned to be more than a toy." Gellian's voice had a tremor of unease. "It was still growing, until we cut away that husk. Our Geiger counters show that uranium is being concentrated inside the hull, possibly for fuel."

"You don't mean—" Dane paused to stare at the tiny ship, breath-taken.

"I think it was meant to grow into a real ship of space." Gellian peered at it apprehensively. "The not-men are already uneasy, I should imagine, under our attacks. I think they're looking for a fortress on some other planet, beyond our reach."

"These mutants—" Dane turned at last from the metallic plant, frowning over that more disturbing puzzle. "How do you identify them?"

"That's a problem I hope you can help us solve," Gellian said. "A difficult thing, because the mutants were so cleverly shaped to hide among men. They're somewhat tougher and quicker and stronger than we are, and apparently immune to most diseases, but the older ones are already cunning enough to conceal such physical differences, as well as their stranger mental endowments."

"And—the mental differences?"

"High intelligence," the gaunt man said. "An average I.Q. probably twice ours. A remarkable acuity of the senses—from the images she used in her poems, that blind child must have been able to smell the red color of a rose, and to hear the molecular vibration of heat. But the gift that makes them so dangerous, and so difficult to trap, is ESP."

"Extrasensory perception?" Dane shook his head uneasily. "Are you certain?"

Gellian nodded.

"We haven't had any not-men in the laboratory. Not alive. We don't know the extent or the limits of their psychophysical capacities. But nothing else could account for that girl's escapes from all our traps.

"I hope they all aren't so gifted," he went on huskily. "But that one female thing seems to know our plans before we do. Besides evading all our efforts to kill or capture her, she has been able to warn and hide quite a number of suspected children before we could take them."

"Is that the worst thing she has done?" Dane inquired. "Rescuing children doesn't seem so reprehensible—"

"She's deadly!" Gellian stiffened angrily. "She is armed with weapons more dangerous than that convict's H-bomb—because they're more subtle. Several of our best operatives have disappeared on her trail. By sheer good luck, we found what she had done to the last one."

Dane stood listening uneasily.

"The chief investigator for our Canberra office," Gellian went on grimly. "An able man, trained and loyal, armed as well as we could arm him. He went out alone, two months ago, to check a newspaper story about this gifted eight-year-old. He didn't come back.

"Investigating a possible mutant takes time and caution, and he had been gone three days before the branch manager got alarmed enough to look for him. The manager couldn't find him, or the mutant child, or any other clue. It's just an accident that one of our operatives on another case recognized him last week, washing dishes in a waterfront joint up in Darwin."

"Then this girl didn't kill him?"

"Not physically." Gellian seemed to shiver again. "But his mind had been destroyed. Memory wiped out. He was using a different name, and apparently he was quite content with his dishwashing job. He recalled nothing of his work with the agency—didn't even know the old friend who found him."

"Amnesia?"

"Not any common kind." Gellian shook his head uneasily. "Our medical experts say that he has Craven's disease—a rare type of encephalitis, first reported a dozen years ago by a mission doctor in New Guinea. A brain infection that destroys the memory—permanently. All the evidence shows that he had been deliberately infected with the virus—probably by this mutant girl."

Dane nodded uncomfortably. The chill of danger hung

cold in the room, and he wondered for an instant if what his senses had detected could be the working of some other secret weapon, strange as that virus.

"That's the sort of thing we're up against," Gellian went on. "Such biological warfare could destroy us before we know we've been attacked, yet it's perfectly safe for the not-men, because of their natural immunity to disease. You can see why we need such experts as you are."

"I'm not sure." Dane shook his head. "It looks to me as if the mutants used that virus only in self-defense—"

"A hellish weapon!" Gellian broke in. "But we could learn to cope with weapons. What worries me isn't any weapon, or even the terrible cunning of the not-men, but their psychophysical gifts. While I suppose some human beings do have some feeble extrasensory perceptions, those mutant psi capacities are as strange and dangerous to us as the new mutation of human reason must have been, long ago, to the last dull near-men."

Dane shivered a little, awed in spite of himself.

"That's the danger." Gellian's haunted eyes looked hard at him. "Now will you join us?"

Dane hesitated uncomfortably. The bitter taste of danger burned his tongue again. Refusal was going to be awkward, yet he knew he must refuse. Sparring for time to decide what to say, he asked uneasily:

"Just what would you want me to do?"

"Help us trap the maker, first," Gellian said grimly. "That trail's too cold to be of much more use." He gestured restlessly at the wall map. "We're going to set a geneticist to catch one."

"I couldn't be much help with that." Dane was thinking uneasily of the letters he had brought from San Francisco, but he carefully kept from looking at his scuffed briefcase, where he had set it on the floor.

"Anyhow," he said defensively, "I don't see much sense in trying to run down Kendrew. He'd be a harmless old man, by this time. Or very likely already dead—if that last mutant was born eight years ago."

"He's still alive," Gellian insisted flatly. "If he can create new species, he can certainly protect his own health. And he's our logical point of attack—just because he's human. Whatever he has created, I doubt that he was able to make himself a superman. If we can catch him alive, we have the means to make him tell who all the not-men are and how he mutated them. Perhaps we can destroy them, with the same science that made them."

He straightened aggressively.

"That's your job, Belfast. Are you ready to begin?"

"I don't think so." Flinching from Gellian's gaze, Dane turned uncertainly back to that bright rocket growing on the mutant tree. "This is all—tremendous!" he whispered. "More exciting than atomic fission ever was, because it's a creative art. But I think you're unduly alarmed."

He swung earnestly back to face Gellian's stare.

"If Kendrew's discoveries have fallen into the wrong hands, I'm anxious to do something about it," he added quickly. "I want more information—there're a number of things I don't understand. But I don't see any reason for panic. Certainly, I'm not ready to start slaughtering children!"

Gellian's breath caught sharply.

"You phrase it too harshly." Anger snapped in his hard voice. "But you've no choice, however you put it. Not if you're a man!"

"I'm human," he whispered sharply. "I want to be loyal. But I've been following Kendrew's great dream all my life. I can't turn my back on it, without even taking time to think—"

"We have no time. If we fail now, while the not-men are young, they won't give us another chance." A sudden exasperation shook his voice. "Didn't you say you could feel them—observing us with their strange senses?"

"I do feel—something."

That sourceless blaze of danger lay darker on Gellian's sunken cheeks, now when he looked. The frost of it seemed colder in the air, and its bite sharper on his tongue.

"Something—but I don't know what it is," he whispered uneasily. "Perhaps it is a reaction to some sort of unconscious awareness of the psychophysical powers of those mutants—if they're really as vicious as you think. Perhaps it's something else. Anyhow, it's still too vague and fitful to act on. I need time to find out what it is."

Gellian shrugged impatiently.

"Better consider your own position, while you're taking time," he said softly. "Although our agents satisfied themselves that you're a man, don't forget that your father was a friend of Kendrew's. That might become an awkward fact, if you refuse to join us."

Dane stepped backward apprehensively.

"Please don't threaten me," he muttered huskily. "Can't you give me a little time to think?"

"Normally, we couldn't." Gellian peered at him disconcertingly, and then nodded in decision. "But since we need you so badly, I'll make an exception. If you decide to come back, be here at eight tomorrow morning."

"Or else I become another black pin on the wall?"

"I didn't want to be so blunt." Glancing soberly up at the wall map, Gellian seemed almost apologetic. "I'm quite sure you're human. I know the maker left San Francisco many years before your birth."

His fevered eyes swept back to Dane.

"I'm not threatening you," he added quietly. "I'm simply stating an ugly situation. You're either with us or against us. This is war, and that's the way it has to be."

Deliberately putting down a surge of panic, Dane made himself pause to look at his watch. Ten-thirty. He still had time to find out what that girl wanted, at the Sanderson Service, before he tried to see Messenger. He bent to pick up his briefcase, trying not to seem too uneasy with it, and turned quickly toward the door.

"By eight in the morning," Gellian repeated gently behind him. "I hope you decide to come back."

He went out to the elevator, trying not to hurry. The glare and reek and chill of enmity went with him. He clutched the brief case desperately, afraid for a moment that Gellian's agents would try to stop him. But they let him go.

FIVE

He found a cab at the corner. Sitting uneasily straight as it crawled back uptown through the heavy mid-morning traffic, toward the Fortieth Street address of the Sanderson Service, he tried to decide what to do.

He couldn't go back. Kendrew's old dream had grown into a stubborn purpose of his own, rooted perhaps in his father's crusading idealism and his mother's vivid Eurasian loveliness. In spite of Gellian's fears, the promise of genetic engineering still seemed too splendid to be destroyed.

If his mother's blood had been all Caucasian, it occurred to him now, he might have grown up well content with the world as he found it. The pain of genetic accident must have been what forged his own eager hopes of genetic revolution.

And it had kindled a defiant independence in him that wouldn't easily yield to Gellian's ultimatum.

For Tanya de Jong had carried the chaos of the age written in her genes. Her dark beauty and her sensitive intelligence and her quick emotions had been the gifts of many races. Moody with the restless longings of homeless generations, she came of White Russian fugitives from violence and Dutch Colonial wanderers of commerce, of yellow people and brown driven from their ancient ways by the white man's passing triumph and already rebellious in exile.

She had been a laboratory technician in one of Manila's bomb-scarred hospitals when Dr. Philip Belfast arrived there in 1945, an Army surgeon, worn and lonely from the long ordeal of all the islands behind. They fell in love. Deaf to the shocked friends who said it wouldn't work out, he wanted to marry her.

"But she ran away." His father's voice came back to him now, edged with the sad bewilderment with which the old doctor had always spoken of that event and its aftermath.

"She quit her job, and wrote me a desperate little note to say she was going because she didn't want to hurt me.

"I thought the trouble was only her worry about our racial difference, though we had already agreed that we wouldn't let that matter—not too much. But I was ordered on to Okinawa before I could talk to her, and I didn't see her again until I went back to look for her, after the war.

"I found her then, back at work in the same hospital. I could see she still loved me, even though I was American. There hadn't been any other man. But still she wouldn't marry me—not until after I made her tell me what the trouble was.

"She thought she was psychic—maybe she was, though I laughed at the notion, then. She claimed she had prophetic dreams. She insisted she had seen her parents die in her dreams, when she was a little girl, the same way they really died in the first air raid on Manila.

"In the dream that had frightened her away from me, she thought she saw me kneeling, torn with grief, beside an operating table where she lay dead. She was convinced that she was doomed to die young, and she didn't want to hurt me the way I had been hurt in the dream.

"I didn't take much stock in any sort of extrasensory perception—not then. I thought she was just a little unstrung from all that had happened to her and her people in the war. Though I don't think I ever really shook her conviction of that fate waiting, I finally made her understand that her hysterical flight had hurt me as much as anything could.

"Anyhow, she married me." Dane could see the old surgeon's wistful smile again, lighted even in his memory with an undying love. "We came back to San Francisco before you were born. She promised to forget those dreams, and I think she did—at least for a while."

Frowning thoughtfully now in the cab, trying to forget the cold cloud of sensed hostility around him, Dane tried to weigh the consequences of their marriage. It must have damaged his father's career. He knew his mother had been deeply hurt, many times. Yet neither, he felt, had ever really been sorry.

His mother died the year he was ten. The racial snobs were not to blame for that. The cause had been crushingly incomprehensible to him then—though when he learned about her precognitions later, it occurred to him that the very effort to deny her doom had helped to cause it, by keeping her as silent about the warning symptoms of her illness as she had learned to be about her dreams.

She died of cancer.

He remembered the smiling hope and the veiled despair, the tight-lipped silences of pain, the desperate surgery. The last day of her life came back to him now with a painful clarity: the pale grace of her emaciated hand waving to him almost gaily as she was wheeled away to the operating room; the rank sweetness of ether in the lonely, busy corridors where he waited forever; the hoarse agony in his father's voice, saying she would never wake up, because her heart had stopped while she lay under Dr. Huber's scalpel.

"Why did you let him do it?" In his numbed dismay, he must have been thoughtlessly accusing. "Everybody says you're the top surgeon here. Why did you let Huber kill her?"

He saw his father's gray face stiffen, and knew his bitter tone had hurt.

"Huber didn't kill her, Dane." His father's low voice seemed tired and very kind. "The cancer did, and it had already spread too far before that first operation. I watched Huber today, and nobody could have done better. Tanya didn't have a chance."

"Why didn't she?" He felt the cruelty of his questions, yet he couldn't check their tortured urgency. "You're a fine doctor. I know you loved her. Why didn't you—why didn't somebody give her a chance?"

"Because nobody's good enough." The surgeon took his hand gently, to lead him away from the shrunken, sheet-covered body being wheeled out of the operating room. "Because medicine is not yet really a science. We know too many facts, without enough understanding."

They came out of the hospital, away from the dim hush of death into the sunlit street and the clean wind from the sea. Feeling miserably regretful for his bitter questions, Dane clung hard to his father's cold fingers, silent until they were in the parking lot.

"But couldn't there be a science of life?" he whispered hopefully, then. "So that people would never have to be sick, or suffer, or die before they were ready?"

"Someday, maybe." His father nodded wearily, walking on beyond the parked car as if he hadn't seen it. "Once I had a friend who dreamed of such a science. I even tried for years to help him work it out. His name for it was genetic engineering."

"Did he ever do it?"

"I don't know." His father kept walking on, away from the car, and still Dane didn't stop him. "Once he wrote me that he almost had it. But then a tragedy wrecked his life. He disappeared. I never found out where he went, but it looks as if he failed to conquer disease and pain and death. Because people still—"

His father turned suddenly back toward the car, asking in a softer voice if he wouldn't like to stay with Dr. Huber's sons until after the funeral. But people still died. Even people like his mother, who had wanted so terribly to keep on living.

"No, Dad, I'll go on home with you," he said quickly. "But I'm not going to be a surgeon, after all. I want to be a geneticist, like that old friend of yours. I want to finish the job you worked on with him—so that people needn't die the way mother did."

"She always said you'd do something very wonderful." Fumbling clumsily with the keys, as if he had forgotten how to start the car, his father tried to smile. "But I'm afraid you'll find the same difficulty in biological research we have in medicine—too many facts illuminated with too little understanding."

That was the first Dane ever heard of Charles Kendrew. It must have been about that time that his father began to notice those new clues to the fate of the missing geneticist, for it was later that same year that he retired to open the Kendrew Memorial Laboratory.

Already in slowly failing health, the old surgeon had worked there as desperately as if determined to conquer death before he died. His failure was due, Dane thought now, to that foreseen difficulty. The many related sciences of biology consisted of more facts than any mind could grasp, without some deeper understanding to bring them into focus.

In his own turn, Dane tried just as hard. Too hard, perhaps, completing the thesis for his doctorate before he was 23, and replacing his father as research director not a year later. Though he still felt fit enough, he wondered for a moment if the strain and the failure of intense effort might be half the matter with him today.

He knew their defeats had killed his father, and he had begun to wonder what had turned the successful surgeon back to that once abandoned undertaking, when he found the letters that were in his brief case now. His father had written Messenger the same year Tanya died, as a tattered carbon copy showed:

"Once I had a friend who was trying to mutate new species to order. He disappeared in Mexico, nearly twenty years ago, after a crushing family tragedy. I had believed him dead—until I began to see the recent advertisements of Cadmus, Inc.

"I have since examined some of the remarkable plant products your corporation is shipping from New Guinea. Cotton stronger than nylon. Latex better than any synthetic. Timber superior to mahogany and teak—from trees no botanist has ever described.

"While I know that cultivated plants are always being improved, your amazing progress in New Guinea makes me believe your products must come from entirely new plant species, of the sort my lost friend hoped to create by directed mutation. I am most anxious for news of him. Any confidence will be respected. His name was Charles Kendrew."

Messenger's prompt reply to that inquiry was typed on a crisply expensive gold-colored bond, beneath the New York address of the corporation and a green engraving of the dragon and the demigod that formed the Cadmus trademark.

"The origins of the eccentric expert who bred our improved plant strains have always been a mystery to me," the financier had written. "I'm indeed grateful for your suggestion that he may be your missing friend, and I regret very deeply that it comes several years too late.

"The few pertinent facts I know are these: The man is obviously American. I first met him in Darwin, Australia, when I was there as an Air Forces meteorologist in 1944—some five years, I believe, after your friend vanished. While he was always evasive about his past, he behaved like the victim of some overwhelming misfortune. He never wanted to come home, not even after his health seemed to require a change of climate. While he calls himself Charles Potter, that is probably a *nom de guerre.*

"Unfortunately, I am unable to make any positive identification from the photographs and physical description you enclosed. The height and the bone structure of the face seem about right, but Charles Potter's health had already been wrecked, when I first met him, by excessive drinking, and his face disfigured by tropical skin diseases.

"Tragically, the man himself is no longer able to tell us anything. While he is still living in New Guinea, at our experimental plantation on the upper Fly, his mind is hopelessly gone. He is receiving every possible care, but I'm afraid he can't live much longer.

"That's all I know, and I leave the conclusion to you. The

open possibility that this sick man may be your lost friend, however, leads me to mention something else which ought to interest you. Ever since Potter became ill, we in the company have wanted to set up a laboratory in which his unfinished researches can be carried on, and his papers edited for publication.

"In view of your past experience, as well as your personal interest, I am venturing to ask your advice. If you are interested, wire me at once."

That promise of Charles Potter's papers must have been enough to win his father. Though Dane had found no copy of any reply, it was later that same year that the surgeon turned for the second time from his practice to research, becoming director of the new laboratory.

There were other letters, written later. Carbons of his father's discouraged reports. Brief notes of encouragement from Messenger, always promising money for some new project. But no other mention, strangely, of Kendrew or Potter or the Cadmus exports from New Guinea. Those omissions worried Dane.

Had all the financier's generous gifts to the laboratory been only a cynical device to bribe his father into forgetting the vanished geneticist? He had been trying vainly to avoid that painful suspicion, ever since the unexpected failure of his father's heart plunged him into the shocking disorder of the old surgeon's papers and affairs.

His father hadn't been dishonest. In spite of the auditors, Dane knew that. Never a successful businessman, he had simply failed to keep any adequate accounts, or limit expenses to the endowment funds. Dane had to sell all the precious equipment, besides using the most of his own savings, to meet accumulated bills.

Yet, if those donations hadn't been some sort of bribe, why had Messenger cut them off so abruptly when his father died? And why else had that correspondence remained hidden in his father's desk, unmentioned even after Dane became research director?

Those were the questions Dane meant to ask Messenger, when he could see the financier, and he was trying to reserve judgment until he had heard the answers. All his clues were inconclusive. He was hoping for an innocent explanation of his father's silence, and perhaps even a look at the Potter papers.

Cadmus had grown greater than ever, in these twelve years since Philip Belfast first inquired about his missing friend. Nowadays, the sleek advertising of the corporation no longer mentioned the exciting novelty of its New Guinea products, but only their accepted excellence. Cadmus copra and cotton and latex and hardwoods were staples of world commerce, and even Dane himself had once taken them for granted.

Since his talk with Gellian, however, those profitable exports from New Guinea had become as disturbing to him as that iron tree and its peculiar fruit. His hopes for an honest understanding with Messenger began to flicker. If Charles Kendrew had really been the man Gellian called the maker—and whom Messenger called Charles Potter—and if all the vast wealth of Cadmus had grown from a secret exploitation of genetic engineering—

The consequences of that proposition became too alarming to pursue, and Dane felt relieved to escape them for the time, when his taxi stopped below the tall new office building on Fortieth, at Nan Sanderson's business address.

SIX

The small reception room on the nineteenth floor was empty when he entered, yet it seemed a sanctuary. Dane Belfast escaped that haunting danger-sense at the door, as if he had come somehow into a safe refuge. He was looking at the neat glass desk and the chrome-and-plastic chairs, trying to surmise the nature of the Sanderson Service, when a tall girl walked out of the room beyond.

"Dane!" She looked at him with a curiously anxious intentness, and then smiled approvingly. "I'm Nan Sanderson."

He smiled back, at the friendly light in her eyes. He liked the clean planes of her tan face and the smooth up-sweep of her red-brown hair and the trim simplicity of her gray business suit, but those surface things couldn't explain the way she made him feel.

Somehow, she made a tremendous sense of relieved security well up inside him. That surge of feeling took his breath and closed his throat, so that for a moment he couldn't speak. He stood staring blankly at her tawny loveliness, thinking of something that had happened long ago in San Francisco.

He didn't know why he should think of it now, because it was one of the painful childhood incidents he had always tried to forget. Nine years old, he had been invited to a children's party at Dr. Huber's home. Two small girls were choosing sides for some game on the lawn, and they left him standing alone at the end, unchosen. He started uneasily toward the one he thought would have to take him, but she shook her prim curls scornfully.

"We don't want you." The agony of that rejection had returned in his dreams for many years, and even now he winced again from her shrill cruelty. " 'Cause you ain't white!"

"But I am too white!" He held out his hands indignantly to show they were no darker than her own. "My father's Dr. Belfast, and he's white as yours."

"But your mama ain't," she informed him stonily. "And so

you ain't—no matter how you look." All the children were turning to stare, the way cruel bystanders were later to stare in his dreams. "And my mama says it's a shame Dr. Belfast threw himself away on her," the pitiless child went on. " 'Cause she's part Chinaman and part nigger and part God knows what!" Her curls tossed haughtily. "And that's why we don't want you."

Speechless with shock and pain, he had been dimly aware of flustered adults trying to smooth the incident over. His mother wasn't Negro at all, but only part Eurasian. The children must let him play because he was Dr. Belfast's boy, and anyhow his mother was cultured and charming and half Caucasian. The other little girl grudgingly agreed to choose him, but suddenly he didn't want to play. His mother was as good as anybody, and he didn't want apologies or pity. He said politely that it was time for him to go home, and thanked Mrs. Huber and his little hostess properly, and walked stiffly away alone.

He had never told anybody about that, not even his mother, because he knew it would hurt her the way it did him; but he remembered studying himself in the mirror often afterwards, when he knew he was alone, uneasily glad his gray eyes didn't show the slight Chinese cast of his mother's, half sick with fear that his lean face might tan too darkly, wishing forlornly that his straight brown hair had been a sandy red, like his father's.

Time had slowly worn most of the old pain away. Most people must have forgotten about his mother, after she was dead. In science, he had found a world where men of all races could meet equally on the common ground of honest intellectual effort, and presently his own research had kept him too busy to think much about anything else.

Now, however, Nan Sanderson somehow made all that

come back. The cruel hostility of those small children had been as incredible to him then as this awareness of unseen hate around him today, and the enormous relief that relaxed him when she smiled was the same secure feeling of unquestioning acceptance he always found with his mother.

"Well?" the tall girl was saying. "Aren't you Dr. Belfast?"

"Dane Belfast." Gulping at the lump in his throat, he yielded to his impulse to explain, because her serene blue eyes seemed so understanding. "I didn't mean to stare, but you just gave me the oddest feeling."

"Yes?" She waited, interested.

"I don't quite know what's wrong with me today." He looked at her hopefully. "Since just before you called, I've had the queerest feelings. Of danger. I can't be sure it's anything real, yet the sensations are so vivid they frighten me. I seem to see danger, like dark fire, and feel it, like a cold wind—if you can imagine that. It somehow comes and goes, but it followed me all the way here. But suddenly, when I saw you, I felt—well, safe."

He had paused, afraid of what she might think, but she was nodding soberly.

"The danger's real enough," she said quietly. "But we'll try to make you safe."

"What sort of danger?" He couldn't help glancing back toward the empty corridor outside. "And how are you going to make me safe?"

She shook her head. "Before I can tell you anything, you must establish your right to our service."

"How do I do that?"

"You answer questions, and you pass a test." She turned to the door behind her. "Come on inside."

He followed eagerly, lifted by a curious confidence that he could answer any question, and pass every test. The tastefully plain room beyond might have been the office of a successful psychoanalyst, but nothing about it told him the object of the Sanderson Service. The girl beckoned him toward a chair and turned to take a wide blue card from a filing cabinet.

"First we must check your record." She studied the card thoughtfully. "Dane Belfast. Race: white. Birthplace: San Francisco. Father: Dr. Philip Belfast, surgeon and biochemist. Mother: Tanya de Jong Belfast." Her liquid eyes lifted. "Is all that correct?"

"All—almost." An unexpected wave of feeling shook him and choked him, so that he had to swallow. "All except the race."

His own words frightened him. He hadn't thought of his mixed ancestry for a long time until today, because it didn't seem to matter in the tolerant world of science, but now that old bewildered fear came back to seize him as if it had been haunting his unconscious all the time.

"I—I'm not entirely white." He didn't want to tell Nan Sanderson the truth; he was terribly afraid the fact would shatter her quiet friendliness, yet somehow he had to speak. His voice trembled, and his eyes fell from hers. "My mother was Eurasian. A quarter Chinese. An eighth each Javanese and Filipino. The rest was white, Russian and Colonial-Dutch."

"That's the way we have it." When he dared look up, she was calmly checking something on the card. "Now, your university records—"

"Doesn't that matter?" He couldn't help his hoarse interruption. "That Eurasian blood?"

"Not to us." Her blue eyes were innocently wide. "No racial strain is really pure, anyhow. I'm an eighth Cherokee, myself." Smiling, her lean face was a warm golden brown. "Do you mind that?"

He could only shake his head, because that hard constriction had closed his throat again. She had somehow awakened that old pain, which must have been rankling just beneath the level of his consciousness all the years when he thought it forgotten. Accepting him now, she had helped to heal those old injuries.

"Any racial stock can contribute very useful genes." She was studying the card again, as if she had looked away from him out of respect for the privacy of his emotions. "But we're interested now in qualifications of an entirely different sort."

She didn't say where she had found the information, but the card listed his biology degrees from Stanford, and his doctorate in biochemistry from Caltech, and even his two years as research director at the Kendrew Memorial. She asked about the common diseases of childhood, and seemed pleased when he said he had escaped them.

"Now come with me," she said, and he followed her back into a small laboratory, where she took his blood pressure and deftly stabbed his finger for a blood specimen. Watching in perplexed impatience while she entered something on the card, he asked:

"Am I going to qualify?"

"I don't know yet." She spoke half absently, turning to study a smear of his blood under a microscope. "Because all this is just preliminary. The physical data is no more important than your racial background, really. The essential tests are mental."

He almost gasped. That curious sense of sanctuary had swept away his first faint notion that she might be one of the mutants Gellian hunted, but this brought that suspicion back, with a shattering force of conviction. Recovering from his involuntary start, he studied her searchingly.

Still busy, to his relief, with the microscope, her fine face wistfully intent and the cold north light turned warm on her hair, she looked entirely and enchantingly human. But all the maker's creatures, in Gellian's disturbing theory, had been cunningly shaped to hide among men.

Dane nodded, shaken. For all he knew, she could be that most evasive, most dangerous thing. Yet, oddly, he felt no revulsion or fear. He was enormously interested, instead; fascinated by her veiled strangeness and breathless to discover her mutant gifts. A quick pity touched him, too, when he thought of her as a lonely alien, bravely fighting her human hunters.

That flashing suspicion made the nature of her business seem suddenly clear. She must be looking for her kinsmen, scattered along the maker's trail, to warn and aid them against Gellian's exterminators. The Sanderson Service, it struck him, must exist to serve not-men only. And these tests were designed to find them!

For one strange moment, Dane wished that he could pass. The drama of the girl's desperate position had already stirred him, and now for one wild instant in his imagination they stood side by side, heroic and alone, the hunted but undaunted Eve and Adam of a noble new race.

Impatiently, he discarded that fantasy. He didn't want to be a misfit, and he tried to guard himself against such neurotic wishes. He had merely surmised that she might be a mutant, anyhow, he reminded himself. Even if she were, she could have had no reason for picking him for these tests, except his father's old friendship with Charles Kendrew; and his own birth had come many years too late for that to signify.

"Well?" He saw her turning from the microscope, and tried to cover his awed wonder with that casual query. "How am I doing?"

"Well enough." Nodding approvingly, she brought two sharpened pencils to the little table where she had seated him.

"Now we come to the psychological tests."

Psychology was one of the biological sciences, and he knew all the standard tests. These were unfamiliar, however, and the most difficult he had seen. For the next hour, while the girl held a stopwatch and marked his papers, he sweated through increasingly intricate riddles.

"Do I have to be a genius?" he finally demanded.

"It wouldn't hurt your chances." Smiling slightly, she glanced at his scores on the card. "But you have qualified for the final test."

While he waited, tapping with a pencil in an effort to disguise the taut intensity of his expectation, she set up a wooden screen before him on the table.

"I'm going to shuffle these, and deal them out of your sight." She showed him a thin deck of cards, printed with simple geometric figures. "I want you to call them as they fall."

Trying too hard to seem at ease, he heard the pencil point snap beneath his tightened fingers. For he knew the cards; the standard ESP deck, devised years ago for the parapsychology research at Duke University. Extrasensory perception, Gellian had said, was the mark of the mutants.

"I can't," he whispered. "I'm not psychic."

Investigating that new frontier of the widening sciences of life, he had sometimes found challenging signs of a real psi capacity—an inexplicable reach of the mind beyond the range of any known senses or physical faculties—but only now and then, unpredictably erratic as his mother's glimpses of tragedy to come, always in other subjects. Never in himself.

"Please!" The anxiety in his own voice surprised him. "Can't we skip this?"

"This is the one you have to pass." But her warm eyes gave him a grave encouragement. "I think you will. This feeling of danger you mention—I think that's an actual perception, of a very actual peril."

He nodded, reluctantly. That cold dry glow of evil over everything outside this puzzling haven must be evidence of—something. He straightened in the chair, waiting nervously for her to go ahead.

"Ready?" She sat down behind the screen, where he couldn't see her. "Here's the first card, face down on the table. Just take your time, and try to tell me what it is."

SEVEN

He tried hard enough, surely. That faint, unfriendly glow from outside the window was still distracting, however, even when he closed his eyes. All he could visualize was her face, changed in his mind to a lovely but somehow inhuman mask of lean-carved ivory, her long eyes turning slowly hostile as if they had narrowed against that penetrating glare.

"Call the one in your mind," she urged at last. "You'll hit it."

He could only guess, desperately, "Is it—a star?"

"I don't know, until we finish the run. Now just relax, and take your time, and tell me what you see. Ready?"

"It's—probably a cross?"

She dealt again, and he kept on guessing wildly. He couldn't expect to qualify, he reminded himself. He shouldn't even try, because success would only mark him for Gellian's executioners. In spite of himself, however, the thing he feared was failure. And even though he was afraid that fear itself might make him fail, he couldn't stop the anxious sweat that felt cold on his forehead and clammy on his hands, or evade that pitiless pale reflection from the gray sky outside.

"Why take it so hard?" She rose when the run was finished, shaking her head in reproof at his breathless tensity. "Why don't you smoke, while I check your score?"

He was a light smoker, because he had worked so much in sterile laboratories where nicotine was contraband, but he found a cigarette and pulled on it nervously until he heard her shuffling the cards again.

"How'd I do?" he asked huskily.

"Well enough." But he caught the disappointment in her voice. "Let's try another run."

He tried again, but still he felt no truth in his desperate guesses. And he saw the trouble on her tawny face when she rose, her faint smile forced and foreboding.

"I'm terribly sorry, Dr. Belfast." He felt the chill of a new formality in her voice. "I was sure you'd qualify, and I can't understand your failure."

"I'm trying." That cruel dry light was suddenly stronger in the room, turning her somehow coldly pale and stern. He knew she was about to turn him out of this unaccountable refuge. "Trying too hard, probably." An illogical alarm shook his voice. "Please don't turn me down without another chance."

"That wouldn't help." Remote from him, she shook her head wearily. "Not unless your psi capacity had been disturbed by some emotional shock." Her blue eyes turned piercing, and something hushed her voice. "Have you seen the man I mentioned?" she whispered sharply. "John Gellian?"

Meeting her probing stare, watching for her reaction, Dane nodded slowly. "He found me in the lobby of my hotel, an hour after you called. He took me around to his office, and told me a story, and offered me a job."

Her tawny body seemed to freeze. Cold as that glare outside, her wary eyes searched him again before she demanded: "Did you take it?"

"Not yet." Curiously relieved to discover that her mutant perception didn't tell her everything—if she were a mutant—Dane relaxed a little. "What he told me was too much to deal with, all at once," he added. "I'm thinking it over, till eight in the morning."

"He told you I'm something strange?" she breathed faintly. "Something—monstrous?"

"He talked about genetic mutations," Dane admitted uncomfortably. "A strange story. I don't quite know what to think—"

"Don't believe him!" The ice in her voice thawed suddenly, to a hot vehemence. "I know that horrible story, and it isn't true. That man's sick. He has those hideous delusions. They make him dangerous—to you as well as to me."

She sat down suddenly on the edge of the little table that held the screen, as if weak with her troubled emotion. Her long eyes were suddenly too innocent.

"No wonder you bungled the tests—if you believed Gellian's insane lies!" She smiled at him, with a wan relief. "Trust me, Dane. Just ask me anything you want to know."

"All right." He leaned a little forward, watching her anxiously. "Just tell me who you are."

"Nobody very exciting." She spoke flatly, suddenly withdrawn again. "Just an ordinary business girl."

"I—I do want to know you, Nan." A flood of feeling surged up against his own reserve, an urgent impulse he didn't clearly understand, born perhaps of that sense of sanctuary and his fear of losing it. "Please tell me all about you. Just imagine I'm making out a blue card for you."

"If you like." Her red mouth was smiling slightly, but her

eyes stayed veiled and distant. "Father was a mining engineer, and Mother a schoolteacher he met in Montana. I was born in Anaconda. He's retired now, and they live on a half-acre ranch near San Diego."

"And—you?"

"Nothing unusual." She shrugged, too casually. "Dull little mining towns, where Father worked. College. Two or three men who thought they loved me. A few jobs that didn't matter. Including this one—"

"But this one does matter," Dane objected quickly. "If you're going to tell the truth, I want to know something about the Sanderson Service."

"Sorry," she said curtly. "I'm not permitted to discuss our service with people who fail to qualify."

"I know something about it, anyhow," he said. "Gellian told me you're busy locating and helping other not-men." He studied her. "Is that your service?"

"Gellian's wrong!" Her lifted voice turned bitterly vehement. "His sick imagination has twisted the facts into a shocking lie. But I see that I must tell you something."

"I think you'd better."

"You won't repeat it?" Her long eyes turned dark with troubled pleading. "Not even to Gellian? Particularly, not to him!"

"All right," he agreed slowly. "You have my word."

Nodding for him to follow, she walked back into her office and sat down wearily. Not looking at him, she leaned absently to straighten the penstand and calendar and clock, and then brushed automatically at some invisible fleck of dust.

"Well?" He waited, standing impatiently in front of her desk.

"You see, I'm a geneticist, too," she said at last. "I'm helping conduct a tremendous experiment in human genetics. The service is part of that."

"Your object?"

"To rescue the human race from civilization."

He waited, puzzled.

"We feel that modern civilization, by sheltering the unfit, has stopped the forward evolution of the individual. Perhaps even turned it backward. We're trying to replace the missing care of nature. To evolve an improved human type, by a process of intelligent artificial selection."

"Kendrew's process?" Dane whispered huskily. "Genetic engineering?"

"Kendrew?" Her blue eyes widened innocently. "No, our process isn't genetic engineering. We're using the same simple method men have always used to improve any breed. We select individuals who have desirable traits, and cause them to marry and have children." Aimlessly, her long golden fingers moved the penstand again. "Among the genes we require," she added at last, "are those for the psi capacity."

"And you qualified?"

She hesitated. For a moment he thought her face had a look of lonely yearning, but then she turned quickly from him, into the merciless thin glare from outside. That washed all feeling from her face, leaving it fixed and cold.

Faintly, she said, "I qualified."

"I see." Almost believing her, Dane yielded to a sudden, troubled impulse. "Once there was a little girl," he muttered. "She said I couldn't play, because my genes weren't all white." He laughed harshly, not sure why he did. "You can't change your genes."

"Quite true." She rose briskly, moving toward the door. "I'm glad you understand, and I'm sure you'll keep your word. Good-by, Dr. Belfast."

"Wait." He stood stubbornly where he was. "Didn't you

promise me another chance?"

"I did intend to give you one." Her unhappy eyes came back to him. "But I can see now that you simply aren't for us. Please forgive my blunder. And go—before you're deeper in danger!"

"From Gellian?"

"From all unthinking people, outside our experiment." Urgency lifted her voice. "From people who mistakenly feel that we're assaulting the Christian ethic, don't you see, and the democratic philosophy that all men are brothers."

"I see." He studied her pale anxiety. "Gellian is only a champion of the old race, jealous and resentful of the superior breed you're creating?"

"If you wish to phrase it that way." She nodded quickly. "That's the danger. The reason you must go now—and never attempt to see me again."

He nodded carefully, trying not to show that he had seen through her lie. But he had. Her story of that vast experiment in applied human genetics had been planned cleverly enough to convince another geneticist. Given the organization, with the money and the devoted leadership to work secretly through several generations, man might be bred into superman, without the need of any new process of genetic engineering.

Her story was quite plausible—but still a lie.

Any such actual experiment, for one thing, running as it must through centuries, would require absolute secrecy to protect its records and its staff and its selected subjects from such hostile men as Gellian. If her story were true, it could be told to no outsider.

Shaken by that consideration, his reluctant belief was swept away entirely when he thought of that metallic tree, which must have been found in one of her own raided refuges. Perhaps she still hoped Gellian had failed to notice anything unusual beneath the holiday disguise, or to connect that plant with the mutant men.

Generations of selective mating would surely produce a superior human breed. Even the psi capacities might be vastly increased, assuming that the genes for those were existing but recessive. But such a new creation as that harmless-seeming Christmas tree might require an impossible million generations of natural mutation and artificial selection. It hadn't been made that way, and it demolished her story entirely.

She had opened the door, waiting for him to go. Still reluctant to leave this sanctuary, before he found what made it so, he paused to look at her hopefully. All he saw was that glare from outside on her tawny face, a strange cruel sheen, inexplicable as ever.

"Good-by, Dane." Her voice was hushed and taut. "Better go on."

Yet still he hesitated. He felt suddenly sorry for her, because of that pathetic lie. Because it showed so clearly the limits of whatever slight psi capacity she might possess, and because it seemed such a flimsy defense against Gellian's killers and all the glowing hate outside.

"May I see you again?" he begged impulsively. "Tonight? Tomorrow? Can't we try that test again?"

"You didn't qualify." Cold beneath that reflected enmity, she had withdrawn even beneath the reach of his pity. "Your failure is final," she added flatly. "And my time limited."

So was his own. At eight in the morning, he must join her hunters, or else be hunted with her. In the few free hours left, he still had Messenger to see, and too many puzzles to solve, and that hard choice to make. He walked out stiffly, driven by that overwhelming urgency, and heard her snap the lock behind him.

EIGHT

Short as his time was, Dane could do nothing before he saw Messenger. Waiting for three o'clock, when the old tycoon might be in, he ate lunch with a forced deliberation and wandered restlessly back to his room to search again through the meager clues in those old letters.

He managed to relax a little in the cab, inching downtown through the wet streets, but all that sense of pitiless attack fell back upon him when he got out at Messenger's address. Unnerved by that impact, he paused on the curb to look for its source.

The enormous tower, all sternly functional glass and granite, had been planted boldly in a somewhat run-down section of shops and lesser office buildings in between the financial district and the sleek, newer developments in the Rockefeller Center area, as if its builders intended to pioneer in New York real estate as they had in New Guinea. The disturbing thing about the building was the plaque of bronze and colored glass above the entrance.

Green glass filled a golden outline of New Guinea, the shape of it a sprawling dragon, the monstrous jaws toothless and spread wide. Against it in high relief stood a bronze figure of Cadmus, the dragon-slayer of that old Greek myth, arms flung out to sow the teeth which took instant root, so the legend went, to grow into men. Beneath the dying dragon, huge golden letters spelled: CADMUS, INC.

That symbol had always seemed harmless enough before, in the company advertising and on Messenger's letterhead: a natural reference to the beastlike shape of that great island on the map, the triumphant giant standing for the corporation, sowing those vast new plantations. Now, however, it had become a disquieting hint of the maker's superhuman creations.

That hueless glare of evil shone cold on the plaque, and the dusty reek of unseen deadliness seemed stronger than the bitter traffic fumes. Retreating again from the snarl of the street, Dane pushed through the massive glass doors.

"Yes, sir?" A pale, bulky man challenged him from the glass-and-granite fortress of a desk which guarded the elevators. "May I assist you, sir?"

"Dane Belfast to see Mr. Messenger," he said. "I left my name this morning."

The pale man might have been a retired detective. He studied Belfast with opaque cold eyes as if trying to recall him from some police line-up, before he reached for the telephone. But as he listened, his tight-lipped disapproval changed, surprisingly, to a wintry smile.

"Go on up." He nodded toward the elevators. "Mr. Messenger wants to see you right away."

All that unaccountable feel of crouching peril seemed to fall away from Dane, as the express elevator lifted him, so that he was almost at ease again when a blond receptionist cooed his name into an office interphone, and then came gliding with a sullen grace to guide him past empty desks into a long, luxurious room beyond.

"Well, Dr. Belfast!" An enormous, ugly, weather-beaten man, J. D. Messenger came waddling laboriously around a magnificent desk made of pale New Guinea silverwood, to grasp his hand with an entirely unexpected warmth. "I've been expecting you. Sit down and have a cigar."

Dane declined the cigar, but he sat down gratefully in a huge leather chair, trying to get over his instant liking for Messenger. Prepared to meet some human reflection of this cold fortress of a building and the unobtrusive power of Cadmus, he wanted to mistrust this genial reception.

"What's on your mind?"

But Dane sat hesitantly silent, watching Messenger move with an elaborate and laborious caution back to his chair. Old and overweight and obviously ill, the financier still had a certain surprising felicity of action, and even a kind of charm. The history of an active life lived nearly to the end was written on his calmly massive face, in ancient scars and unhealthy purple blotches and sagging yellow wattles of loose skin, yet his shrewd blue eyes were smiling serenely.

"Good to see you." Already puffing, the old man paused as if the task of sitting down took all his effort. "Admired your father. Interested in your research. Deeply. Sorry I had to cut the money off."

That beaming cordiality made Dane feel awkward about the questions he had to ask, and he hastily reviewed his plans. Logically, Messenger ought to know both Nan Sanderson and Gellian. Milking his vast fortune from those mutant plants, he had certainly learned something about the maker's more ambitious creations. And Gellian's implacable hunt for the not-men, covering Australia, had surely also reached New Guinea. Yet Messenger's cheery innocence made him doubt that the man was involved with either of them. For an instant, he questioned even the evidence that the financier had bought or tricked his father.

"Well?" Settled now behind the desk, hands locked over his belly, Messenger seemed disarmingly patient. "If you want something, young man, let's talk about it."

"I do want something." That scarred smile had begun to reassure Dane, even about those awkward questions. "Something you promised my father, when you first endowed the laboratory." He watched uncomfortably for the big man's reaction. "If you can arrange it, I'd like to see Charles Potter's notes."

Those battered features showed no flicker of surprise.

"Sorry, but I can't arrange it." Messenger shook his head, with a ponderous bland regret. "Poor old Potter was eccentric, you know. Trusted nobody. We found all his papers destroyed, after he died."

"Died?" Dane had half expected that blow, yet he flinched. "When?"

"Let me see." Messenger scrutinized his flat blue thumbs. "Must have been last year—no, two years ago. Out in New Guinea. The old bird would never hear of coming back to civilization, not even to die."

"Did my father ever know?"

"I doubt it." Messenger shrugged, with a patient huge indifference. "Old Potter had squandered all he ever made, on drugs and drink and experiments that failed. Alienated all his friends outside the company. Had no relatives. Seemed to hate mankind. I don't think anybody cared—"

"My father was never alienated," Dane broke in quickly. "I know he cared because Charles Potter—Charles Kendrew—was his oldest friend." He stared at the genial financier, searchingly. "What I don't know is why he never told me that your plant breeder was his missing friend."

"Because he wasn't, probably." Messenger's small, pale eyes lifted lazily. "What gave you any such idea?"

"My father's papers. Letters to him from Kendrew. A letter of your own." Accusations would do no good, and Dane tried to soften his voice. "Didn't you think Potter was actually Kendrew when you endowed the Kendrew Memorial?"

"Your father's notion." Messenger peered idly down at his restless thumbs. "Before he knew anything about Potter. I thought he might be right, until I learned more about Kendrew. We both agreed, then, that his missing humanitarian couldn't very likely be my twisted misanthrope dying in New Guinea. We knew he wasn't, when your father failed—as you have also done—to turn Kendrew's ambitious theories even into Potter's very modest practical results."

The humanitarian might have been changed into the bitter recluse by that tragedy in Albuquerque. Dane was about to suggest that when a sudden suspicion shook him. Had Messenger killed the missing geneticist?

Still gasping a little for his breath, this jovial fat man didn't look like a murderer for profit. Yet he and his associates had been the only known beneficiaries from those tremendous discoveries. Messenger's guilt could explain the generous arrangements to insure his father's silence, and this present glib insistence that his plant breeder had not been Kendrew.

"No regrets about the millions we poured into your research," the financier was wheezing. "No hard feelings, understand." He shrugged good-naturedly. "We bet on a losing hand. I'm just sorry we couldn't afford to go on losing."

This was not the time or place to make any unproved accusations. Dane sat frowning, wondering how to get the most information at the least risk.

"A bad year for the company, you see." Messenger's fat, mottled hands gestured apologetically above the polished silverwood. "Floods in New Guinea. And a bad time for me," he added wryly. "My last wife's lawyers are bleeding me dry."

"But we can carry on our research, without much money," Dane insisted. "Even if your expert burned all his papers, there's still a record of his process—in the genes of the plants he bred for you."

"Sorry, Belfast." Pursing fat blue lips, Messenger shook his head. "Your father used to want specimens, but we can't ship live plants. Company policy."

"Then I'll go to New Guinea," Dane offered—grasping eagerly at that possible escape from Gellian. "I can study them better on the spot, anyhow—"

"Impossible!" The warmth had gone from Messenger's eyes, leaving them cold and flat and somehow too small for that enormous, mottled, sagging face. "My associates wouldn't consider that."

"I don't intend to steal your secrets." Dane half rose, drawn taut with anxiety. "But I believe those plants are directed mutations—no matter who Potter was. If we knew how he made them, we could make—anything! Specialized mutant viruses, for instance, to wipe out disease germs." He looked hard at Messenger's own sick face. "Would that be against your policy?"

The old man's small eyes met Dane's for a moment, surprisingly keen, before they fell sleepily again to his cradled paunch.

"I organized Cadmus more than twenty years ago, to operate mines and plantations in New Guinea." He spoke slowly, economizing his wheezing breath. "We needed plants adapted to the nasty climate there, and I hired this Charles Potter to breed them for us. He did it, without telling anybody how. Then he threw away his slice of the profits, and devoted himself to his own peculiar method of slow suicide. We gave him all we promised, and that transaction is closed. Our policy now is simply to protect and develop our enormous investment in New Guinea."

His eyes flickered at Dane, hard as lumps of ice beneath the swollen, drooping lids.

"Cadmus is a legitimate business," he went on doggedly. "Our exports average billions of dollars a year. We pay enormous taxes and concession fees and dividends. Our employees—white-collared accountants here or naked Kanakas in the jungle—get decent treatment and excellent pay. The wealth we create benefits all the world." He caught a rasping breath. "Isn't that enough?"

"Not for me," Dane blurted impulsively. "Not if you're hiding and exploiting those wonderful discoveries Kendrew hoped to make. Not if you're guilty of—that."

Murder, he had wanted to say. Murder of a newborn science, and its unfortunate inventor. But this shrewd old man had betrayed nothing, and such charges would be obviously unwise. Dane checked his outburst, and tried to soften his bitter voice.

"Sorry I troubled you," he muttered stiffly. "Thanks for all the help you gave my father."

Trembling, he turned to go.

"Wait!" Messenger boomed behind him. "We haven't talked about that job."

The financier was standing when he turned, swaying ponderously beyond the desk, smiling with that shattered charm which still somehow transformed his gross bulk and redeemed his scarred and mottled ugliness. Dane came slowly back, asking blankly, "What job?"

"Didn't you come to ask for a position with the company?" Genial again, those faded little eyes peered innocently out of their deep wells of bloated flesh. "Knowing something of your circumstances, I took that for granted. How would you like a place in our public relations division?"

"I didn't suppose you wanted much publicity."

"We don't." Messenger's slow grin was almost likeable. "Half the work of any press agent is preventing bad publicity."

Dane stood thinking of that other job waiting, at the Gellian Agency. Hoping Messenger might yet somehow rescue him from that pressing dilemma of whether to become hunter or hunted, he tried to tell himself that the cunning old tycoon looked too bluff and hearty to be entirely bad.

"People envy our success," the financier was wheezing.

"They start malicious rumors, and attempt to meddle in our private affairs, and try to steal our trade secrets. Your job will be to fight such interference."

Belfast stared incredulously. "To help conceal the very facts I want to learn?"

"Put it that way if you like." Messenger nodded cheerfully. "Be here at ten in the morning, if you want to go to work. Your pay starts at three hundred a week."

Dane stiffened at that improbable figure, wondering if Messenger hoped to buy him off, as he thought his father had been bought.

"A lot of money," he said. "How do I earn it?"

"Relax, and I'll tell you all about it." Beaming as expansively as if he had already accepted, the fat man offered dark New Guinea cigars in a heavy silver humidor, and lighted one himself. "You'll have an office down the corridor—though most of your work will be outside. You can set your own hours, and you'll find us liberal about expenses. We try to make our people happy, Dr. Belfast."

Declining the cigar, he waited mistrustfully.

"Cadmus spends millions of dollars a year to create a favorable public opinion," Messenger went on. "We hire expert professional publicists, and we buy every kind of advertising. But, in our special case, that isn't enough."

Dane shook his head. This job already looked as ugly as Gellian's.

"Unfortunately, occasional matters come up that are too delicate to be handled in any ordinary way." The shrewd old eyes didn't seem to see his silent protest. "I want you to join the small staff of skilled specialists we employ to care for such extraordinary cases as they come up, by whatever methods they may require."

Including—murder?

The thought opened that wide room for a moment to a sudden glare of danger, which turned the pale New Guinea hardwood cold as actual metal. The smoke of Messenger's cigar had a sudden bitter bite of deadliness. Belfast shifted uncomfortably where he stood, wondering if this offer might be as difficult to decline as Gellian's.

"As such a specialist," Messenger continued blandly, "you will work directly under me. You will receive your assignments from me personally, and report their accomplishment to me alone—there must be no failures. Miss Falk will pay your salary and expenses in cash, but you aren't to discuss your work with her or anyone else. Get that?"

"But I haven't taken the job."

"A necessary precaution," the fat man panted. "And you will take it, when you hear about your first assignment."

Dane listened uncomfortably, certain Messenger would never tell him so much, except as a warning to forget what he already knew.

"A tricky affair." Worry erased the financier's ponderous confidence. "There's a newspaper reporter—a filthy little rat—prying into our private business with a stupid persistence and no legitimate reason. He has even been to New Guinea, trespassing on our concessions. Now he's back in New York City, ready to expose us—as he puts it. Your first job will be to gag him."

"How?" Belfast rasped harshly. "Am I to cut his throat?"

"Don't joke." A pained reproof stiffened Messenger's red, ugly slab of a face. "Didn't I tell you we're strictly legitimate? That's the peculiar difficulty of this job. Your methods must always be entirely honest."

"If a man is writing the truth," Dane said flatly, "how can you gag him—honestly?"

"Your problem," Messenger murmured. "Although we

can assist you with unlimited funds and a staff of clever specialists who have solved many such problems with never an incident to stain the good name of Cadmus!" The faded eyes peered sharply through gray cigar smoke. "Is that perfectly clear?"

"Perfectly," Dane said. "Even though I can't take the job."

"Better think it over." The fat man was blinking at him sleepily, and he felt danger like a cold liquid dripping down the back of his neck. "Come back in the morning, if you change your mind. I'll hold it open until ten."

"I'll think it over," Dane agreed. "But I've had another offer that's even harder to refuse."

"Better watch your step," Messenger warned, with an air of lazily friendly concern. "These people trying to steal our secrets don't stop at anything. Bits of accidental information about our business have cost a number of men their lives."

"Thanks." Nodding ironically, Dane turned to the door. "I'll try to be on guard."

NINE

Dark uncertainty followed him out of the building, past the sullen blond receptionist and the pale man guarding the elevators; and that snarl of unseen danger met him again when he came out into the windy street.

The taste of hostility was once more a dry bitterness in his mouth, and the feel of it a cold weight at the back of his skull. Alarm was a soundless siren, cutting through the thunder of traffic. The scent of hate was a nauseous reek, and he had to squint against a driving glare of black malignance.

That awareness couldn't be real—but it was. For a panicky instant, in spite of Nan Sanderson's tests, he wondered if it could be some actual perception of Messenger's specialists or Gellian's executioners or even Kendrew's inhuman creations; and he turned back suddenly, trying to catch some murderous stalker by surprise.

The people he saw were harmless to the eye: a few clerks and office girls, shrinking timidly from the raw east wind and ignoring him entirely. Yet that colorless cast of danger made all their pale faces equally gray and wary and implacably intent.

Rain was beginning to fall, and he failed to signal a taxi. Shoulders hunched against the wind-driven drops, he hurried to the subway entrance at the corner, wondering desperately what to do.

Of these two jobs he didn't want, the one with Cadmus seemed faintly preferable. That, at least, wouldn't place him among the exterminators of Nan Sanderson's new race. But neither position seemed to offer any immunity from the unpleasant consequences of not taking the other, and he started down the subway steps as eagerly as if escaping the need to decide.

That suffocating reek of danger checked him again on the stair, stronger than ever underground. Retreating confusedly, he stumbled back outside and started plodding back through the thin rain toward his hotel, groping dazedly for anything to do.

Give it up and get away, common sense was urging. But it had been too late for that, he knew, ever since Gellian spoke to him in the lobby. Perhaps ever since Nan Sanderson called. There was nowhere to go, beyond the reach of Gellian's men, or Messenger's. If the mutants were causing this danger-sense, they might be anywhere.

Anyhow, even now, he didn't want to run away. The

amazing art which had shaped that metallic plant was worth any possible risk. The wealth of Cadmus was merely a hint of what it could do. Here was the goal of all his life, too near and real to be abandoned now.

Yet, what else was possible?

The police were unlikely to believe anything he might say about murder in New Guinea, or not-men in New York, or even about that bitter taste of danger on his tongue. Messenger was secure in the impregnable fortress of his corporation, and Gellian's operations were evidently within and above the law.

He couldn't help thinking wistfully of the comforting sense of safety he had found at the Sanderson Service, but even that uncertain sanctuary was closed to him now. The hunted girl had made it plain that she would class him with her human hunters, since he had failed to qualify.

He had no money to hire bodyguards, or to finance any investigation of his own. Feeling more than ever a stranger in New York, he could think of no man or woman to whom he could turn—except, perhaps, that unknown newspaperman Messenger was planning to gag.

Bedraggled in the storm, Broadway was jammed now with the first homeward rush of shoppers and office workers, raucous with horns and police whistles and the squeal of wet brakes. All the remembered color and glamor of the street was gone, since he had seen it with his parents so long ago, and it lay gray and cold and ugly now beneath that chill dry glare.

He was still plodding north, too aimless even to signal at the taxis passing in the rain, when his harried thoughts turned to that nameless reporter. He wanted to know what the man had discovered in New Guinea, but he could see no way to find out. He shook his head wearily—and noticed the change in that pall of overhanging danger.

Before, that colorless glow of something not light had seemed to burn uniformly over all the inhospitable city, but now it seemed to fade and flow, condensing into an ominous column east of him.

At the next corner, he turned uncertainly toward it. For that sudden shift was at least another hint that it came from something outside his troubled mind, from something more than his own fatigue and strain and the cruelty of that small girl, so long ago, who wouldn't let him play because she said he wasn't white. If he could find its actual source, here and now, he thought that might turn out to be the key to all his riddles.

Leaning against the whipping wind, he followed that dark column two blocks east, watching it slowly fade from above the shabby streets ahead, until it was entirely gone. He stopped at the corner to search again, but that gray glare seemed once more sourceless, diffused everywhere. Shivering in his damp clothing, he turned heavily back toward Broadway.

He had no better clue to follow, and there was nothing else to do. He felt worn out, too tired to wonder any longer. He wanted the dry warmth of his hotel room, and yet felt suddenly afraid to go back to it, because he thought Messenger's men or Gellian's might already be waiting for him there.

He wished again that he could find the man from New Guinea. But that enterprising journalist, with such excellent reasons for avoiding the Cadmus specialists, was no doubt already in hiding, lost beyond any search he could make—

The glare ahead was fading. Staring blankly, he saw that dark illumination move again, flowing away from Broadway to gather over one grimy block on the side street behind him.

He turned back toward it once more, driven by a breathless urgency.

For the change in that strange radiation had come as he wondered how to find that hiding man—almost as if it had been a searchlight, focused to guide him. Now he noticed that it seemed to fade and spread while he wondered what it was, and to gather again when his mind came back to that nameless newsman.

Dimming and returning with every shift of his thoughts, that inexplicable beacon hung over the same dilapidated block until he reached it, and then the ominous reflection of it seemed to pick out the gloomy doorway of a cheap transient hotel. Trying not to breathe the strong reek of menace seeping out of the narrow lobby, he pushed eagerly inside.

"Sorry, mister." The sad-faced red-haired youth at the desk looked up mistrustfully at his empty-handed dampness. "No vacancy here."

"I just want to see one of your guests. A newspaperman, just back from New Guinea." Anxiety caught his breath. "I don't know his name, but don't you know the one I mean?"

The clerk's sad eyes brightened at Dane's five-dollar bill.

"We do have a funny little guy up in five-eleven," he admitted. "Name of—" He paused to peer at the dog-eared register. "Name of Nicholas Venn. Sunburned, from some hot country. Typing, up in his room. Would he be your party?"

"Let me talk to him."

The clerk picked up the five, and nodded at the ancient automatic elevator. A typewriter stopped, when Dane knocked at the locked door of 511, but he had to wait a long half-minute before it was opened on a chain to a cautious slit. A tired nasal voice asked harshly who he was.

"Nobody you know," he said. "But who I'm not might interest you. I'm not a Cadmus expert. I think that gives us something in common. May I come in?"

After another uncertain half-minute, Nicholas Venn unchained the door. A nervous, shabby, hungry-faced little man, he secured the door again before he turned to face Belfast, with a glitter of puzzled mistrust in his narrowed eyes.

"All right," he rasped uneasily. "Tell me what we have in common."

"Danger," Belfast said. "From Messenger's specialists."

And he turned to look around that musty cell of a room, which opened on a dark airshaft. Stronger than the light of the naked bulb at the ceiling, that hueless glare of peril washed the stained walls and the ramshackle dresser and the battered suitcase half under the unmade bed.

Catching an apprehensive movement behind him, he swung back to see the worn bolo on the dresser, now in easy reach of Venn's poised hand. A forlorn, unshaven little fugitive, in his wrinkled tropical suit and high boots still caked with dried red clay, as if he had been pressed too hard to clean them ever since he left the swamps of New Guinea, the man looked more alarmed than alarming, yet that dark fire shimmered on the long jungle knife with the glint of death itself.

"Well?" Venn stood peering at him fearfully. "How do I know you really aren't a Cadmus man?"

"I'm a geneticist. I want to talk about those mutant plants in New Guinea. I've some papers—" Dane had stooped to open the briefcase, but he stopped as Venn's thin, dirty-nailed hand darted for the bolo. "Just papers."

Dane took off his damp topcoat to show that he had no weapon, and the little man put down the jungle blade with an apologetic grimace.

"Guess I'm jittery." Venn's blood-shot eyes narrowed again. "But how did you get here, unless Messenger put you on my trail?"

"He did, in a way." Dane decided to say nothing of that guiding column of dark fire, just yet, though he still hoped to find the source of it in something here. "When he was trying to hire me."

"If you aren't working for him—why not?"

"Because I think he's exploiting a discovery stolen from a friend of my father's. A way to mutate new species. If you've really been to New Guinea, I think we can help each other."

"I've been there, all right." Venn nodded wearily. "I do need help. From a geneticist, especially." He nodded at the only chair. "Sit down, and let's talk things over."

Removing an empty milk carton and a full ashtray, Dane sat down in the chair. "What can a geneticist do?"

"Examine something I brought back." The haggard little man came limping quickly to sit on the edge of the untidy bed. His cautious voice turned harshly vehement. "Then he can help me smash Messenger's gang!"

"Something from New Guinea?" Dane had to catch his breath. "A specimen?"

"I don't know what it is." Venn frowned uneasily. "That's why I need an expert. It was already dead when I found it, floating on the Mamberamo."

"Let me see it." Eagerness brought him out of the lumpy chair. "If it's any sort of mutant plant, it ought to tell us something about genetic engineering—the process I think Messenger got from my father's murdered friend."

"It might be a mutant." The frightened man had nodded with a quick alertness in his hollowed eyes, and Dane began to see the sane intelligence and defiant courage with which he faced some pursuing terror. "But it isn't a plant—not altogether, anyhow."

"May I examine it?"

"I think we ought to get acquainted, first." A weary watchfulness came back to Venn's sleepless eyes. "Let me see your papers, now."

Belfast showed the contents of the briefcase and his wallet, and spent the next half hour answering shrewdly searching queries about his scientific training and Kendrew's old dream of rebuilding the genes of life at will and his own recent meeting with Messenger.

"Okay, Belfast." He gave Dane a thin smile of approval. "You'll see why I had to be safe, when you know what I've been through."

"That specimen—may I see it now?"

"Later." Venn grinned wearily at his restless anxiety. "But the thing isn't even whole. It won't mean much until you know how I got it."

"Then let's hear about it." Sitting impatiently back to listen, Dane lighted a cigarette, hoping the tobacco might help cover that bitter scent of hostility still hanging in the room. He saw the sudden glitter of hunger in Venn's red eyes, and offered the package.

"Thanks!" Venn's soiled, broken-nailed fingers quivered with the match. "I'm all out of tobacco." He lowered his voice, glancing sharply at the door. "Because I'm afraid to leave this room to buy any more. Or even to eat. I'll tell you why—if you're willing to take the risk of a cut throat, for knowing."

TEN

Belfast shivered. Venn had hung his wet overcoat on the head of the bed, but the chill of the windy street had struck deep into him, and the icy feel of something else against his spine was colder still.

"I'm listening." Peering uneasily at the defiant little man hunched before him on the side of the bed, he restlessly stubbed out the cigarette, which had failed to kill the dusty scent of menace in the room. "Though I am afraid."

"You had better be!"

"It's hard to believe Messenger could afford to murder anybody." Feebly, he argued against his own haunting apprehensions. "After all, Cadmus is a respectable business firm."

"Think so?" Venn shook his head. "You're wrong."

Glancing sharply at the door, he dropped his voice again.

"An accident I got on the trail. Couple years ago, I began doing a series of features on business leaders. I did the top men of General Motors and General Electric and U.S. Steel. I came to J. D. Messenger, and the big wheels told me to cross him off the list.

"The Cadmus advertising account was worth a hundred thousand dollars a year, they told me, but the company didn't like free publicity. A smarter man might have quit, but I didn't. I've got a nose for crooks. Cadmus had a funny smell, and I began digging.

"The job wasn't easy. Most people didn't know anything. The few that did were getting rich out of keeping quiet. But I followed my nose. In spite of all the friendly advice, I kept asking questions. I even went around to the Cadmus Building.

"The company press agents made me a little too welcome. They took me up to a private bar to load me with good Scotch and glittering statistics. Millions of acres of plantation cut out of the jungle. Millions of tons of copra and rubber and lumber and cotton and sugar and oil. Millions of ounces of fine gold. Billions paid out to the lucky investors.

"They seemed to feel I was insulting their hospitality when I wanted to know where Messenger came from and how he got his business start and why his competitors have all gone under. Nobody would tell me much, not even Messenger himself.

"A tough old bird to interview. Tried to ask all the questions himself. Insisted he was just a hired man for the big bankers on the board of directors, men like Zwiedeineck and Ryling and Jones. When I didn't fall for that, he offered me twice what I was making to write advertising copy for Cadmus.

"I turned him down, because I had already been to see those bankers. I didn't like the way they had told me to lay off the story. Besides I had begun to pick up rumors."

"Huh?" Dane straightened breathlessly.

"Just a word here and a hint there," the shabby man said. "Mostly from other people who had wondered about Cadmus, and been bluffed or paid to lay off. It was one of Messenger's own publicity men who told me why the company doesn't have any labor problem in New Guinea—after he'd had too much of his own Scotch."

"They hire native labor?"

Venn shook his head. "I was trying to learn how Messenger had run Cadmus from a shoestring to the top of the list, in twenty years. I kept pumping everybody I could reach, about his production methods and labor relations and sales policies. What I finally learned isn't anything you might expect."

Belfast waited painfully, while Venn kicked absently at that worn suitcase, pushing it farther under the bed.

"Cadmus doesn't use Kanaka labor," he said. "A returned missionary had told me most of the natives have been shut up in a few reservations near the coast. But it can't be imported labor either—because the statistics don't show any immigration to New Guinea from anywhere. Interesting problem, don't you think?"

"Machinery?" Dane suggested impatiently. "Mechanized farming?"

" 'Mules.' So our drunk friend said."

"Mules?" Dane stared. "Don't mules need drivers?"

"These aren't the braying kind. A sort of tame iguana, the press agent said, that a man named Potter found in an unknown valley on the upper Fly. Smarter than elephants, but still too dumb to join labor unions. The climate doesn't hurt them, and they'll work until they drop—I guess that's why they're called 'mules.' "

"I wonder if Potter really found them." Dane was thinking of the Cadmus trademark—that bronze giant scattering the dying dragon's teeth, which in the myth had grown into men. "I wonder if he didn't make them?"

Venn peered at him oddly.

"The mutation process probably works on animals, as well as plants." Gellian's not-men were evidence of that, but Dane decided not to mention them, just yet. He looked eagerly at the suitcase under the bed. "Did you bring back one of those mules?"

"Something. I don't know what it is."

Waiting, Dane fumbled mechanically for another cigarette, and Venn reached greedily for the pack.

"Mold spoiled ours, there on the Mamberamo. There were times when Messenger might have bought me off with one good smoke."

"So you went to New Guinea?"

"In the end." Venn inhaled again, avidly. "That Cadmus man convinced me he had told the truth about the mules, after he sobered up—with the panicky way he insisted they were just a crazy rumor. I drew out my savings for expenses—and learned you can't buy a ticket to New Guinea."

"Company policy," Dane quoted sardonically.

"So I went to Australia, first. Got across to the island on a government cutter, with an official party out from Canberra to inspect the native reservation west of Moresby. That still didn't get me into the Cadmus concessions, but I stayed ashore. I tried to hire native guides, but the company property is taboo, and the Kanakas are all scared to death of the little-fella green-fella devil-fella—that seems to be the pidgin term for Potter's lizards.

"Finally I found a discouraged missionary who wanted to get back to the States, and swapped him my return ticket for a leaky motor launch. I meant to go up the Fly, west of the reservation, and take a quiet look around Messenger's back yard."

Dane looked up expectantly from that mud-stained suitcase. "And—did you?"

"Bad luck from the start." Venn sucked the last possible breath of smoke out of the cigarette, and crushed the tiny stub regretfully. "The Fly's more river than you'd expect to find on any island. I was lost for a week among the mangrove islets in the estuary. Never did get far upriver, or find anything except mosquitoes and crocodiles and wide miles of muddy water.

"Native constabulary cutter picked me up, after I ran out of gasoline. It turned out the unconverted missionary had stolen the launch from the company, and I spent three months in a stinking native jail before a Cadmus man came around to get me out.

"Nice of him!" Venn grinned sardonically. "Under the concession agreements, Cadmus pays all the reservation expenses, which makes any company man a little tin god. This one was friendly and apologetic. He got my case dismissed and offered to pay my way back home.

"I told him I was too sick for the trip. He sent me to a

Darwin hospital, at company expense, to get over the malaria and fungus infections I had picked up on the Fly. I got out without a dime, and worked my way around to Manila to try the back door."

Feeling an increasing admiration for the stubborn tenacity of this frightened, grimy little man, Dane inquired, "How'd you get on, without money?"

"Cadmus has made a lot of people curious," Venn said. "I found men ready to pay for what I knew, and willing to risk their lives to find out more. A little group of us joined forces, to go back.

"We had among us all sorts of theories about the prosperity and secretiveness of Cadmus. A majority thought the company had found uranium and developed private atomic power to reclaim the jungle. One man, a little Frenchman named Lambeau, had a theory the company was using uranium rays to breed new plants. A few were after diamonds or gold. What I wanted, by that time, was one of Potter's mules.

"We used to meet in the back room of a grimy little Manila bar, to pool the pesos and rumors we had managed to collect. Took months to get started, but we finally hired a fishing boat to smuggle us ashore on the north coast, west of Humbolt Bay, where the jungles are a little too wild even for the company's native guards—"

Venn paused abruptly, listening as footsteps approached along the corridor outside. Sweat broke out on his thin sallow face, but he relaxed as the feet moved on outside, and reached eagerly again for Dane's cigarettes.

"And what did you find?"

"Nothing pleasant." Venn inhaled thirstily. "We managed to avoid the company launches on the rivers and the constabulary lookout towers on the headlands and the patrols that fly along the coast, but New Guinea beat us. Mosquitoes and leeches and jungle rot." He shook his head ruefully. "Malaria and typhus and dysentery. Jungle vines and mountain ranges and river swamps and rain that never ends. That island isn't fit for human beings. I suppose we needed a gang of those domesticated lizards!"

He paused to finish the cigarette, sucking on it greedily and uneasily watching the door.

"Did you get inland?"

"Part of us." The worn man shrugged. "You'd think we already had troubles enough, what with the company guards and New Guinea itself, but we had to fight one another. Our organization went to pieces. Most of the men balked at the coastal range—some were already too sick to travel and the rest lost interest in everything else when they found a few flakes of gold.

"Just three of us went on across the range, into the Mamberamo country. That little Frenchman, and a big Dutchman named Heemskirk who looked soft as tallow and turned out to be indestructible—almost. Lambeau had a Geiger counter, and they were looking for uranium.

"We three split up again at the Mamberamo. They had heard so many native tales that they didn't want to meet the little-fella green-fella devil-fella. They got across the river on a log raft one night, going on toward the great central range, and I started upriver in a little inflated plastic boat.

"Patrol planes were droning over pretty often by that time—I suppose somebody had got wind of us. I had to keep close to the riverbank, under the edge of the jungle, with mosquitoes eating me alive. A constabulary launch finally ran me off the river altogether. I struck overland for the fence around the Mamberamo concession. Never got there."

Sitting hunched on the bed, Venn shivered. "Stinking swamps alive with leeches. Flooded tributary streams full of crocodiles, and hills that are rain forests tipped on edge, and more nipa swamps beyond. I ran out of food and atabrine. Malaria hit me again. Finally gave it up.

"I was three-quarters dead, the day I came paddling back down that tributary into the Mamberamo—too weak and groggy to know where I was or to care who saw me—and found the dead thing floating."

"A mutant iguana?" Belfast whispered.

"Maybe you can tell what it is." Smiling with a haggard triumph, Venn got down on his knees to pull the travel-scarred suitcase from under the bed. He unlocked it, and dug beneath soiled shirts and underwear to come up with a heavy, strong-smelling package.

"The boat." He began unrolling layers of tough, transparent plastic from around something shaped unpleasantly like the body of a child. "I cut it up for wrapping."

The thing he unwrapped was neither human nor lizard nor anything else Dane could name. The color of it was a shiny, greenish black, and the heavy, penetrating odor of it became part of that reek of danger in the room.

"It doesn't decay." An awed puzzlement slowed Venn's voice. "I was too sick the night I dragged it out of the water to use the preservatives I had brought, and next day I could see they weren't needed." He looked up sharply. "Do you know what it is?"

Kneeling beside him on the floor, carefully turning and prodding that queer, crumpled thing, Dane shook his head dazedly. The creature had been a biped, he could see, with slender three-fingered hands and a long, egg-shaped head. Its sleek, dark armor was somewhat like the chitinous exterior skeletons of insects and crustaceans, and the small masses of dried, brittle tissue on the back resembled vestigial wings. The rest of it was incomprehensible.

"Well?" Venn whispered anxiously. "What is it?"

"Something new." Dane frowned blankly at the curiously smooth oval of its head. "Something I don't understand. No mouth, you see. No jaws. Eyes, but no external ears. No nostrils—though it must have had some respiratory arrangement to live at all. No evidence of any sort of alimentary tract, or even of reproductive organs."

He bent to peer and prod again, and finally shrugged with bafflement. "It's no iguana, certainly. No more a lizard than it is a man. The fact that it doesn't decay—and its odor—suggests an entirely different chemistry of life."

He rose at last, turning slowly back to Venn.

"The thing's exciting," he said. "It proves that somebody is creating entirely new kinds of life in New Guinea. It may even tell us something about the method they're using, though I'll need time and equipment for any real examination." He glanced at the suitcase, asking hopefully, "You didn't bring anything else?"

"No." The haggard man hesitated, frowning at that reeking green thing. "There was something else," he admitted reluctantly. "Something stranger than the mule. I didn't mean to mention it, because it's something you won't want to believe."

ELEVEN

Waiting impatiently, Dane watched Nicholas Venn wrap that dead green creature back in the sheets of plastic, and bury it once more under his soiled laundry.

"Let's see this other thing," he whispered anxiously.

"I didn't bring it back." Nervously, Venn pushed the suitcase back under the bed. "I was afraid to bring it," he confessed. "It's somewhere on the bottom of the Mamberamo, now."

"What was it?"

"Just a twig." Restlessly, Venn helped himself to Dane's last cigarette. "Just a twig from a tree."

"And what made it so strange?"

"It was heavy as iron. Really mostly iron, I think, because it was highly magnetic." Venn peered at him uncertainly, nervously burning up the cigarette. "Maybe you'll believe me when you've heard about the tree where it grew."

"Go ahead."

"Heemskirk and Lambeau found the tree," Venn began, "growing somewhere up near the snow line on the slopes of Mt. Carstensz. So that durable Dutchman said—Lambeau's mind was blank as a baby's when Heemskirk came packing him back to our rendezvous, and even the Dutchman himself was half out of his head. They had lost the Geiger counter, and everything else except that twig. A wonder they got back at all!"

"Malaria?"

"Malaria—and something else. We all knew a little jungle medicine by that time, but Heemskirk couldn't tell me much about what had hit them. He was half delirious, raving about thickets of thorny scrub they had crossed in the lower valleys, and queer black flies that stung them, and that peculiar tree."

"The tree?"

"It grows along some high valley beyond the thorns and the flies and the glaciers," the haggard man said. "If you want to believe the Dutchman—he muttered and shouted and screamed about that tree, day and night, until his fever broke. It shines at night, with a cold blue glow. He used to gibber about that glow, and he called it the color of death. The tree rattled the counter, he kept saying, as if it grew out of the mother lode of all the uranium on Earth. But the tree itself was iron."

"Huh?" Dane felt that pressure on his spine turn colder. "Iron?"

"I didn't want to tell you," Venn shook his head apologetically. "I can't expect you to believe me."

"But I do."

Recalling that queerly similar metallic plant in Gellian's office, Dane sat for a moment wondering uneasily what would be the fruit of that hidden tree. What, beyond mutant men, had been the ultimate logical aim of the maker's art? The stars?

"Every living thing is partly metal," he assured Venn, soberly. "That green mule seems to me a more radical mutation, though I'd like to know why that tree was designed to assimilate uranium and such large amounts of iron. I do wish you had brought that twig."

"It frightened me," Venn confessed huskily. "It was still radioactive enough to glow in the dark. When I saw that, and saw how sick its rays had made those two men, I threw it in the river. Too late." He shrugged regretfully. "Heemskirk and Lambeau are both in a Manila hospital now, with total amnesia."

"Amnesia isn't a common result of radiation sickness," Dane said. "There's a virus encephalitis endemic in New Guinea that destroys the memory. I wonder if your friends didn't pick that up. Perhaps it's carried by those stinging flies."

"A convenient virus, for Messenger's company!" Venn's red eyes narrowed. "Another mutation, you think?"

"Likely enough." Nodding uncomfortably, Dane thought of Gellian's investigator infected with that same virus. "I don't think it had ever been reported before Messenger's outfit went in there, and only a few isolated cases have ever appeared anywhere else. Not much is known about it, not even how it spreads. It ought to make an effective biological weapon."

"I'd never heard of it," Venn muttered apologetically. "Sorry I threw away the twig, but just then things were getting pretty desperate."

"You were lucky to get out with the mule," Dane agreed. "It's enough to prove that Cadmus is using some process for directing mutation."

"Will you help me do that?" Venn's shadowed eyes searched him anxiously. "Prove to the public what Messenger and his gang are up to?"

"I'll do anything I can." Dane nodded quickly. "Because I'm pretty well convinced they murdered my father's old friend, to get that process. I want to recover it. Kendrew intended to enrich the whole world with it, not just a few bankers."

"Then let's decide what to do."

"You might do more without me," Dane warned him. "I'm afraid I'd be a dangerous asset."

"Don't worry too much about Messenger's specialists." A feverish purpose glittered in Venn's weary eyes, and quivered in his rasping voice. "Because we can run those vermin to cover now. I've smashed other rackets with press campaigns—though none quite so vicious. I know how to use publicity."

"So does Messenger," Dane said grimly. "But I'm going to be in trouble with another group, besides. A private detective agency, hunting mutant men supposed to have been made by this same process. I've refused to join them—and they're going to be looking for me, after eight in the morning."

"Mutant men, huh?" Staring forebodingly, Venn seemed to listen again for footsteps in the hallway. "Is there no limit to what that process can make?"

"It can unlock all the latent powers of life," Dane said soberly. "And the limits of life have never been reached."

"Anyhow, we still have tonight." Venn shrugged abruptly, as if trying to shake off his fears. "You can examine the mule again, and describe it for the scientists. I'll fix up a press release. We'll have a press conference—at seven in the morning!"

Nodding in agreement, Dane felt hope come back.

"I know how to manage that." Venn's weary voice was confident again. "I'll invite reporters and photographers enough so Messenger can't intimidate them all. We'll have copies of our release ready for the wire. You can display the mule for the photographers, and answer questions for the science editors. We'll have Messenger running for cover, by eight o'clock. The glare of publicity ought to protect us from him—and everybody else."

"I'm not sure Messenger'll run," Dane objected uncertainly. "He struck me as a pretty tough customer. And I'm still afraid of Gellian. Though I think he's too much alarmed about the mutants, he evidently does have a wide and powerful organization."

"Can you suggest a better plan?"

"No." Dane shook his head soberly. "I don't see much more we can do."

"Then let's get at it, now." Venn got up impatiently from his seat on the bed. "The first thing—" His haggard face turned anxious. "I hope you have some money?"

"Not enough. Around a hundred dollars."

"That should do it." Venn frowned thoughtfully. "We'll need to rent a duplicating machine to run off our press release. Paper and supplies. A few dollars for tips, to get word around. Money to hire a larger room, somewhere, for our press reception."

"At my hotel," Dane suggested. "I'll call about it."

"Good. My welcome here's about worn out." The shabby man grinned wryly. "Even the room service doesn't seem to trust me for a pack of cigarettes."

"Oh." Dane saw then that he must be hungry. "Let's go somewhere to eat."

"I do need food." Venn nodded at the empty milk carton. "That was yesterday. But I'm afraid to go outside. Just bring me something when you come back—and be careful yourself, in case anybody's already watching."

And Dane went down again to the street, which seemed more friendly now than Venn's beleaguered room. The rain had stopped, and that gray glare was paler in the twilight. Facing the raw east wind, he inhaled gratefully, glad to escape that bitter reek of something more than the dead green mule.

He walked three blocks, watching shop windows, without finding either business machines for rent or the laboratory equipment he needed for his own examination of the mule. Deciding to shop by telephone, he turned back, stopping at a delicatessen to buy cold meats and a loaf of bread and containers of hot coffee.

Night had fallen, in the half hour since he came out, and now the city lights shone sickly pink against the low, wind-torn clouds. That colorless dark fire seemed to settle and clot once more around the bedraggled old hotel, as he approached it, and that dusty reek met him again in the lobby, grown suffocatingly strong.

The red-haired clerk watched him suspiciously over a tattered comic magazine, as he carried his packages into the automatic elevator. The fifth floor seemed too silent, and its hush set that soundless alarm to throbbing again in his mind. He hurried to knock, and the door swung open from his hand.

The odor of death came out to meet him, overwhelming now. Holding his breath against it, he stumbled inside. The light was out, but that harsh glare of something else revealed Nicholas Venn, sprawled across the unmade bed, beheaded.

Fighting panic, Dane set his packages on the dresser and shut the door and snapped on the light. Merciless as that other dark illumination, the light showed him Venn's head, more than ever pinched and pale, staring from its own black pool on the sheets.

He turned quickly from it, feeling ill, to look for the briefcase, which he had left on the dresser. It wasn't there. He started across the room to look for it, and stumbled against the suitcase. It lay open on the floor, Venn's dirty shirts dumped out and one of them soiled again with wiped red smears.

The plastic-wrapped package was also gone.

He bent to search for it under the bed, but his groping fingers failed to reach the mule. What he found felt cold as death itself, and what he saw when he drew it out was Venn's long jungle-knife, red-spattered and blazing with that dark fire in his hand.

TWELVE

Swaying from his shock, Dane stood for dragging seconds in that gloomy room, aware only of the dry scent of deadliness, and the sticky chill of the bolo hilt in his hand, and the somber glare of something inexplicable which shone on the beheaded body of Nicholas Venn.

Pity made a painful tightness in his throat; and then he

began trembling with a cold anger at the killers of this shabby little man, whose only offense had been his stubborn effort to learn and tell the truth about Cadmus, Inc.

A shaken impulse swung him to the telephone, to notify the hotel management and the police. For Messenger's specialists in preventing publicity had overreached themselves. Not even all the Cadmus billions, he thought, could buy immunity for such things as this.

His hasty fingers caught the receiver—and the touch of it rocked him with an almost physical impact of alarm. The hueless bloom of death darkened in the room, and its dusty bitterness choked him. He let go the instrument, staggering back from it dazedly.

The harsh consequences of that act were suddenly as clear as if he had already endured them. Messenger would suavely deny any charges against his men, hinting shrewdly that the rascals trying to steal his priceless trade secrets had fallen out among themselves.

Cadmus would remain impregnable. For the fingerprints stamped in Venn's blood on the bolo hilt and the telephone were now his own. He shivered to a sudden icy certainty that Messenger's efficient experts had followed him here from the Cadmus building, and deliberately arranged this final disposition of the Venn case so that it would also dispose of his own.

A sense of trapped futility held him helpless for a moment.

But he hadn't completed the call. Warned by that puzzling awareness, he still had time and freedom to fight. The green mule would make a powerful weapon in court, the thought steadied him, if he could somehow recover it.

Calmer now, he nerved himself to examine the body and the head. At first he saw no mark of anything except the jungle knife, but the twisted oddness of the head's grisly grin drew him back to find a faint swollen discoloration of the upper lip, from some slight injury which must have been inflicted while Venn was still alive. It appeared to be no ordinary bruise, because tiny beads of blood had oozed from the punctured skin. Yet he could discover no other cause for it.

Frowning at that, he hurried on to inspect the lock and chain. They were intact, as if Venn himself had opened the door. But how had that frightened man been induced to let his killer come in? Searching the narrow room, he found no explanation.

He listened anxiously at the door and started to open it, in a mounting panic to escape this glare and reek of death before Messenger's men could arrange to have him found here with Venn's blood drying on his hands, but he fought fear down again, and made himself turn back.

Too much haste could destroy him now, as surely as the Cadmus killers. Deliberately, he took time to wipe the telephone and the inside doorknob with another of Venn's soiled shirts. He used his handkerchief to open the drawers of the dresser, dimly hopeful of finding whatever Venn had been writing. Messenger's experts must have been far too efficient to leave such evidence against the company, however; the drawers were empty.

Gathering up the bag of food and cartons of cooling coffee he had set on the dresser, he bent to listen and opened the door with his handkerchief, and paused again to wipe the outer knob. The automatic elevator was an endless time coming. It took him down alone.

Three decayed and elderly men were sitting in the row of worn chairs along the lobby wall, idly watching a florid fat man who was asking at the desk for the sample room on the fifth floor. None of the three looked vigorous enough to have beheaded Venn, and the other, still damp and flushed from the weather, had obviously just come in.

Belfast waited for the salesman to limp toward the elevator with a heavy sample case. He knew the sullen youth at the desk would soon be recalling everything about him for the police, but he decided to take the risk of leaving a stronger impression.

"I came here to buy some valuable plant specimens that Mr. Venn brought back from New Guinea," he began carefully. "He told me to come back later, because he was expecting another bid. Now he doesn't answer my knock." He looked sharply at the clerk. "I wonder if the other bidder came?"

The clerk shrugged, with a weary indifference.

"I think somebody's about to beat me out of a big commission." He showed a twenty-dollar bill. "Can you remember anybody who called on Mr. Venn while I was out?"

"Nobody." The sallow youth eyed the money wistfully. "That little guy never had no callers. You're the only party seen him since he checked in."

Dane tried not to shiver visibly.

"Somebody must have bought those tropical plants," he insisted. "Maybe somebody staying here. Probably carried them out, while I was gone. Has anybody left with baggage since I was here before?"

"Couple of salesmen checking in. Nobody checking out. Unless—" The clerk looked back at the twenty, hopefully. "Unless your party could be a girl?"

Belfast began to shake his head, and changed his mind. "Might be." He tried not to seem too desperately concerned. "If she left in the last hour, with baggage or a large package."

"She did."

The clerk was holding out his pale hand, but Dane hesitated. No ordinary woman would have strength and skill to decapitate a man with one slash of a knife. But the not-men, he recalled that warning of Gellian's, were quicker and stronger than men. He released the bill.

"When was she here?"

"Came in just after you asked about Venn." The clerk crumpled the money into his pocket. "Wanted a room on the fifth floor. All we had was the sample room and an inside single. She took the single."

"But she's already gone?"

"Checked out ten minutes ago. Said she'd changed her plans."

"And she had luggage?"

"A big white rawhide bag. She tipped me a dollar just to set it out on the sidewalk and flag a taxi for her."

"What did she look like?"

"Tall, I'd say." The clerk pushed the money deeper in his pocket, defensively. "Not bad-looking."

"Did she have blue eyes and reddish-brown hair?" Dane's voice was dry with strain. "Skin just faintly olive—as if she had a little Indian blood? Was she wearing a gray business suit?"

"That's right," the clerk agreed eagerly. "Except that she changed the suit upstairs. She came down in a low-necked evening dress and a thousand dollars' worth of fur."

He must have swayed, for he felt cold and sick inside. He found himself clutching at the desk with a sweaty hand, and drew back apprehensively, hoping the police wouldn't check for fingerprints there.

His first warm liking for Nan Sanderson made it hard to imagine her in this murderous role, yet the evidence already had a sickening weight. Messenger had probably known of the human mutants from the beginning, and that cunning tycoon couldn't fail to see the advantages of employing such superior specialists.

Why, he wondered, had she changed clothes upstairs? To charm her way into Venn's room, with that low-necked gown? Or had she taken off the gray business suit after it was already spattered with his blood?

"May I see her name?" he muttered huskily. "The way she wrote it on the register?"

Grudgingly, as if afraid he would want the twenty dollars back, the clerk pushed the worn book toward him, pointing. *Evelyn Barker, Chicago.* The name and the vague address meant nothing at all, but he had seen Nan Sanderson's handwriting when he took that test in her office, and this neat script was the same.

"Thanks," he whispered bleakly. And then, recalling his commercial role, he lamely tried to grin. "It begins to look like Miss Barker has beaten me out of that commission."

Nodding with a veiled hostility, anxious to be rid of him now, the clerk watched sharply as he gathered up his parcels and plodded out to meet the leer of the streets. The sullen youth would recall him very clearly, when the police came.

He stuffed his dangerously conspicuous burden of food and cold coffee into a trash can at the nearest corner, and hastily flagged a taxi there. He kept it for only a few blocks, then walked across the street and caught another cab.

The dark shine and the hateful reek of pursuing peril followed him all the way to his own hotel, however, and he was shaken to see his unshaven haggardness in the bathroom mirror. With his gray suit shapeless from the rain and his face pinched and drawn beneath that frosty glare, he looked the hunted fugitive he soon would be.

A thin illusion of safety let him sink into a chair, feeling too tired to move. But the room was no refuge, and the merciless spur of danger drove him on again. Delaying only to bathe and shave and change into his other suit, a dark blue that wouldn't fit the clerk's description, he went out again to look for that green mule.

Flinching from the harsh-lit streets, he couldn't help wishing for some simpler weapon, something solid and deadly in his hands. But any effort to buy a gun would doubtless put the police on his trail. And that bolo, he warned himself, had failed to save Nicholas Venn.

Wet from the rain, Madison Avenue was puddled with pale reflections of colored signs, and strange with that other, colorless glow. That dark illumination seemed the same in all directions, until, experimentally, he began to look for the stolen mule. The effort made it shift again, as he had half expected. It became the glow of a hueless moon, low beyond the buildings to the south, in the direction of Nan Sanderson's office.

Facing that dark beacon, he stood frozen for a moment in puzzled fear. The strange way it guided him to Venn's hotel had made him believe it might be some incredible, newborn power of his own. Now, however, recalling the deadly trap into which it had lured him there, he thought it more likely some unknown weapon or power of the not-men, designed for defense against their human hunters.

Anyhow, whatever the truth, Nan Sanderson's office seemed a logical place to look for the missing mule. Still trying not to leave too plain a trail, he took one taxi back to Times Square, and another east on Forty-second Street, and walked the last two blocks south to Fortieth.

The building looked dark, but a sleepy-eyed elevator operator took him to the nineteenth floor and waited while he rapped at the door of the Sanderson Service. To his surprise, it opened instantly.

"Why, Dane!" Smiling, the tall girl looked past him to meet the questioning glance of the man in the elevator. "It's all right, Kaptina," she called. "Dr. Belfast is one of our clients."

She let him in, and locked the door. He stared at her uneasily. She still had on the evening gown she had worn from Venn's hotel. The luminous blue of it turned her eyes violet again, and her olive skin to tawny gold. She looked lovely, and strangely afraid.

"Why did you come back, Dane?" Her tapered, graceful hands had risen apprehensively when she saw him, and her breathless voice held a wounded reproof. "Didn't I warn you?"

"You warned me."

And he recoiled a little, watching her nervous hands go on from that apprehensive gesture to smooth back her damply shining, red-brown hair. She looked so entirely and appealingly human that he tried for an instant to believe she was—and somehow blameless. Perhaps a helpless tool of Messenger's. Or more likely an innocent captive of the mutants, trapped in that same web of terror he had felt around him all day.

Reluctantly, he discarded that idea. It failed to explain away all the evidence that she herself was a desperate superhuman being—probably one of the first flawed creations of a fumbling maker, lost and frightened and therefore deadly. He gulped uncomfortably.

"I came back for a biological specimen." Watching her lean-drawn loveliness, he saw terror crawl up to drain the blood from her lips and the light from her eyes. "The body of a small greenish creature, called a mule. I think you have it here."

"Please—won't you leave me alone?" Her pale hands made a violent protesting gesture. "And get out of town, while you can!"

"Sorry." He grinned at her stiffly. "But it's much too late for that. I've talked to Messenger, you see, as well as John Gellian. And I've just seen poor little Venn with his head off."

She nodded, shrinking from him, her low eyes narrow and greenish seeming now. Her hands were folded, ivory-white and trembling. She seemed to wait for his accusation, and he made it hoarsely:

"You killed him—didn't you?"

She flinched, and seemed to catch her breath. The line of her pale lips drew harder, expressing neither admission nor denial.

"Anyhow," he added harshly, "I want that mule."

She stood for a long time motionless, her tawny body taut. She seemed at bay, desperate and dangerous. He supposed she must be planning a new disposition of his case, since he had avoided that other trap, yet he couldn't escape a pang of pity for the ultimate loneliness he felt in her.

"I have it," she admitted at last. "Back in the lab."

He moved forward quickly. "Let me see it."

"Please, Dane." She stepped in front of him. "Don't!"

Her fine hands were open and empty, and he had brought her no bolo. Yet he stopped uneasily. "I need that mule," he insisted huskily. "To save my life!"

"It didn't save Venn's." Her low voice trembled with anxiety. "It wouldn't save yours. But I can still help—if you'll only try to get away."

Determinedly shaking his head, he watched her turn impulsively to pick up her plastic bag on the reception desk. Blue to match her shining gown, it was far too small to hold a bolo, or even any ordinary dagger or gun, but he swung toward her quickly, poised to snatch at any weapon. What she got out was only a key.

"Won't you take my car?" She thrust the key at him

quickly. "A maroon convertible, parked across the street. I think it will get you out of town, if you go at once."

"Not without that mule."

Still blocking the door, she studied him with a tortured indecision dark in her eyes. "I'm sorry," she whispered at last. "I really wanted to help you get away." She dropped the key back in the blue bag, moving regretfully out of his way. "Come on in, if you must see the mule."

He followed her back to the little laboratory where he had failed to qualify for the benefits of the Sanderson Service. Choking fumes brought him gasping to the sink. There he found the creature from the Mamberamo, reduced to a few dark shapeless scraps dissolving in a greenish acid froth.

"I'm sorry, Dane." Her low voice swung him back. "I didn't plan it this way—"

That was all he heard. He caught one glimpse of the weapon she had found in the moment while his back was turned: a thin metal tube little longer than the key. Though it looked too tiny to be dangerous, he snatched at it desperately. It clicked very softly in her golden fingers before he could reach it, stabbing out a fine jet that stung his forearm like a hot blade. That was all he knew.

THIRTEEN

Somebody was shaking him. "Wake up!" It was a girl, bending over him anxiously. "Can't you wake up, now?"

She was beautiful in shimmering blue, reddish-haired and tawny-limbed, but he didn't recognize her. He didn't know this dim-lit office room. His head ached intolerably when he tried to lift it, and his right arm throbbed, and he couldn't wake up.

"Who are you?" She kept on shaking him, without mercy. "What's your name?"

He couldn't remember anything at all, but he was too deeply asleep to speak or even shake his head. She stopped at last, to slip a cold thermometer under his tongue. She stabbed his finger with a painful little needle to take a drop of his blood, and even lifted his eyelids open again, with a deft, cool thumb, to probe his eyes with a thin blade of light. The light hurt, but still he couldn't wake.

Later a telephone rang near his head. Still too drowsy to move, he heard the girl's quick footsteps, and her low voice speaking.

"No, I'm still waiting," she said. "I've packed what we can take, and destroyed what might harm us. I'm ready to go, as soon as our visitor is able."

The answering voice was too faint for him to hear.

"The usual satisfactory reaction to the jet injection." The girl spoke briskly again. "He crumpled up, before he ever knew what hit him. Pulse still accelerated and temperature high. He's a clean page, by this time."

Dimly, he wondered what her words could mean, but he couldn't remember anything. Feeling too heavy to move, too blank even to ask who he was or what had happened to him, he kept on listening.

"Two hours, probably," the girl said. "He's still unconscious. We can't move him yet, without the risk of greater damage to his brain. I had better stay with him, until the fever breaks."

He felt feebly grateful, because his head was still bursting.

"Leave him behind?" Her voice lifted protestingly. "He's worth all the danger to us. And he wouldn't have a chance, if they ever found him here."

He wondered vaguely who "they" were, and why he wouldn't have a chance.

"A raid?" Her voice turned faint with fear. "At four? No, I didn't know. I'm too tired tonight to see that far ahead."

The other voice murmured in the instrument.

"But we can't just abandon him." Cool resolution steadied her tone. "We need him too much with his mind undamaged. I'm afraid to move him yet, but I think I can delay that raid."

He thought the other voice objected.

"I'm going out now, to make a diversion," the girl said firmly. "If I get away with it, I'll come back here in two hours for our new recruit. We ought to reach your place by five—if we get there at all."

She hung up the telephone. He felt the thermometer in his mouth again, and the sting of a cold swab against a painful spot on his swollen arm. Then her quick footsteps receded. A door opened and closed, and she was gone. Wondering dimly whose that other voice had been, he went back to sleep.

What woke him was a shock of sheer alarm. It brought him to his feet, dazed and trembling. The movement hurt his head and left him giddy. He leaned weakly against the office desk, hands lifted to his throbbing temples, trying to remember anything.

He had been lying on the floor, with a blanket spread over him and a coat folded under his head. He thought he must have been somehow hurt, but he could find no injury except a small swollen discoloration on his right forearm. His shirtsleeve had been rolled above it, and the spot had been swabbed with some dark antiseptic.

He looked around him blankly, but he didn't recognize the desk or filing cabinet or the doorway beyond. All he knew was the fact of deadly danger, which didn't need remembering, because it was dusty bitterness hanging in the air, and a frosty bloom on the anonymous walls, and an urgent cold pressure at the back of his head.

Shivering, he put on the coat. Driven by those sensations of alarm, he tiptoed through the doorway into a small reception room, which looked equally strange and felt equally dangerous. He slipped out through another door, into a dark corridor.

Even in the darkness, that cold glow of something not light showed him the stair. He ran down flight after flight, as silently as possible, until at last he came to a closed door at the bottom. He reached to try it, and a shock of new alarm numbed his throbbing arm.

Drawing back confusedly, breathless and trembling, he could hear heavy feet beyond the door, and cautious low voices, and the muffled clicks of guns being loaded. Those sounds passed on, and the danger behind spurred him to try the door again.

It let him out, into a wider hallway. He ran silently along it toward the gray light from the street, until once more the feel of danger caught him. That cold force held him flattened back against a closed door while two men with short automatic rifles burst in from the street and ran crouching past him to enter the stair door from which he had just emerged.

That frosty clutch of warning let him go again, as the riflemen disappeared, and he ran out the way they had come, into the street. It was a gloomy canyon, the distant lamps veiled in rain. Afraid to run, he started walking briskly past the cars parked at the entrance, toward the nearest corner.

No sound of alarm or pursuit came from behind, but he knew suddenly that those armed men had reached that room and found him gone. A warning reverberation echoed in his throbbing brain, and the bitter reek of hate exploded all around him, and the whole building shone with a dreadful dark luminosity.

He ran from it, then, frantically.

The sensations of danger faded slowly, as he ran. That warning bite went out of the air he gasped, and that dark reflection dimmed behind him, and that driving reverberation ceased. He was plodding along the empty sidewalk, three blocks away, shivering only from the thin rain, when the sudden headlamps of a car struck him from behind.

He almost ran again. That white glare was merely light, however, and he could feel nothing colder than the rain. He held himself from flight, even when the car pulled up to the curb beside him.

"Hello, there." The girl from the office was at the wheel. She leaned quickly to open the car door for him. In the faint glow from the instrument panel, he could see the reddish color of her hair and the warm ivory tones of her lean face.

"I'm Nan Sanderson," she whispered. "I've come to help you get away."

Something made him hesitate. The glow against her face was only light, however, and he could feel no danger around her. Something made her car a sort of sanctuary. Gratefully, he got in beside her.

She drove rapidly at first through the rain, uneasily watching the dark streets behind in the rear view mirror and frowning sometimes at the panel clock, whose hands stood at five. She leaned to turn on the car heater when he sneezed, but seemed to give him no other attention.

Chilled and dripping, he relaxed in the blast of warm air, watching her sleepily. The pale, increasing light of dawn gave her a look of childish, troubled innocence. He liked her, and he felt safe with her. The danger he had fled was drowned in the dripping dark behind, and he could feel no pursuit.

Once, however, she pulled into a narrow alley, snapped off the lights, and waited there, uneasily watching the clock. After what seemed a long time, a police car came racing the way they had come, siren moaning and red light glaring.

She backed out of the alley when it was gone, and followed it more slowly. Rain-dimmed daylight had come by the time a tollgate stopped them, at the end of a long bridge. She paid from a small blue plastic bag, and she no longer watched the mirror as they went on, but smiled at him as if her fear had all been left beyond the river.

"We've made it!" He liked the friendly warmth of her voice. "Now I suppose you'd like to know where we're going?"

"I—I suppose." That was all he said, for words, like everything else, were curiously hard for him to recall. He didn't care, really, where they went. He was with her, and that colorless glare of enmity was left somewhere far behind.

"We're going to Mr. Messenger's estate on Long Island," she said. "Don't you remember him?"

He shook his head drowsily.

"Don't you even know your own name?"

But he didn't remember anything. He didn't even want to try, because the effort hurt his head. All that mattered was the moment, and the girl's warm presence. He didn't want this trip with her to end anywhere.

"Fallon." Her tawny smile heightened his dreamy content. "You're Dr. Donovan Fallon."

"Fallon?" The syllables seemed somehow stiffly unfamiliar, but all words came awkwardly to him now. He repeated carefully, "Dr. Donovan Fallon."

"Now, Don Fallon, would you like to have a job?"

"I don't know." The future was as blank as the past. "I don't know—anything."

"You need a job." Her lean face was gravely concerned. "You've been sick, and you're in serious trouble now. You've no family. No friends. No money. But Mr. Messenger can help you, if you're willing to work for him."

"What kind of job?" He looked down at his hands, flexing them doubtfully. "I can't remember—what I ever did."

"Don't worry about that." Her golden smile thawed his cold uncertainty. "Part of your memory was destroyed forever by this illness—it was a rare type of virus encephalitis. You'll have to start all over again. But your manual skills weren't harmed. And the damage to the memory is usually quite shallow, so that you can probably relearn most of what you used to know very quickly."

He answered her smile, trying hard to follow.

"Anyhow," she assured him, "Mr. Messenger will understand your difficulties. He makes a hobby, you see, of helping people stricken with that encephalitis, because he thinks the virus was accidentally imported by his own company." Her smile widened confidently. "You'll like Mr. Messenger."

He nodded, gratefully, but a lingering unease made him inquire: "What's this trouble I'm in?"

"You're a geneticist." Her long blue eyes looked up at him from the road, full of a troubled innocence. "You were working with this encephalitis virus, trying to identify it as a fresh mutation, when you had a laboratory accident. A young woman assistant was also infected, when you were. She died. You are accused of her murder."

"Murder?" He stared at her blankly. "Can Mr. Messenger get me out of that?"

"He'll take you to New Guinea," she said. "We're going there to undertake some very important laboratory work for the company. When you've recovered enough of your old knowledge and skill, Mr. Messenger wants you to be his laboratory technician."

"If it was all an accident, why must I run away?"

"Because the girl was pregnant. The police believe she had been the unwilling subject of some illegal experiment in human genetics. They think you deliberately gave her a deadly injection of the virus, to cover it up, taking a safe dose yourself to divert suspicion."

"But—I didn't do that!" He watched her searchingly. "Did I?"

"You're innocent." Her calm smile reassured him. "But such charges stir up a great deal of feeling, and the authorities have circumstantial evidence enough to send you to the chair. We can't help you in court, and obviously you can't testify in your own defense."

Groping in the blankness of his mind, he found no fact to help him.

"But you'll be safe enough in New Guinea." She was still smiling, yet her sidelong glance seemed oddly anxious. "If you want to come with us?"

"Then you're going, too?"

"I am." She nodded. "As Mr. Messenger's secretary."

That decided him. This new life was not two hours old, and she was still the center of it. He relaxed, content to be anywhere with her.

"I want to come," he told her. "If we can get away."

FOURTEEN

She slowed the car at last, to turn from the highway into a broad drive which curved between massive masonry pillars toward a long mansion which loomed massive as a fortress in the rain.

"Mr. Messenger's place," she said. "We're to pick him up. His private plane is waiting at the airport." He heard the tremor of urgency in her voice. "We must get off the ground before the police broadcast your description. That gives us not quite an hour."

He wondered how she knew, but a faint alarm whispered in his mind, warning him not to ask. He turned restlessly to study that dark building, dimly awed by its frowning bulk.

"Mr. Messenger must be sad about giving up the place," she said. "But he had to sell it, to help save Cadmus."

"Cadmus?"

"I'd forgotten." She smiled apologetically. "That's Mr. Messenger's company. It operates plantations in New Guinea. It used to be enormously successful, but production has fallen to nothing. Your job now is to help us breed new plants, to get the company back on its feet."

She parked at a side door of the mansion and slipped out of the car, nodding for him to follow. Unlocking the door, she hurried him up a wide stair to a huge bedroom, where an enormous man sat waiting.

"Nan, I thought you'd never come!" The big man tried to rise from his chair, and sprawled back helplessly. "What made you so long?"

"I went to that detective agency, trying to help Dr. Fallon." The girl moved quickly as she spoke to lift the fat man's wrist, and paused to take his pulse. "I did destroy that Christmas tree and several other damaging exhibits, but I was almost trapped. Dr. Fallon's place was already surrounded before I could get back there, but he had wandered outside. I found him on the street—and he wants to go with us."

"Glad you're going, Fallon!" A genial smile swept all the scarred ugliness and the mottled illness from the huge man's sagging face, and he held out his hand. "My name's Messenger."

Wondering how a Christmas tree could be a damaging exhibit, he took Messenger's flabby yellow hand. The girl gave him no time to ask about anything.

"Your heart's worse." She bent over the swollen wrist, frowning in concern as she counted the pulse again. "I'm afraid you shouldn't risk the flight."

"I'm tough as a mule," Messenger wheezed. "And I've already burned our bridges behind." Grasping a silverwood cane, he leaned laboriously to stir ashes and charred papers in a metal wastebasket. A scuffed briefcase lay open and empty on the floor beside it. "Our baggage is already on the plane." His pale, small eyes lifted uneasily. "Can we still make it?"

The girl glanced at her watch. "We've forty minutes," she said, "before the airport authorities receive Dr. Fallon's description."

"Then help me get up."

They both helped. He came ponderously upright, gasping alarmingly, yet moving with a surprising ease and dignity once his feet were under him. At the car, he heaved himself into the rear seat, and seemed to fall asleep.

The girl drove the treacherous wet streets with a silent concentration until the air terminal buildings emerged from the gray veil of rain ahead. She slowed the car then, to turn with a low-voiced warning:

"Be careful, here. You're Dr. Donovan Fallon—that's all you'll need to say. Mr. Messenger has your passport, and we'll take care of any questions."

The time now was six. He could feel her mounting strain as they approached the customs and immigration men, but Messenger aroused himself with an appearance of lazy patience to display their papers, and the officials waved them on.

The pilot of the waiting plane waved cheerfully from the high cockpit as they started toward it, and a small brown crewman stood waiting to help them aboard, grinning an amiable welcome.

"Well, Dr. Fallon." The girl touched his arm, whispering softly. "I think you're safe."

He followed her eagerly until he saw the insigne painted on the bright aluminum flank of the craft. Terror checked him then, with an icy suspicion that he wasn't safe at all. He paused uneasily, looking up at the emblem.

A green dragon, outlined in gold, gaped and hissed as it died from the red wounds twisting across it like rivers on a map. A tall bronze giant towered above it, arms flung wide as if sowing seed. An ominous dark glow shone over those figures, out of his own lost past. He thought he could almost remember—

"Coming, Dr. Fallon?"

The girl's warm voice shattered that moment of dread. Returning her smile, he hurried to overtake her. The dark steward was already helping Messenger up the ramp. They followed, and the brown man closed the cabin door, and the plane began to move at once.

He could see the girl's elation as the great craft lifted them through the pounding turbulence of the clouds, but he was no longer sure he shared it. His glimpse of that green dragon had somehow thinned the veil across his memory, and now he was suddenly afraid of what lay just beyond.

"Just thirty hours aloft!" She was showing him the sleek luxury of the lounge and the staterooms, the gaunt strain on her bronze face relaxing into loveliness now. "Fuel stops at two or three Pacific islands—and we'll be at Edentown."

"Eden—What?"

"Our experimental plantation on the Fly River, deep inside New Guinea," she explained. "Where all the wealth of the company was born—and where we must create it again." She caught his arm. "Now let's go meet the rest of the crew."

He turned with her, and shivered when he saw the dying dragon and the giant again, this time on the bulkhead at the end of the lounge. Glowing with pale danger, that emblem seemed the key to his forgotten past. He stood frowning at it, trying to remember.

"That dragon is the map of New Guinea." She stepped to touch a jagged red wound across its belly. "The Fly. Edentown's right about here." She smiled. "You'll be quite safe, there."

Not sure of that, he turned quickly to keep her from seeing his uncertainty. They went forward, into the comfortable quarters of the crew. The pilot and the navigator on duty and the two men waiting to relieve them were all tanned and cheery. Somehow, with their smiling competence, they reminded him of that triumphant giant standing over the dragon.

"Another lotus-eater." So the girl introduced him. "Dr. Donovan Fallon."

He blinked at the phrase, but each man grinned and gripped his hand with a hearty warmth, as if the phrase had established a special bond between them. Mounting doubts were nibbling away his first deep liking for the girl, however, so that he was suddenly afraid to ask her what a lotus-eater was.

"Now I'm going to my room," she told him. "Better get some rest, yourself, because we've a lot of work to do."

She called the steward, Medina, to install him in his cabin. As soon as she was gone, he asked uneasily, "Just what is a lotus-eater?"

"Most of us are," the little brown man said. "Nearly all the company people who ever see New Guinea. We get the jungle jobs, you see, because we're immune.

"Immune to what?"

"Virus encephalitis." Medina looked at him curiously. "Not many people get it, here in the States. You must have picked it up from a fly we shipped in by accident."

"I don't know." A thin panic crept into his voice. "I can't remember anything."

"You never will." The steward shrugged unconcernedly. "But don't fret about it. The company will take care of you, no matter how you caught the bug. You'll never have to worry again."

"I can almost remember," he muttered uncomfortably. "Something—not very pleasant."

"We all feel that way at first." Medina grinned. "You'll get over it. All you've really lost is your troubles. Mr. Messenger always says he wishes he could pick up the bug himself, because he says we lotus-eaters are the happiest men on earth."

Dane shook his head uncertainly.

"Look at my case," Medina insisted cheerfully. "I used to be a Filipino." He spoke as if the virus had obliterated his nationality as well as his past. "I am told that I came to New Guinea, hoping to rob the company. A man must be unhappy, to face such desperate risks for the sake of an unknown gain. All of us feel better now, as loyal servants of the company, than we could possibly have been before. You'll soon be happy as the rest of us."

"I don't think so."

"You're just tired." Medina shrugged cheerily. "Call me if you want anything."

He woke suddenly, sweating and shivering in his berth. For a moment he thought some shocking memory had come back as he slept, but each detail vanished as he groped for it, until only a haunting recollection of terror was left. He sat up at last, flinching from a thin needle of pain at the back of his head.

The plane was steady now, droning through stable air, and the bright sunlight soon swept away the lingering dread of the dream. Even that tiny ache was gone from his head, by the time he had washed his face and left his room to look for breakfast.

"Good morning, Dr. Fallon." Startled by that genial hail, he found Nan Sanderson and the financier sitting over coffee cups in the lounge. Beaming at him, Messenger's fat, splotched face seemed to have a better color, and the girl was radiant.

"Feeling better, Don?" She nodded at the ports. "Now you can see you're really safe."

Turning uneasily to look out, he saw an endless rolling plain of white stratus clouds below, bright as new snow beneath the morning sun but fissured here and there with chasms floored with dark, wind-wrinkled water.

"The Pacific," she said. "We're not three hours from Hawaii. Your old troubles won't overtake you now."

"But can't I be traced?" He stared at her, wondering uncomfortably if she had been part of that forgotten dream. "The people at the airport have my name."

"Donovan Fallon is a new name, to fit your new life." Her quiet friendliness brushed away his apprehensions. "Don't worry over the old." She rang for the steward. "Eat your breakfast, and let's get started with your re-education."

The grinning former Filipino brought a tray which made a little table beside his chair, and Dane emptied the plastic dishes with a relish which surprised him. Before he had finished, Nan Sanderson came back with an armful of heavy books. He frowned at the titles.

Microbiology. Mechanisms of Mitosis. Proteins, Viruses, and Genes. Evolution of Mankind. And another, that somehow recalled the haunting unease of his dream: *Biochemistry of Mutation.*

"Better begin with that one," Nan said. "It's by one of the best young men in the field, Dane Belfast." The name made him shiver inside, but he didn't know why. "I think you'll find them all easy reading, because your memory is really only half erased."

He read all day, alone in his cabin, skimming that book and the others until his eyes blurred and his head ached again, looking for the past he had lost. He was disappointed. The briefest glance recalled the meaning of each page, like something known before, but that was all. The books opened their limited area of technical knowledge across that stubborn barrier of forgetfulness, but all his groping efforts failed to find anything beyond.

Once, when the plane landed, he looked out to see a fringe of palms beyond the taxiways, and pink stucco bungalows buried in purple bougainvilleas. He left his books uneasily, to ask where they were.

"Potter Field," the steward told him. "Near Honolulu." Beyond the ports on the other side of the lounge, Medina showed him huge freighters docked, and rows of long warehouses all bearing the emblem of the dragon and the giant. "And Potter Harbor."

"All this belongs to Cadmus?"

"We're an enormous enterprise." The little brown lotus-eater beamed as proudly as Messenger himself. "The sun never sets on the dragon. We're all very lucky, to be with such a company."

Nodding dubiously, he went back to the books.

That night he slept badly, while the plane lurched and

shuddered through rain squalls along the tropical front. He dreamed another dreadful dream, in which Nan Sanderson and Messenger were generous friends no longer, but sly and dangerous enemies.

He woke in the dark, his ears clicking painfully from the pressure change as the plane came down to land. A thin pain pulsed in his head again, and his mouth tasted bitter and dry. He lay sweating and trembling in his berth, almost afraid to breathe. For that nightmare had followed him out of sleep, no longer a dream. He was no longer Donovan Fallon, groping to find himself in a strange world one day old.

He was Dane Belfast.

FIFTEEN

Rubber barked against hard coral as the wheels struck a landing strip, and he stumbled to the small round window of his cabin as the plane taxied through sudden damp heat toward a lighted hangar and a waiting fuel truck. He searched the dark field, frantically.

Still sick and shuddering from the terror of that nightmare turned real, he could think only of the need to reach John Gellian with his apologetic warning that Messenger was an ally of the not-men, and New Guinea their fortress—an impregnable citadel defended by that virus of forgetfulness, and by all the men it had robbed of their humanity, and doubtless by deadlier creations of the maker's stolen science.

And this, panic whispered, might be his last chance. Escape from those guarded concessions had proved impossible for many another man before him; and the next time these enemies of men removed his memory, their means would surely be something more primitive and permanent than that mutant virus.

He dressed quickly in the dark, and came back to measure the little porthole. It was far too small to let him out, and the glass was securely fastened. Peering out anxiously as the craft rolled to a halt and the engines died, he recoiled from another barrier.

Painted above the hangar doors was the Cadmus trademark, the dragon-shape of that enormous island and the victorious golden giant sowing dark human seed. This Pacific islet must be another company station, operated by lotus-eaters too cheerily loyal to give him any aid.

"Three hours?" Nan Sanderson was saying. "Then let's ask Dr. Fallon to join us."

He couldn't help an apprehensive start when he heard the steward knock, but he tried not to look so hopelessly trapped as he felt when he came out into the lounge, where the girl and Messenger and one of the pilots sat drinking coffee.

"I heard you moving, Don." She was smiling, but her words frightened him. He had been very quiet. How keen, he wondered, were her mutant perceptions? How long could he hide his escape from forgetfulness?

"Time we were up, anyhow," she went on brightly.

"Though it's only midnight here, we're almost keeping up with the sun—or we were, until this engine quit. While they're changing it, how about a walk on the beach?" She looked at Dane, inquiringly. Suddenly too confused to speak, he nodded hastily. He saw that she didn't know his memory had come back, and for a moment this looked like the chance he wanted. Feverishly, his imagination seized it.

Now he could wait to make his break for freedom until they were alone on the beach. Though she herself might be a deadly thing, tougher and quicker and stronger than any human woman, he could hope to offset her mutant faculties with the advantage of surprise.

Once away from her, he would have the cover of the dark even though the odds might be still overwhelmingly against him, he could try to find some sort of craft to carry him off this enemy islet. And any man he met should be his ally—any except those grinning slaves of forgetfulness. All he needed was to reach one man—the captain of a liner or the humblest beachcomber—faithful enough to take his warning to Gellian.

"How about it?" Nan had turned to Messenger. "Feel like coming with Don and me?"

He heard the utter trust with which she spoke his name—and it struck him then that his present status as a supposed lotus-eater was an accidental weapon in his hands, worth far more than all the information he could take to Gellian, even if he got away.

He knew too little.

How many not-men were gathered in New Guinea? Where were their weapons and their plans? Were they fighting to dominate mankind, or only to save their own lives? Was Nan Sanderson the leader she had seemed in New York or merely a minor agent?

What of Messenger? Was that sick financier the dupe of the not-men, the unsuspecting human screen for a spreading alien empire? Or a willing ally? Or had he used the youthful mutants as innocent tools of his own shrewd schemes?

Those were the questions Gellian would ask—for that efficient detective ought to know about as much as he did, by this time, from the clues Messenger and the girl must have left. Choosing the human side, Dane saw his duty to look for the answers. And he ought to find them in his hands, if he could only conceal his recovery.

He might do even more. For the danger driving Messenger and Nan Sanderson back to New Guinea must be something more grave than Gellian's raids. He thought it might turn out to be a crisis in the fortunes of the not-men that could be used to end this war of races with some just peace.

The role of a happy captive of the virus would be hard to play. The difficulties and the dangers he saw waiting in New Guinea made that discarded scheme for escape seem cowardly. Yet he was suddenly eager to go on, hoping to learn Charles Potter's actual fate, and even to discover the final secrets of life which had been his own goal from the beginning.

He turned to Nan, and contrived a hopeful smile.

"You two go ahead," Messenger was wheezing, already breathless and dripping in the moist heat. "I'm all right—tough as a mule—but I'll wait here."

Leaving the steward to look after him, Dane and the girl got off the plane together. She led the way almost gaily along the narrow slope of coral and wet sand between the airstrip and the sea, showing a childish pleasure in the starry tropic night and the luminous breakers on the reef.

Following, trying to conceal his own dangerous constraint, he had time to wonder what she was. In spite of himself, he liked her, and her warm charm now made him think for a moment that she might be after all a normal human girl, caught as he had been in the not-men's secret web and controlled by some device as sinister as that mutant virus.

"Careful, Don!"

Watching her dim figure in the dark, he hadn't seen the sharp coral ledge that tripped him. Before he could fall, she had turned back to catch his arm and help him get his balance back.

"Thanks," he whispered hoarsely.

Terror had taken his breath, because her flashing quickness and her effortless strength recalled all the evidence that she was a mutant enemy. Even her disarming loveliness was merely one more weapon, he thought grimly, used to camouflage her deadliness.

Walking silently on beside her, he couldn't escape his awareness of that charm, however, nor help feeling a reluctant admiration for the daring and the skill with which she was fighting for the survival of her race. She must have stood off Gellian's whole organization in New York, single-handed. From her cryptic report to Messenger, she must have raided the agency offices alone to destroy that metallic tree and those other accumulated evidences of the maker's work.

Still human, however, he shivered again at the picture of her cunning strength matched against the hopeless exhaustion of little Nicholas Venn. If she were truly superhuman, the cold thought struck him, that killing must have been no more to her than the necessary disposition of a dangerous animal. She would doubtless destroy him with as little compunction, if she happened to read his thoughts.

"Don." Terror touched him when she turned toward him in the dark. Her quiet tone reassured him, and then frightened him again, when he recalled how deftly Venn must have been disarmed. "Did you finish the Belfast book?"

"And most of the others." He managed to breathe again. "It seemed more like remembering than learning."

"You're lucky," she told him. "The amnesia is generally deeper. Death is uncommon, but more often there is permanent damage to the mind. I'm glad you're doing so well, because we need your best to save the company."

She went on to ask a few questions about the bioluminescent organisms which made cold fire in the lapping water at their feet, as if testing his recovered knowledge, and then they walked on silently again. Afraid to ask how his best could save the company, he was trying hard to assume the patient content of those men without pasts.

He was faintly startled to recognize the crooked Southern Cross, which he had seen only on star maps before, now standing low over the pale surf ahead, but he looked away from it quickly, afraid that even a second glance might betray him. Those books had included no texts on astronomy.

The girl didn't seem to notice. She caught his arm while they scrambled over another coral ledge, and let it go as they crossed the patch of dark sand beyond, walking on in thoughtful silence. He supposed she must be planning her defense of the not-men and the company, until she said quietly:

"Sometimes it gives me an awed feeling—almost a religious feeling, I think—to walk on a tropical beach. Because it must have been in a place like this that the life on Earth was first created."

She nodded at a hollow in the rock beside them, where starlight shone pale on a pool of still water.

"In some natural test tube like that," she went on softly. "In one of the billions which the waves and tides had washed and filled again, times without number, with different trial solutions that were heated under the sun and cooled by radiation, concentrated by evaporation and diluted again with rain, stirred with the wind and bombarded with natural radioactivity—until at last the patient chemistry of chance put our first parent molecule together, in such a way that it could endure and reproduce itself and undergo mutation into all the forms of life we know."

"Chance alone created life?"

He regretted that whispered question instantly, but he had been thinking of the riddle of her own origin, and of the logical necessity of the maker's unknown art to take the place of the many generations of normal mutation and natural selection required to create a new species in nature.

"Chance alone." Her quiet reply showed that she had caught no reference to herself. "But that action of chance doesn't dim the wonder of the universe for me. Probability is involved in the structure of every atom, and the possibility of life must have existed in matter from the beginning of time, waiting to be revealed."

"I think I understand."

I could share the solemn feeling she expressed, and it made him less reluctant to take her hand when they came again to broken footing. For they both belonged to the same common stream of life, which had flowed down all the ages since it first sprang from that ancient tidal pool. For an instant he almost forgot that he was human and she was not.

For a moment they were kin—and then the feeling frightened him. He let go her hand uneasily, when they came to smoother going, and tried to guard himself against her deadly charm by asking technical questions about her theory of that chance creation.

Where, precisely, was the threshold of animation, at which that original molecule crossed the borderline of life? What had made it a living template, able to shape inert matter into perfect copies of itself? How had mutation begun changing the templates, to launch evolution?

Her answers made a shield against that dangerous sense of kinship, until they came back to the plane. Her knowledge of genetics made him wonder if Charles Potter had been her teacher, and it frightened him. If the mutants ever learned to direct mutation—he was afraid to think of that.

Saying he was sleepy, he retreated to his cabin.

SIXTEEN

They were again in flight when the hot sunlight of another morning woke him. Looking from his cabin window, he saw only sky and clouds and sea: the sky an infinite bright chasm of milky light in which the droning plane hung motionless; the clouds remote cumulus, luminous and topless and somehow palely unreal; the sea a dull mirror for the clouds and the sea, equally infinite and equally unreal.

The sea washing an island beach had meaning, because it had been the mother of life, but this remote blank unbounded surface was alien as outer space must be. He turned away from it uneasily, to wash and dress and look for breakfast.

He found Nan Sanderson standing in the lounge, staring somberly out at that empty sky and lonely sea. That perilous kinship they had found on the beach made her seem entirely human for an instant, when he saw the trouble in her eyes.

"Something wrong?"

"Mr. Messenger." Her brown face was gaunt with worry. "I'm afraid the altitude changes have been too much for his heart in spite of the pressurized cabin." She smiled soberly. "Though he still insists he's tough as a mule!"

He had been tough, Dane thought bleakly. The fantastic buccaneer who had stolen the science of creation, and allied himself with the alien enemies of his race to build and defend the empire of Cadmus—death in bed, of coronary thrombosis, would be a somewhat anticlimactic fate for J. D. Messenger.

Her sad eyes came back to him, and Dane felt cold inside. Trying hastily to mold his face into the bovine calm of the lotus-eaters, he tried not to wonder if her mutant perceptions included any power of mindreading. If they did, such a thought might kill him.

"We'll soon be over New Guinea," she was saying. "Shall we eat while we wait to see it?"

She rang for the steward. Before they had finished breakfast, the shape of land began emerging into that featureless bright void, first a pale shadow beneath the tall pillars of shining cloud ahead, and then a sudden green reality, edged raggedly with a thin white line of beach and broken water, and trailing reddish stains from muddy rivers far out into the clean dark sea.

"That red is like the dragon's blood." The girl nodded sadly at the long stains. "And Cadmus is dying, really—unless we can grow another crop of Potter's mules."

He caught his breath to inquire how Potter's mules were grown, and abruptly swallowed the question. Too easily, he could betray too much knowledge about the dead green creature Nicholas Venn had died for possessing, and too much emotion for a man without a past.

Turning quickly, he looked again at the land ahead, which here rose steeply from the sea, dark with the dense green forest which seemed to express the ruthless drive of life to survive, in the way it clung to every broken surface, soaring and thrusting seaward and skyward in competition for space and light.

That visible conflict for the means of survival, the uneasy thought struck him, must have begun in that same quiet tidal pool where life was born. The first fission of that original living molecule had created two equal rivals for the lean resources of the then sterile planet. The first mutation, introducing unequal advantage, had made that unending struggle still more deadly.

This cruel clash of men and not-men, he saw, was only the inevitable continuation of that same conflict, which he thought must go on until life expired. The stern reality of that eternal war was the reason for John Gellian's implacable intolerance, and also for this slender girl's resolute ability to behead a man with a jungle knife.

"We've left the coasts as they were," she was saying. "Except for improving a few seaports, and moving the natives into reservations away from the flies that carry that encephalitis.

"The jungle is a very convenient screen," she added innocently. "Against the people who try to steal our business secrets—and generally become faithful employees, after the virus hits them."

Belfast nodded, carefully keeping his face toward the window and striving for the calm of one who had forgotten everything and therefore could be surprised by nothing. Defending himself against her tawny fascination, he began to think they had to be enemies, not because she was wicked nor because he was, but simply because they were both alive and she a new mutation. The barrier between them was a law of nature, old as life.

After all his rationalizing, however, she still disturbed him. If she had been obeying some such primordial law, all her acts became forgivable. He wanted to like her, in spite of everything—but nothing could ever bridge that genetic gulf between them. Afraid to look at her, he stood watching the dark jungle silently, and he felt vastly relieved when she left him to see how Messenger was feeling.

The sick man came shuffling laboriously back with her, wheezing for his breath. His puffy flesh looked sallow and blotched and almost cadaverous, but he was able to grin a genial greeting at Belfast, and soon he was leaning ponderously to inspect the company concessions which came into view beyond the coastal range, his shrewd eyes anxious.

Those concessions made Dane almost forget his careful

calm. Broad highways cut the deep rain forest, leaping canyons and rivers on long steel bridges. Tall white dams backed blue lakes against frowning mountains. The sun glanced on railway steel. Unending rows of cultivated trees made ranks and files across vast plantations.

"The mules have done all that," the girl remarked. "With only a few lotus-eaters like yourself to supervise them."

He nodded stiffly, trying hard to conceal the dismay which had followed his first amazement. This was literally an empire, created and controlled by that stolen science of genetic engineering. What could one man hope to accomplish against it?

"Look!" Messenger was muttering gloomily. "Won't you look at that?"

And Dane forgot his dismay, staring at the financier in deep bewilderment. For Messenger seemed to find no pleasure in the look of this immense green domain. Shaking his puffy head, he was making dull clucking sounds of regret, and his small eyes had filled with bitter tears.

"What's wrong?" Dane whispered.

"The mules," the fat man gasped. "Dying."

"Where?" They were flying far too high to distinguish those small green creatures of the maker. Dane was puzzled, and almost sorry for the sick man. "I can't see anything."

"Nothing." Messenger nodded sadly. "No tractors working the plantations. No trucks on the roads. No trains. No shipping on the rivers. The mules are dying—and everything has stopped."

"But we'll soon grow another crop of mules." The girl brought Messenger a small white pill and a glass of water. "Now take this, and sit down. We're climbing again, to cross those mountains, and you must rest your heart."

She stayed to watch him anxiously while the plane swayed

through turbulent clouds over a formidable range. For a time he had to fight for his breath, but he seemed more comfortable again after they dropped into another immense valley beyond, and Nan went back to her room. Left alone with Messenger, Belfast decided to risk some of the questions he was afraid to ask the girl.

"There isn't much about mules in those books," he began cautiously. "Aren't they a kind of hybrid?"

"Potter's mules are different."

"Won't I need to know something more about them?"

Messenger nodded, and he waited painfully, trying to cover the naked intensity of his interest with the serene cheer of those men without trouble.

"Potter's mules conquered New Guinea." The sick man nodded somberly at the jungle-choked canyons below the descending craft. "This damned island's no place for men, and there was too much work for men to do."

"Who is Potter?"

"Dead." The only emotion Messenger betrayed was concern for his labored breath. "He was my first associate in the company. A queer old duck. But he knew how to take the genes apart and put them back together to grow whatever he wanted."

The financier paused, glancing at Belfast with tired, watery, blood-shot little eyes which still seemed disturbingly keen. His sudden question was disconcerting:

"How much do you know?"

Dane drew a careful breath, trying hard to hold that mask of quiet. "I read those books," he said slowly. "Each page seemed to come back as soon as I saw it, but there must be a great deal more I can't remember—"

"Good," the big man broke in. "I just wanted to be sure you could follow. Anyhow, I first came out here to investigate the assets of a bankrupt gold mine. I was going back to report that the claims couldn't be worked profitably with native labor, when I met Charles Potter in Sydney."

This wasn't what Messenger had written his father, Dane recalled. He had been an Air Force meteorologist, in that other account, and that meeting in Darwin. One story had to be a lie. Had he told it to cover the murder of his first associate? Nothing in his bloated yellow face seemed to answer that. Dane discovered that his own hands were clenched, and relaxed them apprehensively.

"Potter was peculiar." Smiling at the oddities of the maker, Messenger's scarred ugliness became almost likable. "A creator—a god, almost—begging on the waterfront. He had pasteboard in his shoes to patch the holes. I bought him a drink and his dinner and a pair of shoes. We talked all night in my hotel room, and next day we started back to New Guinea."

Messenger's swollen hand made a feeble gesture toward the ragged mountains westward.

"The mine was somewhere yonder, near the head of the Fly. Potter's mules dug four million ounces of fine gold out of it, the year we started. Just the beginning! I had to show him what that trick of his was worth. Even then, he was sometimes stubborn. Just a genius, I guess."

Pausing as if to reflect on the regrettable illogic of genius, Messenger fumbled at his coat pocket and found it empty.

"My cigars." He grinned ruefully. "The doctors have been after me, and now Nan's trying to wean me. I'll have her give you the box—if you smoke?"

"I—I don't know." Belfast caught himself in time to shake his head blankly, wondering if that suave query had been intended as a trap. "I don't remember."

"Try them, anyhow," the big man rumbled heartily. "A

special brand, grown from a new tobacco that Potter mutated to suit my own taste."

"Thanks." Dane decided to chance another question. "How did Potter cause mutations?"

"I wish we knew!" Messenger shook his head gloomily. "A queer, twisted sort. Must have hated his own guts. Drunk half the time, when he wasn't full of drugs. Never trusted any assistants. He would never even tell me much, and I didn't know enough genetics to follow the little he did."

"That's too bad," Dane said carefully.

"Calamitous!" Messenger gasped. "Unless you and Miss Sanderson know enough genetics to grow another crop of mules."

"What did he mutate them from?"

"A motile alga, he called it." The fat face frowned. "I don't remember the Latin name he used, but it's a simple, one-celled plant that swims in fresh water ponds under its own power. He changed the genes to make the cells develop into obedient little bipeds, about half as tall as men. They can't talk, but they're intelligent enough for most kinds of labor. And they don't eat—that's a touch of Potter's genius."

Belfast tried to breathe again, reminding himself that to a man without memory such creatures might seem no more remarkable than the common green scum from which they had been made.

"Potter kept the chlorophyll, you see," Messenger was wheezing. "But mutated, too, to store up eighty percent of the energy of sunlight, instead of one percent. All those mules need for food is air and water and sunshine."

Dane nodded, as blankly as possible.

"I don't suppose you fully appreciate that," the financier rumbled. "But it means free labor, in an age when the human worker wants more and more for less and less. We could have taken over the world—if old Potter had made mules enough."

"But don't they breed?"

"Mules are sterile," Messenger wheezed. "That's why he picked the name. He made them that way on purpose—for the same reason he made them so short-lived and so small. Afraid they'd get out of hand. He was a twisted little human wreck, I told you. No better head for business than he had for whisky. Didn't even trust himself."

The fat man paused to peer gloomily out at the clouds piling up toward the dark mountains westward, all their bases level as if they stood on some transparent floor, the summits billowing far up into the milky brightness of the tropic sky. Dane waited impatiently, afraid to prompt him.

"Potter made the mules to live just two years," he went on bitterly. "The last crop came out of his lab just before he died, nearly two years ago. That's why we've got to grow another."

Dane opened his clenched hands again, and inhaled deliberately. "Those books tell you how to cause a few mutations at will," he said carefully. "But those few are all simple special cases. There's no general formula. I wouldn't know how to begin trying to breed anything like that. Unless—"

He looked up at Messenger, trying not to seem too anxious. "Unless Potter happened to leave some record of his process?"

"Unreasonable, I told you." The bulging head shook heavily. "He burned every scrap of paper in the lab."

"Then I don't see much hope—"

"Miss Sanderson knows something," the financier said. "I sent her out here to help nurse old Potter, and she finally won his trust. He tried to tell her how, toward the end—after he was already too far gone, it seems, to remember all the steps."

Had he trusted her, really? Dane looked down at the jungle again, to cover that sudden doubt. Had Potter really talked—or had she just attempted to pick the priceless secret from his mind, with some mutant but still imperfect mental perception?

"She tried a batch of mules, after he was dead," Messenger wheezed sadly. "They looked all right—until they died in the vats. But she's been studying in New York, and now she has you to help. Maybe you two can do it, together. We're ruined if you fail."

Gloomily, he elaborated. "Production falling, the last two years, as the dying mules were not replaced. Export shipments at a standstill, now—with overhead and dividends eating up our capital reserves, until the company's about to crash."

Recalling the haughty façade of the Cadmus Building in New York, Dane found it difficult to veil his astonishment.

"Everybody outside still thinks we're solid as Gibraltar," Messenger went on. "I've floated bonds and borrowed money to keep up a convincing front, but that's played out. Our own directors want to come out here to see what's wrong. I can't stall them off much longer. If we haven't got production to show them, that's the end of Cadmus."

Emotion shuddered in the shallow voice. "That's the situation, Dr. Fallon. A grave predicament for all of us—and especially for you lotus-eaters, who depend so much on the company. You understand why you must give your utmost?"

Belfast nodded as calmly as he could. "I think so."

"Then help me get up!"

He tugged while Messenger heaved, and then stood watching the huge man move out of the lounge with that laborious slow shuffle, which still somehow had dignity and grace. Peering out and down again at the flat, sun-parched barrens now unfolding beyond the forest, he considered the story of the mules with a puzzled scowl.

Most of his questions remained unanswered. The number and the aims of the not-men were yet to be discovered, but the collapse of the company which had aided and concealed them would be a profound crisis in their affairs. Whatever the outcome of that, he was almost inside their stronghold, and he still could hope to learn Potter's process of creation.

SEVENTEEN

Belfast saw the mules half an hour later, when the landing plane taxied to a jolting stop on a muddy airstrip at Edentown. Recent floods had slashed raw canyons into the strip and the taxiways, and the mules were repairing the damage.

Silent, busy pygmies, toiling with toy spades or struggling by twos and threes to lift small stones, they came scarcely to the waist of their overseer, a tanned lotus-eater who towered above them like a golden giant. The green of their queer, slim bodies was glossy and almost black, and they worked with an unceasing haste. Some of them spread graceful membranes which he first thought were wings.

"Can they fly?" he asked Nan Sanderson, following her toward a mud-splashed jeep in which another smiling, sunburned man sat waiting.

She shook her head, and he could see already that those slender, fringed appendages were too delicate for flight. They were specialized tissues, she said, which served as swimming organs while the mules were in the embryonic stage, growing in the vats. In these mature individuals, they had been modified to drink in the energy of light.

He nodded silently, pausing to gape. An astonishing triumph of biological engineering, the mules were living protoplasm shaped for one specific purpose—to deliver free labor.

Designed with all the free ingenuity that other sorts of engineers had always used in building their simpler mechanisms of dead metal, they amazed him and they frightened him.

"Coming, Don?" the girl called back.

He hurried after her, uneasily. They caught up with Messenger, who was gasping painfully and mopping feebly at the sweat already shining on his bloated flesh. Moving with that careful poise which always seemed a triumph of mind over gross matter, he was dolefully shaking his head.

"Look at everything!" he panted sadly. "Holes in the road. Bridges out. Boats tied up. Factories stopped and warehouses empty and machines gone to rust. Plantations buried in lawyer vines and *kunai* grass. Nothing but ruin anywhere!"

"But the mules we can grow from one mutant cell will change everything." The girl took his puffy arm, her gesture quick and tender. "They can cut the weeds and mend the roads and save the company."

"If we can only make them!"

"We can," she promised him softly.

The jeep driver came to meet Messenger. "Mr. Van Doon wanted to be here," he apologized. "But he has been up at the gold mines, and the bad roads must have delayed him."

"Vic Van Doon's our New Guinea manager," the girl told Dane. "An old lotus-eater, and one of the best. You'll like to work with Vic."

The warmth of her tone caught him with a twinge of irrational jealousy. Far from sure he would like Van Doon, he turned to help the driver haul Messenger into the front seat of the jeep, and then climbed in to sit with Nan on the luggage in the rear.

She had undressed for the tropic heat, her long body golden beneath blue shorts and halter, and for a moment he couldn't take his eyes from her lithe loveliness. In spite of himself, he suddenly wanted to have her and hold her and defend her forever, even against his fellow men.

But then she looked at him. A faint smile warmed her cool blue eyes, as if she had sensed his surge of emotion. She seemed aloofly pleased—but a dark terror brushed him. If she could read his unwilling admiration, she would surely soon perceive some more dangerous thought.

He turned away quickly, grateful for the pitching of the jeep in the muddy ruts that flung them apart and kept them busy hanging on. Afraid to say anything, he sat sweating in the damp heat, his clothing already adhesive.

Her tawny allure was only one more weapon, he warned himself. She probably used it as deliberately as she did that mutant virus, to keep the loyalty of these men who had forgotten other women—but even that thought might be his last, if she were to pick it up.

"Look around you, Fallon." Messenger's breathless voice brought him a welcome escape. "You'll see how much we need the mules."

Relieved to turn his thoughts from the girl's inhuman charm, he looked out at a young plantation already choked with grass and vines.

"Potter's last creation," the financier gasped laboriously. "A mutant kind of rubber tree. The latex is a thermosetting plastic, clear as glass and strong as steel. This one plantation might save Cadmus, if we had mules enough to hold the jungle back."

The only mules Dane could see, however, were a few carrying rocks and earth in tiny baskets, to fill a gully where flood water had cut the road. He was watching one small creature when it paused and staggered with its burden. Its flightless wings fluttered and collapsed. Silently, ignored by the others, it sank down in the mud.

"They die that way," the girl said. "As quietly as they live."

The long bridge across the Fly was still intact, but the flood had cut one approach with a wide ravine, spanned now with a makeshift wooden scaffold which swayed alarmingly under the jeep. Downstream, an abandoned dredge lay where it must have run aground, canted across a red sandbar. Beyond the river, a few more mules were toiling, ineffectually as ants, to remove a great tree which had fallen across the road.

"A sad thing to see," Messenger puffed, as the jeep jolted around the tree. "These old mules are used up, the way I am. You should have been here two years ago, when they were young and strong and swarming. New Guinea looked like a billion dollars, then."

"And it will again!" The girl spoke too vehemently, as if trying to convince herself. Dane felt almost sorry for her and the sick man, until he reminded himself that even the driver had been a victim of their strange alliance, robbed of memory and nation and family to serve against his race.

"Edentown." Messenger gestured feebly at a cluster of straggling buildings by the road ahead. "Our New Guinea headquarters. You'll live at the Cadmus House."

The Cadmus House had a look of decayed luxury. The ornamental woodwork of the long verandas needed new paint. A rank forest of papayas had overrun the grounds, and creeping vines were smothering the hibiscus and frangipani along the walks.

The jeep driver started to turn in toward it, but Messenger waved him on. They passed a hospital and a few straggling shops and warehouses and one tall office building. Beyond that forlorn outpost of the company, the forest closed in to wall the road again, until the jeep emerged on a grassy plateau that rose like an island from the jungle sea, two miles from the river.

"Old Potter's house." Messenger nodded heavily toward a rambling stone mansion, scarlet with bougainvillea, at the end of a muddy driveway. "That's where he died."

"Mr. Van Doon has it ready for your party." Approaching the turn, the driver slowed again. "The air-conditioner's running—"

"Drive on." Messenger's swollen hand lifted, with a painful urgency. "I want to get started."

The battered vehicle splashed ahead again, and Nan's golden arm lifted toward a low structure of white concrete, which stood isolated beyond a barbed wire fence ahead.

"The mutation lab," she told Dane. "The biological engineering section, where Potter used to produce all his mutations."

Trying to veil the taut agony of his interest, he leaned to study the building where that lonely genius had made the mules, and probably that virus of forgetfulness, and possibly even Nan Sanderson herself. The massive windowless walls gave it the look of a fortress, and he was not surprised to see two brown riflemen outside.

"Notice them, Fallon!" Messenger's voice had a sudden flat vehemence. "That area's taboo—even to you lotus-eaters. Keep out. Those guards shoot to kill."

"Outsiders want our secret processes," the girl said more quietly. "Some of them are ingenious and persistent. We have to protect the company."

Dane nodded as calmly as he could, trying not to flinch when he recalled how she had protected the company from one persistent and ingenious outsider named Nicholas Venn.

"The production section." The fat man gestured heavily. "Your domain, Fallon."

Just across the muddy ruts from the mutation lab, the production section was another long building roofed with sheet aluminum. Beyond it, a series of broad shallow concrete tanks spread fan-like down the slope toward the jungle-clotted river.

"That looks strange." Cautiously, Dane probed again for the secret of creation. "Do I know enough to run it?"

"Not yet," Messenger gasped at Nan. "Tell him."

Dane forced himself to breathe again. Afraid the girl would see the raw violence of his anxiety, he turned to frown again at the puzzling construction of those empty tanks. For here must be the tremendous secret he had sought from the beginning.

"Potter grew each crop of mules from a single mutant cell," she began briskly. "He let it multiply in a sterile food-solution until he had as many billion germ cells as he wanted. Then he added a reagent to stop the fission, and start each cell developing into a mature mule.

"But you won't be concerned with that."

Numb with disappointment, Belfast turned with a careful show of expectation toward the building above the empty vats.

"Here's where we'll bring you the swimmers—the microscopic embryonic mules. Your job is to keep them alive. Though the grown mules are hardy enough, the swimmers are quite delicate. The last ones we made died in the tanks—killed, I think, by some blunder. With your skill, perhaps, we can grow them to maturity."

Dane looked at her doubtfully. "I'm afraid those books didn't say anything about growing swimmers."

"I'll bring you a memo on the process." Her voice was intense, her blue eyes dark and grave; her lean ivory loveliness caught him so painfully that he had to turn away.

"The first stages are critical," she added. "The vat solutions must be kept uncontaminated, exactly balanced chemically, and irradiated with just the right intensity of light—since the swimmers live on light, even a few moments of darkness can kill them, by stopping photosynthesis.

"An exacting job, you see." She looked at him keenly. "Can you do it?"

"I think so." He tried desperately to mold his face into the stolid good humor of a lotus-eater. "I know I can!"

"Good." She gave him a quick little smile of confidence. "The larger swimmers aren't quite so delicate. When they're old enough to leave the sterile vats inside, they develop an instinct which guides them on through the growing tanks outside. There, they need only sunlight and a few days of time to become adults, ready to climb out and dry their swimming membranes and go to work for the company."

Belfast mopped at the sweat on his face and studied the empty tanks again. Perhaps this elaborate process for the manufacture of intelligent slaves shouldn't seem remarkable to a man who remembered nothing else, but he found it hard to hide his dazed amazement. He felt grateful for the interruption, when another jeep came splashing up behind them.

"It's Vic Van Doon." And the girl called gladly, "Hi, Vic!"

A muscular, sun-browned man in faded shorts and shapeless pith helmet came wading through the mud to shake hands with her and the panting financier.

"Nan! J.D.! Good to see you!" His voice was bluff and vigorous, and his broad face was smooth with oblivion. "I wanted to meet you at the plane," he said, "but the jeep got stuck in a wash-out, up in the hills."

"The mines?" Messenger asked. "Did you get them running?"

Momentarily grave, Van Doon shook his head. "I took the best mules I had up there, but they're all too weak and old to do the work. And dying like flies."

"We'll soon have more." Nan turned. "Vic, this is Don Fallon. Our newest lotus-eater. He's to be in charge of the production section."

"Hello, Fallon." Van Doon caught his hand with a bone-cracking grip. "You'll never be sorry the black flies bit you. I've been with the company three years, and never a regret. That virus is a sure cure for trouble-makers." He chuckled genially. "I believe I came to murder Mr. Potter and break the company—right, J.D.?"

"Right," Messenger said. "Nearly did it, too."

Belfast looked away from Van Doon's smiling pride in that conversion, trying not to shiver. It made him sick to see how that virus had turned such a determined enemy of the company into this loyal slave, and for a moment his own plans seemed hopeless.

"No time to squander." Messenger straightened impatiently. "Let's get to work!"

Dane nodded, trying feebly to smile again. No matter how many before him had failed, his purpose was still undetected. Though he was disappointed to be shut out of the mutation lab, the products of it might tell him something about the process. And—in spite of Messenger's taboo—he still hoped to find a way inside.

"I'll bring you that memo, as soon as I can," Nan told him. "But you might start looking over the plant right away. We ought to have the first batch of swimmers ready by morning. You'll have to have everything sterile, and fresh solutions mixed."

"Wait here, Fallon," Van Doon added. "I'll send your assistants out with the keys." He turned to Messenger and the girl. "I've got the old Potter house ready for you. Nan, won't you ride over with me?"

She let him help her out of the jeep. Belfast climbed hastily out on the other side, to hide his flush of unwilling resentment. Let her go, he advised himself bitterly. She meant nothing to him except alien strangeness and shocking danger. The lotus-eater was welcome to her!

Left alone when the two jeeps lurched away, he walked stiffly out of the driving sun into the hot shade under the eaves of the production building. Waiting there, feeling the drops of sweat creeping like insects down his flanks and legs, he cautiously surveyed the mutation lab across the road.

The two riflemen returned his gaze suspiciously. He swung as casually as possible to examine the slope behind him, where those tiers of empty tanks dropped toward the river bottom. Searching for a back path to that fenced and guarded fortress, he paused abruptly when another riddle challenged him.

Danger seethed all around him. He knew it was there—but he couldn't feel it, not in the way he had sensed the hostility of New York. The jungle was alive with crocodiles and deadly insects and internal parasites and a hundred other shapes of death, but it had no warning glow of evil. The faint dankness of the river swamps was not that bitter reek of hate. The harsh cries of unseen birds in the trees below him were strange enough, but they rang no alarm in his mind.

Glancing uncomfortably at the guards across the road, whose restless guns needed nothing more than light to show their deadly readiness, he frowned at the riddle of that lost danger-sense—or had it been a sense?

For that seeming awareness of peril had never led him to actual safety. Coming upon him just before Nan Sanderson first called, it had guided him twice—or three times, really—

into her mantraps. It had brought him here, into ever-mounting jeopardy.

Nan Sanderson had been the common factor, it struck him, in all of those baffling experiences. She must have somehow caused those sensations. Had what he felt been her mutant mind, reaching out to read his thoughts and even to influence his actions?

He nodded uneasily. That would explain the absence those feelings now—she had naturally relaxed her unknown faculties, when she thought the virus had made him her harmless tool. But when those sensations returned, they would mean she had decided to pick his mind again.

He shivered when he recognized her in the jeep, coming back with Messenger from the old Potter house. Her cheerful wave of greeting startled him unpleasantly. He managed to answer it stiffly, but he felt relieved when she drove past him, into the fenced grounds of the mutation lab.

Four more lotus-eaters came up from the town in a rusty truck, with keys to the production section. Dane went in with his new assistants to explore the building. What he found was a long row of stainless steel vats, each larger than the next, all linked with a bewildering web of pipes and pumps and valves. Before he could finish inspecting the intricate auxiliary equipment of boilers and filters and flood-lamps and thermostats and air-conditioning units, one of the men called him back to the door.

"Don?" A thin dread touched him when he heard Nan Sanderson's voice, but he relaxed a little when he saw the folded papers in her hand. "The memo."

He took it silently.

"Follow it exactly," she told him. "Remember, an error of one minute or one degree or one percent might be enough to kill the swimmers."

Memo to Dr. Fallon, the first page was headed, in blue-black ink which had not yet darkened. The hand-printed characters staggered wearily, but they were stubbornly legible. In the first step, he read, the embryonic swimmers must be kept for eight minutes in ten liters of sterile water at 38 degrees Centigrade, under 96 foot-candles of filtered light. In step two—

Dane started, and then tried hard to stop the trembling of the pages in his fingers. For he had seen that same hand printing neater and more vigorous, but still the same—in letters written long ago. For all that wavering weakness, the slanted bar at the top of the *A* and the curved oblique stroke across the *f* and the back-slanted tails of the *g* and the *y* made it unmistakable.

The writing was Charles Kendrew's.

EIGHTEEN

Nan Sanderson made him come with her down the descending row of vats. Pausing to show him how to operate each one, she let him study the instructions in that memo and then shot rapid questions to be sure he understood.

Dane followed her dazedly. His forced responses seemed painfully mechanical to him, but she appeared not to notice his disturbance. When they left the bottom vat, where the growing swimmers were expected to leap a low barrier to the tanks outside, she turned anxiously.

"Think you can do it?"

Huskily, he said he thought he understood everything. He walked with her out to the jeep, and watched her drive back toward that squat building beyond the barbed wire, which had the look of a prison now.

Stumbling slowly back to begin his own task, he studied that unsteady hand-printing again. No, he couldn't be mistaken—the writing was Kendrew's. The implications staggered him.

The memo proved that Messenger's eccentric plant breeder was actually Charles Kendrew—as his father had once suspected, before the financier somehow bribed or tricked him into forgetting the notion. Charles Potter was the missing maker of the not-men, whom Gellian was hunting.

And he was still alive!

Messenger and Nan Sanderson must have lied about his illness and death, to discourage inquiries about him. That fresh ink and the words *Memo to Fallon* were sufficient evidence that the maker was not only still alive, but well and sane enough today to write these elaborate instructions for the care of his creations.

Alive—but the helpless prisoner, obviously, of the man who had been his friend and the inhuman creatures he had made. Somehow, Dane decided, they had compelled him to write this paper. Right now, no doubt, they were trying to make him create that mutant cell they needed so desperately.

But how could a creator be confined?

Dane frowned again at the memo, and the answer seemed clear enough, between the wavering lines. For no process of reshaping genes could turn a human geneticist into a god. Whatever the maker's method, it had limitations—the initial weakness of the mutant cells showed that. He thought it unpleasantly significant, too, that the maker was not allowed to control the whole process of growing even the harmless mules.

Trying to read the history of his father's missing friend in those scrawled pages, Dane shivered again, even in the sticky tropic heat. He knew Messenger's ruthless shrewdness, and he recalled his chilly awareness of Nan Sanderson's mutant faculties. Merely human, the maker must have trusted them—his friend and his splendid new creation. He must have been too stunned to save himself, when they joined against him.

Scowling at the memo, Dane tried to puzzle out the circumstances. Perhaps the personal tragedy that drove Kendrew to leave America had broken his vision and his purpose, leaving him the abject tool of the financier. That might help explain the virus of forgetfulness!

He nodded over the pages, in bleak understanding. Pursued even to this far wilderness by some unendurable memory, the maker could have created that virus to wipe out his own unhappiness and so unwittingly surrendered his new science to Messenger and the mutants he had made. If that were true, the guarded mutation lab might be the only world he now knew, and the art of biological engineering all he had cared to remember.

Whatever the truth, the maker must be rescued. The present plight of his captors seemed to prove that they had not yet fully learned his arts. He must be set free before the not-men had extorted knowledge enough to make them forever invincible.

"What's wrong, Fallon?"

Startled by that loud voice, he turned to find Van Doon behind him in the doorway.

"Sick?" the brown man boomed. "Or why aren't you busy?"

"Nan just brought this." He showed the memo, and tried to recover his lost calm. "Instructions, for me to read."

"Miss Sanderson, to you." Van Doon seemed curiously curt, for a lotus-eater. "And you had better get to work."

He went to work. All that breathless day and half the stifling night, he toiled with his crew to prepare the vats for those mutant cells. His mind was busier—turning over shadowy surmises and unsure conclusions, trying to imagine the maker's present situation and to plan a rescue.

Charles Kendrew would be an old man by now, he reminded himself, perhaps as feeble as Messenger. The halt in the creation of new mules, two years ago, could have come from infirmity instead of rebellion. Whatever had happened, Nan Sanderson was evidently learning the art of mutation now, with the maker her tutor.

In that circumstance Dane thought he saw a stern time limit. With her superior intelligence and her possible mind-reading ability, the mutant girl would surely soon learn the science that had shaped her. When she did, the not-men might have no further reason to keep their creator alive.

Too much haste, however, could be as fatal as delay. Pursued by his dread of the absent slip of the tongue or the unthinking gesture that might unmask him instantly, he strove for the tireless patience of the true slaves of oblivion, while he scoured vats and pipes and tested valves and pumps, and smiled at the pitiless heat.

The production unit was air-conditioned—but not, he found, for human comfort. The sterile, humid, super-heated atmosphere required by the growing mules was even more distressing than the fitful breath of the dying monsoon outside. By midnight, when at last the vats were ready to receive those strange seeds, he was limp and reeling with fatigue.

But the broken prisoner in that low fortress across the road had become real and pitiable in his mind by now; he could smell the dungeon odor and see the festered sores the chains had worn and hear the stubborn moans of torture. Despite his exhaustion, the maker couldn't wait.

He picked one man from his cheerful crew to watch the instruments inside that steamy incubator, and posted another on guard inside the airlock that kept out contaminated breezes. The others he sent back to their quarters in the river village.

"Stand by," he told the guard. "I'm going to catch a nap in the stock-room. Call me if anything comes from the mutation lab."

The dark stockroom, outside the airlock, seemed incredibly cool and dry and comfortable. Lying on a cot, he heard the truck depart. The blowers of the air system droned softly, and rain hissed ceaselessly on the sheet metal roof. Occasional faint strange cries came from some jungle bird, and he could hear the muted steady thudding of the diesel plant down by the town.

Those quiet sounds encouraged him. After a long half-hour of listening, he rolled silently off the cot, selected a pair of wire-cutting pliers from the tool-bins beside the door, and walked cautiously back into the dim hallway.

He glanced toward the airlock. The man on guard inside stood where he had left him, stolidly faithful, safely out of view but casting a broad, patient shadow through the glass door.

Silently, yet trying not to seem furtive, he let himself out of the building into the rain. Pouring straight down from a windless black sky, drumming on the metal roof, it fell with a surprising cold force that took his breath and made his teeth chatter for a moment.

Lights on four tall steel masts flooded the fenced laboratory beyond the road, silhouetting the two motionless riflemen at the gate. He retreated from them quickly, into the long black shadow of the production building, which reached back to the straggling fringe of tall grass that edged the plateau.

That screened his path to a point on the other side of the clearing, where he was shielded from the guards by the low bulk of the mutation lab itself. He caught his breath there, and ran crouching out to the barbed wire.

For a moment, sprawled cautiously flat in the rain-beaten mud and reaching for the wire-cutters, he felt almost victorious. In his mind, he was already past the fence and the concrete walls ahead, inside the maker's prison.

He could see no lights within that windowless building, but the jeep parked outside assured him that Nan Sanderson and Messenger were still there, and his hot imagination saw them busy wringing the secret of creation from the man they had betrayed.

Creeping forward to cut the wire, he weighed the heavy pliers thoughtfully. Not much of a weapon—but he hoped to come silently upon those two; he must learn all he could before he struck. Messenger was a feeble old man. Nan, for all her unknown gifts, was still a girl. With a reasonable run of luck—

Alarm struck him.

The shock of it came when he touched the barbed wire, so abrupt that he thought for an instant that he had been hit by high voltage current. He recoiled, gasping for breath. The taste of danger bit his tongue again, and the sweetish jungle smell of wet decay was drowned under bitter deadliness. He lay still in the cold muck, too stunned to move. But the wires were not insulated to carry current: that shock had been something else. It had lighted a dark blaze of jeopardy all around the building ahead, and it had chilled the rain on his back with the icy finality of death.

Was it Nan Sanderson's mind? He felt suddenly sure it was—and panic shook him. If he could feel the unknown power of her mutant brain, reaching out to guard the laboratory, she could doubtless sense his presence too. Once she found him here at the fence she wouldn't need to read his thoughts to learn that he was no true lotus-eater. A word to those riflemen would send him back into oblivion, to stay.

He crushed out that panic, and reached for the wire again. He was only guessing, after all, that her mind caused those danger-sensations. He might be wrong. Or even if she had perceived him, she wasn't omnipotent. His pliers touched the fence—and that shock struck again.

It stopped his breath and numbed his arm, so that he dropped the tool. It blinded him, with a wild flare of peril like a great sudden light. It closed his throat with the bitter dustiness of death.

As soon as he could move, he started crawling away. For he had failed—and thrown his life away for nothing, if this venture were discovered. Whatever the nature of that barrier, it was impregnable. Halfway back to the jungle fringe, he tried to rise and run. As he came to his knees, however, that danger-shock struck again. It flattened him back to the mud and pinned him down there, shivering and breathless under the driving rain.

Nan Sanderson had really found him, he thought then. He thought she was holding him for the guards—the way she had held little Venn, no doubt, while she struck with the bolo. There was nothing he could do about it, except lie waiting for a bullet or a knife.

But no one came out to kill him. Once he heard a door open and presently close again at the laboratory, but that was all. After a long time that dreadful dark illumination began to fade behind him, and that icy pressure on him slowly relaxed. The danger was passing.

That was the way he felt, and he began to wonder again if those sensations could really be what they seemed: an actual awareness of danger. He recalled his mother's belief that she was psychic, and her seeming foreknowledge of her own death. Had he inherited that uncomfortable trait?

He wanted to reject the notion. He had always doubted the reality of such supernormal experiences. Though his mother had died as she expected, he thought the expectation itself had killed her. Certainly no tests—not even Nan Sanderson's—had ever showed any psychophysical capacities in himself.

Searching for a more acceptable explanation, he turned to that virus encephalitis. Evidently that synthetic disease did more than merely erase the memories of its victims: the industrious obedience of all these men who had come to rob or break the corporation showed that it changed personalities. He wondered suddenly if it also sharpened the senses.

The virus was designed to convert the enemies of the notmen into useful tools of the company. Lowered thresholds of sensation might make the slaves more efficiently alert. It was barely possible that he had been already infected at the time he first felt that danger-sense—for all he knew, a droplet of the virus might have been left for him somewhere, perhaps on the glass in his hotel room.

But the idea seemed unlikely. He shook his head slightly—and even that tiny movement renewed the crushing pressure of danger. The shock and flash and reek of menace were things too violently real and terribly near to be easily rationalized into anything else. Impatiently, he pushed the notion of virus-sharpened senses out of his mind.

For that weight of cold hostility was lifting. Experimentally, he raised his head. This time nothing forced him down. He crawled on again, toward the ragged curtain of grass, and nothing stopped him. Still shivering from something colder than the rain, he started back to his post in the production section.

Reflected light from the clearing showed his path dimly, and even that fading glow of danger seemed to help him find the way. Once the dark shine of it picked out a fallen log that would have tripped him, and again the faint feel of peril checked him at the brink of a dark gully he had not seen. Whatever their cause, those sensations seemed more and more a useful gift of his own.

He knelt once in a shallow rain-torrent to wash most of the clinging mud from his hands and knees and shoes. And he hurried on again, hoping now to get back unseen to his cot in the stockroom. He had almost reached the production lab, running silently up the black shadow behind it, when that feel of menace challenged him again.

Pausing to listen, he heard a door slam. Feet splashed in the rain-puddles. A starter growled, and a motor coughed, and gears clashed. He swung to run for the jungle, but the cold touch of danger froze him where he stood. The sweeping headlamps found him.

He was grateful then for the warning that had restrained his impulse to run, for he couldn't have reached any cover in time. The slightest false movement could destroy him now. He could only stride on toward the blinding lights, trying not to scowl too painfully, striving to recover his thin mask of forgetfulness.

"Well, Fallon." The loud voice of Van Doon halted him. "Where've you been?"

"Walking." He tried to shrug. "Just up the road."

"Walking—in this rain?" Van Doon's voice seemed too brittle with anger for a lotus-eater's. "Why?"

"It's hot inside." He tried to seem merely tired and annoyed. "And we've got the vats ready. Just standing by. I tried to get a nap, but I couldn't sleep. I thought the rain would cool me off."

He came on as if to pass the jeep.

"Stay where I can see you," Van Doon rapped. "Tell me exactly where you went."

"Just up the road. Out past the old Potter house to the edge of the jungle." He let himself shiver. "Maybe I went too far; I'm cold now."

"Weren't you trying to spy on the mutation lab?"

"What makes you think that?" He let resentment tinge his tone. "Mr. Messenger told me it's taboo."

"Sorry, Fallon." A surprising mildness softened that bleak voice. "You see, I woke up half an hour ago, feeling that something was wrong. When I called from town, the men found you gone. I was naturally upset, don't you see?"

Squinting against the headlamps, Dane quivered to a stab of suspicion. Real lotus-eaters were unlikely to be awakened by worry, it occurred to him. And this sudden conciliatory calm was overdone—as if Van Doon were another pretender, reminding himself to act like a slave of the virus. Too serenely, he was asking now:

"Do you know the reason for that taboo?"

"To protect the secret of mutation—"

"To save our lives," Van Doon said softly. "That fenced area has been infected, you see, with a hundred kinds of deadly mutant organisms. Mr. Potter immunized Miss Sanderson and Mr. Messenger against them, but no intruder could get back outside that fence alive. Do you see why I was so upset about you?"

That was probably a lie, Dane thought, invented to keep people away from the mutation lab.

"Thanks," he said. "I'll stay away."

Trying not to frown, he stood wondering about Van

Doon. The man had seemed a little too vigorous and stern from the first, it seemed to him now, and too possessive about Nan Sanderson—he stiffened in the light, and tried not to stare too narrowly.

He had expected to find other members of the new race cornered here. Not many; Gellian's map of the maker's trail had shown intervals of weeks or months between mutations, and he thought most of Kendrew's first creations must have been flawed beings, too imperfect to discover they weren't human.

But Nan Sanderson must have taken those brilliant children somewhere, when she rescued them from the Gellian Agency. And, among all the maker's early efforts, others besides Nan must have been successful enough to see what they were and to escape Gellian's hunters. With the Sanderson Service, she had probably been able to find and gather at least a few of them.

Trying hard to hold his composure, Dane shuddered in the glare of the headlamps. Van Doon's tireless competence and carefully veiled alertness seemed more than human to him now. If Nan were the golden Eve of the variant race, Van Doon must be a dark Adam!

Hiding in his guise of forgetfulness, he must have been the keeper of this jungle fortress, and the maker's jailer, while Nan and Messenger were away. He was fighting beside them now, it seemed clear to Dane, in jealous defense of his mate and his race.

"Sorry, Fallon." His voice was far too friendly now. "I hope you understand—and please be careful, for your own sake. Now I think you had better get some rest, to be ready when you're needed."

The jeep lurched away at last, and Dane stumbled heavily back into the production lab. He was chilled, and his knees felt weak, and failure lay heavy on him. Mutant or not, Van Doon was unlikely to let him make another attempt to reach the mutation lab. The maker seemed remote from him as a man already dead.

NINETEEN

The lotus-eater guarding the airlock met Belfast with a look of reproof. "Please don't go out alone, Dr. Fallon." His brown calm seemed disturbed. "We thought you were asleep, until Mr. Van Doon called. Are you all right?"

"Of course I'm all right." Dane tried to match his even tone. "Just walking, because I couldn't sleep."

"We aren't permitted to go about alone, here near the lab," the guard said. "We're to look out for each other, because of the danger of mutant infection. Mr. Van Doon's orders."

"I see." Dane nodded stiffly. "Thanks."

Back on his cot in the stockroom, he lay sleepless for a long time, trying to devise some way to reach the maker. He needed John Gellian, but the New York office of that zealous enemy of the mutants was precisely as inaccessible as Kendrew's prison, just across the muddy road. Now that all the company exports had ceased, he saw no chance even to smuggle out a message.

A dark mood of hopeless desperation came to crush all his efforts to frame some plan of action. Exhausted and afraid, his mind saw mankind already doomed, as surely as the last shambling sub-men had been when Homo sapiens evolved. Those last slow ape-men must have been as helplessly bewildered before human intelligence, he reflected bitterly, as he was now before the unknown faculties of the new race.

He fell at last into vague dreams of dreadful Armageddons in which all the armies of mankind were stunned and destroyed by something unseen, while Nan Sanderson and Vic Van Doon strolled untroubled among the scattered human dead, bathed in a dark and dreadful fire.

"Please, Dr. Fallon." The air-lock attendant was shaking him apologetically. "Miss Sanderson just telephoned, and they're nearly ready with the germ cells. We're to stand by."

The men on his day shift had come back in the truck, bringing his breakfast in a cardboard box from the Cadmus House. With the diligence of a true servant of the company, he set them to cleaning the growing tanks outside before he paused to eat. He was waiting at the door when Nan Sanderson and Messenger came across from the mutation lab, where they must have been all night.

The financier waved feebly from the jeep as the girl parked it, as if too exhausted or ill to get out. His blotched puffy face looked almost cadaverous, and his breath was a shallow, noisy gasping. Dane couldn't help feeling faintly sorry for him.

"Ready, Don?" Nan came wading through pools of yellow water, gingerly carrying a vacuum bottle. Fatigue had hollowed her tawny cheeks, but her eyes had a burning expectation. He looked quickly away from the glints of rain on her reddish hair, afraid even of her loveliness.

"We're ready."

She put on a surgical mask and sterile gloves and boots and gown, and came with him through the airlock into the main room. Frowning against the painful bluish glare of the germicidal lamps, she carefully opened the vacuum bottle to remove a stoppered, gauze-wrapped test tube.

"The next crop of mules." She handed Dane the test tube, half full of a greenish liquid. "Steady. You're holding the company's future—and your own."

He poured the liquid carefully into the solution ready in the first vat, and methodically set down the time and temperature. She stood watching silently, her eyes dark and anxious above the white mask. A fear that she might read his thoughts made him ask:

"Can't we make another batch, if anything goes wrong?"

"We've no time." She shook her head uneasily. "Vic just telephoned."

He waited, afraid to think anything.

"Vic had been talking with New York," she said. "Bad news. Somebody found out that Mr. Messenger had left the States. Rumors that the company was in trouble started a foolish panic on the stock exchanges. Our directors managed to stop the wave of selling, but now *they're* scared."

"Our own directors—" He reminded himself to show no knowledge of Wall Street. "Won't they help?"

"They did form a pool—three of the original investors. They bought enough of our shares and securities to stop the break, but now they're afraid to hold them. Vic says they're coming out here in a chartered plane, to see what's wrong."

He nodded carefully, waiting.

"They weren't to do that." Anxiety quivered in her muffled voice. "Mr. Messenger never allowed any outsiders here. It wasn't hard to keep people out, so long as we were making billions. But these three bankers will be flying in here tomorrow morning. They'll want to see something more than mud holes and dead mules."

The first eight minutes had gone. He opened a valve and started a pump to lift the solution into the larger second vat. Watching his deliberate care, the girl smiled approvingly.

"Now I must go see about Mr. Messenger," she said. "Last night was almost too much for him." Above the mask, her blue eyes were luminous with an appealing trust which made Belfast almost wish his memory had not come back. "Take good care of the mules!"

"I will," he promised.

Curiously, he really wanted to. Notwithstanding all the ugly evidence against these two, he couldn't help an unwilling admiration for Messenger's shrewdly stubborn courage, nor could he entirely deny his liking for this lovely, lonely enemy of men.

Letting the girl out through the airlock, he found himself trembling. She had left the future of Cadmus in his hands. The act of sabotage would be quite simple. He could kill the young swimmers by simply turning off a light for two or three minutes.

Yet that was impossible.

He had accomplished too little. And any attempt at sabotage would destroy his chance to reach the maker or to learn the aims and numbers of the mutants. He saw instantly that he must do his best to grow the mules.

His reluctant admiration for Messenger and his pity for the troubled girl had nothing to do with that sound decision. So he told himself; yet a dull mistrust of his own motives kept nagging at him until he began to feel that Nan's strange charm could serve as insidiously as that virus to turn her victims against mankind.

Haunted by that dark uncertainty of himself, he spent all day sweltering inside that humid incubator, faithfully reading dials and keeping records and turning valves to move the greenish spawn from each vat to the next, on schedule. The others on his crew were at work outside, filling the outdoor tanks.

Late that afternoon, while he was pumping the still-invisible swimmers into the last indoor vat, he heard a knock at the sealed glass door at the rear of the building, and turned to see Nan Sanderson and Messenger outside. Touching his mask, he shook his head and signaled for them to come around to the airlock.

The girl beckoned him closer.

"You can let us in," she called through the heavy glass. "No contamination should hurt the swimmers now. They're ready for the tanks outside, and those aren't sterile, anyway."

Grasping for the patient obedience of a lotus-eater, he unsealed the door. Rest had erased the girl's fatigue, and the financier seemed himself again, carrying his flabby bulk with that old, surprising poise.

He asked anxiously, "How are they growing, Fallon?"

"I've followed that memo," Dane said. "That's all I know."

Bending laboriously to study the pale green solution beneath the blazing lamps, Messenger nodded with a massive approval.

"The color's all right." He gestured at a low-power microscope on a little bench beside the vat. "Let's see a sample."

Dane dipped a little of the solution into a Petri dish, and placed it below the lenses. The mutant creatures were instantly visible: tiny graceful fish-like shapes, swimming with swift undulations of those filmy membranes which would be modified into wing-like organs for photosynthesis in the grown mules. Fascinated, he kept looking until Messenger nudged him anxiously.

"Good!" the fat man whispered. "Potter's were just like that."

He gave his place to Nan, who smiled with such eagerness that Dane almost shared her joy. "They seem sound," she agreed. "They ought to be leaping soon."

The swimmers had now come to the stage when their own

instincts should begin drive to them on from each vessel to the next. Dane unsealed the slit that would let them leap into the tank outside, while the girl was counting the individuals in the sample.

Messenger glanced at the figures she was setting down.

"Eighty-nine?" Triumph lit his yellow face. "The way Potter used to figure, that means nearly five billion in the batch! Enough to turn all the island back into a garden. And start the dollars and pounds and francs and marks and pesos and rubles to rolling in again!"

"They can save Cadmus," Nan said. "And more."

What else they could save, she didn't say. But Dane dared a glance at her as she stood watching the thin blade of stainless steel the tiny swimmers must jump. He could see her hope like a bright flame along it, and the darkness of her loneliness and her dread all around it, and he understood.

Cadmus was the fortress of her race. The mules had built it, and it had been falling into ruin since as they died. This new generation of those small slaves could make it powerful again—and Dane found it hard not to share her eagerness.

"They'll make a green mist over the blade," Messenger was whispering. "The billions of them crossing. I've seen it many times."

Dane adjusted the shining barrier to stand precisely at the level of the liquid. He snapped on the blue light above it, to trigger that phototrophic instinct, and raised the metal hood outside to protect the tiny swimmers as they fell into the tank.

And they waited.

The strain turned Nan's face ivory-pale and gaunt again. It shortened the fat man's shallow breath, and spread a yellow cast across his mottled, swollen flesh. And it drew Dane taut, so that he started more violently than any victim of oblivion should when Van Doon brushed against him, coming silently to stand beside the girl.

They waited, and saw no swimmers leaping.

Dane was afraid to look at the illness creeping over Messenger. He tried not to see the girl's haggardness, or her quiet glance of gratitude when Van Doon's hard brown hand touched her shoulder with a small caress of intimate assurance.

No swimmers leapt, and after a long time Dane saw tiny bubbles beginning to rise through the liquid, leaving an oily, green scum where they burst. He leaned to look closer, and caught a faint but sickening stench. Pointing at that foul broth, he turned inquiringly to Messenger.

"Rotting . . ." The financier's lax blue lips framed word silently, and his puffy face sagged into a dreadful cadaverous emptiness. "Rotting alive . . ."

He staggered. The spots on his face turned a darker purple. He began coughing and gasping and rattling in his throat, fighting for air. But he shook off Dane and Van Doon when they tried to help him.

"Don't mind me." He swayed to the microscope bench and lowered his cumbrous bulk to the stool there, clinging to the bench with his swollen hands as frantically as he clutched life itself. "Still tough—as a mule!" His face twisted queerly, trying to grin. "Just find out—what's wrong."

White-lipped, Nan turned back to the evil-smelling vat, but Van Doon swung upon Dane in a savage ferocity.

"I'm going to kill you, Fallon, if you're to blame for this!"

"Wait," Messenger panted feebly. "Let's wait and see."

Dane turned carefully to watch the pale girl. He tried not to think of anything else, while she read the temperature of the vat and checked the intensity of the light above it and tested the green solution. Her trembling hands spilled one sample, and all he felt at last was pity for her quiet desperation.

"There's nothing wrong with the solution." Her bloodless hand pushed the rack of test tubes slowly from her. "Except that the swimmers are dying in it."

Messenger had leaned to study the specimen in the Petri dish, and now he straightened heavily. "These too," he said. "Rotting—while they swim."

"His doing?" Van Doon glared at Dane, with an animosity strange in a lotus-eater. "If he sabotaged them—"

"It's our fault, Vic," the girl broke in. "Another imperfection mutation. The developing swimmers should become immune to the organisms of decay before they reach this stage. These didn't—and they were destroyed by the first contamination."

She turned gravely to Dane.

"This is a terrible blow to the company, Dr. Fallon. But you aren't responsible, in any way. Please forgive Vic. He's naturally upset."

"That's all right," Dane muttered uncomfortably.

"Drain off that slop," Messenger rasped at him. "Sterilize the vats, and stand by." He swung ponderously from Dane to Van Doon and the girl. "Because we're going to try again tonight."

"What's the use?" Nan said bitterly. "Those bankers will be here by daylight. Even if the next lot lives, we won't have anything ready to show—"

"I'll take care of them." Messenger's breath was coming back, and contempt edged his returning voice. "Ryling and Zwiedeineck and Jones—I'll sell them a spoonful of some green scum, whether the next lot lives or rots!" He clutched the bench again, to drag himself upright. "I've been bluffing those old buzzards ever since Potter died. I can do it again."

Declining any aid, he lumbered heavily away. Every labored breath and footstep seemed such a triumph of purpose over time and dissolution that Dane stood looking after him with an unwilling awed respect, in spite of all his frauds.

TWENTY

Dane was waiting in the hot still of dawn when Messenger and Nan Sanderson emerged again from the guarded mutation laboratory. He went out to meet them, as she parked the jeep.

"We're standing by," he said. "Everything sterile again—"

Her tawny shoulders rose and fell, in a tired little gesture of empty defeat. "Vic mutated another cell," she said. "It seemed all right, at first. It lived—but it failed to multiply. Worthless. Now we've nothing at all to show those bankers."

"But we'll bluff 'em, anyhow!" A sallow color of fatigue lay over Messenger's sagging jowls. He looked too feeble to help himself out of the jeep, yet his shallow voice had an undertone of invincible confidence. "Right, Dr. Fallon?"

"Right," Dane said, striving hard for a lotus-eater's calm.

"Here they are." Messenger turned laboriously to point, and Dane saw three jeeps bouncing up the muddy road from the river. "Van Doon called an hour ago to say they were landing. I told him to leave their luggage at the Cadmus House, and bring them right on up."

He lurched feebly forward in the seat.

"So get me out to meet the greedy fools! I've made them billions enough. You might think they'd be content without flocking in to pick our bones, now we're down. What they need is a shot of lotus-juice." He gave the girl a spotted grin. "Got your jet-needle handy?"

"We can't do that!" The girl caught his puffy arm, to help Dane lift him out of the seat. "Cadmus is already getting bad publicity, and we couldn't get away with such important men. The uproar—"

"Don't you worry!" Messenger chuckled. Every breath seemed to cost him a great effort. He was clutching at the jeep for support, yet he balanced his bloated bulk with an air of invincible audacity. "These titans of finance are fellow-thieves of mine, and I can talk their lingo."

The three jeeps jolted to a stop, and the bankers climbed gingerly down into the red mud, followed by the attorneys and accountants and engineers they had brought to support them against the aged invalid who faced them now with an expression of bland inquiry.

"Hello, gentlemen," Messenger said. "So you had to see New Guinea?"

The newcomers had gathered into a silent huddle, as if for defense. They looked uncertainly at Messenger, and apprehensively at the fringes of jungle around them, and defiantly back at the fat man. Three of them came uneasily forward at last, squeamishly skirting the deeper mud, to shake his flabby hand. His shrewd eyes blinked, and his lax lips moved as if with a secret amusement. The three retreated.

"I know you didn't want us out here, Messenger." The speaker was plump and florid. He had dressed for the jungle in the shiny boots and gaudy shirt and white sombrero of a dude cowboy, and he looked uncomfortable in them now. "Now I see why."

"Please, Mr. Zwiedeineck," Messenger said mildly. "I know things did run down while I was away, but now I'm back." His small eyes studied the others, with a pale insolence. "Before you start anything, gentlemen, let me remind you that I've made you just about the richest men alive."

"Huh!" That impatient snort came from a gaunt, uncompromising man, still dressed in the same severe dark suit and stiff white shirt he must have worn on Wall Street. "Let's get down to facts, J.D. You know what we want."

"A few more billions, I suppose. But you don't see them here—do you, Mr. Jones? You'll have to wait and let me make them for you."

"I've waited long enough." Jones gestured impatiently with a black notebook. "I've been trying for two years to learn why our exports were slumping. Already I see the reasons—machinery rusting and plantations abandoned and things in general gone to wrack. I think we need new blood out here, J.D."

"You're right," Messenger said. "Green blood. That's what we're trying to manufacture. Want to see our plant?" He swung toward the third banker, a tiny wisp of a man in shorts and white sun helmet, who was shrinking back toward the jeeps. "What's wrong, Mr. Ryling?"

"Maybe you can tell us." Ryling's high voice stuck, and he cleared his throat nervously. "But I don't like this damned island—the heat and diseases and bugs, and the way the jungles are growing back over everything. Or the look of those little green monsters working on the roads!"

"You don't like the mules?" Messenger blinked at him incredulously. "Not even after they've made you hundreds of millions out of that beggarly eighteen thousand you scraped up to put in the company?"

"I don't like your sneers, Mr. Messenger." Ryling's bright, black eyes looked vulturine. "Or your secret, scheming business methods. Or your people out here—those damned flat grins are getting on my nerves. I'm getting out of Cadmus!" He fell back farther toward his own little group of experts. "I'm going to demand the liquidation of the company and division of the assets."

"You're a little late with that idea, Mr. Ryling." Messenger chuckled innocently. "I've already used all our working capital and reserves to pay overhead and dividends—and nearly a billion of borrowed money, besides. The corporation has no physical assets left to liquidate."

Ryling crouched warily back among his supporters. Zwiedeineck lunged forward angrily, forgetting to skirt the mud, and stopped as if injured when it splashed his cowboy boots. Jones was the one who spoke, anger striking a harsh Yankee twang in his voice.

"A shocking admission, Messenger! If that's a fact, how do you intend to keep Cadmus afloat—and your own fat carcass out of jail? Or do you?"

"I do." Messenger beamed benevolently at his wrath. "Bad as things are, I still have two intangible but important assets. One is the enormous extent of our insolvency. The other is a unique bit of technical know-how."

"Insolvency?" Jones glared. "How is that an asset?"

"You can't help yourselves by cutting up a corpse." He paused to blink genially at Ryling and Zwiedeineck. "You'll never make another penny out of Cadmus—none of you—unless you let me bring it back to life."

The gaunt banker turned to stare down at the bend of the Fly, where wild green walls overhung the sullen chocolate water. Perhaps his imagination saw the mosquitoes and leeches and crocodiles there. Dane thought he shivered.

"You think you can beat this jungle?"

"I did it once," Messenger said. "With that bit of know-how."

"So?" Jones watched him distrustfully.

"A process of mutation." His eyes flickered toward that windowless building beyond the barbed wire barrier. "The creative power of a god, almost."

Jones spat skeptically. "Let's see your creator."

"If that process were yours, would you take chances?" Blandly, Messenger shook his head. "But you've seen its products—our exports, and those mules Mr. Ryling doesn't like."

"You've got to show us something."

"If you wish." Messenger nodded at Dane. "Our Dr. Fallon, gentlemen. In charge of the production section. He'll show you how we grow the mutant germ cells into useful mules."

"Fine," said Jones. "But how do you make the mutant cells?"

"You wouldn't be sucking up to me in this stinking mud hole if you knew that." Messenger gave him a spotted grin. "You'd be busy building another private empire, all your own."

"Maybe." The lean man studied the dark river again, where that abandoned dredge lay washed aground. "But then we wouldn't be here, if you were really growing anything. We'd be back in New York clipping our coupons." His suspicious eyes flashed back at Messenger. "Are you having trouble with your 'god'?"

"Yes, we've had trouble." Messenger nodded regretfully. "The original creator, you see, was our old associate, Potter. Potter's dead."

"Dead?" The Yankee voice twanged again, with a nasal concern. "And his process is lost?"

"Only temporarily." Messenger paused to beam at little Ryling's fearful greed. "We've had our technical difficulties, but Dr. Fallon and Miss Sanderson are getting them licked. We'll soon have New Guinea swarming with new mules, gentlemen, and your billions rolling in again."

"You'd better!" The banker watched him avidly. "Where

are you producing these mutations?"

"Yonder." He shrugged toward the fenced laboratory.

"Let's have a look." Jones swung aggressively.

And Dane hoped for an instant that these suspicious men would force their way inside the building.

"You won't want to go in there." Messenger's mild, asthmatic voice shattered his hope. "Not when you know how poor old Potter died."

The banker turned back watchfully. "How?"

"Insane," Messenger said. "A god gone mad!"

"How is that?"

"An insane creator." Messenger's fat shoulders quivered, in a deploring shrug. "Afraid of his own creations. Afraid to share his process, until he lay dying. Afraid of being murdered for it—as men enough had tried to do. I suppose he was trying to defend himself, in his own twisted way. Toward the end he made himself some strange allies."

Messenger glanced at Ryling with a pale-eyed pity that made the tiny man cringe, as if he shrank from the jungle around him and the mud underfoot and even the air he breathed.

Jones asked harshly, "Just what are you driving at?"

"I suppose you know New Guinea's no health resort." Messenger had begun to shudder with exhaustion, Dane could see, yet he still contrived to beam urbanely. "Malaria," he murmured. "Typhus and filariasis. Yaws and leprosy and jungle rot."

The others had all retreated toward the jeeps, leaving Jones alone.

"What do you mean?" His voice was husky. "Potter didn't have—all those diseases?"

"None of them," Messenger said. "He had studied the organisms that cause them, back when his mind was better, and he had made himself immune."

"Then I don't see—"

"Those organisms are all alive."

Messenger paused, swaying where he stood. Dane came quickly to take his arm, but he shook off the offered support. He had to struggle for his breath, but at last he was able to go on, his careful shallow voice barely audible, yet oddly calm.

"They're all alive," he repeated. "Plasmodia. Rickettsiae. Nematode worms. Spirochetes. The microorganisms of leprosy. Malignant fungi. They're alive—and old Potter could shift the genes in anything alive, to make it into what he wanted." Messenger gestured feebly at the fenced laboratory.

"I told you he was crazy." Messenger had to gasp for air again. "Spent his last years locked up there, mutating new diseases. He immunized himself against each one, and then deliberately contaminated the whole area with persistent cysts and spores—his last dreadful gift to the world he feared and hated."

"If that's true," Jones said bleakly, "how can you work there yourself?"

"He had to immunize a few of us," Messenger said smoothly. "People he halfway trusted, so that we could come in to care for him. But he poured all his serums down the drain, before he died." His shrewd eyes swept the gray-faced group. "Now do you want to see the mutation lab?"

Pale now, sweating through the cowboy shirt, Zwiedeineck shook his head. Ryling scrambled back into his jeep, as hastily as if he thought those cysts and spores had spread across the road. Jones stood his ground, however, scowling thoughtfully—and in his opaque, slate-colored eyes, Dane glimpsed the fleeting shape of opportunity. Jones looked like a good poker player.

Doubtfully, he was repeating, "If that's all true—"

Without looking around, Dane was vividly aware of Messenger's shrewd alertness, and Nan Sanderson's deadly perfection. He could feel the veiled desperation beyond Van Doon's bright brown calm. If any of the three caught his gesture—he was glad he had no time to consider what would happen then.

The banker's hard narrowed eyes had moved from Messenger to the girl and Van Doon. They both smiled, and Dane thought the gaunt man shivered. His suspicious glance came on to Dane. Clutching desperately at his fragile mask of calm, Dane shook his head quickly.

The bleak eyes paused, inquiringly. Swiftly, lifting his hand as if to brush away a gnat, Dane let his fingers touch his lips. Nodding as if in abrupt decision, Jones swung back to Messenger.

"I don't want any of those mutant germs and parasites," he said. "But I will inspect Dr. Fallon's department—if there's no danger."

"None at all," Messenger purred. "Only a little discomfort. The place is an incubator, you understand. Pretty warm and humid."

"That's all right." Jones was already sweating through coat and collar and tie, but he shrugged defiantly. "Let's have a look."

For one breathless instant, as he waited for Messenger's assent, Dane hoped for a chance to talk alone with Jones, but then he heard the sick man urging cordially:

"Ryling, Zwiedeineck—won't you go along? No danger at all. Too hot in there for my old heart, but Van Doon and Miss Sanderson will help Dr. Fallon show you through."

Dane stiffened, and tried to walk on steadily, afraid to wonder whether Messenger had seen his signals. Little Ryling refused to leave the jeep, and the girl stayed with Messenger, but Zwiedeineck and Van Doon followed, so close that he had no chance to whisper anything.

The lab was sterile, he explained, and he waited for all the party to put on boots and gowns and masks before he let them into the blue glare of that super-heated room where the shining vats waited for mutant life. He tried unobtrusively to draw Jones ahead, but Van Doon hurried the other banker to keep up with them.

"You tell 'em, Fallon!" He wondered if that was a veiled, sardonic warning. "Tell 'em how it works."

"The original germ cell multiplies by binary fission," he began nervously, already wet and limp with perspiration. "But that happens over in the mutation lab. Miss Sanderson has stopped the fission process, before she brings the cells to me. In this first vat, we start the multicellular growth—"

"I'm interested," Jones kept rasping through the mask. "Tell me all about it."

No chance came, however, until they had come back to the airlock. Zwiedeineck caught Van Doon's arm, pointing at his mask, and Jones beckoned impatiently at Dane.

"Give me a hand with this infernal gag."

Dane was afraid to wonder whether Van Doon had any mutant acuity of hearing.

"Messenger's lying!" He breathed the words into the gaunt man's ear, his own mask covering the movement of his lips. "About Potter—the creator. I don't know anything about those mutant diseases. But the mutation-maker is still alive, locked up in that laboratory!"

He felt Jones stiffen under the gown, and he heard that Yankee twang come back to his nasal voice.

"Hurry, can't you?"

"This twisted strap—" Fumbling at the knot, Dane leaned to breathe again: "Get out while you can! Go to the Gellian

Agency. In New York City, just off Madison Square. Get that?"

Struggling impatiently with the white gown, Jones moved his head slightly.

"Tell John Gellian where the maker is. Tell him the mutant men are using Cadmus for a front. Tell him Nan Sanderson is out here—learning to be another maker! Tell him she isn't alone. And tell him to strike—"

Jones joggled his arm, and he saw Van Doon swinging toward him.

"Trouble, Fallon?"

"No trouble." The words came hoarsely, and he was grateful for the mask still hiding his own face.

"Here, Fallon." Van Doon flung him the robe Zwiedeineck had worn. "Hang this up, and I'll take care of Mr. Jones."

Dane took the robe and turned way. Outside the building, Van Doon hurried the two perspiring bankers back to Messenger, who challenged them:

"Well, gentlemen?"

Jones drew Zwiedeineck aside, to the jeep where Ryling sat. They whispered together, the plump man slapping at insects with his cowboy hat, and Ryling's eyes watching the mutation laboratory with a glitter of frightened cupidity.

Dane tried not to stare at them too anxiously. Mopping at the hot rivulets of sweat crawling down his own taut body, he tried not to listen too breathlessly when Jones came back alone.

"We'll give you three more months, J.D." His tone seemed calm enough, but Dane could hear the Yankee rasp of veiled emotion. "But if you aren't producing in three months, we're unloading. That clear?"

"Clear enough, and fair enough." Messenger grinned painfully. "Shake on it!"

Jones took his hand gingerly, and turned abruptly away. Without a glance at Dane, he strode back to his apprehensive satellites. They all climbed hastily into the jeeps, and Van Doon escorted them down to the Cadmus House.

"Well, Fallon!" Messenger had dropped that mask of bland assurance, as the jeeps lurched out of view between the walls of creepers. He looked shockingly ill, yet his hoarse whisper seemed elated. "What do you think of that?"

Dane gulped uncomfortably. He couldn't even be sure that Jones had heard his cautious whisper, and now a perverse impulse of pity made him almost wish the banker hadn't heard. He didn't quite know what to think, and he was afraid to think anything at all. He felt relieved when Messenger didn't wait for him to answer.

"We're safe!" the sick man gasped. "Three months ought to be all the time we need."

TWENTY-ONE

The bankers' chartered plane took off two hours later. Dane heard its engines, and he came to the door of the production section to watch it rise beyond the river. It wheeled once above the brown bend of the Fly and then turned east. In a few minutes it was gone, and he went back to wait for another batch of mutant cells, wondering whether John Gellian would ever get his message.

Messenger and Nan Sanderson had returned to the mutation laboratory. The brief, hot dusk had fallen before he saw them emerge again, the man so feeble that he had to try three times before he could climb in the jeep, even with her aid. They drove past him toward the old Potter dwelling without stopping, but Nan glanced at him as they passed. She told him, with a tired shake of her head, that they had failed again.

The men on his night shift brought word from Van Doon that he wouldn't be needed until morning, and he went back to the company town with the cheery lotus-eaters of his day crew, trying hard to be one of them. That night, lying in the windy chill of his air-conditioned room in the Cadmus House, he was a long time going to sleep.

A troubled uncertainty came back to dull his hope that Gellian would get his warning. Even now, he didn't want to help exterminate the mutant race—not at least without some fair and open trial. Yet the plight of their betrayed maker still haunted his imagination. He was afraid Gellian would be too ruthless, but whatever the cost, they must reach the prisoner in that guarded laboratory and find out the truth.

"Dr. Fallon! Everybody out!"

He had been asleep at last, when that urgent voice disturbed him. He looked at his watch; it was three in the morning. Somebody began shaking the door of his room, and he got out of bed to open it. The man in the hall was one of the sunburned lotus-eaters he had seen guarding the mutation laboratory.

"What's up?" He felt too dull and heavy with sleep to face any fresh crisis. "Van Doon sent word they wouldn't need me—"

"Everybody out!" the brown man broke in sharply. "Go straight to your post, and stand by for orders."

"To the production section, you mean?"

"If that's your post." The guard shrugged impatiently. "And stand by."

His breath caught. "Is—is anything wrong?"

"An emergency alert." Even the lotus-eater looked somewhat upset. "There must be trouble somewhere, but that's all I know. You had better get moving."

The man went on, to shout at the next door.

Dane dressed, trying sleepily to guess what sort of crisis had come up and what he ought to do. Several men ran past his door, but when he came out into the hall the old building seemed already empty. The muted roar of the air-conditioning system drowned the sounds from outside, but he could see the flicker of swiftly moving headlamps on the thicket of papayas that screened the windows.

Wondering what he must face, he hurried out through the abandoned lobby into the warm tropic night. Outside, he found urgent activity. It wasn't exactly panic—the lotus-eaters were too calm for panic. Yet he caught a sense of frightened desperation.

Jeeps and trucks were jolting along the worn pavement, driven too fast. A bonfire was blazing against the dark two blocks away, in front of the company office building, and he saw hurried men tossing desks and chairs and bundled papers into the flames. From the airstrip across the river, he could hear the muffled thunder of motors being warmed up.

He went back to the parking area behind the building, but the jeep his crew had used was already gone. After a moment of indecision, he started walking out toward the production section, still trying to understand, and to shape some plan.

Was his whispered warning to Jones the cause of this emergency? He considered that possibility, but dropped it. The bankers had been gone only eighteen hours; they were probably still somewhere over the Pacific. Even if they had radioed his message to Gellian, he thought it unlikely that any action could have followed so soon.

Yet the crisis was obviously grave. At the edge of the town, he came to a warehouse burning. Nothing told him whether the fire was accidental or deliberate, but the great pillar of roaring flame rose straight into the still night, unattended.

The drivers of the passing trucks and jeeps had no time to watch or fight it.

He went on by, obeying orders like another lotus-eater. Beyond the end of the pavement, he was plodding through the mud beside the deep-cut ruts when a jeep stopped beside him.

"Where to, Dr. Fallon?"

The calm friendly voice seemed familiar, and he recognized the driver who had brought him from the airstrip, the morning he came in Messenger's plane. He said he was going to the post at the production section.

"Jump in," the driver said. "I'm going out to the old Potter house."

He wiped his feet and climbed in gratefully.

"What's happening?" he asked. "Is the company in trouble?"

"Can't say." The driver shrugged, with a calm acceptance of whatever came. "But everybody's standing by for something. I've got to pick up somebody at the Potter place. That's all I know."

He got out at the production section. The two men on duty there were sitting patiently in the airlock. They had heard nothing of any alarm, and they appeared undisturbed when he told them what he had seen. He inspected the equipment quickly, and went back to the door to wait for something to happen.

Another jeep was already coming back from the direction of the old Potter house. In the floodlights from the mutation laboratory, he recognized Van Doon and Nan Sanderson. Her luggage was piled in the rear. Van Doon was driving, and he stopped the vehicle across the road, at the gate in the laboratory fence.

Dane was standing in the open, outside the door of his

own building, but they gave him no attention. Van Doon called the two guards to the jeep. While he sat talking to them, the girl got out. She was wearing white coveralls. Without a glance at Dane, she ran up the gravel drive and disappeared inside the laboratory.

She was gone perhaps five minutes, Dane thought, though the time seemed longer. After their brief talk with Van Doon, the two riflemen got in the jeep, to sit on the luggage in the back. Waiting at the wheel, Van Doon sat watching the drive impatiently.

Dane was taut with a troubled expectation. The smoky flames of that burning warehouse still flickered above the jungle, subsiding now, and he could see hurrying headlamps on the road across the river. Aircraft engines still thundered dully in the night; he saw the lifting lights of one plane taking off. Nan's luggage, with all those other signs of hurried departure, made him think the mutants must be retreating again, even from this hidden fastness.

He tried for a moment to imagine where they might be going, but that puzzle was swept from his mind by a quick concern for the maker. He had seen men burning papers outside the company office building, but surely that creative brain was a record too precious to be destroyed. He waited with a painful anxiety for Nan to emerge with her prisoner—and he felt sick when he saw her running back alone.

She got into the jeep with Van Doon and the two riflemen. The idling motor roared instantly. The little vehicle skidded back into the muddy ruts, and the red tail lamps fled into the dark with what seemed a guilty haste. Dane turned back toward the now unguarded laboratory, afraid to wonder what her errand there had been.

"What's the matter, Dr. Fallon?"

That quiet voice frightened him. He had already started

impulsively toward the floodlit building across the road, but he turned back awkwardly. He found the knuckles of his clenched hand pressed hard against his teeth, but he tried to relax. He grinned sheepishly at the calm lotus-eater coming out of the airlock behind him.

"I don't know what's wrong." His voice was hoarse and trembling. He swung hastily again to hide his face, and made a sick effort to stop his mind from seeing the beheaded body of Nicholas Venn. He swallowed to wet his dry throat.

"But there's trouble, somewhere," he went on carefully. "I see Mr. Van Doon has taken the guards off the mutation lab. I wonder why?"

"No business of ours." The brown man shrugged. "Anyhow," he added, "it's still well enough defended. Those mutant diseases will kill anybody who goes inside the fence."

Dane wasn't sure of that. Although the virus of forgetfulness was proof enough that the maker could manufacture new diseases, it would have been more difficult to keep wind and rain from spreading such mutant organisms outside the fence.

Even if those deadly cysts and spores were merely a mental hazard, however, there were other barriers to pass. Besides the paralyzing shock that had stopped him at the barbed wire before, there was the single-minded loyalty of these two lotus-eaters with him.

"We're standing by," he told the one who had followed him outside. "I want to keep everything ready for another batch of swimmers. Please go inside and check all the instruments again."

"Right away, Dr. Fallon."

The man turned obediently.

Glancing after him through the glass door, Dane saw him putting on mask and gown, preparing to go inside the sterile room. The other still sat watching through the glass, however, patiently alert to keep him from risking his life across the road.

Dane was still wondering how to escape that cheerful solicitude, when a raucous horn called him back outside. Another jeep was jolting back from the old Potter dwelling. He recognized the driver who had picked him up on the road.

"Here, Fallon!" Messenger spoke faintly from the rear seat. His face looked gray and cadaverous when Dane saw him in the dimness.

"We're closing the production section," he whispered asthmatically. "Send your men out here, and we'll take them to the airstrip. Before you leave, I want you to burn all your papers. That technical memo. All your records on the swimmers you processed. Any notes you've made. Everything! Is that clear?"

"It's clear."

"Then call your men," Messenger said. "I'll send a jeep back for you."

Dane went to the door and asked the lotus-eater in the airlock to call the inside.

"They're coming," he told Messenger. "Is something wrong?"

"Everything." Messenger's voice was husky with despair. "Those bankers double-crossed me, before they ever got back to the States. Radioed orders to sell Cadmus short. Broke the market—and smashed the company!"

"I thought they gave us three more months."

"I thought so." Messenger's voice was sick. "I thought I had those three buzzards under my thumb. But they came unbluffed—I don't know why."

Dane knew, and the knowledge felt uncomfortable in him. Listening to his breathed warning without a facial sign, Jones had played an excellent game of poker. Those few hurried words must have already broken Cadmus. But now, watching Messenger's despair, Dane felt little elation.

"They sold us out," the shallow voice toiled on. "Van Doon got the news, when he called New York tonight. Headlines in all the papers—New Guinea bubble bursts! Rumors and lies. Petitions in involuntary bankruptcy. Charges of grand fraud. But all that isn't the worst."

Dane quit trying to swallow his anxiety, for this news ought to be disturbing, even to a lotus-eater.

"What else?" he whispered.

"We've an enemy," Messenger said. "A man who thinks we've misused the art of mutation. We've stood him off for years. Fought his influence with company money, and captured his agents with the virus, and foxed him the way I used to fox those bankers. His name is Gellian."

"Gellian?" Dane tried to speak as if he had never heard the name. "What can he do?"

"Plenty!" Messenger said bitterly. "He has convinced a good many political and military leaders that we are manufacturing superhuman mutants that are dangerous to mankind. They are sending a military expedition out to destroy us."

Dane waited, while the sick man struggled to breathe.

"The code name for it is Operation Survival," Messenger went on at last. "Men from several nations are taking part. Most of them have been told that they're wiping out an illicit private atomic research center—a lie evidently intended to confuse people who might oppose genocide.

"The strike had been already planned. It seems that Gellian was waiting only for the information those bankers brought back. Van Doon says military aircraft are already headed this way from several Australian and island bases. We're trying to evacuate everybody before they arrive."

Dane wet his lips. "Where—where are we going?"

"You lotus-eaters will be scattered here and there about our other New Guinea installations," Messenger said. "Van Doon has given the orders for that—but the less any of you remember, when Gellian gets hold of you, the better."

He nudged the driver impatiently. "Honk that horn!"

The horn blared again, and the two men came running at last from the building, the one who had been in the sterile section still shedding boots and mask and gown. They got in the jeep, and it shot forward instantly.

"Burn your papers," Messenger called back. "And wait here."

Dane crumpled all the notes and records he had made into a quick little blaze on the concrete floor of the stockroom, but he saved that memo in the writing of Charles Kendrew. If the mutants ever got the just and public trial he wanted them to have, that might be an important bit of evidence. He was about to hide it in a can among the shelved chemicals, when it occurred to him that the building might be burned. He put it in his hip pocket.

In spite of himself, that act of disobedience added to a growing sense of guilt. He couldn't help feeling that his whispered warning to Jones had been a cowardly stab in Nan Sanderson's back. But, whatever the consequences, he had opened a way at last to that building across the road.

Back at the door, he peered cautiously up and down those muddy ruts. The smoky glare of that dying fire still shone above the jungle, and busy traffic still crawled along the road between the airstrip and the town, but he saw no nearer lights. He caught his breath, and ran across the road.

This time nothing stopped him. No shock of danger dazed him. He saw no dark blaze of evil, and met no dusty deadliness, and felt no chill of warning. If any mutant cysts or spores were taking root in his flesh, he was not aware of them.

Surprisingly, Nan Sanderson had left the door unlocked. It opened to his trembling touch. Darkness met him, and empty silence. He wanted to call out, but his throat was suddenly too dry. He groped beside the door, and found a switch. Light struck him, cruel as a blow.

For it showed him no prisoner, but a shocking riddle instead. The whole building was only one long room. Stumbling out to the center of it, he peered around him at the naked concrete walls. He gulped and wet his lips and shook his head.

He saw no bars to hold the aged prisoner of his imagination. No chains; no sign of violence; no arrangements for any sort of long-continued occupancy. It gave him an irrational relief to know that Nan Sanderson had not come back to kill the maker—because obviously there had been nobody here to kill.

The room was queerly bare, neither prison nor fortress nor even laboratory. A white-enameled kitchen table stood near the center of the clean concrete floor, with two kitchen chairs beside it. Arranged on the table were half a dozen empty test tubes in a small wooden rack, a tiny alcohol burner, a few sealed ampules of sterile water, and a stain of green slime drying in a Petri dish—a culture of that alga, perhaps, from which the green mules had been mutated.

That was all. He saw an old army cot where Messenger must have rested, and empty plastic containers in which Nan Sanderson must have brought sandwiches and coffee. Near the table was a little pile of ashes, where papers had been burned—that, he thought, must have been what Nan came back to do.

But he found no equipment for the unknown art of genetic engineering. No sterile incubators. No carboys of chemicals.

No centrifuges or electron microscopes or X-ray machines. He knew a dozen methods of causing useless random mutations, but he saw no apparatus even for those inadequate processes.

"Well, Dane."

He thought he had closed the door, and he hadn't heard it open, but Nan was standing in it when he turned. Framed against the dark, she looked slim but not boyish in the white coveralls. Her tawny face was haggard with trouble. Her level voice seemed disarming, but he thought she had come to kill him.

TWENTY-TWO

Dane had picked up a scrap of fragile ash, from where the papers had been burned on the floor. He was peering at it when she spoke, trying to read the traces of writing. His fingers crushed it with a sudden tension of alarm, but he tried to recover his mask of forgetfulness.

"Mr. Messenger told me to burn all our papers." He grinned feebly, with a sick imitation of a lotus-eater. "I just came across the road to see—"

His voice shuddered to a stop, for he realized then that she had called him Dane. That meant she knew he had his memory back. He retreated a little, absently wiping the black ash from his fingers, watching her with a bleak expectation.

Her ivory hands hung open and empty, but that was not reassuring when he recalled the inconspicuous weapon with which she had knocked him out before. No doubt she was adequately armed, but still she made no threatening gesture, and it struck him that she wasn't ready to kill him, yet.

His presence here was enough to prove him no faithful

slave of the company. It was almost a confession of his warning to Jones. But she would want to know how much he knew and what else he had done, before she erased his memory again—and this time surely his life.

She was asking quietly, "What were you doing here?"

He straightened defiantly. No deception was likely to succeed again, and he said evenly, "I came to look for Charles Kendrew."

Her nostrils flared slightly, as she had caught her breath. Her ivory face tightened, but her long eyes told him nothing. She nodded at the empty room around them, and her low-voiced question was a challenge.

"Did you find him?"

"I—I don't know."

He stiffened, and looked at her searchingly. For that faintly mocking query had set his mind to work at last, on the new fact of this empty room. Although this was not the maker's prison, and obviously had never been, she had brought the mutant cells from here, and that memo—

"I'm not quite sure I found Kendrew." He spoke slowly, watching her pale hostility, waiting to see her reaction. "But I'd like to see a sample of Mr. Messenger's writing."

He thought her eyes narrowed slightly.

"That's impossible." She looked at the crushed black ash on his fingers and the small pile of it on the floor. "I burned all the papers we had here," she said. "And Mr. Messenger himself is already on his plane, waiting to leave. You aren't apt to see him again."

Dane nodded, accepting that hard fact. He would fight when the time came, with anything he found, but he could see no real hope of winning. Trying to make the most of these uncertain moments before she was ready to kill him, he groped again for the implications of this empty laboratory, but her low voice broke in upon his searching thoughts.

"So you think he is Charles Kendrew?" She was frowning at him as if with a troubled astonishment, but still she had revealed no weapon. "Why?"

"I know Kendrew's alive," he said. "Because I recognized his writing on that *Memo to Fallon.* You brought it from this building, and the only man here was Messenger. He's about the right age, when you come to think of it. Though he doesn't resemble the pictures I've seen of Kendrew as a young man, you'd hardly expect him to. Kendrew was disfigured by burns about the time he disappeared—and Messenger's face is scarred!"

She shook her head. "Pretty inadequate evidence."

"There's more than that." Conviction steadied his voice. "A great deal more, when you come to see it. Messenger has always controlled Kendrew's discoveries. He was unexpectedly generous to my father—who had been Kendrew's friend. He is still fighting with all his cunning to defend Kendrew's creations. Isn't he?"

He paused again, watching the girl, but she failed to answer. Her troubled eyes seemed to weigh him, narrowing with doubt. Waiting for her to decide when to erase his inconvenient recollections, he returned to the logical consequences of this empty room—and they startled him.

"Nan!" He caught his breath. "When I accused you of murdering Nicholas Venn—why didn't you deny it?"

"No denial would have made any difference to you then." He saw the flicker of intense wonder in her troubled eyes, but her voice kept strangely calm. "Would it matter now?"

"It would." Disturbed emotion made a kind of roaring in his brain, or it seemed to, so that his own voice was suddenly a faint sound far away. "I felt sure you had killed him, then. Now I'm just as sure you didn't."

If she hadn't murdered Venn, his harried thoughts ran on, she might not kill him. He looked at her eagerly, but her cold aloofness froze his hopeful grin.

"With too little evidence for either conclusion," she said.

"I had reason enough to believe you killed him, then," he said defensively. "You were in his room within a few minutes of his death. You knocked him out with the same sort of shot you used on me—his upper lip had oozed blood where it struck. You robbed him of that dead mule. You took the manuscript he was writing, and my briefcase.

"But now I know you didn't kill him."

"You do?" Her searching, impersonal gaze reminded him that he was only human, and she something more. "How do you know?"

"Because Messenger is Charles Kendrew."

"How does that apply?"

He started to answer and paused uncomfortably before her probing gaze. She had stepped a little toward him out of the black rectangle of the doorway—and he thought from the way she studied him that his words meant less to her than the unconscious reactions of voice and face and gesture that he could not control.

"Messenger didn't murder Venn," she said quietly. "Neither did Charles Kendrew. Neither, in fact, did I. But the question is why you've decided I didn't."

"You aren't human."

The words struck fear in Dane, even as he spoke them. For that was a dreadful accusation. The tone of his own voice brought back the shrill voice of a child from long ago, saying that he wasn't white. He felt that Nan would be wounded and angered, and he couldn't go on.

"I am a mutant." Her voice was brisk and cool. She didn't seem offended, but that wary aloofness veiled whatever she felt. "But we were talking about murder," she said. "And why you changed your mind."

"I knew you were a mutant," Dane said huskily. "Though I suppose Kendrew had good reasons for changing his name and inventing Potter, all his lies had me pretty well convinced that you and Messenger had robbed and probably murdered him. It makes a difference—"

Dane didn't understand quite what took his voice. He was looking at the wistful loneliness on her face. Even in the shapeless white coveralls, she seemed transfigured with a sudden, tragic loveliness. He thought he was only sorry for her, but he had to gulp and catch his breath.

"It makes a difference, when I know that you have been faithful to Kendrew," he went on awkwardly. "It isn't so easy now to accuse you of killing anybody."

"But Nicholas Venn was no friend of Messenger's." She stood watching him with the same remote acuity, as if his pity mattered no more to her than his terror. "He had learned too much, and we had to keep him quiet."

"But you didn't kill him." Even though she didn't seem to care what he said, that fact was now enormously important to him. "Because you didn't need to. That virus you shot into his face would have wiped out all he knew, and made him another loyal employee of the company. Wouldn't it?"

She stood watching him as if looking for something more significant than anything he could say, and it took her a long time to answer.

"Perhaps." Her voice was curiously casual, as if it didn't really matter what he thought about her guilt. "But somebody killed him."

"If you didn't, it must have been Gellian's men." He nodded slowly, accepting that notion. "They must have followed me away from Gellian's office in New York that morning—to run me down in case I decided not to join them." He felt cold inside. "Probably I'm the one who led them to poor little Venn."

"Possibly." She seemed half absent. "But why would they want to kill him?"

"Gellian's business is exterminating mutants—or people he thinks are mutants," Dane said. "It's hard to pick them out, and he's afraid to take chances. If you aren't with him, you're against him. Venn wasn't with him."

"But Venn wasn't a mutant," the girl said. "Even as a human being, he had no gifts great enough to place him in danger. The Sanderson Service was investigating every gifted individual who could possibly be a mutant, but we had nothing in our files on Venn."

"I don't imagine Gellian's men required much evidence," Dane answered. "If they were shadowing me that day, they must have seen me visit your office, and then Messenger's, before I found Venn. I don't know exactly what they knew about you and Messenger at that time, but it was surely enough to make them suspicious of anybody else I called on."

He paused, frowning at her, trying to picture the event.

"Venn must have looked like another mutant in hiding," he said. "If their investigation uncovered any facts about that green mule, they probably thought it was some unsuccessful creation of his own. When they found him unconscious in his room—I suppose they thought he was only asleep—the chance seemed too good to waste." He looked at her keenly. "Doesn't that make sense?"

Somewhat to his surprise, she nodded.

"That's more or less what happened." She spoke offhandedly, her mind still on something else. "Though Gellian's killers had a better reason for thinking Venn was a mutant."

He stared, and tried not to shiver. "You—know what happened?"

"I saw the report of the two operatives who handled the case," she said quietly. "It was lying in a basket on Gellian's desk when I raided the agency, the night we left New York. The one who killed him had been watching from a room across the hall for several days, waiting to see his contacts. The other checked in immediately after the killing, posing as a traveling salesman. They carried the body out in a sample case."

"I saw that salesman—asking for the sample room!" Dane studied the girl again, and a sense of her alien gifts brushed him with cold awe. "I suppose my visit clinched the case against him. But why were they watching him—why did they take him for a mutant?"

Nan didn't answer at once. She had come halfway toward him across the empty room, and now she paused again, surveying him with a critical alertness. She frowned a little, and nodded slightly, as if making up her mind.

"Venn had come back from New Guinea with his memory undamaged," she said at last. "The others who went inland with him lost theirs, from virus encephalitis. Gellian's men believed that Venn had been exposed, too, although in fact he had never reached an infected area. They thought he was immune."

"I don't quite see the connection." Dane shook his head. "You mean they killed him because the virus didn't hit him?"

"You see, we mutants are naturally immune." Her low voice seemed faintly malicious. "In cases where the psi capacity is still dormant, that virus is sometimes the only positive test to tell our kind from men," she added softly. "Too drastic, however, for general use."

Dane started back from her, but something froze him. For a long time he couldn't move or speak or even breathe. The white-walled room seemed to blur and darken and spin around him insanely, so that all he could see clearly was her lean-lined ivory loveliness.

"I—" He couldn't speak, but his dry lips moved silently. "I must be immune!"

The fact was monstrous, but he could not escape. The clues pursued him through the flickering darkness of his mind. All the things he had known before, the signs he had been afraid to see: His mixed blood, like Nan's. His father's old friendship with the maker. His mother's psychic gift. His own danger-sense—was that some hidden psychophysical gift, just beginning to stir in him?

He wanted to deny it all, as desperately as he had wanted long ago to deny the mixture of his race. The same helpless rage came back to shake him; he hated Nan, the way he once had hated that yellow-haired child. But there was nothing he could do. White or dark, human or not, you couldn't change your own genetic heritage.

"You're immune." She was nodding soberly. "You're another mutant."

"It can't be true," he muttered feebly. "You tested me yourself—and you said I didn't pass."

"But I didn't try the virus on you—not that time." She was smiling slightly now, and she seemed less remote. "No other test is definite, in cases like yours where the psi capacity is still latent."

He wet his lips, and shook his head unbelievingly.

"We were designed, you see, to hide among mankind until we are old enough to protect ourselves." She seemed amused at his confusion, yet her faint little smile was not unkind. "That's what makes it so hard to tell you from a man your age. The difference is that the man is grown."

"Aren't—aren't we?"

"Physically, yes. But Mr. Messenger says we're all still children, mentally. He says the gifts he tried to give us have only begun unfolding."

"It's too much to accept, all at once." He stared at her dazedly. "I need time to get adjusted—"

She checked him with troubled gesture. They listened, and he heard the faint beep of a horn outside. He looked at her uneasily.

"I'm afraid you'll have to do your adjusting on the run." She turned quickly toward the door. "And it's time now for us to start, because the first aircraft of Gellian's Operation Survival will be here by dawn."

He followed her out into the night. Now he understood why she had been observing him so critically. She had been testing him again, to decide whether he belonged to her new race and whether he would do to trust. This time he had passed.

TWENTY-THREE

From the laboratory door, Dane saw the jeep waiting under the floodlight at the foot of the gravel drive. Van Doon sat at the wheel, impatiently erect. The horn blared again.

"We should have been gone already." Nan caught his arm to hurry him toward the jeep. "We were already at the airstrip when I had a feeling about you—that I ought to come back. An extrasensory perception, I suppose, though my own psi capacity is still pretty erratic. Anyhow, I made Vic bring me to see about you."

He glanced aside at her uncertainly.

"And now you want me to come with you—where?"

"We've one last refuge," she said. "Another place where we can hide—if we get there before Gellian overtakes us. I can't tell anybody where it is, until we reach it."

An excited expectation took his breath. He wanted desperately to see that secret sanctuary of the mutants—but he had no right to go there.

"We're taking a company plane," she was saying. "The same one we came in from New York. Mr. Messenger's aboard by now, and we ought to take off right away. This time, Vic will be our pilot."

They were almost to the jeep. He caught her arm to stop her, and he lowered his voice, because he didn't want Van Doon to hear.

"Before we start," he said, "there's something I ought to tell you."

"Well?" She paused restively. "We've no time to waste."

"Maybe you know this already." His voice was husky with confused emotion. "But I want to tell you now that I'm to blame for this attack. I sent a message to Gellian, by that banker, Jones."

She drew back quickly, as if shocked, but in a moment she nodded bleakly.

"You're getting fast results!" She gave him a bitter little smile. "But I'm the one to blame." She seemed honestly apologetic. "I should have recognized you sooner. But we've had too many other troubles, and your ESP score was too completely negative, and your first reaction to the virus seemed too human."

She urged him toward the jeep again. "Let's get along."

He hesitated, still half doubtful. "If you still want me—"

"Please, Dane!" She swung back to face him earnestly. "There are only a few of us. We're fighting for our lives—or running for them. If we don't stand together now, Gellian will destroy all Mr. Messenger had tried to do. We need your loyalty, desperately—and we aren't going to blame you for anything you've done. Now, let's go!"

Nodding gratefully, he went on with her to the jeep. Van Doon sat watching him with a wary mistrust. He felt reasonably certain that the sunburned lotus-eater was actually a fellow mutant. He tried to like him now, but a wave of fear and hate overwhelmed his feeble effort to smile.

"Well, Fallon!" Van Doon spoke harshly. "So we trust you alone for fifteen minutes—and you try to rob the company!" He turned sternly to Nan. "How do you want him punished?"

"I don't," she said. "Dr. Fallon was only doing what he thought we wanted. He's coming with us, Vic, in Mr. Messenger's plane."

"Huh?" Van Doon stared at him coldly, and nodded at the rear seat with an evident reluctance. "Then climb in, Fallon."

Dane climbed in. Uncomfortably, he watched the girl swing into the front seat with Van Doon. Hanging on, as the jeep pitched back into the rutted road, he wondered uneasily why she still called him Dr. Fallon.

Had he been wrong in placing Van Doon among the mutants? His mind was still shaken from all he had discovered in the mutation laboratory, but he tried to calm his thoughts enough to reconsider the status of Van Doon. The brown man still seemed a little more alert and emotional than the other lotus-eaters, but that was all he really knew. It wasn't enough to justify any sort of action.

A silent constraint had settled on them in the jeep. Van Doon drove rapidly, with a grim concentration. Nan sat taut and straight beside him, holding to the side of the lurching vehicle. Dane was afraid to ask the questions in his mind, and he sat trying to guess her thoughts.

Suppose the three of them were the only grown mutants left alive? There were the children she had rescued from Gellian—hidden, perhaps, in that secret refuge—but he had seen no evidence of any other adults, here or anywhere. Three would be an awkward number. He wondered if Nan had put off telling Van Doon about him, for fear of jealousy between them.

A fantastic notion, he tried to tell himself. As the last three survivors of the new race, they surely had other enemies enough, without turning on one another. Aiming at perfection, the maker surely hadn't left them capable of fighting like savages over a girl. For all his trying, however, he still couldn't trust Van Doon.

The jungle town looked abandoned as they jolted through it. All the lights were out, and that warehouse had burned to red embers. The airstrip beyond the long bridge was still lighted, however, and the muddy roads around it still crowded with lotus-eaters sitting patiently in their jeeps and trucks, waiting to be evacuated.

Messenger's plane was standing at the end of the strip, with half a dozen other company aircraft drawn up behind it. Cheerful brown men put them quickly aboard. Van Doon hurried forward to the cockpit, and the plane began to move at once.

They found Messenger himself in the lounge, sprawled helplessly back in a chair. Dane peered at him, shaken with a mixture of emotions. Age and sickness and his strange conflict with his fellow men all had left their ugly scars upon him. His eyes were pale and cold in their deep yellow wells of bloated flesh, and he peered up at Dane with an air of sleepy hostility.

Yet he was the maker.

"I went back to look for Dr. Belfast." Nan lowered her

voice as if to be certain Van Doon didn't hear. "I found him in the mutation lab, looking for your handwriting on the ash of the papers I burned. He remembers everything. He's immune—another one of us."

"That's wonderful!" Hitching his gross bulk laboriously forward, he gave Dane his feeble hand. "Your father was my best friend. I was terribly disappointed in New York, when Nan told me you had failed the psi test. It makes me feel better to have you with us now."

"I'll have to get used to all this." Dane smiled uncertainly, and some lingering doubt made him ask, "If you don't mind—may I see a sample of your writing?"

"I don't blame you!" The old man's smile made the shattered bits of his lost charm seem almost whole again. "Find me a piece of paper."

Dane fumbled in his pockets. What he found was the folded *Memo to Fallon.* He gave that to the fat man with his pen, and watched the swollen fingers write painfully:

Charles Kendrew, alias Charles Potter, alias J. D. Messenger.

He unfolded the memo to compare the two specimens, and set them both against the old letters in his memory. They were all the same. The *t*'s in Potter were crossed in Kendrew's way, and the tails of the *g*'s were all alike. He began tearing the memo into fine scraps, and he whispered huskily:

"Thank you—Dr. Kendrew."

"Please call me Messenger," the big man gasped. "A safer name to wear!"

"It must be," Dane agreed feelingly. "So long as men like Gellian are hunting Charles Kendrew."

"More useful, too," the sick man whispered soberly. "Kendrew, with his naïve approach, had failed Homo excellens. Messenger, the financier, with his new personality and his indirect methods, was able to create Cadmus to shelter them."

"So you walked into these jungles as Charles Kendrew, and came out again—"

"But forget all that," Nan put in warningly. "Even when we're alone, we make it a rule to keep up the fiction that Kendrew changed his name to Potter and died there on the Fly."

"You have been pretty consistent with that deception." Dane smiled. "Talking to me about Potter, as if he had been a real person, even when you thought I was another faithful lotus-eater."

"The lotus-eaters must believe the story, because so many of our enemies are always trying to pump them. And we must believe it ourselves, as nearly as we can," she added quietly. "Just one slip could kill us all."

The plane was taking off now, roaring along the strip and jolting unexpectedly into holes the green mules had failed to fill. Messenger clung to the arms of his chair, breathless and pale, as if the jolts had hurt him. Nan moved anxiously to stand by his side until they were aloft, and stooped then to take his pulse.

"Dr. Belfast is trying to blame himself for our troubles," she told him absently. "He says he sent word about us back to Gellian, by our old friend Jones."

Messenger blinked sharply at him and then shrugged with a weary apprehension.

"I'm sorry," Dane muttered. "I wish I had known sooner."

"Never worry about the past." Messenger gave him a feeble smile. "The future's where all our dangers are. Now that you're on our side, I hope you can help us get away from Gellian."

"I'll do what I can," he promised uneasily. "But everything seems too new and strange, and there's still too much I don't know. I'm confused, and nothing seems quite real."

Messenger nodded sympathetically. "What else do you want to know?"

"A great many things," Dane said. "My father told me a little about you long ago, the day my mother died—that was when I decided to be a geneticist. But I don't understand what you've done and why you did it. I wish you'd bring me up to date."

"I'll try," Messenger promised. "If Gellian gives us time."

"More than anything, I want to know about your process." Bewilderment slowed Dane's eager voice. "I was expecting to find that mutation lab filled with some sort of apparatus for genetic engineering—but there was almost nothing."

"That's right." Messenger nodded. "I used to try all the complicated equipment anybody ever did, for causing directed mutations. None of it worked."

"Then how do you do it?" Dane bent toward him breathlessly.

"I don't, any more." Messenger shrugged heavily. "You saw what happened to those mules we tried to make."

"Have you forgotten?" The sick thought struck Dane that Messenger had been accidentally stricken with his own virus of oblivion. "Have you lost the process?"

"Not entirely," Messenger said. "I'll tell you all about it."

Nan shook her head reprovingly, laying down his wrist.

"Not all at once," she said. "We've a hard flight ahead. We'll be climbing high. Even with the plane pressurized, you'll need all your strength."

"I'll make it—"

"I know you're tough as a mule." She smiled at him gently.

"And you may talk to Dane, if you feel like it, while I give Vic the route to fly."

Dane opened the compartment door for her, wondering again about Van Doon. If he was another mutant—and Dane felt curiously sure he was—why hadn't he been trusted with their route before the plane was in the air? No answer to that was apparent, and Dane turned quickly back to Messenger.

"Well?" The fat man peered at him shrewdly. "Where shall we begin?"

"Anywhere," he said. "I've seen a few of the letters you used to write my father, years before I was born. I know something about what you were trying to do then. Now it seems you've done it—but in a peculiar way." He studied Messenger, with an uneasy bewilderment. "I can't quite see the need for all this secrecy and deception, when you were doing something good."

"Neither could I, in the beginning," Messenger said bitterly. "I didn't understand how Homo sapiens would feel about Homo excellens. Madge was the one who began to teach me that—she was my first wife."

Dane saw the pain on Messenger's splotched face, and he remembered the clippings he had found in his father's files, which told how Margaret Kendrew had tried to kill her husband and then destroyed her child and herself.

"I loved her." Messenger's little eyes were blinking, and Dane thought he saw the gleam of tears. "She was the finest sort of woman. A gifted scientist—without her help, I couldn't have perfected the methods of genetic engineering."

Messenger had to pause, gasping as if emotion had taken his shallow breath.

"My father knew her," Dane said. "He liked her. He used to say he couldn't imagine what happened, there in Albuquerque, unless she lost her mind."

"She was sane," Messenger insisted. "As sane at least as most human beings. And we hadn't quarreled—not over any such common difficulty as money or infidelity. The police and the reporters and her suspicious relatives all failed to guess what was wrong.

"She was human—that was all the trouble."

Dane shivered a little. "She didn't like—us?"

Messenger nodded sadly. "There was a time when she used to share my dream of creating a more perfect race. For years, we worked together toward that great goal. Our own little daughter was the first successfully directed human mutation—a more precocious type than such later ones as you and Nan, because I hadn't learned the danger then. Our next child would have been the second.

"Before it was born, however, Madge began to see mutant gifts we had given the older child. She must have been proud at first, with a normal human pride. But then those gifts began to frighten her, when she realized how far they went beyond humanity.

"For a long time she didn't say anything about it, but I began to notice that she looked unhappy and asked her what was on her mind. She told me, and her bitterness astonished me. She wanted to stop the whole effort, and kill the unborn child.

"Of course I couldn't agree to that. I tried to make her see all the good that Homo excellens could bring mankind, and I thought at the time that she did. She said nothing more about it—she must have been already desperate with her fear of the older child. The thing she did was a hideous surprise to me, but she did it because she was human—I see that now."

Dane shook his head uneasily. "It's hard to understand how any sane woman could murder her own child."

"Human beings have a herd instinct," the maker said. "I suppose it was useful for survival once, and it's still a powerful drive—it was stronger in Madge than her mother love." The small eyes peered at him with a sad intentness. "But I imagine you've already felt the pitiless penalty for being different, with your own Asiatic blood."

It struck Dane then that this wheezy old man knew more about his antecedents than anybody else. He wanted to ask again about the process of directed mutation, but suddenly he was afraid to.

"I've met race prejudice," he said awkwardly, "but never anything quite that drastic."

Yet it had been bad enough. That small girl's voice saying he wasn't white still hurt like a knife, even when he thought of it now.

"You've felt the reaction to a very minor difference," Messenger was saying. "If the human beings who slighted and snubbed you had known you weren't human, most of them would have reacted as ruthlessly as Madge did."

"I can't believe it—"

"Because you aren't burdened with that herd instinct," Messenger said. "It is one of the useless vestiges of the beast that I tried to leave out of the making of Homo excellens." A brief burst of energy gave his voice a sudden vigor. "Intolerance has been the root of all my difficulties," he said bleakly. "It is the explanation of everything I've done—and the sad cause of our failure now."

The sick man paused again with that outburst, as if exhausted by the toil of speech. His swollen yellow hands drooped limply over his knees, and his tired eyes closed behind the folds of sagging flesh. Sprawled back in the chair, he seemed for a moment already dead, until he began to heave and shudder again with the labor of drawing one more breath.

His spotted ugliness and his helpless decay stung Dane to ask, with a sudden unbelief, "If you're the maker—if you can really create Homo excellens—why didn't you do something for yourself?"

At first he didn't seem to hear. His eyes stayed closed while he exhaled, with a raucous snoring sound, and strove to inhale again. But at last he stirred slightly in the chair, peering dimly back at Dane.

"Because I couldn't." His voice was faint and slow, and dull with weariness. "All I ever learned how to do was to rebuild the genes in one cell at a time. Each crop of mules grew from a single germ cell. So did you, Dane—from one cell, in which I rearranged the genes after the instant of fertilization, to enlarge your heritage from Homo sapiens."

Dane wanted to know how that was done, and again he felt curiously hesitant about inquiring.

"The rebuilding of just one cell requires hours of exhausting effort—and usually weeks of observation and preparation." Messenger's gross shoulders shrugged feebly. "There are trillions of cells in my body. I never even hoped to remake myself."

Dane could see that Messenger had already talked too long. He felt touched by the predicament of a creator unable to recreate himself. He knew he ought to let the maker rest, yet he was driven on to ask more questions by a new fear that the sick man had lost the art of creation.

"Back there at the lab—" he said huskily. "Did you forget the process?"

"I'm just too old." Messenger had to fight for breath again, but his feeble voice seemed oddly calm when he went on. "Heart bad. Arteries brittle. Cerebral hemorrhage two years ago, caused by a brain tumor—that's what put the skids under Cadmus. The tumor was removed, but I haven't been able to mutate anything since."

"But now you're teaching Nan?"

"She's learning." He smiled feebly. "She knows the theory already. She's not quite mature enough to work it, yet, but someday she can do more than I ever did—if she gets away from Gellian."

"That's going to take some doing!" Nan spoke from the compartment door behind them, and she was pale with strain when Dane turned to see her. "It seems we were a little slow about taking off."

Dane went toward her uneasily. "What's wrong?"

"Operation Survival seems to be moving about two hours ahead of the time-table we had set up for it," she told him. "Vic has been searching with the radar, and he just picked up a flight of aircraft coming from Australia. Maybe a hundred miles behind us."

"Have they discovered us?"

"They surely have," she said. "But all our company planes are up now, scattering. I hope they won't know which one to follow. Vic's trying to slip out of radar range beyond the mountains, and that means we'll be climbing right away."

She swung urgently to Messenger, but he didn't wait her to speak.

"I'm all right," he gasped. "I don't need my pulse counted, and I don't want to go to bed. Dane and I have been having a most enjoyable talk. I was just about to tell him how I made him."

"Later." Her gentle voice was also firm. "Later—if we get away!"

TWENTY-FOUR

Dane helped Messenger out of the chair, and Nan went with him back to his room. Left alone in the lounge, Dane turned apprehensively to the windows. The night was still dark outside, and even the stars were hidden by a high overcast, so that the plane seemed to hang in its own black universe.

Yet he could see the broad wing above the windows, because it was filmed with a dark fire of danger. He had the feeling of peril nearer and more deadly than the threat of those hostile aircraft lost in the night behind—a feeling that puzzled and frightened him.

He turned from the windows, frowning over the riddle of that danger-sense. He felt sure now that it was neither any sinister influence of Nan's nor any effect of the virus of forgetfulness, but instead some useful new capacity of his own.

He wanted to ask the girl about it, but she hadn't come back from Messenger's room. He glanced uneasily around the lounge, as he stood waiting for her, and he saw that eerie glow again. It shone through the compartment door, as if the metal had been transparent to it.

That hueless illumination gave him a sense of the narrow passage beyond the bulkhead. It showed him the empty bunks in the crew's quarters, and the unoccupied galley, and the navigator's vacant desk. It even let him see Van Doon, alone in the cockpit.

Yet it wasn't any sort of vision. There were no shadows upon shadows, as an X-ray would show. For one strange instant, he simply had a grasp of those things in their places. And then the feeling was gone, a thing so fleeting that it seemed almost a trick of his troubled imagination.

It left him curiously sure, however, that Van Doon was alone. Although he had seen no other crewmen when he came aboard, he had supposed they were busy at their places. That instant of perception left him panic-stricken.

He ought to like Van Doon, he tried to tell himself. If they were both mutants, they ought to stand together against their human hunters. Even if Nan were the only woman of their race, they ought to rise above any rivalry for her. He ought to be ashamed of his distrust—and he began to wonder if that sensation has been a product of his own jealousy.

Impulsively, he opened the compartment door. He was trying to hope that the steward would be busy in the galley, and the relief crew asleep, but everything looked just as he had seemed to sense it.

He started through the doorway, and danger struck him like a cold wind. It made a frosty glitter around him in the dark, and it smothered him with a dusty deadliness in the air. For a moment it paralyzed him, and then he stumbled doggedly up the narrow steps to the cockpit.

Van Doon was really alone, a black silhouette against the lighted instruments. Dane paused uneasily behind him. The automatic pilot was flying the plane, but Van Doon looked busy enough. Headphones were clamped against his ears, and he was leaning to adjust something beside the greenish glow of the radar scope. He swung to face Dane, and snapped impatiently:

"What do you want?"

"I can't see anything outside," Dane said apologetically. "But we seem to be in danger. I was wondering how close it is, and what I can do about it."

"You can't do anything." Van Doon spoke curtly, swinging to watch the radar scope again. "You might as well relax."

"That's hard to do," Dane said. "Are their planes after us?"

"They're coming from all directions."

Van Doon nodded toward the greenish pips scattered across the scope, and bent again to do something with the knobs beside it. He said nothing else, and after a moment

Dane returned to the lounge, feeling more deeply agitated than before.

He went to the windows, but all he could see was darkness and the black fire of danger shining on the wing. He sat down to wait for Nan, intending to ask her about that danger-sense, but she didn't come out of Messenger's room. Waiting became intolerable, and he went back to knock hopefully.

Nan opened the door and shook her head reprovingly.

"Please!" Her tone was hushed and urgent. "Don't disturb Mr. Messenger."

"Then may I talk to you?" He lowered his own voice. "I still don't know much about what's going on, but I've a feeling of things gone wrong." He glanced at her sharply. "I don't trust Van Doon."

"Vic's all right." She smiled faintly. "The trouble you feel is real enough, but he'll fly us out of it if anybody can."

"I don't like him," Dane insisted. "And if this feeling is any sort of real perception—"

He stopped when he heard Messenger's struggle for breath beyond the door, and saw that Nan was no longer listening to him.

"You're just upset." She looked back at him, pale with anxiety. "But try not to worry over Vic. After all, he isn't the one who tipped off Jones. Now I must be looking after Mr. Messenger. He wants to talk to you again, as soon as he feels strong enough."

She closed the door, and Dane went unwillingly back to the lounge. Though Nan had not seemed resentful, he felt hurt by her reminder that he had tipped off Jones. He wanted to repair that blunder. Inactivity had become impossible, yet there was nothing he could do.

Pale daylight drew him back to the windows of the lounge. The plane was still climbing through broken clouds. Though the heated and pressurized cabin was still comfortable, he could see thin ice on the leading edge of the wing. He glimpsed dark peaks ahead, and above them a storm.

He waited uneasily for Van Doon to turn the plane, but it droned on toward those angry clouds. He felt the force of gusty winds, and saw a raindrop on the glass, and then gray mist blotted out everything. He turned and sat down, half-expecting the plane to strike some unseen cliff.

But no crash came. The rain soon stopped, and the air turned smooth again. Van Doon's strategy had been good, he admitted reluctantly. The storm cloud would hide them, and perhaps even confuse radar search. Hopeful again, he went back to the windows.

Behind them, the rain cloud towered above the windward slope of the mountains. Below lay a vast ocean of lower clouds, shining under the cold light of the rising sun, washing the peaks and ridges of the foothills that lifted through it like ragged islands.

The plane was descending now. In a few minutes it sank into that sea of clouds, like a diving submarine. Dane sat down again, wondering when they would reach the refuge ahead. For a moment he felt almost safe—until he thought of Van Doon again, and saw the glow of danger still shining from the cockpit.

Nan came back at last from Messenger's room, and he rose anxiously to meet her. Her face looked gaunt with weariness, but she nodded when she saw the question in his eyes.

"You may talk to him now," she said. "But not too long." She hurried on past him, toward the cockpit. "I must see Vic, about our course." Messenger's door was open. He lay in his bed in the narrow room, propped on pillows under his head and shoulders. The mottled color of his bloated body looked alarming to Dane, but his small eyes seemed to have all their old sharpness.

"Come on in," he called feebly. "If you want to know how I made you."

"I do." Dane came quickly to the side of his bed. "And I'm anxious to ask you about something else—a feeling of danger, that I don't understand. A shock, sometimes. Or a glow or an odor or a taste. Can you explain that?"

"ESP," the sick man whispered. "You'll understand it better when you know more about genetic engineering."

Dane's knees felt weak with his eagerness. He sat down heavily in the chair beside the bed. His heart was pounding, and his breath seemed suddenly as short as Messenger's.

"I've been looking for a way to direct mutations, ever since my father first told me about you," he whispered huskily. "I had decided it was impossible, until I began seeing the things you had made. How do you do it?"

"It isn't easy." Messenger's careful voice was so faint that he had to strain to hear, and agonizingly slow. "I worked for years to untangle the structure of the genes with electron microscopes, but they don't reveal enough. I tried every physical agency that causes mutations. Temperature. Pressure. Radiations. Chemicals. Ultrasonic vibration. None of them offered any promise of the fine control you need to move the atoms in one gene and leave the next one unchanged. I was ready to give up, when Madge helped me perfect a finer tool."

"Huh?" Dane blinked. "What other tool is possible?"

The maker's eyes had closed. He lay motionless for a long time, not even breathing. His blotched flesh seemed bloodless. At last, however, he inhaled again, and looked keenly back at Dane.

"The mind," he whispered. "The mind alone—that is the finest tool. Delicate and quick enough to grasp a single gene and rearrange its atoms in any way you like, with no danger of disturbing anything else in the living cell where you must work."

"The mind alone?" Dane stared at him. "What do you mean by that?"

"My wife was psychic, as people used to put it," he explained laboriously. "Like your own mother. Before we married, she had been a research parapsychologist. She saw my problem, and helped me solve it."

"With psychokinesis?"

"Call it that, if you want." Messenger nodded feebly. "That's a word. I don't know quite what it means to you or to anybody else. What Madge and I discovered is a fact. A process that works—though it may not fit the word, exactly."

"Yes?"

Messenger heaved himself a little higher against the pillows. "Madge had worked with Rhine at Duke University," he went on. "She had already got her great idea, though she hadn't done much with it. That was to link mind and time."

"How's that?"

"The mind works in time," Messenger said. "The flow of consciousness shows a time-factor, and nearly every datum of parapsychology points the same way. With that for a start, Madge had come up with a new explanation of the electrical brain waves recorded by the electroencephalograph."

He had to gasp for air, as if exhausted by that word.

"Those waves are rapid pulsations of voltage in the brain tissue," he continued. "Her idea was that the voltage changes are caused by the rhythmic vibration of atoms or electrons in the plane of time."

Dane leaned nearer, not quite sure what he had heard.

"In time—not space." The faint voice was difficult to hear, but Dane had a sense of the vigorous mind behind it, striving robustly to reach him. "You can see that the electrical effect of such a vibrating particle would fall to zero as it swings away in time, and then increase again as it returns.

"Enough such particles, vibrating in unison, would cause the voltage pulsations we find. The duration of one wave, Madge thought, determines the instant that is *now*. Each new wave, she thought, creates a new *now* and carries the consciousness on from the old, leaving it a part of the past."

Messenger stopped to rest again, limp and almost lifeless on his pillows.

"A simple notion," he toiled on at last. "But it seems to explain many things. The simplest living molecules—the viruses and genes—must be built around single particles vibrating in time. And fission must begin when another particle begins vibrating in unison."

"An exciting idea!" Dane whispered breathlessly. "But—if mental energy can affect physical particles—don't you have trouble about the conservation of energy?"

"That energy in time is still physical," Messenger answered. "I've no time to write the equations, but mind is a function of the energy-flow, back and forth, between space and time. The oldest proof of that is the temperature drop that accompanies any massive psychophysical effect—when heat is drawn from the air to become the literal force of mind.

"The same sort of transfer is going on all the time, in every human brain and every living cell, although it's usually harder to detect, because the amount of heat absorbed is exactly balanced, in the long run, by the new heat generated as the vital energy is spent."

Dane nodded, in awed comprehension.

"So you did prove her theory?"

"A little of it—though the vibration in time is far more rapid than she first thought, and the brain waves seem to be due to a sort of ebb and flow between the spatial and temporal states of energy. Most of the theory is still debatable, as useful theories generally are. But it has served us pretty well."

Messenger closed his eyes to rest again, and it seemed a long time to Dane before he resumed:

"That energy of life obeys its own special laws. Its dual nature gives it a limited independence from both space and time. Though it usually comes from the transformation of heat in our own nerve cells, a receptive brain can sometimes draw it from another—that is telepathy.

"Or a trained and gifted mind can absorb it from any sort of objects at nearly any distance—that is the basis of direct extrasensory perception.

"Usually, we spend it to operate our own nervous systems, but it can be spent on distant objects—that's psychokinesis, if you wish to use the word. A difficult trick, for Homo sapiens!"

The maker lay back to rest again, watching Dane with a look of speculation in his faded eyes. He smiled at last wistfully.

"It ought to be easier for you," he whispered. "But it's so hard for us that Madge had given up proving her theory, before I met her. Even after we tackled it together, it took us years to learn how to apply that actual force of mind to a few atoms in one molecule at a time. And that's all we could ever do."

Dane had been listening too desperately to breathe. He straightened when Messenger paused, and they both gasped for air. He nodded slowly.

"So that's the way you made us?"

"It wasn't quite that simple." Messenger gave him a wry little grin. "There's only a brief critical time, you see, when the genes can be rearranged to make a successful human mutation. That is just after the moment of conception, when the fertilized ovum is ready to begin development."

"I can see that." Dane nodded quickly. "With all the millions of different male gametes competing to reach the egg cell, you couldn't know the combination of available genes until one of them has entered it. And soon afterwards, the cleavage of the fertilized cell would form more genes than you could change."

"Exactly," Messenger panted. "The act of mutation must be completed before the cell division begins. But that crucial time is far too short for all the work that must be done to shape such a complex being as you or Nan. It takes days, or even weeks, to chart all the significant genes involved and discover what traits they carry and work out all the changes to be made."

"But you did it." Wonder quickened Dane's low voice. "How?"

"With training, we were able to focus our new perceptions on a living germ cell," the old man whispered laboriously. "That selected cell could remain undisturbed in the mother's body, because we didn't have to be near it in space. And we were able at last to get around that problem of time, when we learned how to look a little way into the future."

"Prevision?" Dane stiffened with astonishment.

"That follows logically enough from the temporal factor we had already found in life and mind," Messenger insisted patiently. "You and Nan should be better at it, when you grow up, but Madge and I could never see more than just one cell, as it would be no longer than a few weeks ahead.

"In that limited time, we had to complete all our studies of the genetic possibilities of the cell we had chosen, and plan the gene-shifts that would remove all the old hereditary faults and replace them with the gifts of the new race. When the crucial instant came, we had to be ready for the few hours of concentrated effort that would make the coming child Homo excellens."

"So you could plan the work ahead?" Dane nodded, frowning. "But you had to wait for the crucial moment, before you did it?"

"Right," Messenger murmured feebly. "We could see that little way into the future, but we could never reach into it, not even to move one atom. Perhaps we had run into some undiscovered natural law."

"Anyhow, there's something I'd like to know." An awed wonder caught Dane's voice, so that it was a moment before he could go on. "What—just what are the new gifts you gave Nan and me, that make us so different?"

"Can't you wait?" The maker grinned. "For your own safety, I made you to seem as much as possible like members of the old race during your early years, but your differences ought to be showing up quite rapidly from now on. Don't you want to be surprised?"

Anxiously, Dane shook his head.

"All right, if you really want to know," Messenger said ponderously. "Physically, you're stronger than man. You're immune to nearly all diseases. You can expect a normal life-span many times as long as man's. And you'll stay youthful and vigorous, with no reason to fear the senile decay that has overtaken me.

"Mentally, the differences are even more significant. The growth of your intelligence was not arrested at the age of ten or twenty, as a man's is; your intellectual development should continue as long as you live. And your psi capacities, just now beginning to unfold, should vastly widen the promise of your lives—how far, I can't even guess."

Dane sat awed and silent while the maker labored to breathe again.

"And there's something else," the sick man went on at last. "Something greater—because most of your other gifts are only its inevitable consequences. That is something you *don't* have—the hereditary mental and physical flaws and handicaps of Homo sapiens. The potentials were already there, hidden in the genes. The most of what I did was just to clear away the barriers that held them in check. Now that the latent genius of the old race is awakened in you, there are no limits on your future—none at all, so far as I can see."

As if exhausted then, he sank back against the pillows. The eager smile faded from his splotched and swollen face, and he lay silent for a time, except for his raucous breathing. Dane sat watching, humbled and amazed by his glimpse of those dawning wonders, until at last the maker's bright eyes opened again.

"I'm sorry." A sharp pity caught Dane's throat. "Sorry you lost your own gift."

"It had served its turn." Messenger shrugged, with a calm acceptance. "Anyhow, it was never so useful as yours will be. The effort used to leave me sick with exhaustion, even when I was younger. The trouble now, since I had that stroke, is just that I can't keep my inadequate faculties in focus long enough to make a perfect mutation."

"But that must have been a wonderful thing," Dane insisted, still grave with his awe. "Reaching out with just your mind to explore and shift the genes to shape a new species! And all, I suppose, without our parents knowing that anything was happening?"

"It had to be that way." The maker's bloated face was suddenly tired and sad. "Madge taught me that, when she turned against me and tried to wreck our great experiment. I'm afraid the old race is too intolerant to accept the new."

Dane nodded bleakly, thinking of Gellian's campaign of

extermination and the military forces of Operation Survival closing in upon them now. He didn't want to fight the mother race, but he could see no promise of any sort of truce. Genetic engineering seemed to be the only hope for those it had created, and he turned his mind back to that.

"How did Nan come to be looking for the mutants, at the Sanderson Service?" he asked abruptly. "Didn't you already know who we were?"

Laboriously, Messenger shook his head.

"Don't forget the difficulties I had to work against, he panted huskily. "After Madge killed herself and our children, if you want to know the truth, I came near giving up altogether."

Dane nodded sympathetically. "You must have been badly broken up."

"I loved her," Messenger gasped. "I was terribly hurt. And bitterly disillusioned, about all our great plans. More than that, her desperate effort to kill me was a warning of what men like Gellian would ultimately do. I was terrified."

He sobbed for his breath.

"I ran away—from America and our work and the memory of her. For the first two or three years, still running away, all I wanted was escape from men and their cruel world. And I found the means to get away, before I ever dared to pause. A new application of genetic engineering. I could have left the Earth. But I didn't."

His head lifted briefly from the pillows, with a stubborn triumph.

"Because, somehow, I had got back my nerve," he said. "I think that achievement was what made me see that my new powers must be paid for, with whatever good I could make them do. I was still a man, whatever happened, and I would always be. I couldn't abandon my own kind, and still keep my self-respect. I decided to go ahead with the creation of Homo excellens, in spite of all the difficulties."

He dropped limply back to rest again.

"Difficulties!" he wheezed again at last. "I met enough of them. Madge had helped very competently with the first mutations, but now I had to learn to do everything alone. I was afraid to trust another human being, afraid to stay long anywhere. In most cases, too, my subjects had to be stranger or only casual acquaintances, which made it harder to determine their traits and chart the genetic linkages involved—it's no accident that you and Nan, my most successful mutations, were the children of old friends."

He lay silent for a time, watching Dane with a quiet approval.

"Too many of the others turned out badly," he resumed again, with a frown of tired regret. "Because I had to work in secret and keep on the move so constantly—I thought you mutants would be safer, scattered as widely as possible. And then there was my own inexperience at 'creation.' "

He smiled faintly, as if the word embarrassed him.

"I had expected failures, from the first," he whispered, almost apologetically. "Even when Madge was helping, the range of our perceptions was always too narrow, and that crucial period too short for all the genes we had to change. Afterwards, when I was forced to work with strangers, I had to guess about too many traits and their linkages. I knew that blunders were inevitable. But I didn't expect the imperfect mutations to be quite so dangerous, and I wasn't prepared to have their twisted gifts turned against me by such men as Gellian."

He had to pause again, panting noisily, but at last he continued: "Because of all those dangers, I nearly always had to move along again, before the mutant children were born. I couldn't follow them up, to help with their care or even to check the results of my work, without too much risk of exposing them. Nan is one of the few I was able to keep with me."

"Because her parents were your friends?" Dane's breath caught, and he leaned forward suddenly. "I wonder—did you know my mother, too?"

"Before your father ever saw her." The old man smiled fondly. "In the Manila hospital where she worked. When I was there for plastic surgery—getting some of Charles Kendrew's scars erased, to smooth the way for J. D. Messenger.

"Nan's father was a mining engineer," he went on. "I met him while I was in the Philippines on that same trip, and hired him to survey the mines I was buying to work with the mules in New Guinea. I brought him back to the States before he had seen too much, and after he married I managed to keep on friendly terms with the family.

"Nan finished college at sixteen, still believing she was just bright human being. I put her to work as my private secretary—my health was already failing by that time; I wanted her near me and needed her help. When I saw her mutant faculties beginning to develop, I told her what she was. A year ago, I helped her set up the Sanderson Service to find and aid the children I had lost.

"She wasn't really ready for such a dangerous task, because her own variant gifts had only begun unfolding. She's still a child—as you are, Dane. Her psi capacity is still erratic, and I was afraid she would only sacrifice herself.

"But I had made too many blunders." The tired maker paused to sigh. "I had frightened Gellian, with too many defective mutations. His exterminators were beginning to find and kill too many good ones. We had to do something—and I had come to the end of my doing.

"I had tried to make the company a fortress for Homo excellens, but it began to crumble the day my stroke stopped me from mutating new mules. I'd tried to keep Gellian from suspecting that I was the maker—I even contributed money to his agency—but he was collecting clues, mapping the mutations, and slowly closing in.

"We had to do something—and Nan did it. She was able to warn and hide a good many precocious children—more of them probably human than mutants; every bright child was in danger. She kept the agency pretty well disorganized, with raids on the office and clues she planted to draw the hunt from those children to her. She earned us another year of time—"

"And I threw it away!" Dane whispered bitterly. "I wish I had known sooner." He frowned at Messenger. "You must have known I was a mutant. I don't understand why you didn't tell me—or why Nan gave me that test I failed to pass."

"But I didn't know," Messenger protested. "I knew only that you might be. I couldn't keep any records, you see, for fear of men like Gellian, and usually I had no way of learning the circumstances of the birth. When the mutant cell failed to develop, the next ovulation was likely to produce a human child. In many cases—in your own—I had no way of knowing which had happened until Nan could run her tests. When you failed, I was forced to assume that you were Homo sapiens. But I had done everything I could for you and your father—without letting him find out that I been Charles Kendrew."

Dane nodded. "I used to wonder why you endowed that laboratory, for a man you had never met!"

"For several reasons." The sick man smiled faintly. "I hoped your father might find some physical way to direct mutation—I could already see that old age was going to take away my own uncertain psi capacity. Even if he failed, I thought his work would help get men used to the idea—and perhaps make them kinder to Homo excellens. Besides, I wanted to be sure you got a good background in biology."

"I wish Nan's tests had been more accurate."

"She wasn't looking just for mutants," Messenger explained. "A good many of those your age turned out wrong—they're the ones that caused all our trouble with Gellian. Her tests were designed to identify perfect specimens of Homo excellens.

"You can see why that's so difficult to do. I planned all of you to be as hard as possible to tell from men until you come of age—to help you hide among them. Before the psi capacity develops, there's no conclusive test except that encephalitis virus—and you somehow managed to counterfeit the human reaction to that, when Nan had to inoculate you."

"I was pretty sick at first," Dane said. "We were halfway out here in the plane before I began to remember anything."

"The effect of a massive injection, I suppose." Messenger nodded. "The ampules in her jet-gun were loaded with the virus a thousand black flies would carry." He paused to breathe heavily. "Anyhow, it's too bad for all of us that your psi capacity was still too much retarded to let you call those cards."

He lifted his head to blink at Dane.

"But you say it is awakening now?"

"I have this feeling of danger—"

Dane caught his breath and stiffened, for that fitful awareness had come back when he thought of it, overwhelmingly intense. Sudden peril burned his tongue like acid, and it hung like some fuming poison in the air. It chilled him like a sudden wind and it throbbed in his brain like a warning gong.

It was a glare of darkness, flaming over everything around him.

"I feel it now!" His breath and voice were gone, leaving his agitated whisper as faint as Messenger's. "I can taste it and smell it and hear it and see it—coming closer every second."

That dreadful illumination was gathering around the man on the bed, like a visible shadow of approaching jeopardy and death. It turned him cold and cadaverous—and Dane felt sick with dread, because he had begun to feel affection for him. Strangely, however, the maker didn't seem to see that monstrous darkness falling on him.

"The awakening of the psi capacity is sudden and uncertain," he was whispering calmly. "Or it was in Nan's case. I suppose it has to use the images of the other senses at first until it can form those of its own. That gives you the illusion that you are feeling or tasting or smelling or hearing things that are really beyond the reach of your physical senses. When you get that danger-sense, you are probably perceiving the consequences of some possible future event—"

Dane wasn't listening any longer. The throb of approaching peril seemed louder to him now than the engines of the plane. He started to turn, nerving himself to face it, but the chill of danger paralyzed him. He felt the room door open, and he saw that dreadful glare strike through it and fall upon the maker.

Van Doon came in.

TWENTY-FIVE

Messenger seemed unaware of any danger from Van Doon. He turned stiffly on his pillows, and his watery eyes blinked hopefully at the man in the doorway.

"Well, Vic?" he whispered anxiously. "How are we doing, with Operation Survival?"

"We're still surviving." The stocky man grinned easily. "I think we've got away from Gellian. Since we crossed the mountains, the radar shows no aircraft behind." He strode closer to the bed. "How are you by now?"

"I'll be all right," Messenger said. "If you can only fly us where I want to go."

"Can do," Van Doon promised cheerfully. "But you'll have to tell me where it is. Nan's in the cockpit now, watching the radar for me—we're on the automatic pilot. She has been telling me what course to fly, but she says she doesn't know our final destination."

The sick man studied him shrewdly.

"I'll tell you when the time comes," Messenger murmured softly. "Until I do, just fly the course Nan gives you. That will bring us in sight of a certain mountain peak. When we get there, I'll come to the cockpit and show you where to land."

"We're wasting gasoline, flying from point to point," Van Doon protested, with an air of slight impatience. "And Nan's afraid for you to do so much, while we're at high altitude. Hadn't you better just tell me where we're going, so you can relax while I fly us in?"

Messenger shook his head weakly—and Dane shivered to another chill of danger. He could feel the veiled violence behind Van Doon's sunburned smile, and his muscles tightened to meet some murderous attack.

"Our destination's too well hidden for that," the maker was whispering. "I'll have to point it out."

"If you say so." Van Doon nodded casually—too casually, it seemed to Dane. "I was just trying to save trouble for you. I'll have Nan call you, when we see that mountain."

He glanced at Dane, too carelessly, and smiled at Messenger too openly, and slowly turned to go. That icy feel of danger went with him. The glare of darkness faded from around the maker, and Dane gulped for air that now was clean enough to breathe again.

"I'm glad you didn't tell him anything," he whispered impulsively. "I don't trust him—even if he is a mutant."

Messenger stiffened against the pillows.

"Vic Van Doon?" His small eyes blinked painfully beneath the folds of swollen flesh. "What makes you think he's a mutant?"

"The way he behaves." Dane frowned uncertainly, groping for his evidence. "He isn't relaxed, like all the men who've really had that synthetic brain fever. He's desperate—and trying to hide his desperation. I first noticed it when I was pretending to be a lotus-eater, the way I think he is."

"So that's all?" Messenger grinned with relief. "You had me frightened."

"I'm still frightened," Dane insisted. "Since you didn't know he's a mutant, I'm afraid he's working against you. Maybe he isn't grateful for being mutated!"

"You're just worn out and upset." Messenger seemed as cheery as Van Doon had been. "Nan used to imagine all sorts of things, when her psi capacity was beginning to awake. Yours will do you more harm than good, until you learn how to use it. Better forget about Van Doon, and try to get some sleep."

Dane wasn't sleepy, and he couldn't forget Van Doon.

"*Could* he be a mutant?" He looked at the maker, searchingly. "Nan ought to know, if she investigated all your efforts at human mutation."

"She trusts him," Messenger said. "As completely as I do."

"But would she *know?*"

Messenger shook his head, with a mild impatience. "There were a good many of the older ones she failed to trace. In all those years, the parents had often moved or died, and her methods of search were limited by the danger of leaving clues for Gellian."

"Then couldn't Van Doon be one of those she didn't find?"

"A bare possibility." Messenger shrugged. "Though she thought Gellian's men had already quietly disposed of the most of them. Probably the others had discovered their danger and disappeared to escape it."

"Van Doon might be one of them." Dane rubbed his chin uncertainly. "How much do you really know about him?"

"His name used to be Vaughn."

" 'Used to be'?"

"We always renamed the lotus-eaters, besides revising their personal history," Messenger explained. "To avoid the risk that the old names might disturb old memories, in cases of shallow amnesia. And to confuse the outsiders who were always trying to pump our people."

"How old is he?"

"About twenty-eight—he's young enough, at that, to be a mutant." The maker spoke faintly and slowly, saving his breath. "I think he was born in the States, and I know he had a good scientific education. He first came to New Guinea four years ago on a secret mission for an American biological warfare research project—a few reports on our special encephalitis had begun to get into the medical journals, and he was sent out to investigate it for possible military use.

"He posed as a mission doctor, on the Sepik River reservation. He treated several natives who had picked up the virus while they were trespassing on our concessions. Apparently he experimented enough to find that the virus is useless for military purposes—I'd had that danger in mind, when I made it. It is carried only by the mutant flies, and their range is limited to areas where we have concessions. Without the flies, the only way to infect anybody is by hypodermic injection.

"He tried to immunize himself, and he thought he had succeeded. Our people managed to keep him on the reservation, and he didn't get the bug—not that time.

"But he came back, a year later. Our people must have let him learn too much on that first trip, because he came back in command of a private military expedition. He had somehow got hold of three light bombers—surplus army aircraft. They were fully armed, and manned with trained commandos—picked boys, as tough as he was, ready to die for the secret of creation.

"He struck our headquarters at Edentown one day at dawn. Shot up the radio transmitter. Bombed out the roads and telephone lines. Strafed the docks and shops and offices. Seized the airstrip. Took the bridge, and then the town. Finally capture the mutation lab."

Messenger grinned feebly.

"A beautiful raid. Soundly planned and brilliantly executed. Vic was a good man, even then—nobody else had ever got quite so far. But it threw him off his stride when he found nothing in the lab. I was away in New York at the time, and nobody at Edentown knew how to mutate anything. He was looking for Charles Potter—who never existed. For all his planning, the black flies got him and all his men.

"They thought they were immune, but Homo sapiens can't be immunized. The black flies avoid lotus-eaters, but all of those pirates must have been stung before they were on the ground an hour. They were all too sick to fly, by the time they gave up and tried to get away. Three were killed, trying to take off in one plane. All the rest recovered, to become useful employees."

Dane sat frowning doubtfully.

"Three years seems a long time for Van Doon to go on pretending," he conceded. "But the secret of mutation would be worth the effort, if he's still fighting for it." He leaned forward urgently. "Can't we leave him somewhere?"

"Not yet," Messenger muttered feebly. "Later, maybe— I'll talk to Nan about it. But we need him, now, to take us in. Human or not, he's a good pilot, and this is going to be a difficult landing."

Dane shook his head. "I wish we didn't have to trust him—"

He paused when he saw Nan at the door, beckoning.

"Please, Dane," she whispered. "Mr. Messenger needs rest."

"But I'm not tired at all." The maker turned stiffly on the pillows to face her. "I'm feeling unusually fine," he gasped faintly. "We've been having a talk." He winked solemnly at Dane. "A very interesting talk, about creation."

"It's over now," she told him. "And you both need sleep."

Reluctantly, Dane went back to the lounge. He glanced at the windows, but they were filmed with rain and all he could see outside was dense cloud driving past the wings. He sat down wearily, because there was nothing else to do. For a time he fought his aching weariness, but at last he must have fallen asleep.

"Well, Dane!" Nan's voice aroused him. "Here we are."

She stood near him in the lounge, looking outside. The strong light from the windows found all the red in her hair, and it made her fine skin a kind of pink, translucent ivory. She looked flushed and lovely with elation.

"We've got away from Gellian," she said. "This is our

refuge, and now I think we're safe from men."

He hurried to her side, and looked out eagerly. The clouds were gone. Far below them, he could see tangled mountains, all covered with the crowded tufts of great trees which made them seem deceptively soft, like a wrinkled rug. Ahead of the plane, above the vivid green of the sunlit forest, a dark wilderness of tumbled boulders lifted to the foot of a sheer basalt precipice. Above the cliffs, a great peak stood far away, shining against the deep-blue sky of this high altitude with the dazzle of new snow.

"That is Mt. Carstensz." She pointed at the white mountain. "In the Snow Range. Mr. Messenger went to the cockpit, when we sighted it. He'll show Vic where to land."

Dane had caught her sense of victory. He stood watching with a breathless expectation, while the plane climbed to fight the gusts of a windy pass above the cliffs, and skimmed low across new fields of equatorial snow, and wheeled down again over naked boulder slides and patches of sparse grass and lower slopes splashed red and yellow and white with rhododendrons. Something made him clutch her hand, when they saw the canyon.

It was a narrow gorge, cut back into the same dark basaltic formation they had seen below the pass. A glacial stream made a white plume of falling water at its head, plunging into a thin blue fleck of lake, and its foot was guarded by an enormous, solitary tree.

"That's it!" Nan pointed into the canyon. "I know it, from what Mr. Messenger has told me about it. It's the hiding place he found, when he first came to New Guinea to get away from men. It's ours, now."

The plane was diving between the cliffs, and he leaned anxiously to watch. He saw vertical rusty streaks washed down from iron deposits, and a wide black vein that shone with the dull luster of pitchblende, and a yellow patch that must be carnotite.

"That rock looks rich with minerals." His voice was hurried, husky with his wonder. "There are even signs of uranium. But I don't see any buildings." Apprehension caught him. "Or anywhere to land!"

"We'll have to ditch the plane." Her low voice echoed his unease. "That will be dangerous—especially for Mr. Messenger." She nodded quickly at a yellow bale, ready at the door. "A rubber life raft. We'll have to launch it the moment we stop, and get him off the plane before it sinks."

They had already flown the length of the canyon. The plane lifted suddenly to clear the waterfall, and wheeled away over the dark cliffs again, as if to make a new approach.

"I don't much like it." Dane swung uneasily, peering back at that gigantic tree at the mouth of the gorge. "We'd have to come in very low, to lose enough speed, and I don't see space to pass that tree."

"Vic can do it!" She smiled confidently. "He's a wonderful pilot."

Dane dropped her hand, uncomfortably. He wanted to talk to her about Van Doon, but he wasn't sure how to begin. She seemed likely to resent whatever he said, and he decided to wait until they got ashore from the ditching operation. Even then, if Van Doon had brought them safely in, his loyalty would be difficult to challenge.

"We'll be safer, really, by ditching," she was saying quietly. "Because the lake's quite deep, Mr. Messenger says, and the plane ought to sink without leaving any traces for Gellian's fliers to see."

"I wonder if that matters." He turned to look at her, moodily. "Men will soon find us, anyhow, even here. New Guinea will be overrun, now that Cadmus is gone. The secret of mutation will be prize enough to draw them—besides that promise of uranium. I'm afraid we haven't got away."

She faced him, her lean brown face very grave at first. Her eyes met his, candidly probing. A frown drew troubled lines across her tawny forehead, but her quick smile erased them.

"Perhaps I shouldn't tell you, but I'm going to," she moved toward him impulsively. "After all, it's our secret. I thought you ought to know, in case we don't all get ashore after we ditch."

He waited uneasily, trying not to think of Van Doon.

"We'll be gone from here," she went on, "before men can find us."

"But if we ditch the plane—"

"Mr. Messenger has a space ship waiting," she told him. "We won't know how good it is until we try it, but it ought to be better than the rockets men are building, because it has atomic power—there *is* uranium in those cliffs."

"Atomic power? A space ship—" He shook his head, unbelievingly. "It would take hundreds of experts and millions and millions of dollars worth of equipment to build any sort of fission-driven space ship," he protested. "I didn't see any shops, or any such a project."

"Mr. Messenger's the maker," she reminded him, gently. "He doesn't need shops to make machines."

"How else—" Dane gulped, suddenly voiceless with an awed surmise. "You mean that he built a space ship by shifting genes? That he—*grew* it?"

He turned abruptly back to the windows, looking for that enormous tree at the mouth of the gorge. All he saw now was dazzling snow and dark naked rock and the white billows of cumulus clouds building against the windward slopes far below. He couldn't find that tree, and he turned blankly back to Nan.

"It isn't so difficult to grow a machine as you might imagine," she said. "Most living things are a good deal more intricate, when you come to think of it, than most machines. Mr. Messenger says the space ship was an easier problem than you and I were. In fact, he once had me try one, just for practice."

"Was that—" Dane tried to swallow the dry croak in his throat. "Was that what Gellian showed me? A sort of half-metallic Christmas tree, growing out of lumps of iron and rock in a flower pot, with a toy ship hanging on it?"

"My first mutation—except for a new virus or two." She nodded quietly. "I made it last fall in New York. Mr. Messenger was trying to teach me how to mutate the mules, but they were still too difficult. I tried the space ship because he said it would be easier, and because I could already see we were going to need one, to get away from men."

"How did Gellian get it?"

"I left it for him," she said. "Because he was getting too bold. His men were killing too many bright children—human as well as mutant. He was coming too close to Mr. Messenger, with that map and all his other clues. My little Christmas gift unnerved them all, and helped me rescue several children."

A stern little smile crossed her face, when she spoke of that limited victory.

"Gellian had begun to use it for a recruiting device, when he showed it to you," she added. "But I stopped that, the night we left New York. I raided his headquarters and destroyed it, together with most of his other evidences of our existence."

"And we might have been safe—" Dane nodded bitterly. "If I hadn't sent that warning back to him."

"Don't brood over that." She touched his hand sympathetically. "I'm the one to blame. And it won't matter, anyhow, if we reach the ship."

He turned again, gratefully, to watch for that narrow gorge in the cliffs ahead of the wheeling plane. He failed to find it, but a sudden recollection startled him.

"I'd heard about that tree." His troubled gaze came back to Nan. "It shines at night, with a cold blue glow. It is mostly iron, and highly magnetic, but it has uranium enough to rattle a Geiger counter. A man got near enough to carry away a twig."

Her eyes widened apprehensively. "Who told you?"

"Venn—the man I thought you killed."

"He didn't get that far!" she protested. "He'd never have escaped."

"The man who got the twig was a rugged Dutchman named Heemskirk. The black flies had stung him, all right, but he kept his memory long enough to talk about the tree." Dane hesitated, frowning. "He must have examined the tree pretty thoroughly, but he said nothing about any such fruit hanging on it."

"Mr. Messenger was better at mutation than I am," she told him. "His tree's a neater job. It's hollow—you saw how thick it is. The ship was grown inside the trunk—all the parts formed inside sheathing membranes which were later absorbed."

"And it's still hidden there?" Dane shivered with wonder. "How far—" he whispered. "How far will it carry us?"

"I don't know." Her voice was hushed, as if she shared his awe. "Mr. Messenger came back to look at it four years ago—he had left it growing here long before, when he went out to organize the company. He found it fully formed, with the matrix tissues already absorbed. He didn't try to fly it then, but he thinks it can reach Venus or Mars."

Dane stood silent before the prospect of exile to another planet, which would surely be stranger and more hostile even than New Guinea. He shivered again, under a sudden shadow of loneliness and unease, and he reached impulsively to touch Nan's hand.

"It's a desperate thing, I know." Her fingers clung to his, as if she sensed his dread. "But better than waiting for Gellian to kill us. Life on any other world would be hard at first, but we should be able to keep alive aboard the ship until we learn enough genetic engineering to grow a crop of mules—or something like them—to help us begin making a home for our people."

The idea of that bold project took hold of Dane, and it slowly changed his fear to excited eagerness. The colony would be a tiny outpost against the perilous unknown. The sun would be too hot or too cold, the gravity wrong, the air itself probably unbreathable. But Homo excellens would have a chance to survive, he thought, where the older race would die.

"We can do it!" He squeezed her taut hand, reassuringly. "If we can really learn mutation. Even if we meet unfriendly kinds of life, we ought to be immune to infections—and perhaps we could mutate the hostile species into useful ones."

"I think we can." Looking though the windows as if she saw something far beyond the dazzling peak of Mt. Carstensz, Nan smiled confidently. "I think we can build a new sanctuary—and then we must come back for the children."

"I've been wondering where you hid them," Dane said anxiously. "They aren't here?"

She shook her head. "It was hard to decide what to do about them. We were afraid to gather them here in New

Guinea—or anywhere—for fear Gellian might get them all with one raid. I couldn't even tell them much of the truth, when I tried to warn them—too many of those in danger were human, and even the mutants weren't old enough to be sure of."

Worry cut frowning lines around her eyes.

"A difficult problem, and I'm still not sure we found the best solution," she went on. "But still I don't see any other—until we find some safe refuge. The children were made to hide among men until they come of age, and that's where we left them."

"But you did warn them?"

"I talked to the children, and to most of their parents. What I told them was a variation of the same story we had invented for people who failed to qualify for the Sanderson Service."

"About that secret selective breeding project?" Dane grinned wryly. "I remember that."

"I told the parents that their gifted offspring had been selected for a long range experiment in human genetics." She nodded. "I warned them of deadly danger from a murderous opposition group. When they were skeptical, I gave them cash enough to convince them, and to help them guard and educate the children—those gifts helped break Mr. Messenger.

"Also, I saw each child alone. I promised that we would come back with more help, and taught each one a set of recognition signals so that he could tell whom to trust, and armed the ones who seemed responsible—with injectors loaded with the forgetfulness virus.

"They're still in danger." Her troubled glance fell from the bright peak to the dark cliffs marching above the boulder-slopes. "Yet that was all we could do—except for making these diversions, to draw the hunt away from them. I think the most of them will survive until we can come back for them."

Dane was watching that frowning basalt wall, and he pointed suddenly.

"The tree!" he whispered. "Up yonder."

The gorge was a sharp V of sky notched deep into the rim of that ragged black escarpment. The tree stood near the bottom point, looking no stranger than most New Guinea trees, deceptively small in the high distance.

"That canyon looks too narrow," he muttered uneasily. "And I'm afraid we're too low to reach it on this approach."

"Vic can fly us in, if anybody can."

Nan was smiling confidently, but her mention of Van Doon brought Dane a dazing crash of danger. It turned the air to frost around him, and stung his nostrils with a bitter dust of death. It washed Nan herself with a black illumination that made her strange and cold.

"Don't worry, Dane." She seemed to feel his alarm, and her fingers tightened in his own. "We'll soon be safe."

"I don't think so." Dane clung to her taut hand, and he searched her face, which had become a lifeless ivory mask beneath that glare of shocking jeopardy. He sensed the secret unease behind that effort to encourage him and herself, and he glimpsed the depths of her trust in him. Suddenly, he could talk to her about Van Doon.

"I'm afraid of Vic," he whispered. "I've tried hard to like him, because it seems so dreadful for us to fight over you. But I can't trust him, even if he is another mutant."

"But he isn't—" Her voice stumbled, and he saw the dark terror dilating her eyes. "If he is," she whispered huskily, "he's one that went wrong."

"I've got a feeling—" He dropped her hand, and imperative purpose turned him. "I want to see what Van Doon's doing now!"

He ran to the compartment door, and she followed silently. Danger was a biting chill in the narrow passage through the crew's quarters. Its dusty bitterness took his breath and burned his tongue. It roared in his brain, louder than the engines. It glared from the cockpit, stronger than the cold sunlight.

He started up the narrow steps behind the cockpit, and paused when he could see Van Doon and Messenger. He reached back to check Nan, and touched his lips warningly. The aged maker sat slumped far down in the co-pilot's seat, but Van Doon was leaning forward, with the radio headphones over his ears, shouting into the microphone.

"Captain Vaughn to General Soames, Comopsur!" Dane caught the hoarse and frantic words, above the drone of the engines and that louder roaring of alarm. The term *Comopsur* puzzled him for an instant, until he recognized it as military shorthand for *Commander Operation Survival.* Van Doon's name had been Vaughn, and the spy was now reporting.

"Get this!" Dane was stumbling desperately up the steps again, but he felt weak and sick with shock, and that harsh voice raced faster than he could move. "Headquarters of notmen in canyon north of summit. Look for huge solitary tree below basalt cliffs. I'm crashing plane on rocky slope below, to mark spot for you—"

Dane felt half paralyzed. His dazed brain was grasping the enormity of this disaster. He could see a black tangle of fallen boulders ahead. He realized that the plane was already diving toward destruction, but his stunned body seemed too slow to do anything about it.

Moving in what seemed like the agonized slow motion of a nightmare, he came up the steps to the cockpit at last. He snatched the headset and microphone and hurled his body against Van Doon, fighting for the wheel.

He hauled it back, struggling to pull the plane out of suicidal dive, but Van Doon pushed it down again instantly, with a monstrous strength. Rising half out of the seat, the spy lifted an improvised club: a hand fire extinguisher. Dane snatched at the heavy cylinder, but it slid out of his grasp, already slippery with blood.

"Mr. Messenger!" Nan had followed him up the steps, and her sudden scream knifed through his mind. "He has killed Mr. Messenger!"

TWENTY-SIX

Dane still felt trapped in that strange slow motion. When he reached again for Van Doon's weapon, the inertia of his limbs seemed to hold him back. The resistance was like some thick fluid. The shape of disaster was already stark in his mind, but he couldn't move fast enough to do anything about it.

That nightmare feeling was only illusion, he knew. Desperation must have speeded up his mind to a pace that his body couldn't match, for all Van Doon's movements seemed as queerly deliberate as his own. He failed again to grasp that bloodstained club, but he had time to catch the hard bronze arm that held it. He ducked the blow, and twisted to drag Van Doon away from the controls.

"Take the wheel!" His shouted words to Nan seemed to come as slowly as his body moved, and he thought the diving plane would strike the rockslide ahead before she could reach the pilot's seat.

"Pull it back!" he yelled. "Quick!"

Her movements must have been faster than they seemed.

She slipped into the seat with a surprising air of knowing what she was doing. Her feet found the rudden controls, and she swung the wheel as she brought it back, watching the instruments as well as that tumbled boulder-slope ahead. She was trying to turn the plane away from the cliffs above the slope, and for an instant Dane thought she would succeed.

Van Doon gave him no time to watch.

He had always known, without thinking much about it, that he was strong for his size. Without pausing to consider the odds, he had attacked Van Doon with high confidence.

If his strength was a gift of the maker's, however, their contest gave quick evidence that Van Doon was also a mutant. The spy was many pounds heavier, and equally in earnest. His brown arm twisted out of Dane's desperate fingers, like a massive lever of actual bronze. Again it rose and fell with the fire extinguisher, murderously swift.

Dane flung up his hand defensively, but the heavy brass cylinder crushed it down and struck his temple. The blow rocked him backward. Van Doon swung instantly, lifting that red club to strike at the back of Nan's head.

Dane was reeling and half blind with pain, but he swayed forward to clutch at the weapon. It slipped out of his fingers again but he caught Van Doon's elbow and hung on groggily. That feeble effort took all his will. He expected to be flung away, but something made the mutant spy relax.

Dully, he realized that Van Doon had stopped to wait for the crash. The nose of the plane was still coming up. That wilderness of fallen rock had begun to slip aside, as Nan tried to bank and turn before they struck. Abruptly there was blue sky ahead, instead of the cliffs. He thought they would avoid a crash—until the right wingtip struck.

He heard Nan's faint cry of despair, and then the shriek of tearing metal. Sharp pain stabbed his ears, as the air pressure went out of the cabin. He felt the sickening lurch of the lifting plane, and then he was hurled forward against Van Doon when it struck another boulder. They both were flung to the front of the cockpit. Something came against his head . . .

Suddenly, then, everything was very quiet. The cockpit was tipped sharply downward, and he lay crumpled against the instruments. Van Doon's heavy body was sprawled across his legs, still curiously relaxed. He caught a bitter-almond whiff of potassium cyanide.

The agony of death paralyzed him, a shock of emotion more violent than the crash. For one dreadful instant he thought he had felt Nan dying, but then he knew that the death he sensed had been Van Doon's. As clearly as if she had spoken to him, he knew that Nan was still alive and not yet badly hurt.

Not yet—but the fuel would explode.

That sick fear swept over him—and then ebbed abruptly. Even before he had time to try to gather up his bruised and quivering limbs, the calm knowledge came to him that there would be no fire. Grateful to his mutant faculties for that assurance, he sank back to collect his strength and breath.

Yet, even though he and Nan had come through alive, the danger he perceived had not been extinguished. It still burned like a dark phosphorescence in Van Doon's dead flesh, glowing over the shattered cockpit and the silent shape of the maker. Even though there would be no explosion, he and Nan were still trapped in that stranger blaze. The motives and the misdeeds of Van Doon's queer career remained a deadly riddle.

He managed to move a little, and found breath to speak.

"Nan!" he called faintly. "Can you answer?"

"I'm all right." Her shaken whisper came from close beside him. "I—I think I am."

He pushed Van Doon's inert body off his knees. Blood was oozing from the lax lips, and he saw fine shards of glass upon them. The mouth sagged open as the head turned, and that bitter odor was suddenly powerful. He turned away from it, to look for Nan.

She lay almost beside him, crushed against the great inert bulk of Messenger's body. Her lean cheeks were streaked with blood, but that must have come from the long ragged wound in the maker's scalp, for he saw no wound in her face. She smiled at him, with a shaken relief.

"I'm so glad—you're alive!" she sobbed. "Is Vic—"

"Dead," he told her. "I think from an ampule of prussic acid crushed in his teeth."

"He was faithful so long." A troubled wonder edged her shaken voice. "I can't quite believe he was against us all the time."

"But he must have been," Dane said. "I don't think he ever knew he wasn't human. His immunity from the virus protected his memory, and his mutant gifts made him an efficient spy. If you had been in time to find him, with the Sanderson Service, he might have been one of us."

She tried uncertainly to get up but sank back to rub her bruises.

"Not one of us!" She shook her head, quickly. "Or he'd have realized what he was, long ago. He must have been one of those that turned out wrong." Her sick eyes went to the body at Dane's feet, and quickly fled. "I wonder why he took that poison?"

"An accident, I think," Dane said.

He could see how it must have happened. Sharing Gellian's fear of the mutants, the spy must have been prepared for torture. He must have had the poison capsule ready in his mouth, just now, to protect his secrets if he were captured, and the crash must have made him break it.

"I trusted him," Nan whispered. "I even liked him—I suppose he couldn't help showing a little more personality than the real lotus-eaters."

"Even now, I can almost admire him." Dane nodded reluctantly. "We were monstrous enemies, in his imagination. I don't see how he expected to survive this crash, even if his capsule hadn't killed him. He was willing to give his life to kill us—and it may turn out that he succeeded."

"We can't be pessimists." She tried to smile, through her tight-lipped apprehension. "Maybe nobody heard his call. You stopped him before he had time to say much."

"He told where we are," Dane muttered bleakly. "And anyhow that probably wasn't his first call—he must have been reporting our progress every time I got that danger-feeling. I imagine we've been traced by radar, too, all the way from Edentown."

"I guess you're right." Nodding hopelessly, she forgot to smile. "They let us lead them here. Now they'll soon be closing in, with their whole expedition, to finish us off."

"Which means we haven't much time." Dane glanced outside at the huge fallen boulders that walled the wreckage. "We must get out of here—if we can—before they spot us and drop a few bombs, just to make certain of us."

"How far is the tree?" A desperate hope came back to her eyes. "Do you think we can get there on foot?"

"We can try." He frowned doubtfully. "The going will be hard, at this altitude—up this rock-slide and then the cliffs. But perhaps there's a trail." He glanced at Messenger's crumpled body. "Or how did he go there?"

"In a helicopter."

"I think we'll need one," he said. "But we can try." Wincing from the pain of a dozen sprains and bruises of his own, he moved stiffly to help Nan rise from the tilted floor. She stooped to examine the wound in Messenger's scalp, which was still oozing blood.

"It seems so cruel," she whispered, "that he had to be killed by a creature he had made, when all he meant to do was good—" Her breath caught, and she bent lower. "But he isn't dead!"

Messenger was alive, but little more. Breath fluttered his fat lips feebly as they straightened his body on the sloping floor, behind the seats, but it seemed a long time before he struggled to inhale again. Half open beneath the folds of flesh, his faded eyes stared dimly at nothing. The blotches were darker on his swollen face, and his lips already blue.

"There's a medical kit in his room," Nan whispered anxiously. "Or it was there, before we crashed. Gray plastic, with a chrome catch. Will you see if you can find it?"

Dane went back to look for it, scrambling clumsily up the incline of the tilted wreck. Light struck through a wide hole torn in the cabin wall where the galley had been, and he paused to look out uneasily.

Both wings had been sheared off, he saw, when the cabin came between two great boulders. The crumbled wings and the battered engines, ripped from their mounts, were all many yards away. He could see no danger of fire, but his relief at that was forgotten when he glanced up toward the tree.

The boulder-slope stretched up far above the wreck, a forbidding wilderness of broken stones sometimes as large as buildings. Above and beyond, the vertical face of the cliff raised another barrier. Standing in that narrow notch against the sky, the tree looked no larger than a thick-stemmed shrub.

Its promise of safety and escape was suddenly far away. Messenger would never be able to reach it, with all the aid they could give. The climb would be heartbreaking, even for him and Nan. And time was short—Gellian had studied another mutant tree, and he was unlikely to overlook this one.

Dane clambered heavily on through the wreckage. He found the medical kit on the floor of Messenger's room, and a metal canteen nearly full of water. He rolled them up in the blankets from the berth, and slid down with them to the cockpit.

The maker was still unconscious, breathing slowly and very feebly. Nan took the kit silently, to swab his flabby arm and stab it with a hypodermic needle. She felt his pulse and leaned to listen at his chest and finally shook her head.

"It doesn't seem to help," she said. "I'm afraid nothing will, unless we get him back into a pressurized cabin—soon. We must bring the ship down here."

"I'll try to get it," he said. "If you can tell me something about how to operate it."

"I'll have to go," she told him. "Because the ship is—protected. I know how to get inside, and something about how to pilot it—when I was working last year on that mutant tree of my own, I spent months studying the plans and specifications Mr. Messenger had worked out for this one."

"It will be a terrible climb," he protested uneasily. "Shouldn't we tackle it together?"

She looked at Messenger a long time, and shook her head.

"I wish you'd stay," she whispered. "I'm afraid to leave him so long. He'll need another shot in about an hour—I'll show you what to do. Will you stay?"

He hesitated. The aircraft of Operation Survival would be here soon, he knew, and this wreckage was sure to get their first attention.

"You don't know him the way I do," Nan added softly. "I

don't suppose you've learned to love him. But we both owe him a certain debt."

He looked down at the maker, fighting so feebly to breathe. For a moment he stood thinking of Cadmus and the green mules and the virus of forgetfulness, all designed to defend the new race. The debt was there, and he felt abruptly anxious to repay what he could.

"I'll stay," he agreed. "Just tell me what he needs."

She kissed him unexpectedly, and then opened the kit to show him what to do when Messenger's tired heart faltered again. In a few minutes she was ready to go. The cabin door had been crumpled and jammed, but he helped her through the ragged hole where the galley had been. She started away from him toward the jagged face of the first great boulder above, and turned back impulsively.

"I'm glad you're willing to stay." Tears shone in her eyes and all the marks of fatigue and fear were erased from her brown face by a sudden tenderness. "I'm glad you understand."

He wanted to take her in his arms, but they had no time for that. A sharp emotion caught his throat, so that he couldn't even speak. He tried to smile, but his face felt stiff and numb. All he could do was to nod and lift his hand, with an awkward little gesture that seemed to say nothing.

"I'll come back," she whispered. "If I can—"

TWENTY-SEVEN

Nan turned again, to begin the climb. She looked lean and strong in the white coveralls, and she scrambled up the side of that first huge rock with a swift, sure grace. He knew that she had the hardiness of Homo excellens—but a cold shudder struck him when he saw the tree again, so far beyond her.

She was out of sight for a moment, on top of the boulder, and then he glimpsed her again, running along a sharp knife-edge of stone, to jump the wide gap between two rocks. The leap took her out of view, and for a long time he felt a sick fear that she had fallen.

When he saw her again, she was already high above, a tiny white figure toiling upward against barriers and distances that became overwhelming when her smallness showed their scale. For most of the boulder-slope was still ahead of her, and then the cliffs above.

He saw her fall. The boulder she was climbing looked no larger than a pebble in the distance, but it was many times her height. She was halfway up its face when he saw her slip and tumble back. She lay for what seemed a long time in the sunlight blazing on the black ledge below, but at last she rose, and stooped as if to rub her bruised knees, and finally tried again.

She stopped at the place where she had slipped, as if pinned against the rock. He could imagine her precarious groping for some tiny projection strong enough to take her weight, and he felt sick with fear that she would slip again. But she inched her way on to the top of that pebble, and turned to wave to him, and limped quickly on toward the next rock-chimney she must climb.

He watched her out of sight and went uneasily back to look after the injured maker. The cramped space where he lay was getting too warm, as the vertical sun heated the battered cabin, and Dane carried the blankets outside to make him a more comfortable bed on a flat ledge that was shaded by one of the twisted wings.

Messenger was still unconscious, breathing so feebly that his stubborn grip seemed about to slip from the outmost rim of life, and his great weight made him hard to move. Dane ripped a compartment door from inside the cabin to use for a stretcher, and slid him out of the wreckage upon it.

He seemed to breathe more easily in the cooler air outside, and he stirred suddenly while Dane was dressing the wound in his scalp. His trembling hand came up to touch the bandages, and his pale eyes opened again, seeing and sane.

"Well?" he gasped faintly. "What hit me?"

"Van Doon." Dane told him what had happened. "Nan ought to be back with that ship before night," he finished, with more confidence than he felt. "All we've got to do is just hold out till she comes."

"I'm hard to kill." Messenger grinned feebly. "People been trying that for years." He lay silent while Dane fastened the bandage, and then asked for water. He lay back with his eyes closed for a long time afterward, as if exhausted. Dane bent to count his pulse at last, wondering if heart was giving up.

"Not yet!" He pulled his wrist away with an unexpected vigor. "I'll tell you when I need another shot." He lay for a while watching Dane with a kind of relaxed intentness. "So you and Nan are off to the stars?" he whispered at last. "Dane, what do you think of her?"

"I don't know," he began, but then some mute urgency in the maker's faded eyes made him want to be completely honest. "I do know!" he said impulsively. "She's just about perfect—there wasn't any error in the genes you made for her. I'm sorry for some of the things I used to think about her—when I believed she had killed Nicholas Venn, and supposed Van Doon was her mate. Because she's—wonderful! I believe we're in love."

"Puppy stuff!" A faint smile turned Messenger's weather-beaten face fondly wise. "I think myself that I did all right with Nan, and well enough with you. I'm glad you like each other, though that is not surprising. But—love!"

He closed his eyes to rest again, while Dane waited uncertainly.

"You're children, yet," he went on at last. "Both of you—except in size. If you think you're capable of love—think about today again in another twenty years, or forty, after your mutant faculties are more mature. Then you'll know the meaning of love!"

He lay still again, as if worn out.

From the flat ledge where Dane sat beside him, he could see the tree standing in that high gorge. Restlessly, he kept searching the cliffs and boulder-fields below, but Nan was never in sight. He was afraid she had fallen again, but he tried to cover his gnawing apprehension when he saw Messenger's eyes upon him.

The maker turned fretfully, and saw the distant tree. Dane felt him stiffen. "You've cause enough for worry," he whispered. "I didn't know it was such a man-killing climb. Why didn't you go with her?"

"A sprained ankle," Dane said promptly.

"Don't lie," Messenger rasped. "Why don't you say she made you stay to look after me? The dear little fool! You had better follow now—if you know which way she went. She'll need help."

Dane shook his head. "She wants you to be alive when she gets back with the ship."

"I know she does," the maker breathed. "She has already kept me going longer than I had any right to. But I can't live forever—you and Nan were made to stay alive and youthful as long as you can reasonably wish, but I was never able to remake myself."

He lay staring at the distant tree, while he got his breath again.

"Nan has already saved me from one unpleasant disease," he said at last. "And she has been hoping and working to rescue me from old age."

"Is that possible?"

"She thought it was," he said laboriously. "Death is a necessary function of evolving life—to remove the old generations and make way for the new. Growing old seems to be a normal vital process. Nan was hoping to rebuild a few hormone-producing cells, somewhere in my old carcass, and so reverse senility."

Dane nodded silently, awed at the notion of turning back biological time.

"Naturally, I took a friendly interest in her project," the maker's faint voice toiled on. "That was a pleasant dream: to be young again; to go out with you to the moon or Mars to find a sanctuary for Homo excellens; to watch you and Nan and the others grow into the fine beings I planned; to help you if I could."

"It isn't a dream." Dane had stayed for Nan's sake, but suddenly now he felt glad he had stayed, for the maker's. "She'll be back." Hope echoed again in his voice. "Soon we'll have you safe on the ship."

"No." Messenger's puffy hand reached quivering across the blankets, to touch the naked black ledge. "This is where I die."

"Please!" Dane tried not to shiver. "Don't say that."

"It's true." The maker had to gasp for air again. "My old clock's about run down. Nan was trying to wind it up again. She'll know how in a few more years. But today is when it stops."

"Nonsense!" Dane protested sharply. "I know this altitude puts a burden on your heart. Perhaps you need another shot. You've got to relax. Don't try to talk."

"Don't you heckle me," he gasped. "I'll relax when I'm dead. And I do know I die today. I've a better trained psi capacity than yours is yet, you know."

"Huh?" Dane bent to stare. "You think you can really see the future?"

"One cell at a time, a few days or even a few weeks ahead," he whispered calmly. "I can still do that, in spite of my stroke. I've been examining the future condition of my own brain cells. They all die today."

Dane straightened, impressed by his quiet certainty. "How long have you known?"

"Almost a month," he said. "I didn't tell Nan, but that's why I brought her out here in such haste and tried so hard to help mutate those mules." His faded eyes peered keenly up at Dane, not yet vanquished. "I didn't want to leave you unprotected."

The shrewd glint of his eyes gave Dane a puzzled start. His death today was likely enough, from Gellian's bombs if not from the failure of his heart—but he had invented ingenious lies enough in defense of Homo excellens, and this could easily be another.

"So you're wasting your time," he was whispering. "Risking your life for nothing, waiting for Gellian's planes to catch you here. Nan needs you, and you've done about all you can for me. Give me another shot if you like, and then get started."

"No, I'm not going." Dane began swabbing his arm for the needle. "I don't quite trust your forecast, and I'm afraid that looking into the future is a dangerous business."

"Snap it up!" Messenger's faint voice sharpened fretfully. "Get on with it, and get away while you can."

"I was thinking of my mother." Methodically, Dane began filling the syringe. "I suppose you know she had a psychic gift—but did you know it killed her?"

The maker shook his head, with a feeble impatience.

"She had believed since she was a girl that she was going to die on the operating table. When she began to feel the symptoms of cancer, the fear of dying made her put off the operation until too late to save her life. Believing she would die is what killed her."

"But still she died," Messenger whispered, "the way she had foreseen."

"And you're trying to arrange your own death the same way," Dane insisted. "If I leave, you'll probably die before Nan gets back with the ship." He caught up the sallow flesh and thrust the thin needle in. "But I promised Nan I'd stay," he said. "I'm going to."

The maker didn't seem to feel the needle.

"My blunder." His hollowed eyes blinked, as if dim with exhaustion. "Should have made you less a fool. Or should I?" His eyes fluttered and closed, and his tired whisper was barely audible. "You and Nan are throwing your lives away for nothing, but maybe that's because you're Homo excellens. And maybe it isn't quite for nothing—"

His voice was gone. Afraid he was dying, Dane reached quickly to feel his pulse. It was hard to find, alarmingly faint and uncertain at first, but it seemed steadier and stronger as the injection took effect. His slow breathing became easier, and the deathly blue receded a little from his lips.

Hopeful of outwitting the maker's foreseen death, Dane climbed the great boulder that had broken the wing of the plane, to look for Nan. He stared against the hot glare of the noonday sun until his eyes throbbed and blurred with tears, but all he could see was the vast slope of broken basalt blocks, and the tall cliffs from which they had fallen, and the tiny-seeming tree in that distant gap.

He watched the tree, waiting hopefully for the massive trunk to split and fall apart, unfolding like a flower to reveal the ship. His aching eyes strained to see the tall spindle of it standing new in the sun, dazzling and miraculous, and then rising slowly from its splintered shell on white-hot atomic jets.

But nothing burst from the tree, and his troubled imagination began to picture Nan lying broken beneath some treacherous ledge, or turning helplessly back from the foot of some overhanging precipice, or killed in the ship when she tried to fly it. He couldn't help recalling that it had never been tested, or help thinking of all those other mutations that had turned out wrong.

Depressed and tired, he went back to the ledge below. The maker lay unconscious, and time dragged away. The storm he had seen on the windward slopes must have continued to grow, for a scarf of high cloud moved over the sun and turned the air suddenly chill. He spread a blanket over Messenger, and stood up to watch once more for Nan until the tree itself began to fade and waver in his vision. He sat down to wait again, shivering in the cold wind rising.

The clouds were lowering and darker. Distant thunder began to mutter against the cliffs. At first he thought the storm was crossing the summits, but then the quiver of sound in the air became steadier and more alarming than any natural thunder.

It was the drone of aircraft.

"Well, Dane." Messenger was awake again, blinking at him sadly from the blankets on the ledge. "I'm sorry you didn't go, while you had a chance."

TWENTY-EIGHT

Messenger had asked fretfully for Nan, and Dane was anxiously climbing the boulder above their ledge to look for her again when he felt the familiar feel of danger. He turned, and the dark glare of peril led his eyes at once to the helicopter, floating down on quiet rotors out of that thunderous murmur of engines in the sky.

"Hide!" Messenger gasped behind him. "Maybe you can get away, yet."

But he had been seen. The air shuddered to a nearer blast of sound, as the helicopter checked its descent, and he could see machine guns in their turrets already moving to cover him. His empty hands clenched savagely, but the time for action had gone. He went slowly back to wait beside Messenger.

The helicopter circled them, keeping at a cautious distance. It was a heavy military craft, the closed cabin splashed with green-and-gray camouflage. He made out the insignia of the United States Air Force, half covered by the hastily painted black initials of Operation Survival.

The guns didn't fire. After two slow circuits of the wreckage, the helicopter rose a little, and hovered uncertainly, and finally came back to perch on a boulder beyond the broken engines of the plane. Two airmen climbed down to the rock, and a third man in a business suit.

They scrambled down a little way across the torn metal and broken stone, and then paused uncertainly. The civilian began waving a white handkerchief, nervously. Dane beckoned them to come on, and then started uncomfortably when he recognized the man with the handkerchief.

John Gellian!

Dane couldn't help flinching back from that implacable

enemy, but Gellian didn't look victorious. His eyes were hollowed, and his black-stubbled face was drawn thin with something deadlier than anxiety. He appeared as ill as the maker.

"Hullo, Belfast." He paused at the end of the ledge, nodding at the wary airmen behind him. "General Soames and Colonel Humbolt," he said. "General Soames is commander of Operation Survival."

The airmen nodded bleakly, and stood looking around them uneasily while Gellian came on to Dane. He was obviously the real commander, and Dane could see the general's stern disapproval of his unmilitary methods.

"We're looking for Captain Vaughn," he said.

"Your spy?" Dane nodded at the wreck. "You'll find him there."

"Dead?" Gellian's voice was hushed and hoarse. "You killed him."

"He broke a vial of cyanide in his teeth," Dane said. "Before he found out that he'd been fighting on the wrong side."

"You don't mean—" Gellian stepped backward, and shook his gaunt head incredulously. "He was our ablest agent."

"He was a mutant," Dane said. "That was the secret of his success. Men can't be immunized to Craven's disease."

"If that's true, he's well off dead." Gellian swung mistrustfully away from Dane, to stare down at Messenger. "So you're the maker?" His lips tightened with contemptuous hate. "Traitor! But I want to talk to you."

"Better hurry, then." Messenger's bandaged head lifted feebly from the blankets. "I won't be talking long."

Gellian stalked toward him aggressively.

"Can't we get rid of *that?*" He nodded apprehensively at

Dane, his voice thick with hate. "I want to deal with you, not your monsters."

Messenger shook his head, with a comforting grin at Dane.

"Let him stay." Gellian shrugged disdainfully. "He can't do much."

He swung to Dane, his haggard face malevolent.

"We're in constant radio communication with the aircraft above." He nodded grimly at the helicopter, waiting with engines idling and machine guns trained on them. "If anything happens to us—or if anything breaks our radio contact—their orders are to saturate this whole area with H-bombs. Including the canyon above that tree. Keep that in mind, while you plan your mutant tricks."

Dane nodded, and promised helplessly, "There won't be any tricks."

"Just keep that in mind."

Gellian swung nervously back to Messenger, who blinked at him calmly.

"Well, John?"

"I want some information," Gellian rasped. "About these things you've made."

"If you really want the truth—" Messenger lifted his trembling hands. "Help me up, so I can talk."

They took his arms and set him up against the rock behind the ledge. Dane wrapped the blankets back around him. He had to gasp for his breath, but his pale eyes blinked at Gellian with their old patient shrewdness.

"My staff officers wanted to order bombs away without any effort to negotiate with you." The gaunt man nodded impatiently at the general and the colonel, who had moved nearer to listen. "But Captain Vaughn's last report was interrupted, and I'm not satisfied with the visible target."

His savage eyes raked Dane again.

"Is the main colony of the not-men really located in that gorge?" he snapped at Messenger. "We can't find any installations—are they camouflaged?" He leaned intently closer. "What I want is complete information about the numbers and positions and weapons and plans of the enemy."

"Homo excellens is nobody's enemy," the maker answered softly. "But why should I tell you anything?"

"I think you need medical care," Gellian said harshly. "We can give you that—and the opportunity to atone for your crimes against mankind, by helping us destroy these creatures you've made."

"Not a very strong inducement." Messenger grinned feebly. "My appointment to die is already made, and my chief regret is that I wasn't able to make mutants enough to people the fortified colony you're looking for."

"Where is it?"

"It doesn't exist—except in your sick imagination." Messenger shook his head, and strove to breathe again. "You have been waging war on an old man and a girl and a few defenseless children. I'm afraid you've just about finished us."

"You've been lying long enough." Gellian knotted a threatening fist. "I want the truth."

"I don't think so." The maker blinked innocently. "You wouldn't recognize it."

"Tell me where that girl is," Gellian rapped. "And where she hid those children. You can save yourself and this thing from a more severe interrogation." He nodded at Dane, and glanced at his watch. "I'll give you five minutes to talk."

"Thank you, John," Messenger whispered. "I've a thing or two to say—if I can find the breath—about your war on Homo excellens."

"Say it." Gellian's abrupt impatience was edged, Dane

could tell, with physical pain. "Get to the point."

"I'm a biologist," the maker began heavily. "I've wanted for a long time to talk to you, John, about biology and tolerance—because I think you're honest. I believe you mean well. I've seen you show a degree of tolerance—I used to see people of all races working side by side in your offices." He sank back against the rock, and fought for air, and finally gasped, "Why draw the line at Homo excellens?"

"We're men." Gellian stiffened, his dark face haggard and stern with that inner agony. "Black or yellow or white, we're all men together. Your monsters have united us, and we're fighting for survival." His fevered eyes swept Dane warily and came back to Messenger. "There's no use begging for tolerance, because we'd get none if your creatures had us at their mercy."

The maker shook his bandaged head, painfully.

"I think you could depend on justice," he whispered. "But I'm not begging for mercy. I want to call your attention to a scientific fact. I think your fear of Homo excellens is rooted in a misunderstanding of the Darwinian scheme of evolution."

"We aren't concerned with natural evolution," Gellian answered harshly. "We're simply struggling for existence, against your unnatural monsters."

Messenger heaved himself straighter against the rock. Dane could hear the labored rasp of his breathing and see an alarming cyanotic color coming back to his lips. Yet his voice had a sudden desperate vigor.

"You've let those ideas of the struggle for existence and the survival of the fittest dominate your thinking, because you fail to see the whole process of life. Competition is part of it, true. But the biologist can see another great principle, more essential for survival. That's co-operation."

"We're co-operating," Gellian said, "—to kill your creatures while we can!"

"I know." Messenger nodded sadly, still sitting desperately erect. "You are living the ethic of competition, which has made you surrender to a herd instinct that no longer has any survival value. If you'll only look around, you will see that co-operation is the first principle, and competition merely secondary, everywhere in nature. That fact is a scientific basis for an ethic of love instead of hate."

Gellian shrugged impatiently, looking at his watch.

"Darwin knew the role of co-operation," Messenger went on doggedly. "In *The Descent of Man*, I think it is, he deplores the artificial barriers that keep our sympathies from extending to the men of all nations and races. But too many smaller individuals have twisted and perverted his views, to excuse or glorify rivalry and imperialism.

"Vicious little men are always quoting him to prove that nature's whole plan is war, but that is a wicked delusion. Combat and conquest, hatred and killing—they are the dramatic shadows that sometimes hide the great realities of love and mutual aid. Competition is a parasitic thing that can't exist until co-operation has created something for it to destroy."

Dane could feel the truth of that, but he could see that Gellian wasn't listening. The gaunt man had retreated a little toward the silent airmen, and he was restlessly searching that cruel wilderness of broken stone, as if still alert for some treacherous attack.

"Look back to the beginning," the maker begged him huskily. "Life on Earth began with single cells. They lived in competition for the scanty means of survival on a sterile planet—but it was in co-operation that they united to evolve multicellular creatures, and so make survival far simpler."

"A billion years ago!" Gellian shrugged impatiently. "We're fighting to keep alive today."

"You're blindly destroying the very beings who could do the most to help you keep alive," Messenger whispered hoarsely. "The fact is that you're ignoring an important law of competition and co-operation."

"Huh?" Gellian peered at him skeptically.

"It runs against the law of the herd," Messenger gasped. "It proves the folly of herd prejudice, and it lays down a scientific basis for tolerance. Here it is: the field of co-operation extends far beyond the range of competition, which is most bitter among things most alike."

"How's that?"

"I suppose the simplest example of the law in action is the savage competition of males of the same species for females with which they can live in co-operation—the mutual difference is what makes mutual aid both possible and vital."

Messenger sobbed again for his breath.

"Other examples are all around us. The oxygen I need so much is a waste product of plants, and the carbon dioxide I exhale is food for them—is that competition?"

He blinked earnestly at Gellian.

"Or take your own agency. You employ people of every race, and you must have found a great advantage in their wide range of backgrounds and abilities. Your best operative was Captain Vaughn. A mutant, most useful because he was most different."

Messenger collapsed against the rock, and gasped for air again, and went on stubbornly:

"Homo excellens can do as much for all the mother race as that spy did for you. The differences are great enough to place the mutant race almost outside the range of competition. Though those new traits and gifts may offend your herd instinct, they also widen the opportunities for mutual help.

"The mutants were designed to supply many of the things that our race lacks. They can balance the aggressiveness of men with a wider and finer kind of love. I believe they can save our quarrelsome old race from self-destruction, John—if you will only let them live!"

The maker's whisper was sharp with pleading.

"Can't you see the sanity of that?"

Restlessly, Gellian glanced at the lone tree in that distant gap, and peered suspiciously at Dane, and looked at his watch again.

"Time's up," he rapped at Messenger. "I still want to know where to find that girl and the children." He nodded ominously at the waiting helicopter, and gestured impatiently toward the muffled thunder in the sky. "Are you going tell me?"

"I was hoping to." Messenger nodded his head feebly. "But I don't think you're following what I say."

"That's true." The gaunt man nodded quietly. "I'll tell you why." His drawn face looked stern, but his voice was oddly soft. "I'm dying of cancer—cancer of the liver."

"Oh!" Messenger's shallow breath caught. "I see."

"The doctors can't do anything for me," Gellian said. "Drugs don't help any more." He stiffened restlessly, his hollowed face hard. "Can you expect me to follow your scientific arguments—in that agony?"

"But it hasn't stopped your war on Homo excellens."

"If you're a biologist, you know what cancer is." A sudden ruthless violence shattered the quiet of his voice. "It is a colony of mutant cells—as deadly to the body as your mutants are to mankind. I can't do much about the cancer, but I can still eradicate your not-men!"

"I wish I had known sooner." The maker's faded eyes

blinked regretfully. "Because I once had cancer, too. A malignant tumor of the brain." He glanced at Dane. "I told you how it destroyed my skill at mutation. It had spread too far to be cut out, before I knew the trouble was anything more than old age."

"Huh?" Dane looked down at him sharply. "Didn't you say you had it removed?"

"But not by surgery." His bandaged head turned painfully back to Gellian. "That's a wonderful example of the mutual assistance I was talking about. I was beyond the medical aid of Homo sapiens, but Nan Sanderson saved my life."

The haggard man moved toward him with a hungry intentness. "How?"

"She made a special virus," he whispered. "She rebuilt a common bacteriophage, to feed on cancer cells. That was her first successful mutation—done just in time to save my life."

"Bacterio—what?"

" 'Fleas have smaller fleas to bite 'em—ad infinitum.' " The maker grinned wanly. "The bacteriophages are viruses that consume bacteria. Nan modified one of them, to give it an appetite for cancer cells and nothing else."

"And—did it work?"

"It works," Messenger said. "The pain is ended in a few minutes. Every malignant cell is killed and dissolved into harmless wastes which are quickly absorbed. Recovery is rapid, because there is no damage to healthy tissue."

"A wonderful thing!" Gellian breathed eagerly, but then he drew back suspiciously. "If it's such a perfect cure, why didn't you publish it?"

"You were pressing us a little too hard," the maker told him. "The medical profession is skeptical of such radical new treatments—with reason. Any announcement complete enough to win a hearing would have betrayed Homo excellens to you."

Gellian peered at him sharply. "Do you think I'm that inhuman?"

"You've always seemed pretty implacable." Messenger blinked at him thoughtfully. "We were planning to give Nan's invention to the public, as soon as we safely could. If we had known that the pain of cancer was the root of your hatred, we might have offered it to you."

Gellian straightened abruptly, his lean hands clenched. He wet his pale lips nervously, and glanced helplessly at the officers behind him. Dane could see the torment of indecision in his hollowed eyes, a doubt as cruel as his physical agony.

"I won't bargain," he muttered hoarsely. "I won't be stalled or duped. If all this is only one more of your cunning lies, you'll pay for it."

The maker turned feebly to Dane.

"Open the medicine kit. Show him the serum."

Dane fumbled in the plastic kit, and found a small carton marked *Cancerphage*. He opened it, to show six tiny glass ampules, packed carefully. Gellian bent to peer at them, trembling with his hope and fear.

"Take the box," Messenger told him. "The serum should be injected into a vein. One shot is enough. You can prepare more serum from the blood of convalescent patients, taken about twenty-four hours after treatment."

Gellian reached hungrily for the little carton, but checked himself to peer at Messenger fearfully.

"What do you want in return?"

"Nothing," the maker said. "If you're going to wipe out everything else I've tried to do, I want you to save the cancerphage. A gift from Homo excellens."

The gaunt man still hesitated, drawn taut in his torment of uncertainty.

"I don't trust you," his harsh voice rasped. "If this is a scheme to infect our forces with your diabolical encephalitis—"

"Mr. Gellian!" the general broke in. "I'd advise you to take the serum. We can arrange to have it tested. And I think we had better have a talk among ourselves—with Mr. Messenger's permission. Let's go back aboard."

Gellian seized the little carton. He stood for a moment looking up across that broken wilderness of stone at the mutant tree that seemed so small above those high black cliffs, and then he nodded slowly.

"I guess we had better have a talk." He swung back to Messenger. "This ought to make a difference, if you have told the truth. We'll hold off the bombing until we can reach some decision—unless your mutants try some attack."

"A boy and a girl!" Messenger whispered sardonically. "Lost in these mountains, empty-handed against your H-bombs. What could they do?"

"I'm still not sure." Gellian started away, scowling, but he turned abruptly back after the colonel had caught his arm and murmured something in his ear.

"You're in bad shape yourself," he said. "Do you want us to send a stretcher for you? We've oxygen equipment on the helicopter, and we can pressurize the cabin." He nodded grudingly at Dane. "You may even bring—him."

"Thanks just the same." The maker shook his head. "But we'll feel more at home out here, until you decide to trust us." He piped and rattled again, with his laborious breathing. "If you're going to talk about peace," he gasped, "please remember that we have more to offer than the cancerphage."

Gellian waited for his words with a restless impatience,

but Dane saw an enormous interest in the eyes of the two officers.

"There are other diseases that ought to yield to mutant bacteriophages," he went on painfully. "The process of genetic engineering can make the whole world over. Incidentally, Dr. Belfast and Miss Sanderson can help you protect society from any other imperfect mutants still alive—some of them are really dangerous!"

The general stood frowning at Messenger.

"We'll consider that," he promised uneasily. "We came to assault a fortress, and we're hardly prepared to make an alliance. You must give us time. If you won't come aboard, please wait here."

Messenger whispered faintly that they would wait. His face was splotched again with blue, and his breath was a strangled whistling, but he sat stubbornly erect while the three men hurried back across the wreckage and climbed into the helicopter. Then he slumped back against the rock, as if unconscious.

TWENTY-NINE

Dane laid him back on the blankets, and felt for the uncertain flutter of his pulse, and hastily gave him another injection. It failed to take effect. His fight for air seemed hopeless, and his faint pulse began to skip. Dane started impulsively toward the helicopter, after aid.

"Don't!" he gasped. "Come—back!"

"I'm going after their oxygen equipment," Dane told him. "To help you breathe."

"No use." His bandaged head rocked painfully from side to side on the blankets. "No matter. My work—all done!"

"I'm not so sure." So Dane tried to spur his weary will to live. "Gellian still seems pretty hostile."

"He's still sick," Messenger wheezed. "But he'll soon—be well."

"And so will you!" Dane bent to prop his head and shoulders higher on a folded blanket, to help him breathe. "But let me get that oxygen—"

He caught Dane's sleeve, with a sudden frantic strength.

"Listen—" He clung, fighting for breath to go on. "Promise me—you and Nan—you won't forget—the muddling race—the stupid, noble race that made you."

"We won't forget," Dane whispered. "I promise."

"Thank you—both." His convulsive grasp drew Dane closer. "You can't—do much—for me. But you can help—old Homo sap—"

The painful wheezing ceased, and the clutching hand let go. Dane caught it up to feel for the pulse again, but there was none. Stooping to straighten the body and draw the blanket over the sudden repose of that tired face, he felt crushed beneath a total desolation he couldn't understand.

Death was still a final fact, unchangeable even by genetic engineering. He felt a sick regret that he had failed to delay Messenger's foreseen fate. In these last hours, he had come to like and admire this stubborn old creator, yet he was surprised by that overwhelming weight of grief.

But I've known him longer. The sad words were Nan's, and he thought for a moment that she had come back. *I loved him more.*

Dane looked around eagerly, but all he could see was the helicopter with the machine guns still trained upon him, and the tilted waste of shattered basalt, and the high cliffs beneath the mutant tree. Something made him shiver.

"Nan?" he whispered sharply. "Are you—hurt?"

I'm terribly hurt, her words came back. *Because I wanted so much to keep him alive—until we could learn enough to make his body as young again as his mind always was. We needed him, Dane. You and I did, and those other mutant children he made. And the old race needed him, too.*

"But did you fall?" he gasped. "Are you injured?"

Only by his death, she answered. *I've come almost to the top of the cliff. Just above me is a cave that leads back to a hollow root of the tree. That is the way to the ship.*

He knew then that he was really picking up her thoughts, through their unfolding new capacities. She must have perceived the maker's death with his senses, and that sudden overwhelming sadness was her own emotion, shared with him.

"I'm coming to you." He had been waiting too long; the need for action was suddenly imperative in him. "I can't do anything else for Mr. Messenger, and I believe I can get away through these boulders—"

No, you must wait, her warning thought checked his impulse to flight. *You must tell Gellian what we just promised, and arrange for us to begin. There's a great deal we must do for the maker and the mother race before we attempt any expedition to space, even if this new ship flies.*

"I'll wait," he agreed. "I'll talk to Gellian, if he wants to talk—but I'm afraid he wasn't very much moved by anything Mr. Messenger said. I'm afraid we'll have to run for it to save our lives. And work the way the maker did, to keep our promises. I think we'll need a base, somewhere off the Earth."

We'll see, she answered. *Now I'm going aboard the ship, if I can find that cave and pass those barriers. I want to study the controls, so that we'll be ready to launch it when we have a chance.*

The burden of her sorrow was lifted from him then, as their mental contact broke. He still felt the sharp pain of his own regret, but that was balanced now by the knowledge that Nan was safe.

Anxious hope awoke in him, when he saw a man returning from the helicopter. He started eagerly to meet him, expecting word from Gellian, but the man was only a perspiring sergeant, carrying a yellow-painted oxygen bottle with hose and valve and breathing mask.

"For Mr. Messenger," he said nervously. "General Soames sent me—"

He paused at sight of the blanket-wrapped body.

"You're a little late," Dane told him bleakly. "Tell the general Mr. Messenger is dead."

The sergeant retreated in confusion, and Dane waited again. He paced the ledge until he was tired, and sat down to rest, and got up to walk the uneven rock again. He was afraid to watch the mutant tree, because the gunners were still watching him, but now and again he groped with his mind for Nan.

He failed to reach her. It must have been their shared grief for the maker, he decided, that created that momentary bridge between their minds. In time, as their new capacities unfolded, that communion of thought might draw them into a perfect oneness unknown to the older race, but now he could only worry and wait.

The engines of the helicopter had idled noisily for a long time, ready for flight, and it almost startled him when they were cut off. Listening in the sudden quiet, he could hear the dull drum of the unseen aircraft circling above.

That ominous sound seemed to rise and fall, for a time, but then it slowly died away, as if the planes were departing. His hopes lifted again, in that deeper silence, but for another endless time he saw no movement about the helicopter.

The clouds grew darker as the sun went down behind

them, and he was shivering in a cold wind blowing from the snows above, when at last he saw John Gellian coming back. His heart sank when he saw the way the gaunt man stumbled over the rocks and scraps of wreckage. Hopelessly, he thought Gellian must have tried the cancerphage and been stricken by it.

"The maker's dead." He couldn't keep a tired defiance from his voice. "I guess you'll have to talk to me."

"The sergeant told us." Gellian paused beside the covered body, gray-faced and swaying. "It seems such a dreadful thing, and I'm the one to blame."

And he stood helplessly shaking his head.

"Well?" Dane whispered anxiously. "Have you and the general decided what you want to do, about—us?"

"A difficult problem." Gellian kept looking down at Messenger, and he made soft clucking sounds of regret. "It's a terrible thing, hounding such a man to death. If I had known the truth—but that's no use."

He shrugged, and turned soberly to Dane.

"There's one favor we want to ask." His voice was hoarse with weariness, and hushed with a curious humility. "If you and Miss Sanderson don't object, we want to take the body. Do you mind?"

Dane hesitated, but he and Nan could do no more.

"I suppose not," he said.

"Thank you." Gellian's haggard eyes flashed with gratitude. "There's so little we can do, except to bury him."

He was swaying where he stood, but Dane saw now that he didn't look stricken. His face was lined with bone-fatigue, and his hollowed eyes dark with remorse, but that sternness of agony was gone.

"The cancerphage?" Dane asked quickly. "Have you done anything with that?"

"General Soames made me the guinea pig." He smiled a little, and his dark face had a look of peace Dane had not seen there before. "I think he was more impressed than I was, by Messenger's plea, and he pointed out that I had nothing to lose, whatever it did to me."

"What did it do?"

"It stopped the pain, as quickly as he promised." Gellian glanced sadly at the maker's body. "You wouldn't know how much that means. Just now I'm weak as a kitten—reaction, I suppose. But I'm getting well! I expect to sleep tonight—without drugs—a thing I haven't done in months."

"I'm glad," Dane whispered. "I was afraid it had failed." He looked at the gaunt man, anxiously. "But what are going to do about us?"

"I don't know." Worry erased Gellian's tired relief. "Soames and I have been talking with our people in the governments, trying to decide." He shrugged helplessly. "An appalling problem, because it caught us by surprise. I'm sorry we kept you waiting so long, but even yet we don't know what to do."

"What seems to be the trouble?"

"There's so little we *can* do." Gellian hesitated, studying him uncertainly. "And it's impossible to decide what we ought to offer, because so much depends on you. We can't settle anything, until we know what you are going to demand."

Dane caught his breath, astonished. "We aren't demanding anything."

"You're entitled to more than we can give," Gellian insisted urgently. "We can't do much for Messenger except bury him, but we want to do whatever we can for you—because of him."

"So you mean to let us live?" Dane's knees felt suddenly

weak. "That's all we really need."

"I believe your lives are still in danger, but we're doing what we can." Gellian shook his head regretfully. "It will take a long time to uproot all the fear and hatred we've been planting. I know we can't undo all the damage, or bring any of those children back to life. But the witch-hunt is ended."

Dane felt the hot sting of tears in his eyes. He saw Gellian hesitating, as if doubtful of his reaction, but something hurt his throat so that he couldn't speak of his relief.

"Operation Survival is being disbanded," Gellian went on softly. "Our planes are already returning to their bases, and the last of our forces will be out of New Guinea by tomorrow night."

Dane gave him a thin little smile of gratitude.

"Another thing—" He paused again, uncertainly. "I don't know what you and Miss Sanderson are planning, but we're afraid for you to leave New Guinea, now."

Dane couldn't help a troubled glance toward the mutant tree. "I don't know where we're going."

"We're reversing the aims of our organization," Gellian went on nervously. "The new purpose of the agency will be to get justice for Homo excellens, but it won't be easy to tear down all the intolerance we've built. You will probably be in danger for a long time to come."

Dane shrugged, with a sudden cheerful confidence.

"If you give us half a chance, I think we'll get along."

"We've been talking about the company." Gellian frowned at him, doubtfully. "Mr. Messenger's company. I called Jones in New York—the banker. He has been a silent supporter of the agency, and now he has agreed to reorganize Cadmus—that is, if you and Miss Sanderson think you can make it pay again."

"I think we could." Dane nodded thoughtfully. "Nan will

soon be able to make more mules, and other mutations, I'm sure. We'd want the benefits to be spread more widely than they were before. Whatever we do will be for both our races, instead of just for Mr. Jones. But I suppose we do need to make some money—for the children that are still alive."

"Good!" Gellian seemed relieved, though still uneasy. "Splendid! I'll tell him that you agree in principle. You can call him whenever you like, to work the details out."

His tired smile was suddenly too cordial, Dane thought, and his husky voice too loud. Even though the witch-hunt had ended, the chasm of difference remained. Man and not-man, they could be firm allies and warm friends, but never quite alike. Gellian's good intentions left him unmoved and still alone.

"I think that settles everything, in principle." Gellian reached quickly to grasp his hand, and quickly let it go, as if faintly uncomfortable in his presence. "Is there anything else?" He turned restlessly toward the helicopter. "Do you want us to take you back to Edentown?"

Dane shook his head.

"Please leave me here," he said. "Nan's waiting for me, and we've a way to travel. You can leave word that we'll soon be back again, to work on a new crop of mules."

The helicopter lifted a few minutes later, carrying the maker's body and Van Doon's. Dane watched it go out of sight, shivering where he stood in the windy mountain dusk. As soon as it was gone, he started climbing eagerly toward the high black cliffs and the mystery of that mutant tree, glowing faintly blue against the sudden tropic dark, where Nan was waiting for him.

The employees of Five Star hope you have enjoyed this book. All our books are made to last. Other Five Star books are available at your library, through selected bookstores, or directly from us.

For information about titles, please call:

(800) 223-1244

or visit our website at:

www.gale.com/fivestar

To share your comments, please write:

Publisher
Five Star
295 Kennedy Memorial Drive
Waterville, ME 40901